MOMENT OF TRUTH

Lis... ...e John Grisham' by *Pe... ...llers that draw on he... ...with a prestigious Ph... ...er of the Edgar Allen Po... ...fiction, and all of her novels have been best... *...ent of Truth* is her seventh novel. Her books are now published in twenty countries. A native Philadelphian, Scottoline lives with her family in the Philadelphia area and welcomes e-mail through her website, www.scottoline.com.

'An edgy tale, full of surprises'   *USA Today*

'In *Moment of Truth*, as in her previous novels, Scottoline sets off plot lines like firecrackers. She gets a half dozen of them arcing at a time, bedazzling the reader'
Philadelphia Inquirer

'A carefully crafted tale of immorality, dark secrets and family values gone awry'   *New York Post*

'*People Magazine* has called Lisa Scottoline "the female John Grisham". Grisham is fun, but Scottoline is more creative and her latest legal thriller, *Moment of Truth*, is a fresh addition to the genre ... This is a book you pick up and find you can't go to bed until it's finished ... a thriller that delivers'   *San Francisco Examiner*

LISA SCOTTOLINE

MOMENT OF TRUTH

HarperCollins*Publishers*

HarperCollins*Publishers*
77–85 Fulham Palace Road,
Hammersmith, London W6 8JB

www.fireandwater.com

Special overseas edition 2000
1 3 5 7 9 8 6 4 2

First published in Great Britain by
Harper Collins*Publishers* 2000

Copyright © Lisa Scottoline 2000

Lisa Scottoline asserts the moral right to
be identified as the author of this work

ISBN 0 00 710033 7

Set in Sabon

Printed and bound in Australia by
Griffin Press Pty Ltd, Netley, South Australia

To my mother and brother

I never did give anybody hell.
I just told the truth and they thought it was hell.

—HARRY S. TRUMAN

Book One

1

Jack Newlin had no choice but to frame himself for murder. Once he had set his course, his only fear was that he wouldn't get away with it. That he wasn't a good enough liar, even for a lawyer.

The detectives led Jack in handcuffs into a small, windowless room at the Roundhouse, Philadelphia's police administration building. Bolted to the floor at the center of the room was a straight-backed steel chair, which reminded Jack of the electric chair. He looked away.

The walls of the room were a dingy gray and marred by scuff marks as high as wainscoting. A typewriter table topped with a black Smith-Corona stood against the side wall, and in front of the table sat two old wooden chairs. One of the chairs groaned when the heavyset detective, who had introduced himself as Stan Kovich, seated himself and planted his feet wide. "Siddown, Mr. Newlin," Detective Kovich said, gesturing to a wooden chair across from him.

"Thank you." Jack took a seat, noting that the detective had bypassed the steel chair, evidently reserved for murderers who weren't wealthy. Special treatment never suited Jack. A bookkeeper's son, he had worked his way through school to become an estates lawyer who earned seven figures, but even his large partnership draw remained a pittance in comparison to his wife's family money. He had always wished the Buxton money away, but now he was glad of it. Money was always a credible motive for murder.

"You want a soda? A Coke or somethin'?" Kovich asked. The detective wore a short-sleeved white shirt, light for winter-time, and his bullish neck spread his collar open. His shoulders hunched, powerful but gone to fat, and khaki-colored Sans-abelts strained to cover his thighs. A bumpy, working-class nose dominated his face and he had cheekbones so fleshy they pressed against the rims of his glasses, large gold-rimmed avia-tors. Their bifocal windows magnified his eyes, which were earth brown and addressed Jack without apparent judgment.

"No, thanks. Nothing to drink." Jack made deliberate eye con-tact with Detective Kovich, who was closer and seemed friendlier than the other detective. Propped against the wall on a thin Italian loafer, he was black and hadn't said anything except to introduce himself. Hovering over six feet tall, rangy and slim, the detective had a face as narrow as his body, a small, thin mouth, and a nose a shade too long in proportion to high cheekbones. Dark, almost-onyx eyes sat high on his face, like judges atop a dais.

"Let's start by you telling me something about yourself, Mr. Newlin." Kovich smiled, showing teeth stained by coffee. "By the way, just for the record, this interview is being videotaped." He waved vaguely behind the smudgy mirror on the wall, but Jack didn't look, steeling himself to be convincing in his false confession.

"Well, I'm forty-three. I'm a partner at Tribe & Wright, head-ing the estates and trusts department. I attended the University of Pennsylvania Law School, Yale, and Girard before that."

Kovich nodded. "Wow. Impressive."

"Thank you," Jack said. He was proudest of Girard, a board-ing high school established by the trust of Stephen Girard for fatherless boys. Girard was a Philadelphia institution. He never could have made it to Yale or any other university otherwise.

"Where you from?"

"North Philly. Torresdale."

"Your people still up there?"

"No. My father died a long time ago and my mother passed away last year, from lung cancer."

"I know how that goes. I lost my mother two years ago. It's no picnic."

"I'm sorry," Jack said. *No picnic*. It was such a rich understatement, his mouth felt bitter. His mother, gone. His father, so long ago. Now Honor. He cleared his throat. "Maybe we should move on."

"Sure, sure." Kovich nodded quickly. "So, you're a lawyer at the Tribe law firm. Pretty big outfit, right? I read somethin' about them in the paper, how much they bring in a year. They're printin' money."

"Don't believe everything you read. Reporters have to sell newspapers."

"Tell me about it." Kovich laughed, a harsh guttural noise that burst from his throat. He turned to the other detective, still standing against the wall. "Right, Mick?" he asked.

The detective, who had introduced himself as Reginald Brinkley, not Mick, only nodded in response, and the pursing of his lips told Jack he didn't welcome the attention. Brinkley, also middle-aged, wore a well-tailored brown sport coat with a maroon silk tie, still tight despite the late hour and affixed to his white shirt with a gold-toned tie bar. His gaze chilled the room and the uptilt to his chin was distinctly resentful. Jack didn't know what he had done to provoke the detective and only hoped it worked against him.

"So, Mr. Newlin," Kovich was saying, "hey, can I call you Jack?"

"Of course."

"You got any other family, Jack? Kids?"

"One."

"Oh yeah?" Kovich's tone brightened. "What flavor?"

"A girl. A daughter."

"How old?"

"Sixteen."

"I got a sixteen-year-old!" Kovich grinned, showing his bad teeth. "It's a trip, ain't it? Teenagers. You got just the one?"

"Yes."

"Me, I got a thirteen-year-old, too. Also a girl. Houseful of blow dryers. My wife says when they're not in the bathroom, they're in the chat rooms. Yours like that, on the computer?"

Jack cleared his throat again. "I don't mean to be impolite, but is there a reason for this small talk?" He didn't want to go there and it seemed like something a murderer would say.

"Well, uh, next-of-kin notification is our job. Standard procedure, Jack."

He tensed up. He should have thought of that. The police would be the ones to tell Paige. "My daughter lives on her own. I'd hate for her to hear this kind of news from the police. Can't I tell her myself?"

"Sixteen, she's on her own already?"

"She's legally emancipated, with a promising career."

"Legally emancipated, what's 'at?"

"My wife and I filed papers, I drafted them myself, essentially saying that she's legally an adult. She lives on her own and earns her own money. She's a model, and, in any event, I really would prefer to be the one to tell her about . . . her mother." He paused. "I could call her after we talk. I mean, I do want to make a full confession, right now."

Kovich's lips parted slightly, and behind him, Brinkley's eyes narrowed.

Jack's mouth went dry at their reaction. Maybe he'd gone too fast. "I mean, I feel awful, just awful. A horrible thing happened tonight. I can't believe what I've done. I want to get it off my chest."

Kovich nodded encouragingly. "You mean you want to make a statement?"

"Yes. A statement, that's right." Jack's voice sounded authentically shaky, even to him.

"Okay. Good. Bear with me." Kovich turned toward the table, his chair creaking, and picked up a form, thick with old-fashioned carbons. He crammed it behind the typewriter roll, fighting a buckle in the paper. The detective wasn't overly dexterous, his hands more suited to wrestling fullbacks than forms. "Jack, I have to inform you of your Miranda rights. You have the right to remain silent, you—"

"I know my rights."

"Still, I gotta tell you. It's the law." Kovich finished a quick recitation of the Miranda warnings as he smoothed out the unco-operative form, rolled it into the machine, and lined up the title, INVESTIGATION INTERVIEW RECORD, HOMICIDE DIVISION. "You understand your rights?"

"Yes. I don't need a lawyer. I wish to make a statement."

"You mean you're waiving your right to counsel?" Kovich nodded again.

"Yes, I'm waiving my right to counsel."

"Are you under the influence of drugs or alcohol at this time?"

"No. I mean, I had some Scotch earlier. Before."

Kovich frowned behind his big aviators. "You're not intoxi-cated at the present time, are you?"

"No. I only had two and that was a while ago. I'm perfectly sober."

Kovich picked up another form, two pages. "Fine. You gotta sign this, for your waiver. Sign the first page and then you have to write on the second, too." He slid the sheets across the table, and Jack signed the top page, wrote "yes" after each question on the second page, and slid both back. "We'll start with your Q and A, question and answer." Kovich turned and started to type numbers in the box on the right, CASE NUMBER. "It's procedure. Bear with me, okay?"

"Sure." Jack watched Kovich typing and had the sense that confessing to murder, even falsely, could be as mundane as opening a checking account. A bureaucratic occasion; they typed out a form in triplicate and processed you into prison for life.

"State your name and address, please."

"My name is Jack Newlin and my address is 382 Galwith's Alley." Saying it relaxed him. It was going so well, then the black detective cleared his throat.

"Forget the Q and A for a minute, Mr. Newlin," Detective Brinkley said, raising a light palm with long, thin fingers. He straightened and buttoned his jacket at the middle, the simple gesture announcing he was taking charge. "Tell us what happened, in your own words."

Jack swallowed. This would be harder to do. He tried to forget about the hidden video camera and the detective's critical eyes. "I guess I should tell you, my marriage hadn't been going very well lately. For a year, actually. Honor wasn't very happy with me."

"Were you seeing another woman?" Detective Brinkley's question came rapid-fire, rattling Jack.

"Of course not. No. Never."

Kovich, taken suddenly out of the picture, started typing with surprising speed. Capital letters appeared on the black-ruled line: NO. NEVER.

"Was she seeing another man?"

"No, no. Nothing like that. We just had problems, normal problems. Honor drank, for one thing, and it was getting worse."

"Was she alcoholic?"

"Yes, alcoholic." For the past year Jack had been telling himself Honor wasn't an alcoholic, just a heavy drinker, as if the difference mattered. "We fought more and more often, then tonight she told me she wanted to divorce me."

"What did you say?"

"I told her no. I was shocked. I didn't want to. I couldn't imagine it. I love—I *loved*—her."

"Why did she ask you for a divorce?"

"Our problem always came down to the same thing, that she thought I wasn't good enough for her. That she had married down, in me." That much was true. The sore spots in their marriage were as familiar as potholes in a city street and they had been getting harder and harder to steer around.

Brinkley nodded. "What started the fight tonight?"

"Tonight, we were supposed to have a dinner together, just the two of us. But I was late." Guilt choked Jack's voice and it wasn't fraudulent. If he had gotten home on time, none of this would have happened, and that was the least of his mistakes. "She was angry at me for that, furious, and already drunk when I got home. She started shouting as soon as I came in the door."

"Shouting what?"

"That I was late, that I didn't care about anybody but myself, that she hated me. That I'd let her down. I ruined her life." Jack summoned the words from the myths in their marriage and remembered the details of the crime scene he'd staged. He'd found his wife dead when he came home, but as soon as he realized who had killed her and why, he understood that he'd have to make it look as if he did it. He'd suppressed his horror and arranged every detail to point to him as the killer, including downing two full tumblers of Glenfiddich in case the police tested his blood. "I poured myself a drink, then another. I was getting so sick of it. I tried for years to make her happy. No matter what I did I couldn't please her. What happened next was awful. Maybe it was the Scotch. I don't often drink. I became enraged."

"Enraged?" Brinkley cocked his head, his hair cut short and thinning, so that his dark scalp peeked through. "Fancy word, enraged."

"Enraged, yes." Jack willed himself to go with it. "I mean, it set me off, made me angry. Her screaming at me, her insults. Something snapped inside. I lost control." He recalled the other details of the faked crime scene; he had hurled a crystal tumbler to the parquet floor, as if he had been in a murderous rage. "I threw my glass at her but she just laughed. I couldn't stand it, her laughing at me like that. She said she hated me. That she'd file papers first thing in the morning." Jack wracked his brain for more details but came up empty, so he raised his voice. "All I could think was, I can't take this anymore. I hate her threats. I hate *her*. I *hate* her and want her to *shut up*. So I picked up the knife."

"What knife?"

"A butcher knife, Henkels."

Kovich stopped typing, puzzled. "What's Henkels?"

"A fancy knife," Brinkley supplied, but Kovich only frowned. "How do you spell it?"

Jack spelled the word as Kovich tapped it out, but Brinkley wasn't waiting. "Mr. Newlin, where was the knife?" he asked.

"On the dining room table."

"Why was a butcher knife in the dining room?"

"It was with the appetizer, a cold filet mignon. She must have used it to slice the filet. She loved filet, it was her favorite. She'd set it out for an appetizer. The knife was right there and I took it from the table."

"Then what did you do?"

"This is hard to say. I mean, I feel so . . . horrible." Jack's face fell, the sadness deep within, and he suddenly felt every jowl and furrow of middle age. He didn't try to hide his grief. It would look like remorse. "I . . . I . . . grabbed the knife and killed her."

"You stabbed your wife to death."

"Yes, I stabbed my wife to death," Jack repeated, amazed he could form the words. In truth, he had picked up the bloody knife, unaccountably left behind, and wrapped his own fingers around it, obliterating any telltale fingerprints with his own.

"How many times?"

"What?"

"How many times did you stab her?"

Jack shuddered. He hadn't thought of that. "I don't know. Maybe it was the Scotch, I was in kind of a frenzy. Like a trance. I just kept stabbing." At the typewriter, Kovich tapped out, JUST KEPT STABBING.

"And you got blood on your suit and hands."

"Yes." He looked down at the residuum of Honor's blood, spattered on a silk tie of cornflower blue and dry as paper between his fingertips. He had put the blood there himself, kneeling at her side, and the act had sent him to the bathroom, his gorge rising in revulsion.

"Did she scream?"

"She shouted, I think. I don't remember if it was loud," he added, in case they interviewed the neighbors.

"Did she fight you?"

He tasted bile on his teeth. He imagined Honor fighting for her life, her final moments stricken with terror. Realizing she would die, seeing who would kill her. "She fought hard, but not well. She was drunk. She couldn't believe it was happening. That I would really do that to her."

"Then what did you do?"

"I went to the phone. I called nine-one-one. I told them I killed my wife." Jack caught himself. "Wait, I forgot. I went to the bathroom and tried to wash up, but not all the blood came off. I realized there was no way I could hide what I'd done. I had no plan, I hadn't thought it out. I didn't even have a way to get her body out of the house. I realized I was going to get caught. There was no way out. I vomited into the toilet."

Brinkley's eyes narrowed. "Why did you try to wash up?"

"I was trying to wash the blood off. So I wouldn't get caught."

"In your own bathroom?"

"Well, yes." Jack paused, momentarily confused, but Brinkley's glare spurred him on. "It's not like I was thinking clearly, as I said."

Brinkley leaned back against the wall again. "Let's switch gears, Mr. Newlin. What time was it when you came home?"

"Just before eight. I was supposed to be there at seven but I got held up."

"What held you up?"

"I stopped to talk with my partner. The firm's managing partner, William Whittier." Jack had been on his way out when Whittier had stopped him to discuss the Florrman bill. It had taken time to get free, then it was pouring outside and Jack couldn't get a cab. Ironic that the most mundane events, on the wrong night, had ended Honor's life and changed his forever. "I suppose I should have called to say I was late, but I didn't think it would matter. The maid is off on Monday, and we usually eat a late dinner."

"How did you get home?"

"I took a cab."

"What kind?"

"I don't remember."

"Yellow? Gypsy?"

"No clue. I was distracted. The traffic was a mess."

Hunched over the desk, Kovich nodded in agreement. "That accident on Vine," he said, but Brinkley stood up and stretched, almost as if he were bored.

"Not every day we get somebody like you in here, Mr. Newlin. We get dope dealers, gangbangers, rapists. Even had a serial killer last year. But we don't often see the likes of you."

"What do you mean, Detective? I'm like anybody else."

"You? No way. You're what we used to call the man who has everything." Brinkley rubbed his chest. "That's what doesn't make sense, Mr. Newlin. About what you're telling me."

Jack's heart stopped in his chest. Had he blown it? He forced out a single word: "What?"

"You hated your wife enough to kill her, but you didn't want to give her a divorce. That's psycho time, but you're no psycho. Explain it to me." Brinkley crossed his slim arms, and fear shot through Jack like an electrical current.

"You're right," he said, choosing his words carefully. "It doesn't make sense, if you look at it that way. Logically, I mean."

"Logically? That's how I look at it, Mr. Newlin. That's the only way *to* look at it." Brinkley smiled without mirth. "People sit in that chair all the time and they lie to me. None of them look like you or dress like you, that's for damn sure, but you can lie, too. You can lie *better*. You got the words for it. Only thing I got to tell me if you're lying is common sense, and what you're tellin' me don't make sense. It's not, as you say, *logical*."

"No it isn't." Jack caught sight of Honor's blood on his hands, and it was so awful, so impossible to contemplate, that it released the emotions he'd been suppressing all night. Grief. Fear. Horror. Tears brimmed in his eyes, but he blinked them away. He remembered his purpose. "I wasn't thinking logically, I was reacting emotionally. To her shouting, to her insults. To the Scotch. I just did it. I thought I could get away with it, so I tried to clean up, but

I couldn't go through with it. I called nine-one-one, I told them the truth. I did it. It was awful, it *is* awful."

Brinkley's dark eyes remained dubious, and Jack realized his mistake. The rich didn't behave this way. They didn't confess or blubber. They expected to get away with murder. Jack, who had never thought like a rich man and evidently never would, knew instantly what to do to convince him: "Detective, this interview is over," he said abruptly, sitting up straighter. "I want to call my attorney."

The reaction was immediate. Brinkley's dark eyes glittered, his mouth formed a grim line, and he fell into his customary silence. Jack couldn't read the detective completely, but sensed that he had acted in character, in a way that comported with Brinkley's world view, and that would ultimately put his doubts to rest.

In contrast, Kovich deflated at the typewriter, his heavy shoulders slumping, his big fingers stilled. "But, Jack, we can settle this thing right here and now. Make it real easy."

"I think not," Jack said, turning haughty. He knew how to give orders from hearing them given. "I insist on my attorney. I should have called him in the first place."

"But all you gotta do is sign this statement. Once you do that, we're all done here. It'll be easiest on you and your daughter this way." Kovich's eyes burned an earnest brown. "I'm a father, too, Jack, and I know how it is. You gotta think about your kid now."

"No, I've said much too much already. I want my lawyer and we'll take care of notifying Paige. I will not have you at my daughter's home this late at night. It's harassment. I'll handle the notification through my attorney."

Detective Brinkley buttoned his jacket with nimble fingers. "Better get yourself a good mouthpiece, Mr. Newlin," he said, his face a professional mask. He pivoted on a smooth sole, walked out of the interview room, and closed the door behind him.

Once Brinkley had gone, Kovich yanked the sheet from the typewriter roll with a resigned sigh. "Now you did it. You got him mad, askin' for a lawyer. After judges, there's nothin' Mick hates more than lawyers."

"But I am a lawyer."

"Like I said." Kovich laughed his guttural laugh and turned to Jack as warmly as he had at the beginning. "You sure you don't wanna talk to me? I'm the nice one. I like lawyers. It's realtors I hate."

"No thanks," Jack answered, and managed a snotty smile.

2

Mary DiNunzio smoothed a strand of dark blond hair into her French twist and slumped in a swivel chair beside a conference table cluttered with manila folders, trial notes, and stamped exhibits. It was after business hours, but Mary was still at the law offices of Rosato & Associates, watching her friend Judy Carrier work and feeling sorry for herself. The Hemcx trial was finally over and its aftertaste had left Mary hating her job again. Being a lawyer was even worse than people thought it was, if that were possible. "You sure I can't be a pastry chef?" she wondered aloud. "I like cake better than law."

Judy tucked a manila folder into an accordion file. "Are you going to help or are you going to whine?"

"What do you think? Besides, right now I'm busy supervising. That folder doesn't go where you put it. That's a notes folder, so it goes in the notes accordion." Mary pointed at the accordion standing at the far end of the table. "There. Number eleven."

"Oh, really?" Judy picked up another folder and dropped it into the same accordion. Her lemony hair, cut like a soup bowl when she stood upright, hung down when she lowered her head, reminding Mary of a dinner plate. It didn't help that Judy wore silver earrings made of spoon handles. Mary was getting hungry until she noticed her friend slide another folder into the wrong accordion.

"That's wrong, too. That's Gunther deposition exhibits, so it goes in number ten. And aren't you going to fix the other one?"

"No. See? This is a folder of draft contracts, so it belongs in the second accordion." Judy dropped another folder into the accordion. "I put it in the fifteenth. Ask me if I care."

"Don't you?"

"Not in the least." Judy looked up and smiled. Her bright blue eyes smiled, too, emphasized by the cobalt of a large corduroy smock that billowed around her tall, sturdy form. Judy climbed rocks and engaged in other activities Mary found self-destructive, but she was still shapely to Mary's eye, though she dressed to hide it. And Judy's fashion sense wasn't the only thing about her that mystified Mary.

"Why are you messing up the files, girl?"

"Because it doesn't matter. That's the great secret in law firms, even one as cool as ours. Once you send the file to the records room, it doesn't matter if it's out of order. Nothing ever happens."

"That's wrong. People look at the file again."

"For what?"

Mary had to think. "To prepare the bill, for one thing."

"Nah, they just make that up. You know it and I know it." Judy crammed the next folder into the thickening accordion. "See? I file at random. I put the folder wherever there's room. I always do it this way after trial. Nobody ever came after me. The world didn't end."

"You mean all this time we've been packing up after trial, you haven't done it right?"

"Never." Judy grinned. "Didn't you ever wonder why I always finished ahead of you?"

Mary's mouth dropped open. "I thought it was because you're smarter."

"I am, and this is an example of it. It's dopey to put them away right."

"But you're supposed to."

"Oh, you're *supposed* to." Judy misfiled another folder. "It's like permanent records."

"I don't want to hear anything bad about permanent records. My permanent record was spotless."

"Well, mine wasn't and we ended up in the same place, which proves my point. Permanent records and mattress tags. Nothing ever happens. They're just lies they tell you to keep you in line."

"Like heaven."

"I knew you would say that. For a lapsed Catholic, you're not that lapsed."

"*Mea culpa*." Mary crossed her legs and fiddled idly with cultured pearls that peeked from an ivory blouse she wore with a fitted gray suit. She was on the short side, but had a neat, compact figure and avoided lots of great ravioli to keep it that way. "Maybe we should go get dinner. Have a nice salad."

"Girl food." Judy reached for an empty accordion. "Let me finish disorganizing the file, then we can celebrate our victory in the most boring case of all time."

"Don't jinx it. You don't know that we won."

"Yes I do. We were less boring than they were. Bennie couldn't be boring if she tried."

"Bennie Rosato, our boss? Are you kidding? Ever hear her talk about rowing?" Mary gestured at the walls of the conference room. One wall was glass, facing the elevator bank, but the end walls, of eggshell white, were decorated with Eakins prints of rowers on the Schuylkill River. Beside them hung photographs of Penn crews rowing past Boathouse Row, the bank of colorful boathouses lining the river. "She's boring as hell when she talks about rowing. Also golden retrievers. I'm sick of golden retrievers because of Bennie. If she could put a golden retriever in a boat and row it around, she'd have it made."

Judy stopped misfiling. "If you actually got off your butt and did a sport, you'd understand why Bennie likes to talk about hers. As for the dog stuff, I see that too. Bear's a good dog. I've been baby-sitting him for a week and he's fun."

"Good. Have a great time, just don't tell me about it. Or show me dog pictures."

"You like dogs."

"No, I like ravioli, and I'm still pissed that you screwed up our files."

Judy ignored it. "My family had Labs and goldens growing up and they were great. I'm thinking about getting a puppy."

"Wonderful. See it between trials. Pat it on the head." The phone rang on the oak credenza, and Mary looked over. "Do I have to get that?"

"Of course." Judy gathered a stack of folders and dumped them into an empty accordion. "I'm busy wreaking havoc, and you're closer."

"But it's after hours."

The phone rang again, and Judy scowled. "Get it, Mare."

"No. I'm beat. The voice-mail's on."

Brring! "Get it!" Judy said. "You'll feel guilty if you don't. Don't you feel guilty already?"

"Shame on you, guilt-tripping a Catholic. How low will you go?" Mary grabbed the receiver. "Rosato & Associates . . . I'm sorry, Bennie's out of the country for the entire month. Yes, there are associates of hers here." She slipped a small, manicured hand over the phone and caught Judy's eye. "Man needs a criminal defense lawyer. Should I tell him wrong number?"

"Very funny. Ask him what the charge is." So Mary asked, and Judy read the hue of her friend's face. "Tell him we'll take it," she said quickly, but Mary's brown eyes flared in alarm.

"A *murder* case? You and me? By ourselves? We can't do that! We don't have permission, we don't have authority, we don't have expertise, we don't have any of the stuff you're supposed to—"

"We'll apologize later. Tell him yes."

"But we don't know what we're doing." Mary's hand stiffened over the receiver. "We've only done two murder cases and in one *we* almost got murdered."

"I thought you grew up last case."

"Two steps forward, one step back."

"You told me you weren't afraid anymore."

"I lied. I was born afraid."

"Tell him we'll take it, dufus!" Judy dropped the file and crossed to the credenza. "Gimme that phone."

"No!" Mary clutched the receiver to her chest. "We can't do it! We're not smart enough!"

"Speak for yourself," Judy said, and snatched the phone away.

Ten minutes later, they were in a cab jostling down Market Street toward the Roundhouse. The rain had stopped, but the streets were wet and the gutters full of cold, rushing water. Left-over Christmas garlands wreathing the streetlights blew in the wind, and the lights from the Marriott, The Gallery mall, and the shops lining the Market reflected on the slick asphalt in colored orbs, like Christmas lights. To Mary, the city seemed shut down, with everybody recovering from the winter holidays. Even the cab driver was unusually quiet, but Mary and Judy more than made up for him. They had yammered since they left the office. Only God knew how many trial strategies, settlement conferences, and oral arguments had been discussed in the backseats of the city's cabs. By now cabbies could have law degrees, set up practice, and improve the entire profession.

Mary slumped in her trench coat. "I've never tried a murder case, first-chair."

"So what? We were second-chair to Bennie."

"He called Bennie," Mary said.

"No, he didn't. He called the firm. You and me have more criminal experience than anybody at the firm except her."

"Two criminal trials? Please. This is bait-and-switch, with lawyers instead of air conditioners."

"So tell him." Judy shrugged, the gesture buried in a white down coat that encircled her like a sugar-frosted doughnut. "Let the man make his choice. He wants another lawyer, he can get one."

"I *will* tell him," Mary said, as if Judy had disagreed. She looked out the window and watched the city sleep. "How did we get into this?"

"We like to have fun."

"I hate fun. I hate rowing and goldens and fun of all sorts."

"Buck up, Mare. We can handle it. Just use your common sense. Now, who'd Newlin kill? Allegedly?"

Mary blushed, suddenly glad it was dark in the cab. "Uh, I don't know. I didn't ask."

"Smooth move." Judy laughed, but Mary didn't.

"You could've asked him."

"I thought you knew already."

Mary closed her eyes, briefly. "I'm not competent to do this. I'm screwing up before I meet the client. Is that even possible?"

"It's a land speed record," Judy answered, without rancor. "You and me, we get it done, don't we?"

Mary couldn't smile. Malpractice wasn't funny, and murder even less so. She looked out the window as the cab pulled up at the Roundhouse. The rain began to fall again, a freezing downpour, and somehow Mary wasn't completely surprised.

3

Paige Newlin had finally stopped crying and snuggled against the chest of her boyfriend, Trevor, in the folds of his gray Abercrombie sweater. It was scratchier than her own cashmere sweater set, but she needed the comfort. Paige was still tweaking, trying to come down from the drugs. It was the first time she had tried crystal and she never thought it would make her so crazy. It felt like she'd been electrocuted, supercharged. She had hoped it would get her through dinner with her parents. She had been wrong. Her head was still a mess. MTV was on the flat TV across the living room, but Paige could barely focus on the screen.

She shivered though the elegant apartment was warm and the white couch cushy with goose feathers. She had a body that could only have belonged to a young model; rope-slim in a black sweater set and black stretch jeans that made her long legs look like licorice sticks. She had impossibly narrow hips and high, small breasts. Her crying jag had left her azure-blue eyes glistening with tears, tinged her upturned nose pink at its tip, and caused her soft, overlarge mouth to tilt downward.

"You're still shivering a little," Trevor said, holding her on the sofa. Trevor Olanski was a tall, strapping young man with thick, wavy black hair, round greenish eyes, and now, a troubled frown. His jeans were sliced lengthwise down the thigh and he wore brown Doc Martens. "You want me to turn up the heat, or get you a blanket?"

"It's taking too long to come down, Trev." Paige fingered her long ponytail, a deep red color and straight as a line. The ponytail was her trademark, the signature look that her mother thought would put her over the top. Her *mother*. What had happened? Paige's head was pounding. "I don't need a blanket, I need more Special K."

"No, you've taken too much already. Get hugged instead." Trevor held her closer, which she liked, though she kept eyeing his black Jansport book bag on the coffee table in front of them. Out of the unzipped partition had slid his algebra book, a graphing calculator, and a clear vial of Special K. Ketamine, a veterinary tranquilizer that was supposed to mellow her out from the crystal.

"More K would help, Trev. With the hug. Like a side order."

"Be patient, honey. You were so high, it takes time. That's how crystal is."

"You should've told me that."

"I did. You insisted, remember?"

"Oh, yes, maybe you did. I don't remember." Paige's thoughts jumbled together like colored glass in a kaleidoscope, and her muscles relaxed with the K. "I still can't deal with what happened. With my mother."

"Don't think about that now. You've been through too much tonight, way too much." Trevor cuddled her in his arms. "You want something to drink? Some water or something?"

"No."

"How about I turn the TV off? Or make it louder? You like *Pop-Up Video*." Trevor gestured at the TV, but Paige still wasn't able to focus. It looked like Smashmouth doing "Dancing on the Sun," but it could have been any white guys jumping around in knit caps.

"Nah, it's okay."

"You're not hungry or anything? I can make grilled cheese."

"Too fattening." Paige shook her head and felt the K finally cooling her out. The fight with her mother had been the worst one since she'd moved out. She had been so angry, she had screamed at her mother. Then she'd reached for the knife, on the table. No. She couldn't get the pictures out of her head. She felt chilled to the bone. "Trev, can't I please have another bump?"

"I really don't think that's a good idea, babe."

"I do. I think I need two."

"Can you just relax and nod off? I can bring you something to drink."

"Come on." Paige rolled her eyes. "Just one more? Don't be so stingy."

Trevor sighed and gentled her back to the sofa. "All right, but one is enough. I don't want you to overdo it." He leaned over the coffee table, picked up the vial, and screwed off the black lid. He rummaged through his pencil case to find a Bic pen and used it to scoop powder from the vial. "Just one more. That's it."

Paige nodded, but couldn't think clearly. It was all too terrible. She had known the dinner meeting was going to be bad, but it had gone way too far. Her mother dead. The bloody knife hot and slippery in Paige's hand. She had dropped it and started crying.

"Here we go," Trevor said, handing her the pen cap with the K, and she raised it to her nose and snorted, one nostril then the other, and inhaled deeply. Her brain clouded instantly and she dropped the pen cap. She wanted to ask; she didn't want to ask:

"Trev, did I . . . did I . . . really do it?"

"Honey, why are you asking me?" His green eyes looked confused. "Don't you know?"

"No, I guess, I don't remember. The crystal. I remember some of it, but not all." Paige felt sick inside. It couldn't be true, but it was. She hated her mother. She had dreamed her dead a thousand times. "I remember the knife, and her screaming."

"Let's not talk right now. I'm worried you're gonna get a migraine."

"No, I want to know."

"Okay." Trevor sighed and rubbed her shoulder. "Well, she

started in on you about not gaining weight, something about retaining water, whatever that is." He sighed heavily. "And you started yelling at her and when you told her, she hit you and kicked you. You remember that, don't you?"

"Yes." Paige tried to remember the scene. She saw herself on the floor of the dining room, rolling away from her mother's foot. "She kicked me, okay, and yelled. She wouldn't stop."

"I tried to pull her off you but I couldn't. Then, well, it was like you just went crazy. You went after her." Trevor's voice grew hushed. "I never saw you like that. You've never *been* like that. You were completely out of control. You were raging. It was like it got to you all at once or something, and you picked up the knife. Remember the knife, from the table?"

"Yes." Paige shut her eyes to the memory. The knife. It was the knife they always used for filet. How could she have done this? Killed her mother? Was she crazy? Was she a horrible person? How could she do such a thing? She shouldn't have done the crystal. She burst into new tears, and Trevor held her close again as she sobbed. "Oh my God, I can't believe it. My own mother. I . . . killed her."

"Don't think about it, now. Just relax." His arms encircled her shoulders, wrapping her in a warm, woolly cocoon. "It's not your fault. She's been so miserable to you. You couldn't help it."

Paige listened to his quiet words as the K finally came on. Her breathing slowed. The craziness of the crystal disappeared. Calm crept through her body. Her emotions grew remote, as if they didn't belong to her, but her eyes still stung from crying and she couldn't breathe through her nose. She imagined she looked like hell. She'd studied her face like other kids study French. Trevor massaged her shoulders, loosening the muscles, easing the pressure on her head. Once he had prevented a migraine, just by giving her a massage. He took better care of her than her mother ever had.

"That's it, that's my girl," he said, kneading her shoulder.

Paige heard him but her attention was focused on the pictures in her mind, filtering through her consciousness. Not a kaleidoscope anymore, but a book of photographs, one after the other, as if she were thumbing through her own portfolio. Her face in soft light. In backlight. With too little sleep or too many drugs. She was floating now.

"You all right?" Trevor's hands moved to her nape, slipping under her hair. "You better?"

"Definitely," Paige heard herself whisper. The photos in her mind portfolio morphed into her mother. Her mother in Mikimoto pearls. In DKNY sunglasses. With Estée Lauder eye cream. Her mother was a collection of brand names. Paige smiled inside, drifting. She looked like her mother, everyone said so. Her mother's eye cream evaporated and her blue eyes became Paige's blue eyes. Then her mother's face got younger and younger and turned black.

"Babe, you there? Anybody home?"

Paige nodded, smoothing her cheeks to relax them, like her mother had taught her. Her mother was never a model; she was a deb. Her mother had made her into a model. When she was little, she was in diaper ads, then newspaper layouts and catalog work. This year, her mother was trying to get them a shot in *YM* magazine. A sudden fear disturbed Paige's floating. "What if the police are on their way? I mean, they'll be looking for me."

"No, they won't. Don't worry." Trevor held her closer. "They don't know you exist. You don't even live there anymore. How would they even find you?"

"You're right, they can't." Paige squeezed his arm and it felt like an oak tree. What would she do without him? She got that giddy feeling, kind of horny, that she sometimes got with K. "I love you, Trev."

"I love you, too. We're gonna get through this together."

Paige looked up at him with gratitude. She remembered that he had made her wash up after, at a gas station on the way home. He had told her to get the knife but she'd forgotten it, and he hadn't even yelled. "I'm worried about the knife, Trev. Can they get fingerprints from it, like on TV?"

"No, I don't think so. They have to match them to fingerprints they have on file, I think. They don't have your fingerprints at the police station. You've never been arrested or anything."

"What do we do if the cops come?" she asked, but the question sounded like it came from someone else. Someone inside was asking; whoever kept you breathing in and out. She had learned it from her science tutor before winter break; the automatic nervous system? "I mean, what do I say? I was supposed to have dinner at my parents'."

"The cops don't know that, and if they do, just say you were supposed to go over but you didn't. Maybe you can say you had a migraine."

"But what if somebody saw me leave?" Paige closed her eyes and leaned her head back in the soft chair, the drug overwhelming her fear. "That pimply guy at the desk or one of my neighbors?"

"It was the old guy at the desk and he was dozin' again. I didn't sign in, and nobody was out in this weather. Besides, this place has three hundred apartments. Nobody notices what you and I do."

"What if they arrest me?" Paige said the words, but it didn't seem like it could really happen. Not to her. Nothing could happen to her. She was above the clouds. "What if . . . they put me in jail?"

"Why would they even suspect you? As far as the cops know, you haven't seen your mother all day. The last time you saw her was yesterday at the Bonner shoot. She'd been drinking again, you said."

"Like tonight." Her mother had been wasted when Paige got home. Then screaming, fighting. When Paige had picked up the knife, her mother had dropped her glass. Scotch had flown from the tumbler in a golden rope, like a noose. Then Paige realized something. "Wait. What about my father?"

"Your father?"

"Sure. He must have come home and found her. He was supposed to be at dinner." Paige had almost forgotten about him because he hadn't been in her life much until this past year. Her mother had managed her, and her father had his work. He used to spend all his time handling the family's legal matters, until Paige had finally told him she'd had enough of her mother and wanted to move out. It was like it woke him up. "I called him today at work, and he said he'd be there. He even said to leave you home, to come alone to dinner. I told him I would. He said he would see me at seven."

"So your father comes home and sees your mother on the floor. What will he do?"

"I don't know, how am I supposed to know?" Paige heard her voice get high as a little kid's. It kept her out of commercials and her voice coach hadn't been able to get her to lower her register. It drove her mother crazy.

"Will he think you did it?"

"Maybe," she said slowly, and Trevor looked worried for her.

"Will he turn you in?"

Paige didn't know her father very well, but she knew the answer. "Never," she said.

4

The interview room in the basement of the Roundhouse was rectangular and airless, a dingy bank of cubicles where attorneys met with clients. Grimy wood paneling covered the walls, which were plastered with curling notices in English and Spanish. The NO SMOKING sign bore a cigarette burn, the ceiling sagged around the brown water stain in the corner, and the blue-gray paint on the interview cubicles was covered with pen marks. Phone numbers tattooed its surface and the largest scrawling read GLORIA LOVES SMOKEY, TLF.

There were no other lawyers there except Mary and Judy, and they sat on one side of a smudgy sheet of bulletproof plastic while Jack Newlin was brought in on the other. He was so attractive that Mary felt herself straighten involuntarily when she saw him. Newlin was tall, broad-shouldered, and well built; comfortable with himself in an attractive way and handsome but for the anxiety straining his features. A furrowed brow hooded light blue eyes and crow's-feet wrinkled their corners, tugging his expression down into a frown. His full mouth was a flat line, and a shadow the color of driftwood marred his strong jaw. But Jack Newlin was a man who wore even stubble well. He reminded Mary of Kevin Costner, only smart.

"Thanks for coming, ladies," Newlin said, sitting down. Handcuffs linked his wrists in front of him against a white paper jumpsuit. "But you both really didn't have to bother. I only need one lawyer. Which of you answered the telephone?"

"We both talked to you," Mary answered. She introduced herself, then Judy to her right. "For a murder case, we work as a team."

"I appreciate that, but I won't be needing a team. Who did I talk to first on the phone? Was that you, Mary?"

"Uh, yes." Mary looked at Judy, who gave her a go-ahead nod. Still Mary didn't want to go ahead. "But I can't handle this case alone, Mr. Newlin. I don't have much experience with homicide cases, not as much as Bennie Rosato or lots of other lawyers in town."

Newlin smiled easily. "First, please call me Jack. Secondly, you answered my questions honestly on the phone, as you are now, and I don't need a lawyer with decades of experience. I want you to be my lawyer."

Mary felt her neck flush at the praise. That it came from a total hunk gave her a charge she couldn't quite ignore. "Mr. Newlin, Jack—"

"This will be a simple case. I won't need much firepower. I intend to plead guilty. The truth is, I killed my wife. I did it."

Mary fell momentarily speechless. Had she heard him right? His words hung between them in the air. "You did it?" she repeated, in shock.

"Yes. The police questioned me and I told them everything. I confessed."

Mary met his gaze, and though she had never looked into the eyes of a murderer, she didn't expect them to be so gorgeous. Of course, Ted Bundy had gorgeous eyes, too. Maybe gorgeous eyes should be on the killer profile. "Slow up a minute," she said, trying to get her bearings. "You spoke to the police? Why?"

"I was wrong, I guess. Disoriented. Thought I could answer a few questions and be done with it. I know it was stupid. I called them from the scene. Maybe it was the Scotch."

"Scotch?" Mary would never have pegged him for a drinker.

"Maybe it's best if I tell you what happened, from the beginning?"

"Hold on, are you drunk now?"

"No. Hardly."

"Were you drunk when you spoke to the police?"

"Not at all. I had only a few drinks."

"How many?"

"Two, I think. I feel fine. Does it matter, legally?"

Mary had no idea. "Yes, it does. That's why I asked. Now, go on, tell us what you told them." She fumbled for her briefcase and dug around for a ballpoint and a fresh legal pad. "Let me just get it down," she said, uncapping her pen as he started to talk. She recorded everything he said while Judy listened silently. When he was finished, Mary asked, "Did you tell all of this to the police?"

"Yes, I told them everything."

"Did they read you your Miranda warnings?"

"Yes. They gave me a waiver sheet, too. Two sheets, which I signed and answered."

Mary glanced at Judy, who shook her head. Trouble. "I think that means it's a valid confession. Did they take down what you said?"

"Yes, and they videotaped me."

"What else did they do?" She knew only the TV basics of police procedure. The law according to Steven Bochco.

"Fingerprinted me. Took a hair and skin sample. They took pictures of me, in my suit, and of my hands. There's a cut on my hand from the knife. They took twelve pictures of it, I think. They took my clothes, because they had blood on them. They scraped samples of my wife's blood off my hands and clothes."

Mary was appalled, but hid it. Even a short legal career had perfected her false face. "You had your wife's blood on you?"

"Yes." He glanced away, and Mary noticed that when he looked up, he didn't meet her eye. "Also they wrote up a statement, but I didn't sign it."

Mary's pen paused over the paper. "I don't understand. You confessed, but you didn't sign the statement?"

"Yes, and I asked to call a lawyer."

"Why confess, *then* call a lawyer?"

"I changed my mind. All of a sudden, I wasn't sure I should

confess. I realized maybe I couldn't represent myself. I had thought I could handle it, being a lawyer myself, at Tribe."

"You're a lawyer at *Tribe*?" she asked, shocked. Tribe & Wright was law-firm royalty, almost as pretentious as Stalling & Webb, where she and Judy used to work. Jack Newlin had to be very smart, so why had he acted so stupidly? And violently? It didn't square.

"Yes, I head the estates department. After I told the police what had happened, they started asking me questions and I realized I was out of my depth. I wanted to talk to a criminal lawyer before I signed the confession. I figured I could plead guilty, and with a criminal lawyer, I could get the best deal."

"Why did you talk to the police at all? As a lawyer, you had to know not to."

"I was emotional, I was all over the place, but I'm not expecting miracles from you. I don't expect you to get me off. As I said, I'm fully prepared to plead guilty." His tone remained calm and even commanding, but his eyes seemed uneasy to Mary. His jaw clenched and unclenched, suggesting buried emotion.

"Mr. Newlin, Jack, I see why you want to plea bargain. They'll have a ton of evidence against you. But it's kind of premature to talk about pleading anything now."

"Why?"

Mary didn't know. It seemed like common sense. "It's common sense. I'm not sure what kind of deal we can get you at this point. First, you confessed, and they have the videotape, so your bargaining power is already low. Secondly, you have a preliminary hearing coming up, which is where they have to prove they have enough evidence to hold you." She was remembering from her bar review course. Had the Constitution been amended when she wasn't looking? "Why should we try to bargain before then? In the meantime, we can do our own investigation."

"Your investigation?"

"We always do our own investigation for the defense." At least they had on *Steere* and *Connolly*, Mary's universe of experience with murder cases.

"But I told you what happened."

"We have to learn about the evidence against you." For verification, Mary glanced at Judy, who smiled yes. "We have to understand the prosecution's case against you with regard to degree and possible penalties. We need a colorable defense to threaten them with. We can't bargain from weakness."

"Hear me, Mary. I want this over with now." Jack's mouth set in a firm line, and Mary frowned in confusion.

"But it's not usually the defendant who benefits from a rush to judgment, it's the Commonwealth. Rushing hasn't helped you so far. If you had called us before you talked to the police, you wouldn't be in this predicament. We're talking about a possible death penalty, do you realize that?"

He seemed to gloss over the statement. "I want it over with because I want my family affected as little as possible. I have a daughter, Paige, a sixteen-year-old who's a model. She's still got a career if this blows over quickly and quietly. She doesn't even know that her mother is dead. In fact, I'd like you to go to Paige's apartment and tell her. I don't want her to hear it from TV or the police."

"Her apartment? She doesn't live at home?"

"No. Paige has her own place. Her condo is right in Society Hill, it's not far." Jack rattled off an address that Mary jotted down. "Please go after we're finished here. Can you imagine hearing the news from the police?"

Mary met his gaze again, and his eyes focused intently, suddenly lucid with concern. Could someone who had killed his wife worry this much about their daughter? It was confounding. "You want me to tell your daughter? I'm not sure what to say."

"Tell her everything. Tell her the truth. Tell her what I told you tonight."

"I can't do that. What you told us is privileged."

"Not as against her. I waive the privilege as against her."

"You can't." Mary double-checked with Judy, who was already shaking her head no. "It wouldn't be in your best interest. What if they called her as a witness at your trial?"

"What trial? I'm going to plead guilty."

Damn. "You can't be sure you'll plead guilty and we have to preserve your options. That's why I won't tell your daughter any more than necessary. I'll tell her that her mother is dead and that her father is being held by the police."

"But I want Paige to know that I'm owning up to what I did. I want her to know that as awful as I am, at least I'm not so cowardly as to avoid responsibility for my crime." His strong jaw set solidly, but Mary noticed that small muscle near his ear was clenching again. Eyes and jaws, what did it mean? Anything? Nothing?

"Fine, I'll tell her that you're considering a guilty plea, but that's it. The cops will probably leak that much by tomorrow morning. Agreed?"

"Agreed. Also, I have to ask you a personal favor, if I may." Jack looked plainly uncomfortable, which disarmed Mary. A handsome, wealthy killer who acted like a nice guy. Confusing, to say the least.

"Sure, what?"

"Paige will be very upset about this news. If she is, would you stay with her awhile? She doesn't have many friends."

"Yes," Mary answered, though it went without saying. But something didn't jibe. A pretty, rich girl, without friends? What was up with this family? "What about her classmates? Where does she go to school?"

"Paige is not your typical sixteen-year-old. She looks adult, acts adult, and earns money like an adult. She's privately schooled around her work schedule. She left most of her peer group behind a long time ago, and her boyfriend, at least this latest one, isn't much help. Just stay with her until she feels better and see if she wants to come see me. I'd love to see her tonight and try to explain this to her."

"I'll tell her that, too." Mary couldn't imagine the daughter wanting to see her father in these circumstances. She stood up and packed her pad and pen away. "I think we're finished here, for now. The next step for you is an arraignment, which is when they charge you formally and make a bail determination. I would guess they'll do that in the morning, but there's a chance that it could happen tonight." She glanced at Judy, who nodded. "Judy will stay at the Roundhouse until I get back, in case they do. Do you have any questions?" Mary stood up with her packed briefcase, and Jack smiled, which had the effect of making her feel like a grade school kid, her briefcase transformed into a school bag.

"No questions at all. You did pretty well," he said, and she laughed, flushing, as she led Judy to the door.

"Beginner's luck. See you in the morning."

"Take care of Paige," he said, and the slight crack in his voice made Mary pause.

"Don't worry," she heard herself say, without understanding why.

5

When a homicide as big as Honor Newlin's happens in a city as small as Philadelphia, everybody knows about it right away. Emergency dispatch hears first, then homicide detectives, EMS drivers, reporters tuned to police scanners, the M.E., the crime labs, and the deputy police commissioners. Simultaneously the mayor, the police commissioner, and the district attorney get beeped, and the district attorney assigns the case as soon as the call comes in. The assignment, as crucial as it is, doesn't take much thought, because the result is preordained. In death, as in life, everybody has a pecking order; when a nobody gets killed, the case gets assigned to any one of a number of bright young district attorneys, all smart as hell and fungibly ambitious. But the murder of a woman the status of Honor Newlin, by a lawyer the status of Jack Newlin, could go to only one district attorney.

"Go away," Dwight Davis said, picking up the phone.

Even though it was late, Davis was at his desk at the D.A.'s office, putting the finishing touches on a brief. His desk was cluttered, the room harshly bright, and a Day-Glo blue jug of Gatorade sat forgotten on his desk. A marathon runner by hobby, Davis seemed hardwired never to tire. A constant current of nervous energy crackled though his body, and if he missed his daily run, he was unbearable. The secretaries had been known to throw his sneakers at him, a heavy hint to take off, since they thought Davis got away from work by running. They didn't know that when he ran, all he thought about, stride after stride, mile after mile, was work. Murder cases, crime scenes, and jury speeches fueled his longest and best workouts.

"You're shittin' me," Davis said into the phone. "At *Tribe*?"

He often woke up with a legal argument on the tip of his tongue. He thought up his best closing arguments on the john. He told the funniest war stories in the D.A.'s office and laughed the hardest at everyone else's. Nothing thrilled, intrigued, or delighted him as much as being a prosecutor. In short, he loved his job.

"They got it on video? That, plus the nine-one-one tapes? Oh that's beautiful, that's just beautiful!"

Davis burst into merry laughter. At what? At how the mighty had fallen? No, he wasn't mean. He was just happy. Happy to be alive, now, here, to draw the Newlin case. It was the reason he had turned down being promoted every time they'd offered it to him. The pay was better but he didn't want to process vacation requests, count sick days, hire secretaries, or fire paralegals. Why be a desk jockey when you can try cases? Why walk when you can run? And why try birdshit when you can try Jack Newlin?

"They got the knife? They got his prints on the knife? Tell 'em to move their asses down there!"

He couldn't stop smiling, he felt so good. The biggest case in the city, bar none, and Newlin had the bucks to hire the best. Competition thrilled Davis, and he had the best record in the office. Why did he win so much? The question engendered gossip, speculation, and jealousy among the other D.A.s. Some thought he won because he was decent-looking and juries loved him. Not a bad theory. Clear hazel eyes, thick black hair, a well-formed mouth, and a sinewy runner's body. He was just under average height, but even his relative shortness worked in his favor; he managed to appeal to women jurors without threatening male jurors. But his looks weren't why he won.

"Who's on it from Two Squad? Brinkley, Kovich? Excellent!" Davis ran a hand through his hair, cut short for convenience. "Chief, don't let Diego anywhere near that house, you hear? The man's a loose cannon!"

Other D.A.s thought Davis won because he worked his ass off. It was plausible, considering his hours. He lived the job and was there all the time; in the morning when others straggled in and at night when others staggered home. The life of a typical D.A. was a constant battle for time; it was almost impossible to try cases all day in court and still do the paperwork that had to get done, but Davis managed both. Of course, he had no personal life. His marriage didn't survive the first year and they'd had no children. He kept a small, empty apartment in town. He didn't even have a dog to run with. But his dedication wasn't why he won, either.

"Who's Newlin got for representation? Don't tell me it's a P.D., not with his money. Hey, I heard a good joke, Chief— what do a nun and a public defender have in common? *Neither can get you off!*"

The reason Davis won was simple: he won because he loved to win. The man was a self-fulfilling prophecy with a briefcase. He won for the same reason that money comes to the rich and fortune to the lucky. Winning was his favorite thing in the world. Winning was what Davis did for fun.

"Who? DiNunzio? What's a *DiNunzio*?"

He loved to win like a thoroughbred loves to race. As a little boy he'd shoot the moon, playing hearts at the kitchen table, and as a college quarterback he'd try the Hail Mary to the end zone. In court, he did anything he had to do to win, took whatever risks he had to take, and made whatever arguments he had to make. And it was precisely because he took those risks and made those arguments that they became the right risks and the right arguments and he won. Nor was Davis afraid of losing. He knew that losing was proof of being in the game. You couldn't win if you were afraid of losing.

"Oh, oh, only one problem, Chief," he said suddenly. "Bad news. I just realized something. I can't take the Newlin case. I can't take this case for you."

His expression sobered abruptly. His face fell into the lines of nascent middle age, a wrinkle that bracketed his full mouth and a tiny pitchfork that popped in the middle of his forehead. Something chased the delight from his keen eyes. His mouth drooped at the corners.

"Why, you ask? Why can't I take the Newlin case, Chief? I'll tell you why. *Because it's too fuckin' easy!*"

He howled with laughter as he hung up and threw his Bic pen at the dartboard hanging across from his desk. He didn't look to see where the pen had landed because it didn't matter. He rose quickly and grabbed a fresh legal pad, for that clean-slate feeling. Davis didn't have time for games.

He was on his way to a murder scene.

6

Detective Reginald Brinkley stood alone in Two Squad's coffee room, which was shaped like a shoe box on its end. Yellowed panels of fluorescent lighting intensified the grim cast to the room without illuminating it. Sparsely furnished as the rest of the Roundhouse, the coffee room contained a steel-legged table on which rested a Bunn coffee machine and a square brown refrigerator. Everybody used the coffee machine; nobody used the refrigerator. Inside it was an open can of Coke, a white plastic fork, and twenty-odd packets of soy sauce.

To Brinkley the room smelled familiar, like fresh coffee and stale dust, and he felt at home in its institutional gray-green walls, plastered with outdated memos, Polaroid photos from the Squad's softball team, and a black bumper sticker bearing the unofficial motto of the Homicide Division: OUR DAY BEGINS WHEN YOURS ENDS. The slogan also appeared on black sweatshirts and T-shirts under a picture of a smiling Grim Reaper, but the joke had worn thin to Brinkley and the other detectives. They never wore the shirts. They gave them away as gag gifts.

He shook Cremora into his hot coffee, in a thick Pep Boys mug. It was late at night but he hardly needed the caffeine. He tolerated the rotating tours pretty well; like his father he was partial to night work and he was still jiggered up from his interview with Newlin. It was impossible to tell by looking at him that he was jiggered up, which was what his wife, Sheree, used to complain about. *You don't let me in*, she used to say, like a daytime soap opera, and she'd even got him to go to a shrink over it. Brinkley had loved her that much.

He flinched inwardly at those memories. The couple had sat on the soft couch side by side for a full year, while Sheree and the lady shrink discussed Brinkley, his personality, his job, and his feelings. He rarely interrupted their conversation; they had him figured out so good he didn't have to come to the damn party. The therapy was bullshit anyway. Sheree was changing, by then was converting to Muslim, which finished them off. She had moved out over a year ago, and still he couldn't bring himself to answer the letters from her lawyer. Fuckin' lawyers.

He watched the tiny mountain of Cremora dissolve in his coffee, like a white island sinking slowly into a black sea. He hastened its demise by stirring the coffee gingerly with his index finger. The brew was too hot for his taste, and he had to wait for Kovich anyway. Brinkley had come to the coffee room to get away from the noise in the squad room. The guys not out on jobs were talking the Super Bowl pool again, and he had to think. He watched the black vortex in his mug while he thought about one lawyer in particular. Jack Newlin.

Brinkley hated lawyers, but for some reason, Newlin didn't strike him as the typical lawyer, much less the typical killer. Brinkley had sat across from psychos, wise guys, and bangers who'd just as soon cap you as sneeze. It always gave him a cold feeling in his gut when he took their confessions, delivered in a monotone but filled with details that made him sick. Last week he had listened to a punk tell him how he had tortured an old lady to death with a box cutter. The kid had looked stone bored when he told how he'd raped her postmortem.

Brinkley stirred up the coffee again, making a new whirlpool with his finger, and blew on it, preoccupied. Newlin didn't fit the abuser profile, either. Brinkley remembered the ones he'd convicted; Sanchez, McGarroty, Wertelli. Losers, the lot of 'em. They were the opposite of the stone-cold psychos; they had emotion to burn, hearts like speedballs of rage. They usually had a bad employment history, dotted with booze, crack, or coke, and they were repeaters. Newlin didn't fit the bill. He was successful, his emotions tame and controlled, and two Scotches could "enrage" him. Plus Brinkley had double-checked the file of suspected domestic abuse cases from local hospitals. Newlin's wife wasn't in them.

He kept blowing on his coffee, thinking. Then again, Newlin probably was the doer. The man confessed, and so what if the story wasn't smooth? Newlin might have been disoriented by the whole thing; murder had a way of throwing you for a loop. And Newlin was a lawyer and he'd be used to manipulating the system. He did it for a living, got rich doing it. He would bet he could whack his wife and come out smelling like a rose. That was why he'd called his lawyer at the end. Figured the story was confused enough to maybe get him off. Or maybe Newlin wanted to spill his guts, cut a quick deal, and be out in no time.

Brinkley shook his head. He used to think only rich white folks got away with murder until O.J. proved that rich black folks could buy justice, too. It gave a man hope. He sipped his coffee as Kovich entered the room.

"Cold enough?" Kovich asked, making a beeline for the coffeemaker.

"Not yet."

"Don't know how you can drink coffee cold, especially with a fresh pot of hot sittin' right here."

"Where were you? I been waitin' on you." Brinkley held his mug at a distance from his clean suit, mindful of his partner's clumsiness. "I want to get to the scene."

"I know, so do I." Kovich reached for a Styrofoam cup and poured himself coffee. "I was in the little boy's. Shoot me."

"You were not. You were betting the Super Bowl pool."

"Not me. Games of chance are illegal in the Commonwealth." Kovich drank his coffee.

"Hurry up. We should've been to the scene already. It's ass-backwards, talking to the husband first. I sounded like an asshole askin' him where the knife was. It was like shootin' in the dark."

"What were we gonna do? We had no choice. The guy calls nine-one-one and confesses. They had to arrest him on the scene and we had to question him right away. The lieutenant didn't want Newlin on ice. We got a full confession and it's admissible. Shit, he woulda signed if—" Kovich stopped short. Both men knew the end of the sentence. *If you hadn't fucked up, Mick.*

Brinkley let the moment pass. He'd been right to question Newlin, and the lawyer was hardly the first suspect to change his mind about signing a confession. Brinkley didn't want to argue about it. He'd been partners with Kovich for five years and they had fallen into an easy, if distant, relationship. It was the way Brinkley liked it; he would accept Kovich's social invitations when he couldn't get out of it, but had never even asked Kovich why he called Brinkley "Mick" instead of Reg. Or why he always said, "Sorry, Cholly." Or "I guess, Bill."

"Lemme have this one cup, then we go to the scene. Pick up what we need."

"Pick up what we need?" Brinkley asked. "That means you like him?"

"I don't like him, I *love* him." It was code. Detectives talked about which suspects they "liked." If they liked someone, they suspected him of murder. If they "loved" him, he was as guilty as sin. Nobody but Brinkley remarked the irony.

"You know what? I don't think I like him," Brinkley said, surprising even himself, and Kovich stopped drinking his coffee.

"*What?*"

"I don't like him. At least, not yet."

"Oh jeez. Say what? You gotta be kiddin' me, Mick."

"No."

"What're you *talk*in'? It's a duck!" Slang for an easy case. It waddled in the door.

"You heard me. I'm not sure yet."

"Aw, hell. Why don't you like him?"

"Don't know."

"Mick—"

"I'll think of a reason."

"Mick. Honey. Baby. We got him on tape. The scumbag told you the story, hung together just fine. He had her blood on his friggin' hands. The uniforms were right to place him under. The lab's gonna find his prints on the knife."

"It's his knife and his house. Of course they're gonna find his prints."

"In blood?"

"Don't start with me on the knife anyway." Brinkley had thrown a fit when he heard the techs had already bagged the knife. He had wanted to see it where it lay at the scene, and Polaroids weren't as good as the real thing.

"The lab is workin' on a match. Ten to one they get a full print in blood and it's his."

"Did you call again? Any results?"

"In an hour. They know it's a box job." A rush job, reserved for high-profile homicides. Two Squad hadn't seen many murders that were higher profile than Newlin. "They already called the D.A., Mick. We'll be able to arraign Newlin in the morning."

"No." Brinkley had been worrying it would go down this way, the tail wagging the dog. "It's too soon. I'm the assigned, I'm in charge. I call this shot, not them, for Chrissake."

"Look, it's a silver platter. Newlin admitted to dispatch he did her. The uniforms told us there's no sign of robbery, nothing out of place. He came clean with us, right off. He wanted to get it off his chest, you heard him, and he was nervous as shit. I never saw anybody look that guilty, did you?" Kovich glanced out the door and lowered his voice. "Besides, I gotta tell you they want us to clear this case? It's a monster. We arraign Newlin right away, we look sharp by the time it hits the papers. If we don't charge him, we look like we're playing favorites."

"What favorites?"

"He's white, didn't you notice? Here I thought you was a big-time detective." Kovich smiled, but it faded quickly. "I don't get you, buddy. I thought you hated lawyers."

"I do. That's why I don't like being worked by one."

"You think he's working us?" Kovich looked concerned. He wasn't dumb, none of the detectives was. You had to be the elite to reach the detective level under the new commissioner. It was like the whole force came collectively to attention at the appointment. "Setting up his own ass? Why?"

"I don't know that either." Brinkley considered it. "To protect someone."

"Who?"

"The wife gets killed? Maybe he has a girlfriend."

"Come on, Newlin didn't look like he was gettin' any on the side."

"Mick, please." Kovich glanced out the door again. "Everybody but you and me is gettin' some on the side."

"Maybe not a girlfriend, then." Brinkley set down his full mug. He didn't have time for the coffee to cool. "Let's get goin'."

"A boyfriend?" Kovich tossed his cup into the wastebasket, where coffee washed against the sides. "You never know."

"Maybe anybody. We don't know enough."

Kovich scoffed as he tightened his tie. "You know what your problem is?"

"Yeah. Do you?"

"You gotta make everything hard. The coffee comes out hot, you gotta make it cold. The conviction gets handed to you, you gotta look it in the mouth. You know what I mean?"

Brinkley didn't answer. It was just what Sheree used to say. "Hurry up. I need a partner, not a shrink."

7

Mary stepped out of the elevator onto the tenth floor of Colonial Hill Towers, a sleek corridor of slate gray with art deco wall sconces in a platinum color. She slid the paper with the number of Paige Newlin's condo from her jacket pocket and glanced at it, narrowly avoiding a tall young man in ripped jeans who was hurrying down the hall. His black backpack hit her as he hustled by. Mary apologized reflexively, but the youth didn't answer, just shoved past her into the elevator cab. "Didn't your mother teach you manners?" she said sternly, whirling on her heels, but he said nothing as the silver elevator doors closed.

Mary read the apartment number on the paper. Next to it was Paige's phone number. She had called before she came up, a requirement of the security desk in the lobby. She walked down the hall and reached the door at the end, dreading what lay ahead. She was from a close-knit Italian family and though it had its own stresses and strains, it remained a solid source of comfort and love. How could she deliver news like this? Daddy killed Mommy?

Mary knocked reluctantly on the door. If she hated being a lawyer when it was boring, then she hated it even more when it got dramatic. She needed a job with less emotional involvement. Emergency room doctor, perhaps. Or child cancer specialist.

Paige Newlin, dressed in a blue chenille bathrobe covered with oversize coffee cups, slumped sobbing in the middle of the large white sofa. Her sleek head of red hair, knotted back in a shiny ponytail, was buried in Mary's arms, and her bony shoulders shuddered as she wept. She was tall but thin and fine-boned; she struck Mary instantly as the kind of girl for whom the delicate cycle was invented. And she had burst into tears as soon as Mary had told her that her mother had been murdered.

"I can't believe it. My mother, dead?" Paige cried, weeping.

Mary held her closer, and the girl collapsed in her embrace, the two of them sinking like a single stone into the downy cushions of the sofa. Mary sensed the deep grief Paige must be feeling; she had already experienced the loss of her husband. She was just now putting herself back together, two years later, functioning in her job and life without thinking of him constantly. She looked around to regain some professional distance.

The apartment was decorated completely in warm white; even the coffee table and a large entertainment center behind the sofa were a pickled white wood. The center was well stocked with CDs and a stereo system. There were no books in the room other than some glossy coffee-table volumes, and the decor telegraphed resources far surpassing that of most teenagers, if not lawyers. Mary wondered what Paige's singular life must be like and knew instantly she wouldn't want it, no matter the material rewards, as she listened to the girl's crying.

"I was supposed to go over . . . to dinner," Paige said, between sobs. "I didn't. I should have . . . gone."

"Don't think that way now. This wasn't your fault. You had nothing to do with this."

"I just saw her yesterday . . . at the shoot."

"'Shoot'?" Mary didn't get the term.

"A photo shoot downtown, for the newspaper. My mom booked me for Bonner's Department Store, and the shoot was there. *She* was there."

A photo shoot? Not the stuff of most teenager's lives. At sixteen, Mary had been conjugating Latin verbs and rolling the waistband of her kilt to shorten it. She'd be called to the Mother Superior's office and asked to kneel. Not to pray, but to see if her hem touched the linoleum.

"Who would do that? Who?" Paige's shoulders began to shake, and Mary felt a deep pang.

"It gets worse, Paige. There's something terrible I have to tell you."

"Huh?" Paige looked up, her ponytail disheveled and her eyes puffy with tears. Mary saw the pain etched on her flawless face and the red blotches sprouting on her neck, above the V-neck of her bathrobe. Mary got the same blotches when she was upset, and from the itching under her silk blouse, knew she had them right now. She couldn't imagine how she'd feel hearing what Paige was about to hear:

"You should know that your father has been arrested for the murder of your mother, and he intends to plead guilty," Mary said simply.

Paige gasped, her mouth forming a horrified circle. "What . . . did you say?"

"He's going to plead guilty, and we will be representing him. That's why he couldn't come here himself, to tell you. He's in custody now, but he loves you and wants you to know that."

"My father? *My father?*" Her eyes glistening, Paige looked wildly away and back again. "He *confessed*? He's *in custody*? That's not possible."

"I know. It's a shock."

"He didn't do it. He couldn't do it. He could never." Paige kept shaking her head, her ponytail swinging back and forth. "What did he say?"

"He wants to plead guilty, and that's all I'm permitted to tell you." Wetness came to Mary's eyes at the girl's anguish and she gave up trying to convince anybody she was professional. Italian girls were entitled to their emotions.

"I don't understand." The girl broke down, and Mary looped an arm around her lithe, trembling form.

"I can't explain it. If you want, I'll take you to visit your father and you can ask him whatever you want to know."

"My father's really . . . in jail?"

"At the Roundhouse. He should be arraigned tonight or tomorrow. By morning it will be all over the newspapers, and he was very concerned about that, for your sake."

"Oh, my God, my father." Paige's face dropped into her child's hands, and her head buckled on a neck that seemed no stronger than a blade of grass. She cried harder, and Mary vowed, not for the first time, to find another job.

"Mary," Paige said, her voice choked. "Can I have some water?"

"Sure," Mary answered, grateful for a task to perform. She got up, crossed the room, and found her way into the adjoining kitchen. She flicked on the light, illuminating an ultramodern galley kitchen that looked as outfitted, and as clean, as a sample home. Black granite counters, polished stainless steel sink, and a complete absence of foodstuffs. Mary had never seen a kitchen like it outside of a magazine and hated it instantly. She opened the white cabinet next to the sink, stocked with matching glasses, and filled one with water. Next to the sink sat a small photo in a heart-shaped silver frame, and she picked it up out of curiosity.

It was a tiny picture of Paige in summertime, wearing jean shorts and a T-shirt, grinning at the camera. She was being hugged from behind by a young man whose tan, muscular arms were wrapped around her body. Her neck and long hair obscured his face and he seemed to be kissing Paige's nape. It must have been the boyfriend that Newlin mentioned.

"Mary, my water?" Paige called out weakly, and Mary grabbed the glass and left the kitchen with it and the photo. She handed the water to Paige as her crying slowed to hiccups and then to a stop.

"I saw this photo of your boyfriend. Would you like to give him a call? Maybe it would help to have him here."

"What? My boyfriend?"

"Isn't this him? Your father told us about him." Mary turned the picture around to face Paige.

"Yes, it's him."

"What's his name? He seems like a nice guy."

"Trevor. Trevor Olanski."

Mary glanced again at the photo. "That's funny. He reminds me of a kid I just saw in the hall, when I came up tonight."

"No, it can't be." Paige sipped her water. "Trevor wasn't here tonight."

"He wasn't?" Mary blinked. "I think he bumped into me at the elevator."

"Trevor didn't come over tonight," Paige repeated, and wiped her eyes. "I think . . . I'd like to go see my father now." She brushed a strand of hair into place and stood up, arranging the bathrobe around her slender form. Her face and chest were aflame with blotches, gainsaying her apparent composure. "I'll be dressed in a minute."

"Sure," Mary said, nodding, and watched as the teenager padded off in her terry slippers. Confused, she sank into a chair as Paige scuffed down the hall and closed a door behind her.

Mary gazed at the heart-shaped photo. She couldn't see the boyfriend's face. Why did she think it was the kid in the hall? She ran her finger over the picture, and her finger pad ended up on the tear down the thigh of the boyfriend's blue jeans, visible beside Paige's slim hip. The jeans were ripped lengthwise.

Mary looked closer. Everybody's jeans were ripped. People paid extra for them that way. Then she remembered. The kid in the hall had an up-and-down slit, too. Odd. All of Mary's jeans ripped the same way eventually; sideways, not up and down. So this pair must have been cut lengthwise, on purpose. How many kids cut their jeans that way? Some, but not many. But the boy in the hall and the boy in the photo did, both of whom were tall and roughly the same body build.

It puzzled her. Was Paige lying about her boyfriend being here tonight? No, of course not. Why would she? Duh. Okay. Maybe it was personal. Paige lied because she didn't want Mary to know she had boys over. At sixteen, she was way too young for that, and Mary thought instantly of thirty-three nuns who would sign affidavits to that fact. And on this one issue, she would side with her church. Suddenly the door down the hall opened, and Paige reappeared in casual clothes.

Mary set down the photo, but couldn't chase the nuns from her head.

8

Brinkley got out of the Chrysler and scanned the scene in the drizzle. Squad cars, news vans, and black vehicles from the Medical Examiner's office blocked the narrow colonial street of million-dollar town houses, many bearing iron plaques of historic registration. Cops stood around the squad cars talking, their breath making steamy clouds in the chill. The plastic crime-scene tape stretched under the pressure of the media, which pissed Brinkley off. He knew which photo they wanted: the "bag shot." The photo of the dead body in a black plastic bag, being lifted on a stretcher as it was taken from the house to the coroner's van. The bag shot equaled ratings. In the photos, the bag's industrial zipper would be closed tight, its secrecy only encouraging the imagination's dirty work.

Brinkley slammed the car door closed, with Kovich following suit. The detectives exchanged a look over the rain-slick roof, sharing the same thought. If these idiots knew what murder really looked like, they wouldn't anticipate body bags like birthday cakes. They'd react like Brinkley did, with a familiar nausea, every time he smelled the new-car odor that clung to the black vinyl.

He gritted his teeth as he shouldered the spectators aside, flashed his badge needlessly to the uniform at the door, and went inside the Newlin house. Kovich signed them both in at the scene log and he would take his time, since he was writing the scene, in charge of recording everything. As the assigned, Brinkley had an investigation to run. He strode into the entrance hall, where he found himself the dark eye at the center of a crime-detection hurricane. Techs swirled around him, dusting the telephone and furniture for prints, bagging routine items from a coffee table for evidence, and vacuuming the elegant Oriental in the entrance hall for hair and fiber samples. Behind the entrance hall, the strobe lights of the photographers flashed like lightning.

He took out his notebook and followed the strobe into the living room. He had in mind the advice one of the vets had given him. *A good cop needs a toilet brain. When you get to the scene,* the vet had said, *forget your assumptions about what happened. Flush the friggin' toilet.* It was crude but vivid, and since then, Brinkley could never cross the threshold of a crime scene without hearing a toilet flush in his head. It made sense, especially in Newlin, with the husband's arrest and confession coming before Brinkley's visit to the scene.

He scanned the dimensions of the room. It was large by city standards and the living room had two fireplaces, both on the opposite wall. The ceiling was filigreed with white crown molding and scrollwork like a museum. He took out his notebook, wrote down what he saw, and then rendered it faithfully. Though the lab techs would do detailed scaled sketches, he always liked to do his own, too.

He sketched the gray sofa and two matching chairs arranged in front a glass coffee table, which was now blackened as barbecue with smudges of fingerprint dust and something else that caught Brinkley's eye. He squinted, then walked over with pencil poised. On the glossy glass of the table lay a tiny sprinkling of black dirt. It was located halfway up the table, hidden in the shadow of a crystal ashtray that contained a single cigarette butt, pink lipstick encircling the filter. The ashtray must be why the crime techs hadn't seen it, or they weren't finished here, but the dirt was too dark to be cigarette ash. Brinkley eyeballed the distance from the back of the couch to the line of dirt.

Notebook still in hand, he sat down on the sofa and

stretched out his leg in his loafer. His heel, wet with street silt, hovered two or three inches in front of the dirt on the table. In another minute the silt would fall from his heel, right on the spot. He was right. Somebody had put his feet up on the coffee table recently; somebody tall, between five-eleven and six-one. Brinkley got up, grabbed a passing tech, and directed him to photograph and bag the dirt sample and vacuum the sofa.

"Must be nice," Kovich said, catching up with him.

"What?" Brinkley hovered as the tech took Polaroids of the dirt on the coffee table. He wanted no screw-ups on procedure. That was why he hadn't collected the sample himself.

"You know, it's an expression. 'Must be nice.' To have money, huh?"

"You have money," Brinkley said. The tech was finishing with the Polaroids.

"I don't have money like *this*." Kovich gestured, skinny pad in hand. "This is paintings, furniture, crystal shit. That's fresh flowers in that vase. Real roses, I smelled 'em. I mean, that's real money."

"You want real money, you can get real money, too. Their money doesn't take from you. Got no relation to you."

"All right, Mick." Kovich frowned and backed off. "I signed us in. Log shows the D.A. already here."

"Shit. Who caught it?"

"You gotta ask? Davis."

"The Golden Boy. And we're last at the party." Brinkley watched the tech scrape the grit into an evidence Baggie.

"What'cha got in the bag?"

"Dirt from the table."

"Excellent police work. Place like this, dirt on the table is a crime." Kovich laughed.

"Fool," Brinkley said, smiling in spite of himself, then finished his furniture drawing. He drew the coffee table to fill in his feet-on-the-table theory, noticing that its surface glistened where it hadn't been dusted. When had it been polished last? He made a note, then realized something. There were no photos on the table.

He looked around. None in the whole room, not a single one. Not even of the kid, who was a model? "Kovich, you got kids," he said, as he sketched.

"Last time I checked."

"You got pictures of 'em in the living room?"

"Sure. Katie, she puts 'em around. From school."

"No pictures in this living room."

"So what?"

"I'm glad you're here, Kovich. Renews my faith in law enforcement." Brinkley finished his drawing of the table, and Kovich peered over his shoulder.

"That's prettier than mine, Mick. I think I'm in love."

"Fuck you," Brinkley said, without rancor, and strode into the dining room. He had heard the body was in there but would have known anyway. The room had already started to smell, not from decomposition, way too soon for that, but from blood. The air carried the distinctive scent; fresh blood had a sweet aroma before it coagulated and grew stale. He ignored it, surveyed the dining room, and started to draw.

Another big room, another craggy fireplace, a costly mahogany table, lengthwise, with eight high-backed chairs. Two place settings at the table: husband and wife. Two tall champagne flutes next to pristine white china. Appetizer on a fancy platter. Otherwise nothing. No books, photos, clutter. No bills piled up, no newspapers. Nothing to tell Brinkley anything. Maybe its absence told him something. There was no life in this house. There hadn't been, even before the dead body.

"Mick, we should move along," Kovich said, finishing another page of notes. "The M.E. and Davis are with the stiff."

"Gimme a minute." Brinkley ignored the term, which everybody in law enforcement used. He'd been saving the body for last. He made careful drawings of everything; the table oriented east–west and the high ceiling, white and clean. The walls covered with a light pink cloth, shiny in wavy lines. It had a name. Sheree would know what it was called. Brinkley made a mental note to ask her, then remembered she didn't live there anymore.

"Mick? You done yet?" Kovich asked again, and Brinkley nodded. He stepped forward but couldn't see the body because the D.A. and the M.E. blocked the view. Crime techs buzzed around the chalk silhouette of the body, measuring, photographing, and vacuuming the rug. Brinkley got everybody's attention by standing there in tall, dark silence. The techs edged away, the D.A. rose to his feet, and the M.E. closed his bag and stood up.

Davis shook Brinkley's hand over the dead body. "Reg, we having fun yet?" he asked with a grin.

"You tell me, Dwight."

The D.A.'s rep tie was loosened and a legal pad rested in the crook of his arm like a newborn baby. "Heard you did a first-rate job with the hubby."

Brinkley couldn't tell if it was sarcasm. "He didn't sign."

"I'm not jerkin' you, you guys did great work as usual. I don't need a signature. He confessed and we got the video. I don't need a picture of him doing it." Davis nodded at both detectives. "You wanna fill me in on what hubby said?"

Brinkley shut up, and Kovich launched into the blow-by-blow of what happened. Davis took notes and nodded the whole time, getting happier and happier, and Brinkley thought he had never seen anybody so goddamn happy to wear a white hat. Kovich finished the story, and Davis flipped his pad closed. "Sounds good, gentlemen," he said. "I got plenty to work with. Thanks."

"Let's go home then, eh?" It was the M.E., Aaron Hamburg, who turned and squinted through his trifocals. Hamburg was one of the better M.E.s on rotation, a wizened, balding man near retirement. He got along with Brinkley, but right now he looked tired. He wanted to get on with it already. Have Brinkley examine the body so he could tag it, bag it, and slice a bloodless Y into its chest.

"Sorry I'm late, Aaron," Brinkley said, meaning it.

"I understand, I'm just grumpy." Hamburg was a graying head shorter than Brinkley and wore a rumpled gray suit, dark tie, and a blue yarmulke hanging by a tenacious bobby pin. "I know you had to talk to the husband first. Strike while the iron is hot, eh?"

Kovich nodded in agreement, and Brinkley gestured to the chalk line around the body. He hated it when some knuckle-head chalked a body. It could contaminate or move trace evidence. "Who chalked her?"

Hamburg snorted. "It was Dodgett. It's always Dodgett. Makes him feel like a cop."

Brinkley couldn't smile. "When I see that asshole I'll tell him where to stick his chalk. Now, what'd you find, Aaron?"

"You got lucky this job, it's cut-and-dried. I'll tell you what I told Davis. Unofficially, cause of death is multiple stab wounds. I'll clean her up later but it looks to be about five of 'em. The lethal wound bisected the pulmonary artery. From the temp and lividity, time of death is probably between six-thirty and eight-thirty. Easy case." Hamburg clapped Brinkley on the arm, but given their height difference it fell at the detective's elbow. "You live right, my friend."

"Did you see anything unusual?" Brinkley asked, and Davis looked at him with a frown.

"Why you ask, Brinkley? You got a question?" Davis looked concerned. "Lemme know."

Brinkley sighed inwardly. He didn't like talking about his doubts. Actually, he didn't like talking to anyone but Kovich and sometimes he didn't even like talking to Kovich. "I don't know about Newlin, is all."

"Why not?" Davis cocked his head. Behind him, crime techs completed their tasks. The party was winding down. "He confessed, right? On the scene, and to you?"

"Confession ain't a home run."

"Since when? I mean, like they say in the essay tests, 'Explain your answer.'" Davis grinned, and Kovich laughed.

"I always hated that," Kovich joined in. "'Explain your answer.' 'Compare and contrast.' I hated that shit."

Davis was still grinning. "'Show your work.' '*Elaborate*.'"

Brinkley ignored the byplay. He could never forget the body on the floor. Even at wakes, he never joked around or made small talk. Respect for life; respect for death. "It's too soon to tell. His story didn't sit right."

"How so?"

"I don't believe him, maybe that." Brinkley hated being on the spot. "I think Newlin might be lying."

"For real?" Davis folded his arms, hugging the pad to his chest. "Why would hubby lie?"

"I don't know, it's just a feeling. He seemed like he was lying. Could be he's protecting someone, I don't know who."

"You got any evidence of that? Anything to support it?"

"None, but it's early." Brinkley could feel Kovich looking down at his feet. He was too loyal a partner to laugh.

Hamburg was squinting skeptically. "I'm only the M.E., but I don't see anything out of line here, boys. She's got stab wounds, most of the bleeding internal. Some defensive wounds on the fingers. I'd say she grabbed the knife at some point, but she wouldn't put up much of a fight. She was drunk as a skunk. It's coming through the skin." Hamburg winced. A religious man, he disapproved. "I'll know for sure at the post, but I think we lucked out, boys. Sometimes you get the bear."

"Sometimes the bear gets you," Brinkley said, but Davis clapped him on the arm with the pad.

"Cheer up, man. You got it covered. I say it's a duck, but I hear you. If you get anything concrete, lemme know. I'll study the videotape to make sure. I'll have somebody pick up a copy tonight."

Brinkley thought Davis made the videotape sound like film from the big game. Lawyers. "I'll work on it."

"Don't take too long, my friend. Hubby's going down for capital murder in the morning."

"A capital case? Why?" It bugged Brinkley that the D.A. asked for death in almost every case. It was overcharging, but in this political climate, the public ate it up. It was the cops who didn't like it; there were degrees of guilt in the Crimes Code for a reason. "From Newlin's story, there's not even premeditation."

"Savage murder. Lotsa stab wounds. Evidence of torture."

"He didn't *torture* her," Brinkley said.

"The number of stab wounds counts, you know that. Newlin shouldn't get a lighter charge than the average joe."

Brinkley didn't say anything. Everybody knew who the average joe was.

"Why you stickin' up for this scum, Brinkley? He's a cold-blooded wife-killer. Took a butcher knife to a defenseless woman, a drunk who couldn't even fight back."

"I'm not stickin' up for him," Brinkley said. "I think he's a liar."

Hamburg yawned. "I'll let you experts fight this out. I'm going home to bed. I'll open her up tomorrow at noon." He picked up his bag and trundled off, trailing an assistant. Davis said his good-byes and left with him, and Brinkley wasn't unhappy to see him go.

"Move, people," he said brusquely, and the remaining techs scattered. One tech looked back resentfully, and Kovich caught her cold eye.

"What my partner means is, 'Thanks, everybody, you did a great job. Now good night, happy trails, and y'all come back now, ya hear?'"

The tech laughed, which satisfied Kovich, but Brinkley didn't bother to make nice. He lowered himself to one knee beside what used to be Honor Newlin. She lay on her back with her head tilted into the stupid chalk, her refined features lovely even in death. Her dark blond hair made a silky pillow for her head, and her arms had flopped palms up, slashed with defensive wounds. Blood from the gashes had dripped into the lines of her hand, dribbled between the crevices of her fingers, and pooled in her palms, so that in death she cupped her own blood.

He examined the wounds, a cluster of soggy gashes that rent her white silk blouse. Hamburg had said that most of the bleeding was internal, and Brinkley could see that. He slid his pen from his pocket, leaned over, and pressed open the side of a wound, ignoring the smells of blood, cigarettes, and alcohol that wreathed the corpse. He estimated that the cuts looked of average depth, about four to six inches. It told him the doer was strong, but not too strong, and the angle of attack looked slanted, so the doer was taller than Mrs. Newlin. Around six feet tall, maybe? He thought of the silt on the coffee table. Would Newlin put his feet up on a coffee table? Maybe after a few drinks? Surely not during the fight scene he'd described, though.

"Jeez, can you believe this guy?" Kovich said, from the other side of the body. "Nice house, pretty lady, lots of bucks. So he goes and whacks the wife."

Brinkley ignored him and scanned the body, which showed no other injuries. He judged it to weigh about 125 pounds, at five-six or so. With the blouse she wore black pants of some stretchy material and they outlined the slim shape of her legs, ending above the ankle. Her shins narrowed to a small anklebone, and she had on pink shoes. He looked twice at her shoes. They had no backs, a low heel, and a tiny strap in the front, but the strap of the right shoe was torn and the shoe lay just off the foot. "Shoe's broke," he said, making a sketch, and Kovich nodded.

"Probably ripped it when she fell backwards, like when she was being stabbed."

"You'd think it would just fall off. The shoe has no back. Stupid shoes."

"Sexy, though. They do it for me. You know what else I like? I go for those big shoes. What do they call them? Platforms. The ones they wear in porno. I like the white ones with the high heel. Or the red. I love the red."

"You're a highbrow guy, Kovich."

"Damn straight." Kovich knelt closer to the floor and braced himself on his hand. With his butt in the air and his broad nose grazing the rug, he looked like a big dog at play. "You're about to thank me, Mick."

"Why?"

"Look." Kovich pointed beyond the body, on Brinkley's side. In the path of the tech's vacuum cleaner glinted something tiny and gold. It was wedged in the thick wool of the patterned rug, which was why Brinkley hadn't seen it from his angle. Kovich waved off the tech with the vacuum and both detectives leaned closer.

"Wacky-lookin' thing," Brinkley said. A gold twinkle sat embedded in the swirling Persian paisley. It looked like a tiny piece of jewelry. He looked closer but wouldn't move it until it was photographed. "What is it?"

"An earring back. My kid, Kelley, loses them all the time."

"What's an earring back?"

"It's for pierced ears. It holds the earring on. Don't Sheree have pierced ears?"

"No." Brinkley didn't say more. Someday he'd tell Kovich that he and Sheree had separated. Meantime, he looked at Honor Newlin's head at the same time as Kovich. She still had her earrings on; a single, large pearl on each lobe. He leaned over on his hand, peered behind her ear, and squinted. The left earring back was still on. "This one's fine. You check the other."

On his side, Kovich tilted his head like a mechanic under a chassis. "Okay here, too."

"So they're not hers."

"Wrong, skinny." Kovich righted himself. The body lay between them like a broken line. "They could be hers, just not to these earrings."

"Fair enough."

"See? You're not the only dick in the room."

"Just the biggest."

Kovich laughed and stood up, as did Brinkley, hoisting his slacks up with a thumb and giving the body one last going-over. It stuck in his craw that the techs had grabbed the knife. Couldn't leave the murder weapon in place. Had to get it tested stat. That was the problem with a goddamn box job. Everybody rushed around like a chicken and things got messed up. In the most important cases, they should be going the slowest, not the fastest. He looked away in frustration.

At the end of the dining room table sat the two place settings, untouched. It was fancy china, white with a slim black border, and in front of each plate stood wine glasses and water goblets of cut crystal. Brinkley hailed one of the crime techs with a print kit. "There should be a Scotch glass, two of them," he said.

"There were two, Detective. They're already bagged. Rick there"—she waved toward a red-haired young man—"he's got the Polaroids."

"Terrific." Brinkley wanted to scream. He strode to the red-haired tech, got the photos, and examined them one by one. Shots of the body, from every gruesome angle. Where were the glasses?

There. A crystal tumbler lay on its side next to the body, with liquor spilling out like a dark snake. Three separate views. Another Polaroid of a matching tumbler shattered on the parquet floor. Five photos of it. Brinkley glanced automatically at the floor. It had been swept up. "Goddamn it!" he finally exploded.

"What'sa matter?" Kovich asked, appearing at his side.

"They fucking collected the broken glass! I wanted to see where it fell!"

"You got the pictures, and they'll test everything. You know that. We'll get the reports."

"They couldn'ta waited?" Brinkley flipped through the Polaroids, seething. The focus was fuzzy. He couldn't tell squat from the photos. "We're gonna miss shit!"

"Nothing to miss, Mick." Kovich spread his bulky arms, gesturing at the dining room as expansively as if he owned it. "We got the doer. What's to miss?"

"When does Newlin throw up?"

"Who cares?"

"Me! Bad guys don't throw up after."

"Calm down, bro. This ain't your typical bad guy, I'll give you that. Okay, I'll give you that. You're right, but listen and stop bitching. This is how I think it went down." Kovich punched up his aviators at the bridge. "What we got is a guy, a regular guy, a regular *rich* guy who lost it. A lawyer who saw a move and took it without thinking. He's not a punk, so he tosses 'em after. Or like he said, when he sees he ain't gonna get away with it. He's not upset he did it, he's upset he's goin' down for it. Like you said, he's a *lawyer*."

Brinkley considered it. "So you don't think he's the type either."

"Not the normal type doer, I know." Kovich stood closer. "But whether he's the type or not, you know that don't mean shit, Mick. Newlin did it, all right. Just 'cause he's sorry later, or it freaks him out, or turns his stomach, or it's the one time in his life he breaks the law, he don't even jaywalk before he knifes the wife, don't mean he's innocent. I like him, Mick. I really do. He's our boy and everything here jives with it."

Brinkley scanned the crime scene wordlessly. He had to admit Kovich could be right. It was all consistent. The dinner table, set for two. The Scotch glasses. The appetizer platter, untouched. *Cold filet mignon, her favorite*, Newlin had said. The outside of the meat was seared black and the inside was a spongy, tender pink. It was served cold and sliced, and next to it sat a dollop of speckled mustard and knotted rolls with shiny tops.

Kovich followed his partner's eyes. "Jeez, I haven't had a steak like that in a year, not since Billy retired. Remember we took him downtown, to The Palm? Jeez, I love The Palm."

"No." Brinkley stared at the platter. Next to the mustard was a large pool of gloppy, smooth goo. A tan color. It didn't look like a dressing for the steak. "Look at that, Kovich. That's hummus."

"What?"

"Hummus." Brinkley knew it because of Sheree. When she turned Muslim, she started eating all sorts of shit. Out went the greens and pork ribs, in came the bean soup and whole wheat bread. "It's a dip, made with chickpeas and tahini."

"*Tahini?* Isn't that an island, like Hawaii?"

"No, it's a paste. From sesame seeds."

"Looks like baby shit."

"Tastes like baby shit."

"You eat that?"

"Only to save my marriage." They laughed, then Brinkley stopped. "It ain't the kind of appetizer most people put out."

"Like cheese balls."

"Right." Brinkley didn't know what a cheese ball was, but didn't ask. Kovich ate trash. Ring-Dings and hot dogs. "Like cheese balls."

"Okay, so?"

"So why they serving hummus with meat? Wife's got the appetizer out and she's waiting for Newlin to come home to dinner." Brinkley shoved the Polaroids into his pocket and waved at the platter, thinking aloud. "Newlin says the wife likes filet. We know she likes Scotch. They Scotch and meat people, dig?"

"I guess, Bill."

Brinkley let it go. He felt like he was on to something, whether it was something that mattered he didn't know. "So why they got hummus, too? Meat people don't eat hummus. Hummus is a substitute for meat. You eat either hummus or meat."

"I understand. One or the other. So, you think Newlin eats hummus?"

"No. No man eats hummus. Not unless he wants to save his marriage." Brinkley wasn't joking. "People who eat meat don't eat hummus. Don't work that way."

"How the hell do you know that, Mick?"

"I just know." He didn't want to get into it. Sheree's conversion. The white keemar she took to wearing, covering up her fine body. All the time reading the Koran. It was the beginning of the end for them. "The hummus is for somebody else. Whoever else was at dinner tonight."

"*What?*" Kovich pushed up his glasses, leaving red marks on his nose.

"You heard me. Let's check the rest of the house."

Brinkley and Kovich went through the kitchen, where a large dinner salad sat waiting in pink Saran, and then went through the bathroom, noting the bloodstained towels and the toilet where Newlin had vomited. There was no mistaking the smell, and the detectives took notes, made sketches, and went upstairs. The master bedroom was sterile, the closets neat and well stocked, with a wedding picture on the white vanity, the wife in a flowing white gown that trailed like a cloud. The his-and-her bathrooms were in order, and Brinkley took notes and ordered everything bagged.

Everything looked perfect, even the library, and the wife's home office, which contained a slew of photographs of herself, her husband, horses, and a boat, but only a single photo of the daughter. It was a posed publicity shot, and though the girl looked gorgeous, it wasn't personal in the least. Brinkley tagged the files to be boxed and seized, and listened to the messages on the office answering machine, all routine. Nothing he bagged was remotely as intriguing as the earring back.

He located the daughter's room, which looked like a room for the kid who had everything. Big canopy bed, school desk with books, and three shelves of pretty white dolls. He scanned the shelves but the dolls stared back at him blankly, and nothing was out of order. He had that earring back on the brain. He went over to the dresser and eyeballed it for a jewelry box. Bottles of perfume, hair things, and a box of burled wood sat against the mirror, and he probed its lid with a pen. It was locked. The key must be somewhere. Brinkley searched the drawers with his pen. Silk undies, T-shirts, sweaters, all folded in a rainbow of colors. No key to the box, no nothing. He'd get it after it was seized.

He left the dressers, searched under the bed, between the mattress, and then moved on to the bathroom. It was well stocked but nothing looked unusual, except he found a pink plastic wheel of birth control pills. Brinkley had never seen them before; Sheree didn't need them. He turned away at the memory and left the room to find Kovich.

"I keep thinking about that earring back," Brinkley said, as they walked down the grand, carpeted staircase. "Something that falls off easy, by the body. Makes sense it belonged to the killer. Got knocked off during the struggle."

"Give it up, Mick. Like I said, that earring coulda been dropped a long time ago."

"True, or maybe it was dropped by whoever Newlin's lying to protect. Whoever eats hummus and puts their feet up." They reached the bottom of the staircase where the techs were working on their final tasks. A low steel gurney rolled in on wheels that squeaked as they negotiated the thick, costly rugs. One of the coroner's assistants gave Brinkley the high sign, and the detective nodded absently. "Earrings, a vegetarian, and dirty feet on the table? I'm no expert, but it says teenager to me."

"You're serious?"

"Dead serious. I want to talk to the daughter."

"Christ, Mick." Kovich's eyes widened behind the big window of his glasses. "She's Kelley's age."

"Kelley loses her earring backs, too. You just told me that," Brinkley said, but was suddenly distracted by the shouted one-two-three count of the coroner's assistants, the sound of an industrial zipper being closed, then the squeaking of the gurney's wheels back across the rugs. The gurney rattled past the detectives, bearing the black body bag.

"Film at eleven," Kovich said, but Brinkley was making Honor Newlin a secret promise.

I'll get your killer, he told her, and he knew that she heard him, in some other place and time.

9

After Mary had delivered Paige to her father, she went to find Judy in the Roundhouse lobby, busy despite the late hour. Groups of department employees stood chatting in street clothes, oblivious to the activity around them. Two cops hurried to the exit, their gun holsters and waist radios flapping, and three others dragged a vastly overweight drunk between them in handcuffs. The toes of his sneakers squeaked across the polished floor, making the cops at the security desk laugh.

The oval lobby, with its dramatic curved shape, was modern when it was built, but now looked obviously dated, reminding Mary of *The Jetsons* come to life. Wooden acoustic slats ringed the room, the floor was a funky flecked tile, and the walls were covered with oil portraits of police brass, odd in the space-age setting. An American flag and the blue flag of the Commonwealth of Pennsylvania flanked the security desk, the fluorescent lighting glinting dully on their synthetic weave. Mary spotted Judy reading the newspaper across the room and hurried over.

"Yo, come with me," she said, grabbing Judy's arm. "We have to talk." She hustled Judy aside so no one could hear and told her what had happened in Paige's apartment with the photo. "Don't you think it's odd that she lied about being with her boyfriend on the night her mother was killed?"

"You don't know that she lied. You don't know that the kid in the hall was her boyfriend."

"I think he was. So why would she lie?"

"Maybe she doesn't want you to know her business, whiz."

"This is the night the murder was committed, and Paige was supposed to go to dinner at her parents' house, she told me. She let it slip." Mary glanced over her shoulder. A circle of women talked near a display case that contained model squad cars. "What do you think about that?"

"I don't think it means anything. Not much anyway."

"What if she really did go to her parents' tonight? What if her boyfriend went, too? That doesn't mean much?"

"That didn't happen, Mare. Newlin confessed. He called nine-one-one from the scene. He's even willing to take responsibility for the crime, which he should."

"He could be protecting her."

"Set himself up for murder? Who would do that?"

"A loving father," Mary answered without hesitation, and Judy looked at her like she was nuts.

"My father would never do anything like that, and he loves me."

"For real?"

"Of course not. Confess to a murder he didn't commit? He's not like that."

"My father would do it, in a minute." Mary summoned an image of her father's deep brown eyes and soft, round face. "He would do anything for me, make any sacrifice. If he could save us from something terrible, any kind of harm, he would."

"Doesn't right or wrong matter?"

"Wrong is if something bad happens to me or my sister."

Judy shook her head. "Well, it's not a given, and I really doubt that's what happened with Newlin. Don't be distracted by his looks."

"I'm not."

"You are, too. You'd have to be. But like you told him, there's a ton of evidence that he did it and there's no evidence that Paige did it."

"How do you know? We're not looking for any. Nobody is."

The more Mary said it, the more it seemed possible. "The cops bought his story and they're going with it. We bought his story and we're going with it. Jack Newlin is about to plead guilty and go to jail for life, right?"

"Right."

"But what if he's innocent? What if instead of having a client who's telling us he's innocent when he's guilty, we have a client who's telling us he's guilty when he's innocent?"

Jack saw Paige enter the interview area, a reed of a girl wrapped in a chic black leather jacket. Her wet blue eyes took the dirty interview room in with one appalled look and she rushed to the chair in front of him, her expression so anguished it made Jack feel as if she were the one in prison for life. Which now, in a way, she was.

"Dad, I can't let you do this," Paige said, her voice urgent. Tears spilled from her eyes and her brow was a network of premature worry lines. "I can't let you. I won't let you."

"You have to. You have no choice."

"But it's not right. Your job, your life." Paige wiped the tears beginning to streak her cheeks. Her hair, slicked back in the ponytail style Jack favored, was damp from the rain outside. "Dad, they could give you the death penalty!"

"No, they won't." Jack tried to keep calm. He had so many questions for her, but above all, he had to convince her to follow his plan. She could ruin her life in one night. "Listen to me, Paige. If I plead guilty, they won't charge me with the death penalty. That's how it works."

"But Dad, your whole life, in prison? That's terrible."

"Not at all. They'll send me to Woodville with the other rich guys. It's like a country club. Sammy Cott went there last year. Took ten strokes off his game." Jack smiled, but couldn't coax one from Paige. "Come on, honey. I'll be okay."

"No, you won't." Paige began to cry. "The people . . . the other prisoners . . . they'll hurt you."

"That won't happen, not to me. Lawyers get special status in prison, didn't you know that? Jailhouse lawyers are very valuable. Nobody hurts them."

"Yes, they do," Paige blurted through her tears. "I saw it on TV. On HBO . . . there's this show. You should see what they do . . . to them. There's a lawyer in there and they . . . "

"That's only on TV." Jack had to cut her off. She could get hysterical and she had to keep her wits about her. "I'll do fine, honey. I may even like it. I'll finally represent some honest clients, huh?" He smiled again, but Paige was crying too hard to see, her head bent and her lovely face covered by slim hands. Jack felt his heart wrench as he noticed her hands shaking. He loved her so much, this beautiful child. He had just been getting to know her when this happened. "It's all right. Don't cry, sweetie."

"It's not . . . all right."

"It will be. I'll make it all right, you'll see. You can visit me every week, whenever you want to. The world doesn't end because I go to prison. We'll see more of each other than before. Who knows, our relationship may even improve." Jack laughed, then he saw her shoulders finally relax. Her face came up from her hands, bleary-eyed but smiling, and his heart eased. He felt struck at the power of love, even at the most unexpected times. Especially at the most unexpected times.

"Dad, that's not funny."

"Think of the upside. No more suits and ties, which I hate. And they make all my food for me. You know what a lousy cook I am. Remember when I made the tofu turkey for you? And that hummus you love? It came out like spackle."

"That's not funny either." Paige giggled, and Jack beamed.

"It's not meant to be funny. Dad jokes are never funny, everybody knows that."

"You aren't that kind of dad." Paige sniffled.

"I am, too!" Jack said, in mock offense. "I'm no slacker when it comes to bad jokes. Remember the avocado?"

"No. Tell it to me."

"Okay, what did the avocado say to the celery before they got married?" Jack's heart caught in his throat as his daughter replied:

"Avocado never-ending love for you."

"Right," he said, his voice thick. "That's a pretty bad joke, isn't it?"

"It's a terrible joke." She wiped her eyes.

"You would say, 'it sucks.'"

"It sucks *bad*." Paige laughed, and the sound touched Jack so deeply that he kept talking, hoping the congestion in his throat would work itself out.

"Think of this that way, honey. I'm more responsible than anyone for what happened. It was brewing from the day your mom and I married. You don't know all the reasons for it and you don't have to pay for it. I do."

"No, you didn't do it." Paige kneaded her forehead, still creased with worry. "My head is killing me. I should tell the police what happened. I should be the one confessing."

"Don't do that! Don't even say that! I won't allow it," he said sternly, and Paige looked up, startled.

"I could tell them, you know. You couldn't stop me."

"I'd say you were lying to protect me. They would believe me and not you."

"Why?" Paige's eyes bored into his, and Jack knew he needed to be convincing now. He could see she was actually considering it. He should have anticipated that. She always had a soft heart.

"There are lots of reasons. Because I told them a story that implicates me, for one. Because they'll have direct evidence against me, for another."

"How?"

"It's not for you to know."

"Whatever, it doesn't matter. I could tell them the truth."

"No, please. Who would you rather send to prison, a pretty young girl or a lawyer? It's a no-brainer."

"I don't know." Paige was shaking her head. Her skin was mottled from stress. "God, my brain's going to . . . explode."

"Paige, for once in your life, let me do something for you."

"You did things for me. You worked, you had a job."

"That's not something I did for you, and what I made was a drop in the bucket compared to your mother and you know it."

"You were there, Dad."

"True, I was present. I was in attendance."

"I didn't mean it that way—"

"But I did. *I* did." Jack leaned over the counter. "I was there, but that's it. I let your mother run the show. I was just a guy in the background. I was there, at the birthday parties. I was like an actor playing a role—Father. But I really wasn't a father to you, not the way a father should be."

"What's a father?" Paige blinked, her eyes glistening. "A hero?"

"No, not a hero. Just a man," Jack answered, his words suddenly clarifying his thinking. "I will do this for you. I already have. But there is one thing you have to do, in return. You have to tell me the truth about what happened to your mother."

Paige looked down and sighed deeply. "What happened? It's hard to say. I mean, it's like I don't know."

"What do you mean, you don't know?" Jack heard anger creep into his tone. "You were there, weren't you?"

"Yes."

"Was Trevor there?"

"No, he stayed home, like you said."

"Is that the truth?"

"Dad." Paige glared at him, plainly insulted. "Yes, I told you."

"Good." Jack eased forward on his cold seat, watching Paige's hand shake again as she smoothed back her hair. "I know this is hard for you. I know that whatever happened with you and Mom, it's not easy to talk about."

"It's worse than that." She hung her head and her voice sounded so agonized Jack wondered for a moment why he was forcing the issue. He wanted to get the details of his own story straight, in case they questioned him again, but more important, he wanted to make Paige account for it, at least in this small way.

He, and she, owed Honor at least that. He pushed his resentment away when Paige started to cry again.

"I'm sorry, I'm so sorry," she said, between sobs. "It's so hard to know . . . where to start, even."

"At the beginning." Jack remembered her telephone call to him that afternoon. He had been at his desk drafting a letter and was so pleased that Paige had called him at work. Then she had said she was coming home to dinner and told him why, and that she was going to tell Honor that night. Paige had said she needed help to tell her mother. She couldn't know how much.

"Oh, no. Dad." Paige looked down at her hands lying limp in her lap, then she blinked through her tears. "I think . . . I'm getting a migraine. A bad one. Dad."

"Oh, no." Jack felt stricken. Paige had been plagued with migraines ever since she was young. Paralyzing headaches that hit anytime Paige was stressed and sent her to her bedroom, where she'd draw the curtains and sleep for hours. "Did you see the aura?" he asked, anxious. He meant the double vision or glittery lights that warned her.

"I . . . think so. Wait. Hold on." Paige held up her hand and turned it slowly, gazing at it with eyes strangely out of focus. Jack had seen her do it so many times. If she saw an aura, it meant the migraine was on the way and she had only minutes to hurry to bed. She could take Duadrin at the onset of the migraine, which could head off the symptoms if she took it in time.

"Do you have your meds?"

"No," Paige said, and it came out like a soft wail. "When the lawyer told me you were here . . . I just got dressed and left. I didn't think. I didn't even bring my purse." Her hand dropped to her lap. "Uh-oh. It's . . . coming. Waiting for it is the worst."

"Oh God, no meds?" The pain couldn't be prevented, like a freight train racing at his daughter. Jack had seen how fast it could hit; in five to ten minutes Paige would be reduced to incoherence and agony. He couldn't do that to her. "Honey, go home and lie down right away. The lawyers are right upstairs. Go to them."

"No, no, I want to talk to you." Her hand rose to her forehead and she touched it gingerly. "I want to tell you what happened . . . with Mom."

"You should go." Jack was burning to hear what had happened, but he couldn't torture his own child, twist the vise around her head himself. "Please, we'll talk another time. Go home. God knows, I'm not going anywhere."

"No, no . . . I feel able . . . to talk." Paige rubbed her forehead. "It was just me and Mom . . . I came home to dinner . . . I don't know . . . where to start."

"You went over to dinner," Jack supplied, to help her. "I was supposed to meet you there but I was late. I am so sorry."

"It's not your fault." Tears returned to her eyes but she brushed them away with the back of her hand. "I was early. It wasn't going to go well, I knew. So . . . I went home and she was there. I was . . . going to wait for you, to tell her, but . . . she started in. That I was . . . gaining weight." Paige's tears halted and her voice turned bitter. "I was looking fat. I was . . . retaining water. Oh, my God, my head." Paige kneaded her brow. "Shit."

"You should go. Please go."

"No." Paige waved him off, her hand shaking. "She started in . . . on how I couldn't gain weight. How I had to . . . control myself. How I had to watch what I ate . . . now that my big chance . . . was coming up."

Jack winced. As Paige had grown older, Honor had nagged Paige more about her weight. He had argued that it would drive Paige to anorexia or worse, but neither heeded him. It was always as if he were speaking offstage in a drama played out between mother and daughter. "So you and your mom started fighting, right from the beginning."

"Yes. It got me so . . . upset. It was like . . . I knew why I was gaining . . . and she didn't know. And then . . . I felt like who was *she* to tell me, I'm emancipated and I am not a child, and now . . . I was . . . *having* a child."

Jack felt queasy at the words. Paige had told him on the phone, but hearing it said out loud made it undeniable. His child was having a child. *Their* child was having a child. It was bad news for any parents, but worse for Jack and Honor, given their history. He could only imagine how Honor would have taken the news.

"Oh, no. This is going to be a bad one." Paige's forehead buckled in pain and her hand covered it futilely. "Listen . . . I was thinking . . . now she can't tell me anything . . . because I'm going to be a mother. Not just her. *Me*. All of a sudden . . . I was happy about it. Really happy . . . and I wanted to tell her. So it just . . . came out."

Jack visualized the scene. Paige happy about delivering news that was Honor's worst nightmare.

"I said, 'I'm pregnant, Mom . . . that's why I'm so hungry. So I have to eat and . . . there's nothing anybody can do about it. Because I'm going to . . . *have a baby.*' " Paige stopped suddenly. "That's the beginning of the migraine. It's . . . coming. I'll tell it . . . fast. I looked at her expression . . . and I couldn't believe it. Her eyes . . . they were so big . . . and angry. She looked like . . . a witch."

Jack couldn't even guess at the look.

"Then . . . she hit me." Fresh tears came to Paige's eyes and her face flushed with emotion. "She *hit* me . . . right on the face. Like a really hard slap . . . she called me things but she never . . . hit me before. *Ever.* She hit me so hard . . . I fell off the chair. She *knocked me right off the chair* . . . onto the floor. I couldn't believe . . . it."

But Jack could. Though Honor wasn't a violent woman, this news would move her to it. This news would unhinge her, undo all of them. He wanted to tell Paige the truth right then, had the impulse to explain, but fought it. This wasn't the place or the time. She had only a few minutes before the migraine hit full force. She'd become incapable even of speech.

"I got up from the floor . . . my face was hurting, and I started to cry. Then she grabbed me and . . . threw me down again . . . and started *kicking me*. Kicking me . . . Dad . . . *over and over*. Like in my *stomach*." Paige's sobbing started again, and Jack's gut twisted. "She had on her mules . . . with the pointy toes, and she was, like . . . *aiming for my stomach*, Dad. Really *hard* . . .

with the toe. For the . . . *baby*. Like she was trying to . . . *kick it out of me*."

No. Jack just kept shaking his head. No. He didn't know if he had even said it aloud.

"She started yelling . . . 'You kill it or I'll kill it!' . . . 'You kill it or I'll kill it!' Dad . . . my head. I can't . . . I really can't—" Paige covered her face and doubled over, falling forward on the counter and collapsing into tears. "I don't know what . . . happened next. I just don't, Dad . . . I swear." Paige was crying full bore, but trying to talk. "I started to hurt . . . all over, from my belly . . . and my chest. . . . I started to hurt, so much . . . I rolled away from her. I said . . . I wasn't getting an abortion. But she kept . . . coming at me . . . *kicking*."

No. He didn't want to hear any more. He didn't want to put Paige through any more.

"I was so scared . . . and hurt so much . . . I couldn't even see. I mean, I didn't think she'd kill me, I only know I got so angry, for me, for my baby, it was like . . . I was angry for so long, my whole life. Then, I think . . . I got up . . . and grabbed the knife. I remember . . . I grabbed the knife." Paige looked up, tears streaming down a face contorted with pain. "I can't . . . *think*."

Jack blinked away his own tears. It was his fault. He hadn't been there. Not only tonight, but for all of her childhood. He hadn't known how bad it had been, but that was no excuse. He should have known; it was his job to know. He had deserted his own daughter and when he had finally realized it, he was too late. Guilt engulfed him, drowning him like a wave.

"I went kind of . . . *crazy*. I was yelling and crying . . . it was like everything came back at me . . . I mean . . . I knew I was mad at her . . . but I guess I just got out of control . . . and I stabbed her and when I was done, she was . . . she was"—Paige's expression was a frieze of agony—"she was *lying there* . . . on the *floor*. I dropped the . . . knife. It was all . . . bloody. I didn't mean . . . I just left her there . . . and ran out. I just ran . . . I'm sorry, Dad. I'm so *sorry*." Paige's words dissolved into tears, and her shoulders collapsed as easily as a dollhouse.

Jack couldn't help but raise his hands, even handcuffed, to the plastic barrier between them, touching it with his fingertips. It was cold, hard, and lifeless, so unlike the warm, silky hair of his little girl. How often had he touched Paige's head? Not often enough. Now he had to save her. "Paige," he said, "what did you tell the lawyers?"

"I said . . . I wasn't there." Paige was sobbing hard. "That . . . I didn't go over."

"Okay, so you were never there tonight. You never went over. Stick with that story, understand?"

"It's . . . a lie. God, my head. The . . . lights."

"I know it's a lie. I don't care." Jack lowered his hands and leaned forward urgently. "Never, Paige. Never breathe a word. If you do, you and your baby are lost."

"My baby?" Paige looked at him through her tears. Her eyes were red and swollen. Her skin was a mass of hives. "What about my baby?"

"Think about the baby, Paige. We didn't even get to talk about the baby. What are you planning to do?"

"I don't know, for sure." Paige's weeping stilled. "Get married. Trevor wants to."

Jack cringed inwardly. "What about college? You told me you'd set aside modeling for college."

"I'll go later, after the baby."

Jack bit his tongue. "Okay, let's assume for the moment that's the right decision. If you come forward and tell the police what happened, who will raise the baby? Trevor? Of course not. You have to think of your baby, not me. Please don't interfere with me. If the police question you, say you weren't at the house. Say you were surprised by what I did. Don't go to my arraignment or any other court proceeding. Let me do what I have to do."

"I can't."

"Put your hand on your tummy, right now. Do it, Paige." Jack's tone was so commanding he sounded strange even to himself. Something was happening to him. He felt like he was coming into his own. Maybe even redeeming himself. "Put your hand on your tummy."

Paige did as she was told, crying as she rested her slender, pale hand against the slick black leather of her jacket. She was listening to him, Jack could see.

"That's your baby, in there. Inside you. That baby is your first obligation now, not me. You're a mother now. *You* are the mother. *Be* a mother."

"Okay, Dad," Paige said in a whisper, and Jack knew from her eyes that she had yet to think of herself that way. She would do what he said. She owed a responsibility to someone other than herself, as he did. In one horrific, rainy night, she had become a parent.

And so, finally, had Jack.

10

It was late at night when Mary grabbed the C bus, sitting with her Coach bag and briefcase in the blue plastic seats in the front. The bus was one of the new SEPTA models, white and sharply boxy, with advertisements for TV shows sprayed all over, even the windows. At this hour, the bus was almost completely empty and barreled hollowly down Broad Street. The business day was long over, the in-town shoppers had gone home, and Mary, by any account, should have done the same.

Instead she was going to her parents' house, in South Philly. She told herself it was on the way home, but it really wasn't, and in time she stopped trying to justify her decision. After an evening spent glimpsing the interior of the Newlin family, she yearned to be reminded of what a normal family was like, or at least, her family. Where nobody knifed each other and the only serious fights concerned the Pope. Whoever said you can't go home again didn't grow up near the C.

Mary gazed out the bus window in the dark, watching Broad Street change from the marbled-and-mirrored financial district to the neon funkiness of South Street, surrounded by modern rowhouses filled with lawyers, doctors, and accountants. The gentrified district disappeared in five or six blocks, and businesses began to appear among the less desirable rowhouses; nail and funeral parlors, the omnipresent McDonald's, and Dunkin'

Donuts. She was entering the Italian neighborhood in which she grew up, and though it was only fifteen minutes from the center of Philadelphia, it could have been across the country. Still, the streets of her neighborhood felt more real to her than the law firms downtown.

Mary thought about it as she rode along, and the farther south she went, the better she felt. She remembered that Judy was very attached to her hometown in California, and had told her once about something called land memory. Either you have it or the land does, Mary had never been completely sure, but the bottom line was that you felt best on the land you and your family had grown up on, and in time you made it your own. And no matter what happened to you or to the land, you still felt best there. Standing on it. Being there.

The bus rattled ahead and she watched the land change to dingy rowhouses with city grit blown into each crevice, darkening the mortar. The color of the brick managed to fight its way through, showing the spunk of a weed in a sidewalk crack, and each house had been built with a different color brick; some were the yellow of dark marigolds, some even a pumpkin orange, and the conventional dark red. Each rowhouse had different decorative touches in its façade; in some, the bricks at the top were tilted so the ends stuck out and made a cute line of baby teeth, and in others a layer of narrower brick underlined the flat roofline, an inner-city underscoring. The stoops were the focus of the homes, like the smile of each place; there was marble, concrete, and flagstone, a classy touch.

Mary swayed with the bus, her eyes on the cityscape. The houses were only two stories, so the night sky shimmered above as broad as over any grassy plain, and the luster of the stars wasn't diminished by the telephone wires. She smiled to herself. She was going home. The land didn't have to be the soaring, craggy mountains or cool shady forests that Judy had described. The land could be concrete, couldn't it? Grimy, gritty, shitty, too-close-together, gum-spattered South Philadelphia. If you had spent your childhood there—playing, laughing, walking to school—even a city block could be your land, and you had as much right to the land memory as anybody else.

The bus approached her street, and Mary grabbed her brief-case and got up to go. She held the stainless steel bar, reading the curved ads running along the top of the bus, the ever-popular yellow PREGNANT? and RÉSUMÉ SERVICES. The bus lurched to the same sudden stop it had every day since she'd taken it home from high school, guaranteed to hurl Catholic schoolgirls through the windshield.

But Mary wasn't to be outsmarted. She held tight to the pole through the stop and then thanked the driver on the way out, which was something else the nuns had taught her. Turn the other cheek, even when people shit on you for no reason. Mary had had to overcome that thinking to be a lawyer; parochial school hadn't prepared her for anything except sainthood.

And the job openings were so few.

The rooms on the first floor of her parents' rowhouse were strung like beads on a rosary: living room, dining room, and kitchen. The tiny kitchen was the only room in which the DiNunzios spent time. It contained a square Formica table with padded chairs and was ringed with refaced white cabinets and a white counter with water cracks in each corner. Mass cards and Easter palm aged behind bumpy black switch plates, though the faded Pope John photo had fallen off the wall last year and cracked its frame on the thin linoleum. Mary's mother had taken it as a bad sign and made a week of novenas. Mary had declined to remind her that Jesus Christ didn't believe in the evil eye.

"Is it too late to stop by, Dad?" Mary asked, her face brushing against the worn plaid cotton of her father's bathrobe. He was giving Mary a hug in the warm kitchen, and when he pulled away, his eyes looked hurt at the question.

"Whadda you mean, baby?" her father said softly. "Sure, you can always come home, no matter how late. You know I'm up, watchin' TV."

A short, soft man, Mariano DiNunzio was almost seventy-five, with pudgy cheeks in a barely lined face, and full lips with deep laugh lines. Bifocals with dark frames slipped down a bulbous nose and he wore a white sleeveless T-shirt and pajama pants under his bathrobe. Though he had gained weight, he had the build of the tile setter he had been before his back had given out; his body was shaped like a city fireplug and twice as solid. The DiNunzios specialized in low centers of gravity.

"Thanks, Pop," Mary answered. She knew it was exactly what he'd say, and the sound of it comforted her. She had always been her father's favorite and remained close to him as an adult, when she became aware that their conversations included complete paragraphs of call-and-response, like a priest to his congregation. *Et cum spiritu tuo.*

"I'll make the coffee," he said. "You wanna set the table?"

"Sure." Mary smiled, knowing that the question was part of the same Mass, celebrating the making of late-night coffee. While she went to the cabinets to retrieve cups and saucers, her father shuffled to the sink to fill the stainless steel coffeepot with water. The DiNunzios still used a percolator to make coffee, its bottom dent the only signs of wear in thirty-odd years. Progress was something that came to other households. Thank God.

"You should stop by more often, Mare," her father said, as water plunked into the coffeepot. He turned off the water, set the pot on the counter, and pried the plastic lid from the can of Maxwell House, releasing only the faintest aroma. He scooped dry grounds into the pot's basket, and the sound reverberated in the quiet kitchen, as familiar to Mary from her childhood as a toy shovel through wet, dark sand down at the Jersey shore. *Scoop, scoop, scoop.* And though it was only the two of them, her father would make eight cups of coffee. A veritable sandcastle of caffeine.

"Come more often? Dad, I'm here every Sunday, practically, for dinner." Mary snared two cups by their chipped handles and grabbed two saucers in a fake English pattern they had bought at Wanamaker's, a store that didn't exist anymore. They were just perfect, but she couldn't resist teasing. "Think we'll ever get mugs, Pop?"

"Mugs?"

"Coffee mugs. They have them now, with sayings on them. It's a new thing."

"Wise guy," her father scoffed, blinking behind his bifocals. They were thick, but not as thick as her mother's. Her mother could barely see, from a lifetime of piecework sewing in the basement of the house. Her father had good eyes but could barely hear, the result of living with Mary, her twin, and her mother. Mary had bought him two hearing aids before he consented to wear the one he had now. It sat curled in his ear like a brown snail.

"No, really. I could get you a mug that says World's Greatest Father."

"Nah. Mugs, they're not so nice. Not as nice as cups and saucers."

"People use them all the time."

"I see that. I know things. I get out." He smiled, and so did Mary. It was a game they were both playing.

"And computers, they use, too."

"Computers?" Her father cackled. "I see that, on the TV. All the time, computers. You know, Tony. Tony-from-down-the-block. He got on the Internet." Her father wagged the blue scoop at her. "Writes to some lady in Tampa, Florida. How about *that*?"

"There you go. You could have girlfriends in Tampa, too."

"Nah, I'm more interested in my daughter and why she don't go to church with us on Sunday."

"Oh, Pop." Mary went to the silverware drawer for teaspoons. "You gotta start on me?"

"Your mother would like that, if you went with us on Sunday. She was sayin' that to me just tonight, before she went to bed. 'Wouldn't it be nice if Mary came to church with the family?' Angie goes with us now."

"Angie has to. She was a nun." Mary's voice sounded more bitter than she intended, and her father's soft shoulders slumped.

She felt a twinge at disappointing him, and guilt gathered like a puffy gray cloud over her head, ready to storm on her and only her. "Okay, you win. Maybe I will go with you, sometime. How about that, Pop?"

"Good." Her father nodded, one shake of his bald head, with a wispy fringe of matte gray hair. He set the coffeepot on the stove, twisted on the gas, and turned around as it lit with an audible *floom*. The pilot light on the ancient stove was too high again. "This Sunday, you'll come?"

"This Sunday?" Mary plucked two napkins from the plastic holder in the center of the table, where they had slipped to the bottom. "You drive a hard bargain."

"I bid construction, remember?"

She laughed. "Okay, this Sunday." She eased into her chair at the table. It was the one on the far side. "If I don't have to work."

Her father turned to the stove, the better to watch the pot, and Mary noticed his heavy hand touch his lower back. In recent years, back pain kept him up at nights, but he pretended he liked to watch TV until two in the morning, and she had always cooperated in this fiction. To do otherwise seemed cruel, but now she wondered about it. "Dad, how's your back?" she asked.

"No complaints," he said, which was what he always said. *Et cum spiritu tuo.*

"I know you don't want to complain, but tell me. How is your back?"

"It's fine." Her father opened the bread drawer and pulled out a plastic bag with an Italian roll it. He would have bought it at the corner bakery that morning, coming home every day with exactly three rolls; one for him, one for Mary's mother, and one for extra. The rolls would be buttered and dunked in the coffee, leaving veins of melted butter swirling slick on its surface and enriching its flavor. He took the roll out and set it on the counter, then folded the plastic bag in two, then four, and returned it to the drawer, to be reused for tomorrow's rolls. It wasn't about recycling.

"Are you taking your pills, for the pain?"

"Nah, they make me too sleepy." He put the roll on a plate and set it down on the table, near the butter, and Mary knew they would fight over it, each trying to give it to the other.

"Do you do your exercises?"

"I go for the newspaper in the morning, at the corner. In the afternoon, I buy my cigar with Tony-from-down-the-block."

"But your back hurts. How do you sleep with it?"

"With my eyes closed." Her father smiled, but Mary didn't.

"You stay downstairs at night and watch TV. It's not because you like TV, it's because you can't sleep. Isn't that right?"

Her father eased into his chair, leaning on one of his hands. His expression didn't change, a sly smile still traced his lips, but he didn't say anything. They sat at the table and regarded each other over the chipped china.

"Your back hurts," Mary said. "Tell me the truth."

"Why you gotta know that?"

"I don't know. I just want you to tell me."

Her father sighed deeply. "Okay. My back, it hurts."

"At night?"

"Yes."

"When else?"

Her father didn't answer except to purse soft lips. The coffee began to perk in the background, a single eruption like a stray burp.

"All the time?"

"Yes."

"But mostly at night?"

"Only 'cause I got nothing to think about then." His voice was quiet. The coffee burped again, behind him.

"I'm sorry about that. Is there anything I can do?"

"No."

"Maybe we should try new doctors. I could take you back to Penn. They have great doctors there."

"You made me go last year. S'enough already." Her father waved his hand. "Is that why you came here? To talk about the pain in my back?"

"In a way, yes."

"Well, you're givin' me a pain in my ass." He laughed, and so did Mary. She felt oddly better that he had told her the truth, even though it wasn't good news. She would have to hatch a new plan to get him back to the doctor's.

The coffeepot perked in the background, with better manners now, and she caught the first whiff of fresh brew. It was fun to drink coffee late at night, as settled a DiNunzio tradition as fish on Fridays. When her husband Mike had been alive, he used to join them for night coffee. He'd talk baseball with her father and even choked once on a cigar. He'd fit in so well with her family, better at times than she did, and then he was gone. She felt her neck warm with blood, her grief suddenly fresh. She hadn't felt that way for so long, but the Newlin case was dredging up memories.

"Honey, what'sa matter?" her father said, reaching across the table and covering her hand with his. It felt dry and warm. "I was only kidding. You're not a pain, baby."

"I know." Mary blinked wetness from her eyes. "I'm okay."

"You're about to cry, how can you be okay?" He reached for the napkin holder but there were none left, so he started to get up.

Mary grabbed his hand as it left hers. "No, sit. I'm fine. I know I'm not a pain in the ass. Actually, I am, but that's not what I'm upset about." She smiled shakily to convince him. "I was thinking about Mike. You know."

His face fell, his eyebrows sloping suddenly. "Oh. Michael."

"I'm okay, though."

"Me, too."

"Good. How's your back? No complaints?" she asked, and they both laughed. The coffee perked madly in the background, filling the small kitchen with steam and sound. Mary noticed it at the same time as her father did, but beat him to the stove. "I got it," she said, with a final sniffle. She lowered the heat but the gas went out, so she had to start over and relight the burner. "I hate this pilot light, Pop."

"I told you, they can't fix it."

"I'll sue them." She leaned sideways to light the thing, almost singeing her eyelashes with the *floom*. "I can't do anything about your back but I can do something about the fucking stove."

"Your language," her father said, but she could tell without looking that his heart wasn't in it. She turned around to find him still looking sad. Thanks to her, he was thinking about Mike, and suddenly she regretted coming home. Her father was better off with his TV and his back pain.

"Pop, let me ask you something. I got this case, at work. It's a tough one, a murder case."

Her father's round eyes went rounder. "Mare, you said you wouldn't take no more murder cases."

"I know but this is different. This guy is a father, and I think he's innocent. So don't start on me like Mom. It's my job, okay?"

"Okay, okay." Her father put up his hands. "Don't shoot."

"Sorry." She sat down while the kitchen warmed with the aroma of brewing coffee. "Here's the question. If I committed a murder, would you tell the police that you did it, to protect me?"

"If *you* did a murder?" His forehead wrinkled with alarm. "You would never do no murder."

"I know. But if I did, would you go to jail for me?"

Her father didn't hesitate. "Sure, I don't want you in jail. If you did a murder, it would be for a good reason."

Mary thought about it. What could Paige's reason be? "What's a good reason?"

"If you were gonna die and you had to save yourself."

"Self-defense."

"Yeh." He cocked his head. "Or like tonight, I saw on the TV, this lady who killed her husband. He used to beat her up, you know, when he got drunk. Night after night. Then one night he came home after he went fishing and he stuck a fish down her throat. A *fish*, in her *throat*. Almost choked her with it. What a *cavone*." He shuddered. "And finally she got so sick of him doing things like that that she shot him."

"So, if somebody did that to me and I shot him, that would be a good reason."

"If somebody did that to you, *I* would shoot him."

Mary smiled. Her father was such a peaceable man she couldn't imagine it, but the way he said it, maybe she could. He'd been a laborer, not an altar boy. "Now, here's the hard part. What if I told you that the person I killed was my mother?"

"Your mother?" Her father's sparse eyebrows flew up. "Your *mother*?"

"Uh-huh."

"If you killed your own mother?" He ran a dry hand over his smooth head. "Holy God. Well, then I would say your mother musta been doing bad things to you."

"Would you go to jail for me, even then?"

"Sure, in a minute." He buckled his lower lip in thought. "Especially then."

"Why?"

"Because if your mother was doing bad things to you, it would be my fault."

"How so?"

"I woulda let it happen." He pushed the plate with the roll toward her, as the coffee started to bubble madly. "Now, eat, baby."

11

attended the University of Pennsylvania Law School, Yale, and Girard before that."

It was just after two o'clock in the morning but Dwight Davis would be working all night. He was arraigning Newlin at nine and he was watching the videotape for the umpteenth time. His care wasn't only because of what Brinkley had said last night; he was always scrupulous in case preparation. He had written down everything Newlin had said on a pad in front of him. The D.A.'s office didn't have the resources to order a same-day transcript, which any civil law firm could have done, although in criminal cases, it was justice, not money, that hung in the balance. Davis would never accept it.

"Don't believe everything you read. Reporters have to sell newspapers."

He sat alone at one end of the table in the dim light of a small conference room in the D.A.'s offices. Boxes of case files sat stacked against the far wall, a set of trial exhibits on foam-core, and on top rested an open bag of stale Chips Ahoy. Davis didn't mind the mess. He liked having the whole office to himself. He'd had grown up an only child in a happy family and he coveted quiet time to think, plan, and work. As a prosecutor, time without ringing phones became even rarer, and Newlin would demand it. He'd already devoured the lab results, spread out in front of him like a fan.

"I don't mean to be impolite, but is there a reason for this small talk?"

The bloody prints on the knife matched Newlin's. The serology was his, too, and fibers of the wife's silk blouse were found on his jacket, as if from a struggle. The techs had even managed to lift his prints off her blouse and hands. And the photos of Newlin showed a small cut on his right hand, from the knife. The physical evidence was there. But watching Newlin on videotape, Davis's canny eye told him that something was wrong with Newlin's confession. Something about Newlin had betrayed him. His nervousness, or something Davis couldn't put his finger on. The man was lying.

"I guess I should tell you, my marriage hadn't been going very well lately."

Davis had to find his lie. Figure out what it was. Instinct and experience told him it was there. But where? He sat at one end of the table and Newlin, on video, sat at the other, squaring off in the dark. Or almost dark. A four-panel window faced Arch Street and the last blind was cinched up unevenly, like an Oriental fan on its side. The blinds would never be repaired; they were as permanent as the leftover Chips Ahoy.

"For a year, actually. Honor wasn't very happy with me."

The image on the screen was grayish, the focus poor, and the lighting gloomy. Under Newlin's face was a line of changing white numbers, a time clock that ran into split seconds. The numbers were fuzzy. When the hell would they get decent equipment? The same time the blinds got repaired. Money, money, money. Frustrated, Davis picked up the remote, hit STOP, then replayed the sentence. Where was the lie? What was wrong with this confession?

"Something snapped inside. I lost control. I threw my glass at her but she just laughed. I couldn't stand it, her laughing at me like that."

Liar, liar, liar. Then Davis realized Newlin was lying about the way the murder had gone down. It hadn't been a crime of passion, fueled by Scotch or threat of divorce. Newlin wasn't a crime-of-passion kind of guy, all you had to do was look at him to know that. He was an estates lawyer, the kind of man who planned death. Could it be any more obvious? And what kind of pussy threw a glass in anger? Women threw glasses; men threw punches. No, Davis wasn't buying.

"I realized there was no way I could hide what I'd done. I had no plan, I hadn't thought it out. I didn't even have a way to get her body out of the house."

Classic protesting too much, he had seen it over and over again. Davis had Newlin's number. Everybody knew the family, one of the wealthiest in town, and it always was her money, Buxton money. So, follow the money. Newlin must have killed her because he wanted her money, pure and simple, and made a plan. Either he had decided to kill her himself or hired someone to do it for him, but something had gone wrong. Newlin was trying to cover that up, trying to sell that it was a fight that went too far. What had happened? Davis would have to find out, but with this much dough floating around, it had to be premeditated.

"I wasn't thinking logically, I was reacting emotionally. To her shouting, to her insults. To the Scotch. I just did it."

Davis's anger momentarily blinded him to the image of Newlin. He kicked himself for not realizing the scam at the crime scene, which had been too perfect to be real. Newlin had come home, stabbed his wife, and staged the scene to look like a fight. Thrown the crystal glass down after she was dead. Drunk Scotch over her body, to congratulate himself on a job well done. Acted real confused when he washed up his hands. Cried crocodile tears when he called nine-one-one.

"Detective, this interview is over. I want to call my attorney."

Davis couldn't understand Brinkley's problem. Maybe the detective hadn't had the benefit of the lab results, or maybe Brinkley was smelling that Newlin was a liar and mistook what Newlin was lying about. To Davis, Newlin was a selfish, sick, cold-cock murderer. He would have to get to the bottom of Newlin's scam. Learn how he'd planned to get the wife's dough.

"I insist on my attorney."

Davis hated people like Newlin, who were all about money. It was the ultimate perversion of values, and he had witnessed it firsthand. Crack pimps who knifed their more entrepreneurial girls, drug dealers who capped their light-fingered mules, teenage smoke dealers who executed their rivals with one slug from a nine millimeter. Newlin was no different from them; he just dressed better.

"I should have called him in the first place."

Davis stared at the TV without focusing. There was another thing he didn't understand. Why would Newlin say even this much to the detectives? Or botch it so completely? He heard Newlin making demands in a cold, impersonal tone, and he knew the answer immediately. Newlin was a big-time estate lawyer with an ego and a brain to match. He was thumbing his nose at them. He thought he could get away with it. Outsmart the legal system, even if they had a head start.

"I want my lawyer, and we'll take care of notifying Paige."

Davis looked at the filmed image of the corporate lawyer on the screen and knew instinctively that he was dealing with evil in its most seductive form. A nice guy. A partner in a respected firm. The caring father. Davis wasn't fooled by the guise, even if Brinkley was.

"I'll handle the notification through my attorney."

Davis predicted what Newlin's next step would be. He'd ask for a deal. He would have realized he'd said too much and the evidence would incriminate him. He wouldn't want a trial, with the ensuing embarrassment and trauma; he'd want his way greased, as it always had been. Newlin would try to plead down to a voluntary. Figure he'd get twenty and serve eight to ten. Come out a relatively young man with a shitload of his wife's dough. The murder rap would let him out of the insurance, but he'd have tons of bucks already socked away.

"But I am a lawyer."

Davis scowled. A lawyer, killing for money. It brought shame on all of them. Davis had always been proud of his profession and hated Newlin for his crime. On his own behalf, on Honor Newlin's behalf, and on behalf of the people of the Commonwealth. There was only justice to protect all of us. It sounded corny, but anything worth believing in ultimately sounded corny. Davis believed in justice; Newlin believed in money.

"*No thanks,*" the videotaped Newlin answered, and Davis saw the snotty smile that crossed Newlin's face.

It fueled Davis's decision. Suddenly he knew what to do in the case, but he'd need approval for it. It would be an extraordinary request, but this case was extraordinary. In fact, in all his years as a prosecutor, he had asked for such a thing only twice, and the Newlin case was worse than those. This would be the case of Davis's life and Newlin's. There was only one way to go. On the pad in front of him, he wrote:

NO DEALS.

He underlined it in a strong hand. The Commonwealth of Pennsylvania would not offer a plea bargain to Jack Newlin. Newlin would be prosecuted to the fullest extent of the law, like the common killer he was, even in his hundred-dollar tie. He would be tried, convicted, and sentenced to death for the murder of his wife, Davis would see to it.

He switched off the videotape, closed his pad, and stood up. He stretched, flexing every muscle; he'd been up for hours and hadn't run in two days, but he felt suddenly fit and strong. Alert and ready. Psyched. Davis was going to win.

Because he always did.

BOOK TWO

12

It was early the next morning when Mary returned to the interview room at the Roundhouse to meet with Newlin before his arraignment. She sat opposite him in the grim room, a bulletproof barrier between them. She wore a navy suit with a high-necked blouse to hide the blotches that would undoubtedly bloom like roses in court. That she felt them growing now, merely in Jack's presence, was difficult to explain. To herself. She didn't want to even think about explaining it to her client and was sure it breached several ethical canons, at least two disciplinary rules, and perhaps even a commandment.

Mary cleared her throat. "I wanted to see you to touch base. I have a strategy for our defense and I need to prepare you for the arraignment hearing."

"Sure, thanks." Jack seemed tired, too, in his wrinkled jumpsuit, but his good looks shone through fatigue's veneer. His five o'clock shadow had grown to a rougher stubble, which only emphasized how careless he seemed about his good looks. He raked back his sandy hair with a restless hand. "First tell me how everything's going."

"Better than I expected. I'm very encouraged by my research. That's why I'm here."

"No, I meant generally. The case is all over the news. How's Paige taking all of it?"

"Fine," Mary said, noting that his first question was about his daughter. She decided to test the water. "You know, I've been wondering about Paige. Where she was last night, when your wife was killed. Do you know?"

"Home I suppose. What's the difference?" Jack's expression was only mildly curious, and Mary, distracted, couldn't tell if it was an act. She both wanted and didn't want to believe him. She resolved to find uglier clients.

"Paige told me she was supposed to come to dinner with you and your wife, but she canceled. Is that right?"

"Yes, it is."

"She's telling the truth?"

"Of course she is." Jack's blue eyes hardened to ice.

"I ask because I thought teenagers made things up at times."

"Not Paige."

"I see." Mary paused. Was he lying? "You didn't mention that when we met."

"I didn't think it mattered, and it doesn't." Jack frowned. "Who cares who else was supposed to come to dinner the night I murdered my wife?"

"I do, it's my job. I think Paige may have lied to me about something. She told me her boyfriend Trevor wasn't with her last night, and I think he was."

"What? How do you know that?"

"I saw him leaving her apartment when I went to meet her." She checked Jack for a reaction, but he managed to look calm, except for that jaw clenching again. "And you said Paige doesn't lie."

"She doesn't, except when it comes to Trevor. I don't like him, and Paige knows it. That's probably why she said what she did. She wouldn't want me to know he was over there. Paige edits her conversations, like all of us." He appraised her. "You're not a liar, Mary, but I bet you don't tell your father about the men you see, do you?"

Mary squirmed. He was right but she didn't find it persuasive. She considered confronting him about whether he was protecting

Paige, but settled for planting a seed of doubt. "Okay, let's move on. Paige isn't what I came to talk to you about. I've been doing my homework, and the primary evidence against you will be your confession. The videotape."

"They said there would be other evidence, too. Physical evidence. They told me that."

"I know." Mary checked her notes. "But let me make my point. We can argue that you were drunk at the time you confessed."

"Drunk?"

"Yes. You said you had some Scotch. Two drinks, you weren't sure." She rummaged in her briefcase, pulled out her notes, and double-checked the law on point. "You said you weren't used to drinking and that it caused you to throw up. That's legally significant, and throws doubt on the validity of your waiver. The case law is clear that you can't waive your right to counsel when you're drunk."

"But I wasn't drunk."

"You could have had three Scotches."

"Two, I think."

"Isn't it possible you had three? You told me you had a few. A few is three."

"You want me to say three, is that what this is about?" Jack smiled easily, his teeth straight and even. "Are you coaching me, counselor?"

"Of course not." Mary never coached clients, though she had been known to kick them under the table, collar them in the hallway, or tell them to shut up. None of these breached ethical rules, and was, on the contrary, looked upon with favor. "But if you had two or three drinks, your blood alcohol had to be high. We'll get the tests when they turn them over, but frankly, I plan to argue you were impaired when you confessed."

"But you saw me. I wasn't drunk."

"By the time I saw you, maybe you weren't. Besides, I can't tell if someone's drunk in an interview, necessarily."

"This is silly." Jack leaned forward, and the gravity in his tone telegraphed controlled anger. "I'm telling you I wasn't drunk when I spoke to the police. They asked me if I was drunk and I told them no. I even signed and initialed the waiver."

"You're not the judge of whether you're drunk or not." Mary hadn't expected a fight when she was trying to save the man's life, though maybe she should have. The situation was downright perverse. "Lots of drunks think they're sober. That's why they get into cars and drive."

"I *know* I wasn't drunk."

"How can you be sure, Jack? Your actions weren't exactly rational. Beginning the confession, then calling for a lawyer. You weren't thinking clearly. You'd had the Scotch, early on."

"And then I killed my wife. It sobered me up."

"I don't think that's funny," Mary said coolly, though his bravado didn't ring true. "Why are you fighting me on this? This is good news. Without that confession, their case against you is much weaker. I intend to cross the detectives about it at the prelim and file a motion to suppress the confession."

"Don't do that. I don't think it's viable and it will jeopardize my chances for a guilty plea."

"No, it won't. The D.A. will expect a motion to suppress on these facts."

"I don't want to queer the deal."

"There *is* no deal." Mary leaned toward the bulletproof glass. "And don't bet there will be. They have all the cards right now and unless we fight back, they're gonna play them. They're likelier to deal if they think we have a decent defense or will win a suppression motion. They don't want to lose at trial either."

"I see." Jack nodded, dismissively. "I'll think about it and get back to you."

"I hand you a winner and you'll think about it?" Mary squeezed her pen, trying to keep her cool. His stubbornness only encouraged her confidence. If she was right about the truth, then she was fighting him for his own life. "I'm the lawyer, Jack."

"But I'm the client. I make the decisions in the case. In my own practice, I gave legal advice, and the client made the ultimate decision. Plenty of times I disagreed with my clients, and they with me. I did as they decided."

"This isn't an estates matter, where you assume your client's death. My job is to keep you alive."

"In any case, the lawyer is only an agent."

"Not exactly." Mary had crammed last night, after she'd left her father. "A criminal case is different from a civil case. As criminal counsel, I have a duty to file the motion to suppress. You don't determine the scope of your right to counsel, even though it's your right. It's grounded in the Constitution. Ever hear of the Sixth Amendment?" He fell silent, and Mary continued the lecture, on a roll. "If I don't file the motion on these facts, you could have me before an appellate court on a PCRA. That's post conviction relief, for you estates lawyers. I'd be found ineffective per se, which isn't the sort of thing I want on my permanent record card."

"I didn't want to say this, but I guess I have to. Isn't it possible that you're wrong about this motion to suppress?"

"No. I read the law."

"But, as you told me directly, you aren't very experienced with murder cases. Have you ever filed a motion to suppress?"

Mary swallowed hard. "No."

"So isn't it possible that your judgment is wrong? I'm hearing things from the other inmates, who have more experience than you and me put together. They think you're crazy not to pursue the guilty plea right now."

She felt like snarling. She didn't need legal advice from felons. She was right about the plea negotiation and the motion. It wasn't a matter of experience. Or was it? She couldn't think of an immediate reply.

"Mary, I know you're working hard on my behalf and I appreciate it. I hadn't thought about such a defense. It seems wrong on the facts. I need to mull it over. Isn't that reasonable?" He exhaled audibly, and Mary nodded, still off-balance. Maybe she shouldn't have taken this case. Maybe she wasn't experienced enough. She was playing with someone's life. Still.

"No. You can think about it until tomorrow morning. Then call me and tell me you agree."

"I'll call you." Jack rose, his handcuffs linking his arms against his jumpsuit. "Please don't file a motion until we talk again."

"Wait a minute," Mary said, uncertain as she watched him stand up. "I wanted to brief you on the arraignment. Let you know what to expect this morning."

"The arraignment is a detail. I don't care if I make bail or not." Jack walked to the door and called the guard, who came almost immediately and took him away.

It left Mary stumped. She'd never had a client walk out on her, much less one in leg manacles. He had to be protecting his daughter; there was no other explanation. Defending Jack was turning out to be a road strewn with rocks he'd thrown there, and she was becoming the adversary of her own client.

She wanted to win, but feared that if she did, it wouldn't be much of a victory.

13

Davis hit the STOP button to end the videotape of Newlin's confession and eyed his boss, Bill Masterson, the District Attorney of Philadelphia. Masterson sulked in his sunny office, behind a mahogany desk littered with gold-plated awards, commemorative paperweights, and signed photos. The clutter of photos included Masterson with the mayor, various ward leaders, Bozo the Clown, the city council, and Elmo from Sesame Street, in town to open a new Target store. The D.A.s always joked that one-hour photo developing was invented for Bill Masterson.

Davis was concerned. They had viewed the video three times, and Masterson had said nothing except "play it again" at the end. He hadn't reacted at all to Davis's theory of premeditation. At the moment, Masterson was frowning, emphasizing jowls like an English bulldog's. He was a large man, a tall power forward out of LaSalle, big-boned and still fit. Ruddy skin provided the backdrop for round eyes of a ferocious blue, which fought with his large nose to dominate his face. "So what do you think, Chief?" Davis asked.

"I'm not happy."

"You're never happy."

"This we know." Masterson glowered under a thatch of gray-blond hair.

"So what's the problem?"

Masterson gazed out a window in a wall covered with citations, more photos, and framed newspaper articles. MASTERSON WINS AGAIN read one of the headlines, from under glass. The morning sun in a solid square streamed through the window, past the plaudits, and onto the desk, suffusing his crystal paperweights with light. Davis couldn't tell if Masterson was gazing out the window or reading his own press.

"Chief, I know it's early in the game, but I made up my mind. I've only asked twice before, in *Hammer* and in *Bertel*, and you know I was right on both counts. They're dead and they both deserved it. So does Newlin."

Masterson squinted out the window or at his headlines. The tan phone on his desk rang loudly, and he reached over and pushed the intercom button to signal Annette to pick up. Davis, still at the VCR, pressed REWIND for something to do. He was expert in handling Masterson and knew to take it easy.

"You remember, Chief. The public, the papers, they went for it. They agreed. It gave them confidence in this office and in you. I don't have to remind you about *Bertel,* do I?" Davis had the facts, he didn't have to shout. Leon Bertel had murdered a popular pharmacist in Tacony, and his execution, which took place a month before the last election, had clinched Masterson's win. "I say no deals with Newlin. I want your okay before the other side asks me. I got it? Chief?"

Masterson finally looked away from the wall and down at his desk. "It's dirty," he said finally.

"It's murder. All the more reason to crucify this asshole. He whacks the wife and weasels out of it. He's out in no time with his cash, livin' large again. I want to tell the press, too. Right out, from day one. No deals in the Newlin case. We're taking him down. Bringing him to justice."

Masterson began fiddling with a slim gold Cross pen, rolling it across his blotter, back and forth. Sun glinted on the gold pen as it moved. The phone rang again, and the pen stopped rolling while Masterson pressed the intercom button wordlessly.

"I don't see the problem, Chief. This is a no-brainer. We got him cold-cock, blood on his hands. Think down the line. Say Newlin does his time or even makes parole. He'll have a decent case for it, the model prisoner, he'll keep his nose clean. You want him out and walking around? You think the people are gonna like that? The rich getting away with murder, with our, read Bill Masterson's, assist?"

The Cross pen rolled back and forth, so Davis took a cushioned chair across the desk and remained patient. He was one of the few assistants who got this much face time with the Chief. The word count was usually fifteen before the Chief's attention span evaporated, the mayor called, or the game started. Big Five basketball mattered. Masterson had priorities.

"You know he's lying, don't you?" Davis asked.

"Course." Masterson waved the air with a large, fleshy palm. "They all do."

"Then what?"

"Newlin's at Tribe."

"Yeah, so?"

"You know how much Tribe gave the campaign last year?"

Davis blinked. He never thought the Chief would say it out loud. "He did it, Chief. He killed her."

"Understood, but you gotta have your ducks in a row on this one." Masterson didn't look at his subordinate, but watched the pen as if someone else were manipulating it. "You can't go up against Tribe and be wrong."

"I'm not wrong. You know that. You know me."

The Cross pen came to a sudden stop. The phone started ringing, and Masterson looked over. This time instead of pressing the intercom button, he picked up the call, covering the receiver as he glanced at Davis. "Get me more," he barked. "Talk to me after you do."

"You're tellin' me no? That it's conditional?"

"Go!" Masterson said. He swiveled his chair to the side.

Davis rose nimbly, brushed his pant legs down, and took it on the chin. He hadn't expected the Chief to say no, but he wouldn't lie down. On the contrary, he accepted the challenge.

It would make winning that much sweeter, and in a strange way, he would enjoy the delay of gratification. After all, he wasn't a sprinter, he was a marathoner. He had the stuff to go the distance. This was just a chance to let it shine, shine, shine.

So Davis hurried from the District Attorney's office to begin his search for the evidence that would convict, and kill, Jack Newlin.

14

The press mobbed the Criminal Justice Center. News vans, cameramen, and print reporters with skinny notebooks clogged Filbert Street, the narrow, colonial lane that fronted the sleek, modern courthouse. Black TV cables snaked along the sidewalk like inner-city pythons, and microwave transmission poles fought the linden trees surrounding the courthouse for airspace. TV reporters shouted to their crews, their puffs of breath visible in the morning air. The winter cold bit cheeks protected only by pancake makeup, but the reporters forgot the weather when a Yellow cab pulled up and out stepped Assistant District Attorney Dwight Davis.

"Mr. Davis, any comment on the Newlin case?" "Dwight, will the Commonwealth ask for the death penalty?" "Mr. Davis, will you be trying the case?"

"No comment," Davis called out as he climbed the curb. His head was a helmet of dark hair, with sideburns just long enough to be risqué for a D.A. He wore a pinstriped suit and moved nimbly from the cab to the courthouse entrance. The media loved Davis, and the feeling was mutual, just not this morning. His expression was dour, and when the reporters kept blocking his path, he lost any sense of humor whatsoever. "Move the hell out, people!" he called, and hurried into the Criminal Justice Center.

Arriving on foot just after Davis were Mary DiNunzio and Judy Carrier. No press recognized them, much less plagued them for comment. They were merely associates of Bennie Rosato's and one of the throng of young lawyers heading into the Criminal Justice Center. Mary snorted at the ruckus. "Dwight Davis, no less," she said. "They're rollin' out the big guns. They're scared of us."

"Us? You mean you, and they should be." Judy glanced ahead at Davis. "Check it, Barbie. It's Ken, come to life. He's even got his plastic briefcase."

"Look at him run. He knows I studied. It'll take more than a Commonwealth to stop me now." Mary was psyched despite her meeting with Jack. If her client was going to fight her, so be it. She had never felt so good before court. Where were the blotches? "Step lively, little pretty."

Judy laughed as she pushed on the revolving door of the courthouse. "You're ballsy this morning."

"Temporary insanity," Mary said, and grabbed the next door.

Jack found himself handcuffed to a steel chair in a tiled cell, and directly across from him was a large TV monitor on a rickety table. On the wall was a black phone but the cell was otherwise bare. There was nothing in it but Jack and the TV, so the scene felt surreal, as if Jack would be forced to watch bad sitcoms. Gray static blanketed the screen, which emitted an electrical crackling so loud he winced. *Crk-crk-crk-crk.*

He'd been told by the sheriff that he was going to his arraignment, but this was downright odd. He should have let Mary fill him in, but he had been too shaken by what she'd told him. Had Paige lied to him about Trevor's being there? Couldn't be. Her story had been so convincing and it made complete sense. It was how Honor would have reacted, what she would have said, especially when drunk. But did Trevor have anything to do with Honor's murder? Was Paige even there? Had Jack sacrificed everything—*for nothing*?

Crk-crk-crk-crk. He couldn't think for the crackling noise. He kicked himself for rushing to confess before he was sure of the facts. His reaction had been almost reflexive, the instinct of a good father; shelter, protect, fix. Or maybe it had been the instinct of a bad father, overcompensating. If he hadn't felt so responsible for what had happened, would he have been so quick to confess falsely? He couldn't answer that question. He didn't know. He shifted in the hard chair.

"Sit still!" commanded the sheriff, guarding the door. "Else the camera won't get you right!"

"Camera?" Jack said. It must have been some sort of closed-circuit TV system. He scanned the cell. It was dim, lit only by a bare bulb in the hallway and the bright flickering of the TV screen. A camera lens peeked over the top of the TV. *Crk-crk-crk.*

"Sit still, goddammit!"

Suddenly the static noise ceased, the gray blanket on the monitor vanished, and a full-color picture popped onto the screen, divided into four boxes. The upper right box showed a courtroom made miniature and the upper left box was a close-up of a judge, an unassuming man in a tie and cardigan sweater instead of black judicial robes. In the lower left sat a well-dressed woman behind a sign that read COMMONWEALTH; in the lower right was a young man behind a PUBLIC DEFENDER sign. If he hadn't been so preoccupied, he would have laughed. It looked like the Hollywood Squares of Justice.

"Sit up straight!" ordered the sheriff. "Be ready. You're on deck."

The TV courtroom seemed to be waiting for something, but Jack's thoughts raced ahead. He doubted he'd get bail, considering Mary's inexperience. It was why he'd hired her, after all. He didn't want an experienced criminal lawyer who might figure out he was setting himself up. He had never intended to hire Bennie Rosato herself, but one of her rookies, and he'd been delighted by the reluctant voice on the telephone.

But he might have been wrong about Mary. She was evidently suspecting that Paige was involved, and it worried him. Ironic. With her inexperience came energy and she wasn't as callous as an experienced criminal lawyer would have been. She cared too much, and somewhere inside, Jack was touched.

She hardly knew him, yet she was fighting for him. He smiled despite the tight handcuffs, the weird TV, and the fact that he was about to be arraigned for murder.

"Two minutes, Newlin!" the sheriff said.

Jack stopped thinking about Mary. She was his lawyer and she'd better be a lousy one. Her questions threatened to expose Paige and jeopardize his plan. And what she'd learned about Trevor, if it was true, made him crazy, but he couldn't turn back now. He had to stay the course; keep up the charade. He was good at it, from a lifetime of practice, he was coming to realize.

"Okay, Newlin," the sheriff called out. "You're up."

The sharp *crak* of the TV gavel burst from the monitor, and Jack couldn't deny the tension in his gut. He had to know the truth and he'd have to find it out from behind bars.

But right now, it was time for the justice show.

15

Located in the basement of the Criminal Justice Center, the courtroom for arraignment hearings looked like the set of a television show for good reason. It was, essentially. The courtroom was the size and shape of a stage, half as large as a standard courtroom. It was arranged conventionally; from left to right sat a defense table, judge's dais, and prosecutor's table, but a large black camera affixed to the dais dominated the courtroom. Next to the camera sat a TV screen divided into four boxes: judge, courtroom scene, D.A., and P.D. A bulletproof divider protected those behind the bar of the court from the public, who sat in modern seats like a studio audience. The Newlin case was breaking news, packing the gallery with media and spectators wedged tight in their winter coats.

Mary sat with Judy in the gallery, waiting for the Newlin case to be called, and she kept comparing the real courtroom to its TV version. The TV reduced the gleaming brass seal of the Commonwealth to a copper penny and shrank the judge to an ant with glasses. Jack wasn't anywhere on the screen. "This is wrong," she said. Blotches big as paintballs appeared on her neck. "Today a decision gets made about whether my client gets bail or not, and he's in one place and I'm in another. How are we supposed to consult?"

"Lots of states do arraignments by closed circuit now, because it saves money," Judy said. "You can use the phone to talk to him, remember? If you press the red button, the gallery can't hear you."

"But the sheriff guarding him can hear everything he says, and the courtroom and judge would hear everything I say. Wake me up when we get to the right-to-counsel part."

"You think it's unconstitutional?"

"Is the Pope Catholic?" Mary checked the monitor as the boxes vanished and Jack's face appeared, oddly larger than life above the logo PANASONIC. The close-up magnified the strain that dulled the blue of his eyes and tugged their corners down. She gathered she had him worrying with her suspicions about Paige, but that was as it should be. Maybe because he was on TV, or maybe because of the Kevin Costner thing, but she sensed that he was an actor playing a role and his story was more fiction than truth. In any event, her job now was to free him on bail, against the odds. She rose to go.

"Good luck, girl," Judy said.

Mary mouthed her thanks, ignored the itching beginning at her neck, and walked to the door in the bulletproof divider, which a court officer unlocked. It was quiet on the other side, an expectant hush that intimidated her, but she nodded to the public defender, who stood to the side as she took his desk. Across the studio courtroom, Dwight Davis neatly took the D.A.'s desk. He looked more used to it than Mary, and she noticed the two sketch artists drawing him. She understood completely. He was a real lawyer and remarkably unspotted.

At the dais, the bail commissioner pushed up his Atom Ant glasses and pulled his cardigan around him. Bail commissioners weren't judges and some weren't even lawyers, and they rarely saw a private attorney at an arraignment, much less a D.A. the caliber of Davis. Mary had the impression that the bail commissioner was enjoying every ray of the unaccustomed limelight. "Mr. Davis, will you be handling this matter for the Commonwealth?" the commissioner asked, his tone positively momentous.

"Yes, Your Honor," Davis said deferentially. Even Mary knew that most lawyers called him commissioner.

"Good morning, Your Honor." Mary introduced herself, following suit, and the commissioner nodded.

"Excellent. Mr. Newlin, can you hear us?" The commissioner addressed a camera mounted at the back of the courtroom, above a monitor that showed another image of Jack.

"Yes, Your Honor," Jack answered, his voice mechanical through the microphones.

"Mr. Newlin, this is your arraignment," the commissioner said needlessly. "You are arraigned on a general charge of murder in the death of Honor Newlin."

Mary saw Jack wince, the tiny gesture plain on the large TV screen.

"Murder, that is, homicide, is the most serious crime one human being can commit against another. Your preliminary hearing is scheduled for January thirteenth in the Criminal Justice Center. You will be brought down at nine o'clock and taken in turn. Do you understand?"

"Yes, sir."

"Very well. I see you have a private attorney present, so I will not appoint a public defender. Now we come to the question of bail in this matter." The commissioner turned to the D.A. On the screen his miniature face turned, too. "Mr. Davis, I expect you have something to say on the bail issue."

"We do, Your Honor." Davis stood straight as a pencil. "As you know, murder is, as a general rule, not a bailable offense in Philadelphia County. The Commonwealth feels very strongly that the commissioner should follow custom and practice in this matter, for in this case, bail is not in order."

Mary bristled. "Your Honor, bail should be granted. There is precedent for bail in murder cases, as you know. The law is simply that bail isn't automatic, as it is for other offenses. Bail is routinely granted where the defendant is an upstanding member of the community." She had been up all night studying the law. "That is the case with Mr. Newlin. He is a partner at the Tribe firm, a member of the Red Cross Board, and of several charitable trusts. It goes without saying he has no criminal convictions. He is a superb candidate for bail."

"You make a nice point, Ms. DiNunzio." The commissioner mulled it over, rubbing his chin like a miniseries jurist. "It is true, the defendant is well known in the community. Mr. Davis, what say you?"

"Your Honor, in my view, the defendant's prominence cuts both ways. First, he should not be treated better than other defendants merely because of his social status. Secondly, as a wealthy partner in a major law firm, the defendant possesses financial resources far beyond the average person and has a significant family fortune. All of this argues that he poses a significant risk of flight. This individual can use his resources to flee not only the jurisdiction, but the country."

Mary shook her head. "Your Honor, Mr. Newlin poses no flight risk. He has a number of ties to the community and in fact has immediate family here. His daughter, Paige, lives and works in Philadelphia."

Jack flinched at the sound of her name, Mary saw it; his forehead creased in a frisson of fear. He didn't want Paige brought into it, and it conflicted Mary. She had to make the right argument, whether he wanted it or not. She caught the ghost of her own reflection in the glass of the TV, and she looked almost as stressed as Jack.

Davis stifled a laugh. "Your Honor, I find it difficult to understand that defense counsel can argue Mr. Newlin's devotion to his daughter. He is, after all, charged with the murder of her mother."

The bail commissioner looked into the camera lens, as if for a close-up. "Mr. Newlin, I've heard your attorney's arguments, but I must rule against you. There will be no bail in this matter and you are remanded to county jail until your next court date." The bail commissioner closed one pleadings folder and opened another. "That concludes your arraignment, Mr. Newlin. Please sign the subpoena in front of you and the sheriff will escort you back to your cell."

Jack vanished as abruptly as if someone had grabbed the remote and changed the channel, and Mary watched with dismay as the screen returned to its four boxes. She knew, more than she could rightly justify, that he was innocent. All she had to do was prove it.

But her client was her worst enemy, and the first round had gone to him.

16

On the way back to the office, Mary took a detour through the young and hip floor at Bonner's Department Store, which was downtown near the Criminal Justice Center. The floor was actually named Young & Hip, which told Mary instantly that she wasn't allowed to be there. Growing up, she had only been Guilty & Sinful, and as a lawyer had segued right into Guilty & Billable.

She wandered through racks of shirts that looked too small to cover even a single breast and skirts you wouldn't have to roll to shorten. Now what fun was that? And how would you achieve that bumpy effect at the hem? She considered asking where the real clothes were, as opposed to the joke clothes, but she was on a mission. She searched for a salesperson.

"Can you help me?" Mary asked, locating a skinny young woman with about three hundred plastic clips in her hair. Each clip was shaped like a baby butterfly that had landed, quite by magic, on its own clump of hair. Mary addressed the woman without reference to her hair, pretending that a headful of insects was not only normal, but desirable. "I need some information about a photo shoot that took place here Sunday. It was for the store. For a newspaper layout, I think."

"Wait." The saleswoman put a green fingernail to her cheek, and, again, Mary acted as if emerald were a naturally occurring shade in nongangrenous tissue. One couldn't question the Young

& Hip. "You have to ask the manager. She's over there." She pointed, and Mary followed her green fingernail like a traffic light that said Go!

The manager turned out to be the youngest and hippest of all, which Mary should have anticipated; short, canary-colored hair that looked greasy on purpose, no discernible shame about her black roots, and a tongue pierce that created a speech impediment. The manager was otherwise tall and slender, with contacts-blue eyes and a name tag that read TORI!

"Excuse me, were you at the photo shoot at the store this weekend?" Mary asked.

"Sure." Tori! leaned on a chrome rack of Capri pants, NEW FOR SPRING despite the fact it was midwinter. "I'm at all the shoots. They have 'em at the store 'cause it's cheap. Swingin' in the racks, you know."

Mary nodded. "There was a model at the shoot named Paige Newlin. A redhead. Do you remember her?"

"Oh-my-God, her mom was just murdered, right?" Tori! squealed like they used to for Elvis, and Mary looked nervously around. The department was mercifully empty, Philly evidently not being Young & Hip enough. You had to go to New York for that. Mary leaned closer to Tori!

"I'd prefer you keep this confidential. I'm a lawyer working on the case, and I need to know if you saw Paige Newlin at the shoot."

"But that is so weird, that her mom got killed and all. I saw her name in the paper. Newlin. That is sooo *random*."

"Yes. Now, did you see a redhead? Long ponytail?"

"A redhead?" Tori! swirled her tongue around her barbell, which Mary gathered was helping her think. "Uh, no. There were a lot of girls. I didn't think they were so hot."

"Did you happen to meet any of their managers?"

"No, none of the managers come to the shoots."

Mary considered it. Paige had said her mother was there. "What about mothers who are managers? Like Paige's mother, Mrs. Newlin."

"I don't know. I don't remember. I was kinda busy, you know, getting the stock we needed."

Mary sighed. "So you didn't see Paige and her mother?"

"Nope. Can't help you out there." Tori! clicked again, then started waving. "Maybe Fontana can, though. She's our tailor. Fontana!" she called out, and Mary turned to see whom the manager was hailing. Coming at them with ladylike steps was a very short woman, Mary's mother's height. She wore a navy blue suit, a white shirt with a floppy bow tie, and brown shoes with sensible heels. Her glasses looked old and her smile sweet, and Mary knew instantly that they were both Little & Italian.

She fought the impulse to run into her arms.

"I no like to tell bad things," Fontana said, hurrying along on her little legs. The "things" came out like "dings," but Mary could translate easily. If you grew up in South Philly, you could communicate instantly with any tailor, barber, or mobster.

"I don't want you to tell bad things," Mary said, hurrying beside her, matching stride for stride. Fontana Giangiulio had to be pushing seventy but Mary could barely keep up. "I just want you to tell me what you saw."

"I have to do de weddin' dress now. Dey need me dere."

"I'll walk you. I don't want to interrupt your job. Just tell me, please, what you heard. It's very, very important."

"I no like to say." Fontana shook her head in a jittery way as she chugged forward. "Ees no nice. Ees, what dey say, tales outta school."

"No, it's not. If it's the truth, it's not a tale, and you can save someone's life."

"Oh, *Deo*," Fontana said, scurrying along. "I no say."

"You saw the Newlins on Sunday, the mother and the daughter, Paige. You fixed Paige's dress."

"De *seam*, I said. No de dress. De dress, she was fine. *De seam* was no right." Fontana didn't stop to frown. "I put de clip in de back seam, to hold for de picture. Not for permanent, you know, for . . . *come se dice, Maria*?" She waved a tiny hand.

"For temporary," Mary supplied. "For the picture, got it. So you worked with Paige."

"I feex her seam. De customers, dey think we no hear, we no see. But we hear. We see."

"I know, that's true." Mary could imagine little Fontana buzzing around the models, kneeling as she chalked the hem at their feet. The tailors would be ignored because servants were invisible, especially to the likes of the Newlins. "What did you see?"

"Oh, *Madonna mia*!" Fontana waved her hand again as they barreled to the escalator and climbed on. Mary took advantage of the chance to breathe, now that Fontana had to stand still for a minute. "Dey fight, dees two!"

Mary tried to hide her excitement. "A big fight or a little fight?"

"A beeg fight! Dey fight and dey fight! But only in de dressin' room, you see. Not where nobody can see."

"What did they fight about?"

"De mother, she call de daughter alla names. She call her a *puttana*!"

"A *puttana*?" Mary was shocked. It meant a prostitute. A whore.

"*Sì! Sì!* Fontana no can believe!" She shook her head for half a floor, gliding downward with her chin high, upset at the very thought. "Den de daughter, she start to cry, and de mother, she laugh."

"Laugh?"

"*Sì! Sì!* She laugh and she walk allaway out!"

"She left?"

"*Sì! Sì!*" Fontana hopped off the escalator when it reached the second floor and took off past the makeup counter. The bright chrome of Clinique reflected on her glasses, but Mary could see her aged eyes go watery behind them. "But de girl, she start cryin', so sad. De makeup, ees alla mess. De seam, Fontana do again, with de clip. De girl cryin' on her knees, so Fontana help de girl up. She so pretty, like angel." Fontana motored past black and glossy Chanel, but Mary saw it as a dark blur. "And *Fontana*, she hold de girl, hug de girl, until she no cry no more and she get up and she feex her makeup and Fontana feex de seam and she pretend like no ding happen."

Mary tried to visualize it. "Then what?"

"An' den she go out and dey taka her picture. Howa you like *dat*?"

"That's terrible," Mary said, meaning it. She knew there had been something very wrong between mother and daughter. She wondered how long it had gone on, emotional abuse like that. A long time, for Paige's powers of recovery to be so fast, her emotional scars hidden by makeup and a professional smile. Had Jack known about it? Had it been hidden in dressing rooms and behind closed doors, or was Mary making excuses for him? What had her father said, that night over coffee? *If your mother was doing bad things to you, it would be my fault.* "Did anybody else see?"

"*Sí! Sí!* One person know what I say ees true." Fontana stopped in her tracks and held up a finger.

"Who?" Mary asked, breathless.

"Jesus Christ, he know," she said, with a faith that Mary couldn't begin to understand.

For her part, she could never fathom where Jesus Christ was when a mother called her daughter a whore.

17

Jack paced in his holding cell, waiting to use the pay phone outside. The guard said he'd get to it before they left for county jail, but that was an hour ago. He'd made a stink, claiming he had to call his lawyer, but it was a lie. Mary was the last person he'd phone right now. He had to call Trevor and get him down to the prison. Find out where that kid was the night Honor was killed. He'd shake the truth out of him.

"Guard! I need to make that call now!" Jack turned on his heel when he reached the bars of the cell, then turned back. The cells were a lineup of vertical cages, their white-painted bars chipped and peeling. Grime covered a concrete floor that sloped down to a small drain, and there was no toilet. They allegedly took the prisoners out for that, though the stench of urine filled the cell like a zoo.

"Fire! There's a fire!" Jack shouted, but even then there was no answer. An old man in the next cell laughed softly; he had been laughing to himself since they put him in there. Jack paced back and forth, driving himself crazy with what-ifs. What if Trevor had killed Honor? What if he and Paige had done it together? What if Paige had lied to him completely?

The prisoner in the next cell laughed louder, reading Jack's thoughts.

18

M s. DiNunzio," Brinkley said, standing beside Kovich, "before you lay down the law, mind if we sit?"

"There's chairs at the dining table behind you." DiNunzio gestured, and Brinkley looked around Paige Newlin's elegant, feminine apartment. The couch, chairs, and coffee table were decorated in shades of white, and he felt suddenly like an anvil on a cumulus cloud.

"Here we go, Mick," Kovich said jovially, yanking a chair from the dining room to the coffee table, and Brinkley dragged one over for himself. The chairs raked four wiggly lines in the thick white rug. Brinkley and Kovich sat down as the lawyer kept talking.

"Here's the way it goes, Detective Brinkley," DiNunzio was saying, from a seat next to Paige Newlin. She had a pretty face but wore a blue suit with a high collar that made her look tight-assed. "You can ask the questions you need to, but Paige cannot answer if I instruct her not to. She's been through a lot and she's feeling awful. As I told you on the phone, I don't know why you had to meet with her."

"It's just for background information." Brinkley slipped a pad from his breast pocket and flipped it open. Another woman lawyer whose name he forgot sat catty-corner to the sofa in a shapeless corduroy dress. He wasn't surprised that woman lawyers dressed as lousy as men lawyers. "Ms. Newlin," he said, "first let me say how sorry we are for the loss of your mother." Beside him, Kovich nodded in sympathy, like he always did when they did next-of-kin notifications. "Please accept our condolences."

"Thank you."

"I do need to ask you a few questions." Brinkley worked a ballpoint from the spiral of his notebook. "How old are you?"

"Sixteen."

Brinkley was starting with the softballs, to get her talking. He didn't want her threatened and he wanted to observe her. The first thing he observed was that she had pierced ears. She was wearing tiny pearl earrings, smaller versions of her mother's. He thought of the earring back in the rug. "Date of birth?"

She told him, sipped water from a glass, and replaced it on a coaster on the coffee table. Grief weighed each perfect feature and her mouth sagged with pain. She looked obviously bereft, even to his suspicious eye. Still it was hard to ignore her looks. Dressed in blue jeans and a classy white turtleneck, Paige Newlin was a knockout. Big blue eyes, pillow mouth, and glossy red hair that cascaded beyond her shoulders.

Brinkley made a note of her birth date. "Born in Philly?"

"No. Actually, in Switzerland. My parents were traveling."

"You reside here, at Colonial Towers?"

"Yes."

"I understand that you used to live at home with your parents. When did you move here?"

"Early last year."

"Your parents' home is beautiful, by the way. Antiques and such, everything nice." Brinkley gestured vaguely. "It's very well kept. Do your parents have help, for the house?"

"Yes. A maid."

"How often did she come?"

"Twice a week, Monday and Thursday."

"So she had been there yesterday?"

DiNunzio leaned toward Paige. "If you know," she said, and Paige shrugged.

"I don't know. I live here now."

"I see." Brinkley nodded. He was thinking about the dirt on the coffee table. If the maid had come on Monday, it could have been new the night of the murder. "How was it you came to live here?"

DiNunzio interrupted, "Your question isn't clear, Detective, and I'm not sure I see the relevance anyway."

"I'm just trying to get some background information."

"Background or not, she doesn't understand the question, and neither do I."

He shifted his weight and addressed Paige. "I was asking you why you moved out of your parents' house."

"I wanted to be on my own. Live alone. Be independent."

"Did you get along with your parents?"

"Yes."

"With your mother?"

DiNunzio cleared her throat. "She just answered that, Detective Brinkley. Again, I'm not sure it matters who she got along with."

"I'm wondering why she moved out of her house at such a young age. It's unusual, and we like to fill in all the questions the captain will ask us. He gets feisty about the details."

"That's your problem."

Brinkley, his annoyance growing, addressed the daughter. "Did your parents get along?"

DiNunzio cut him off with a chop. "I'm instructing her not to answer that."

Brinkley was getting pissed. He'd never met a lawyer who hadn't interfered with getting to the truth. He couldn't understand that kind of job. "You're disrupting a police investigation, Ms. DiNunzio."

"I disagree, but I won't bother to argue with you." DiNunzio turned to Paige. "Don't answer."

Paige nodded shakily, and Brinkley looked at his notepad. "Did your father ever strike your mother?" he asked, and DiNunzio scoffed again.

"Detective, she's talking to you voluntarily. You wanna continue this line of questioning, you'll have to get a subpoena and we'll meet you at the Roundhouse."

Brinkley exchanged looks with Kovich. Neither wanted the girl taken down. Officially, she was still victim's family. It would look like they were beating on her, with the suspect already placed under. "I don't think that'll be necessary. Paige, when was the last time you saw your mother alive?"

DiNunzio eased back into the cushy sofa, and Paige answered, "Sunday. The day before she . . . you know. We were at a photo shoot."

"You're a model, I understand."

"Yes."

"Why was your mother at your photo shoot?"

"She was my manager."

"Did you ever have another manager?"

"No."

"Did you want another manager?"

"No. She was still my manager, when she—"

"Passed," Brinkley supplied, and Paige nodded jerkily. Brinkley shifted forward on the chair. "What does a model's manager do, exactly?"

"She managed my career, got me the shoots, dealt with the bookers."

Brinkley made a note. "Bookers are what?"

"People who give you modeling jobs," Kovich chirped up, and Brinkley looked over, surprised.

"Okay," he said, and turned slowly back to the daughter. "You know what I don't get?"

"What?" Paige pursed her lips, which trembled slightly. It made Brinkley wonder. He made a mental note of it, then said:

"I don't get how you stay so thin."

"You don't eat!" Paige answered, breaking into a smile that Brinkley thought looked relieved.

"How do you not eat?" he asked. "Me, I love food. Ribs, burgers, shakes. You give all that up?"

"Milk shakes? Uh, hello." She laughed.

Kovich nudged Brinkley's arm heavily. "A lot of models smoke," he said, with a savvy smile. "That's how they stay thin."

Brinkley wanted to hit him, but didn't. "What do you know about getting thin, partner? Look at you!"

The lawyers laughed, and so did the daughter. Brinkley could feel the tension ebb away and the atmosphere warm.

"I know all about this," Kovich said. "I got my finger on the pulse, Mick." He put a thick finger over his wrist in case anybody missed his point, then turned to Paige. "I have daughter, she's your age. She tells me about the models. Who smokes, who doesn't. A lot of 'em smoke but they hide it. Kate Moss smokes. Naomi Campbell, she smokes. Am I right or am I right, Paige?"

"It's true. Their diet is, like, water and Camels." Paige nodded vigorously. "But that's not my diet secret."

Kovich inched forward on his chair. "What's your diet secret?"

"Portion size," Paige said, her tone confidential. "Most people, their portions are way too big. It's all portion size. I figured that out by myself."

"Portion size," Kovich repeated, like it was a goddamn state secret, and Brinkley tried to get back on track. He was getting there, just slowly.

"You can't make a small cheeseburger."

"You can't eat cheeseburgers if you want to lose," Paige said. "No red meat. No butter. No oil."

"No meat?" Brinkley asked casually. "You a vegetarian?"

"Sure am." Paige nodded in satisfaction. "A lot of the supermodels are, too."

Brinkley shook his head, his thoughts elsewhere. That would explain the hummus on the appetizer platter. The daughter *had* been there for dinner. "I'd have to think about it. It's a lot to give up. I love meat."

"You get used to it, you'll see."

"*I* can't get used to that," Kovich said flatly, but Brinkley excused himself and stood up slowly, shaking his pant leg over his ankle holster.

"Ladies, I hate to interrupt, but may I use the facilities? I'll just be a minute."

"Sure," Paige answered. DiNunzio looked unhappy but didn't countermand her, and Brinkley headed off. "First door on the right," Paige called after him, and Brinkley slipped inside and shut the door behind him.

Inside the bathroom, he could hear them talking diet. DiNunzio wouldn't put up with it for long; Brinkley didn't have much time. He lifted the toilet seat loudly and coughed at the same moment as he opened the medicine cabinet. His eyes scanned the shallow shelves, which were almost empty. Glade air freshener, extra guest soaps. There. A comb.

Brinkley picked up the comb by the corner. Silky red filaments of hair were entwined in its teeth. He grabbed some toilet paper, slid the hair from the comb, and put the comb back on the shelf. Then he slipped the paper with the hair carefully into his inside jacket pocket. It wouldn't be admissible in court—the seizure wasn't kosher and the chain of custody nonexistent—but it wasn't for court anyway. He closed the cabinet, flushed the toilet, and opened the door and let himself out of the bathroom. He rejoined the group, which looked as chummy as a hen party. Kovich was good with women. Sheree always said he was like a big teddy bear. "You lose weight yet, partner?"

"I'm on my way," Kovich said, pushing up his glasses. "No more oil for me. Kelley tells me the same thing. It's liquid fat. Right, Coach?"

Paige nodded happily, and Brinkley sat down. "We'll finish up this conversation," he told her. "I don't want to keep you too long." He picked up his notepad from the chair. "I know this is a hard time for you."

"Thanks. I don't feel very well, it's true. I had a pretty bad migraine last night. I had one the night before that, too."

Brinkley thought a minute. "You got it after you heard about what happened—"

"No, I got it before, in the afternoon. I was supposed to have dinner with my parents last night, but I canceled because of the migraine."

DiNunzio waved her hand like a ref calling foul. "I think that's enough now. Detective, you said you were finished here."

But Brinkley couldn't let it go. His hummus theory was in doubt. "I want to clarify that. Did you go to your parents' house last night?"

"No. I was here. I was supposed to go to dinner, but I canceled. I stayed at home in bed."

Brinkley studied Paige's face. Her thin skin colored with agitation, but she would have been upset, in context. It flushed his hummus theory down the drain. "Is there a way we can confirm that?"

"What?"

"Your whereabouts that night?"

DiNunzio stood up abruptly. "I don't see the relevance of the inquiry. I'm instructing Paige not to answer."

"It's one last clarification."

"No it isn't. You've charged her father with the crime. If Paige needs a lawyer, we'll get her one, too. And I don't remember you reading her her rights."

"We don't have to Mirandize her unless it's a custodial interrogation, and she's not in custody."

"It's starting to smell like she is," DiNunzio said, and Paige picked up her water from the coffee table with a shaky hand.

Brinkley stood up, flipped his notebook closed, and returned it to his breast pocket. "I don't think we need to continue this any longer." He looked down at Paige, who, though tall, suddenly seemed to shrink into the couch. "I'm sorry to have bothered you today, Paige. We'll try to handle this without disturbing you again. Feel free to call us if you have any questions."

"She will," DiNunzio said, but Brinkley bit his tongue.

"Please take my card." He slipped a slim hand into his back pocket for his wallet and flipped it open. The heavy gold badge of the Detective Division flashed in the sunny apartment as he extracted a business card, and he noted Paige's slight frown at the sight. A natural reaction? Lots of people reacted to the badge. He knew a cop who said it got him laid, every time. He pulled out a business card and extended it to Paige, but DiNunzio took it instead.

"Thank you," she said, moving to the door. "I'll show you both out."

Kovich got up, and Brinkley grabbed his coat and left, with more questions than before.

"You're outta your mind, Mick," Kovich said, shrugging off the winter chill in his polyester sportjacket. It was a cold clear day, the temperature barely above freezing, but Kovich never wore a coat. It wasn't a macho act; the man never got cold. Brinkley didn't understand it.

"I don't think so." They strode from the tall apartment building toward the Chrysler. Wind gusted down Pine Street, and Brinkley buttoned his black leather topcoat.

"The hummus shit, that washed out. The kid was going over to dinner, Mommy put it out, then the kid canceled."

"Got it."

"She didn't do it, Mick. Plus we got the father locked up, and Davis on the case. What do you think's gonna happen? You got a stray one, and he's gonna let Newlin go? Are you nuts? The paper's already calling him 'No Deal' Davis. The prelim's around the corner."

Brinkley squinted against the cold sun like it hurt. "She doesn't have an alibi."

"She doesn't need one. You saw the lab reports. The prints are his. The fibers, it's all there."

"The lab reports don't mean anything. Not if he staged the scene to protect the daughter."

"Nobody could stage a scene that good!"

"Not even a lawyer?"

"Jesus H. Christ!" Kovich picked up the pace, his breath puffing like a locomotive, and Brinkley could see he was getting worked up. "You're losin' me, Mick."

Brinkley didn't say anything.

"I was workin' with you before but now that I met her, you're losin' me. She's a kid. She's like the girls in the magazines, in Kelley's magazines. She's *Kelley*, for Christ's sake."

"No, she's not. You don't know her."

"Listen to me, I'm a father, Mick. Teenage girls, they're not that different. Didn't you see her? She's all broke up, she got the puffy eyes, the whole thing. Kids her age, they don't take stress that well. Kelley gets a zit, she cries in her room. They're Drama Queens, all of 'em. That kid was upset for real."

"If she did it, she would be. Like you say, she's a teenage girl, not a scumbag."

Kovich snorted. "Anybody who kills their mother is a scumbag. It's automatic."

Brinkley thought that one over as they reached the car. By then, Kovich was breathing easier but not much.

"So what'd you do in the bathroom?" he asked, opening the driver's side door.

"Number one," Brinkley told him. He was thinking about that earring back.

19

Mary and Judy stayed with Paige, lingering in her apartment kitchen after the detectives had left. Mary's doubts about Paige were only encouraged by Detective Brinkley, who was apparently beginning to question Jack's confession and suspect Paige. Mary wondered what he knew and if he had any evidence that Jack was innocent. But Paige could know that, too. "That wasn't much fun, was it?" Mary asked her.

"No." The teenager opened her refrigerator door, retrieved a slim jug of orange juice, and set it down on the black granite counter. "They got mean at the end."

"They make extra for mean."

Paige didn't smile. "What do they want from *me*, though? They were acting like I was the guilty one. Do you think they suspect me or something?"

Mary searched her face, and Paige was plainly upset. "They have to investigate the crime, and we have to permit that, within limits."

"But they have my dad in jail." She took a glass from the glistening cabinet and poured herself a fresh-squeezed orange juice, without offering it to anyone else. "They won't even let him out on bail. Why are they coming to me?"

"They have to check everything out. I thought it would be more pleasant for you to be questioned here, rather than downtown."

"It totally was. I never want to see that place again." Paige wrinkled her small nose. "I swear I saw a rat outside there last night."

Judy smiled. "You did. It's their pet rat. Size of a dog."

Mary looked over, horrified. "Are you serious?"

"Yep. The cop at the desk told me. His name's Coop."

"The rat or the cop?"

"The cop, doof."

"Great," Paige said, with a shudder. "Well, I'm just glad it's over." She sipped her juice, leaving a parabola of pulpy film on the glass. "It's kind of a lot to deal with. I mean, tomorrow is my mother's funeral. I don't suppose they'll let my dad go to that, will they?"

"I doubt it," Mary said, and thought it a strange question. She found her suspicions about Paige confirmed the more time she spent with her. She just didn't have any solid proof. Yet.

"I feel so bad for him. Worried."

"Don't worry." Judy touched Paige's arm. "We'll take care of your father, and you take care of yourself. We'll go the funeral, of course."

"Thanks. That's nice."

"We're happy to." Judy exchanged looks with Mary, who remained dubious. She kept thinking of what Fontana had told her at the store, about Paige's mother calling her a prostitute. She wondered how that would make Paige feel about her mother the next day. Angry enough to kill her? No. But what if there were a lifetime of it? Mary decided to explore it. If she were going to prove Jack's innocence, she couldn't do it through him because he wouldn't let her. Maybe she could do it through Paige.

"I don't know much about being a model," Mary said. "It sounds fun. Glamorous. Do you like it, going to photo shoots and all?"

"Sure, yeah. It's cool. But it's not like you *go* to a photo shoot. It's like you work at one. I mean, it's *work*."

"Well, how? Like take the Bonner shoot, for example. How is that work? Isn't it just fake-smiling in nice clothes? Like being a lawyer."

Paige laughed. "No way. You have to stand for hours and they don't treat you that well."

"How so? I would think models get the star treatment, especially if they have a manager there." Mary was choosing her words with care, and Judy shot her a warning glance.

"No way." Paige nodded, not completely happily. "Sometimes my mother would see things I should have done better, like if my hands looked stupid. I don't always know what to do with my hands." She fell suddenly quiet and just as Mary was about to follow up, Judy interrupted.

"But Paige, I always thought the photographer could make you look better," she said, and Mary knew it wasn't coincidental. Judy was the only person less interested in the modeling profession than Mary.

"No. They tell you how to stand, and that's it," Paige answered, unaware of the tug-of-war over her. "The girl has to do it."

Mary yanked back. "Who are some of the photographers you use, like for the Bonner shoot? I'm thinking about getting my photo taken for work. You know, tough woman lawyer in front of a row of law books."

Judy snorted, and Paige set down her juice. "Caleb Scott shot Bonner, but I wouldn't use him. He's a jerk. Most of the time, like for all the catalog work, we use Vivi Price. She has her own studio in New York. Ever hear of her? She used to be an assistant for Demarchelier."

Mary made a mental note. "Trevor must like having a girl-friend who's a professional model," she said, pushing it.

"Trevor? Yeah. He's cool with it." Paige checked her watch, a silver Rolex that hung loose as a bracelet on her knobby wrist. "Well, I gotta go. I'm gonna meet him for a late lunch. He doesn't have any classes until three, and they have open campus."

"Where does he go to school?"

"Downtown, at Philadelphia Select. He's going to Princeton next year. He's really smart." Paige's smile turned professional. "I should get ready or I'm gonna be late. It takes me forever to get ready."

"Where are you meeting him? Maybe we can drop you off."

"No. I can get a cab. It's just at the Four Seasons. Thanks, anyway."

"Okay." Mary touched Judy's arm. "We'd better get moving then, lady," she said, and tried not to sound too eager. She'd have to hurry to do what she needed.

Mary powered down the sidewalk, hailing cabs as she walked, with no luck. It was so cold that spittle froze on the concrete sidewalk. The trees were dark hands reaching to a stark blue sky. Still she loved Philly in winter. "Don't you wonder about what Paige just said?"

"You're outta your mind." Judy hurried along to keep pace, hauling a heavy brown briefcase, the accordion type that law professors carried. "What is it with you and Paige? Why don't you like her?"

"I think she's selfish. Did you see, she didn't offer us any orange juice, and she barely said thanks. These things matter."

"No, they don't." Judy's mouth flattened to a hyphen, giving a sharp edge to her voice. "Bad manners aren't against the law."

"They're telling details."

"Telling what? We're supposed to be preparing a defense, and this case isn't about her. It's about her father."

"Well, I think he's innocent, so I have to investigate other possibilities." Mary shivered in her cloth trench coat as she tried to hail a cab. She and Judy never argued. It suddenly felt very cold. "Right?"

"Wrong. She's off the point." Judy's eyes became skeptical slits of blue and she stopped in mid-sidewalk, against a backdrop of colonial town houses. The soft melon color of their brick and the bubbles in their mullioned windows testified to their authenticity. "We still have no reason to think Newlin is innocent, or that she did it."

"I told you about the fight Paige had with her mother, in the dressing room." Mary faced her best friend on the street. "I bet it wasn't the first time they fought that way."

"That's not enough. Everybody fights with their mother some-times, probably more often in dressing rooms than anyplace else. They don't just up and kill them."

"Paige just said she wished her father could come to the funeral. If you thought your dad had stabbed your mom to death, would you want him at her funeral?"

Judy sniffed. Her upturned nose was red at the tip, from the chill. "No."

"And aren't you hearing Paige has a lot more sympathy for dad, who tells us he's the bad guy, than for mom, who got killed? I mean, if Paige had killed her mother and was letting her father take the rap, she'd feel guilty, wouldn't she? I can't be the only guilty person in the world."

Judy blinked. "Okay, I admit it, it does seem odd."

"So, to support my theory about Jack covering for Paige, we have to understand a lot about this family in a very short time, and we need to know how they related. We need to reconstruct the events leading up to the murder, to put it in context. Make sense?"

"I guess."

Mary suppressed her surprise. Had she won? Was it that easy? "So you agree with me? You think I'm right?"

"I think you could be."

"Are you sure? I mean, I'm usually not."

Judy laughed. "This time you are. You're growing up, right before my eyes. What do you want to do next, boss? It's your case."

Mary thought a minute, suddenly giddy. "Okay, you go back to the office and find precedent for the preliminary hearing. I was going to follow my lead."

"Your 'lead'?" Judy smiled. "You're a lawyer, not a cop."

"Don't question me, I'm the boss!" An empty Yellow cab whizzed by and Mary waved frantically. "Yo, wait! Stop!"

"Mare!" Judy called after her. "Where are you going?"

"Catch me if you can!" she shouted, running after the cab, and Judy shot off after her, laughing.

20

Brinkley stood beside the stainless steel table with Kovich and Dwight Davis as the autopsy began. Brinkley kept a lid on his testiness at Davis and his distaste at the procedure by listening to the piano music coming from the CD player on the shelf. Hamburg always played Chopin's Nocturnes, and though Brinkley didn't listen to classical music, he appreciated it. The sweet notes of the piano made incongruous background music for the coroner's dictation, into a black orb of a microphone that hung from a wire like a spider on a web.

"This is the case of Honor Buxton Newlin, a forty-five-year-old female," Hamburg began. He was wearing blue pressed scrubs under an immaculate white jacket.

The body of Honor Newlin lay naked on the steel table, her eyes closed and her chest sliced cruelly with the wounds that had killed her. Brinkley tried not to look, in some sense protecting her modesty, and Hamburg evinced a similar respect for the body. His tone was almost rabbinical as he recited her height, weight, sex, age, and eye and hair color into the microphone.

"On January twelfth, the subject was brought to the Philadelphia Medical Examiner's office . . . "

They were only at the beginning of the autopsy; Hamburg had just cut away the woman's clothes, the first step of the external examination. The inspection of her blouse had taken a while, since Hamburg had been so systematic, matching each stab wound to each tear in the white silk and squaring up the bloodstains. The D.A., the detectives, and the medical examiner had pored over the clothes and pink shoe with the torn strap, but Brinkley could draw no new conclusions about the shoe and Davis thought it didn't mean anything.

"Head: The head is normal. There is no evidence of trauma to the head. The scalp hair is . . . "

Brinkley was bumped slightly by Davis, edging him into the green steel cabinets lining the morgue. The area reserved for autopsies was cramped, dominated by a lineup of steel tables with drains in the middle and a deep sink under the head. No other autopsies were being performed, which Brinkley counted as a godsend. He found himself looking away while Hamburg swabbed the dried blood from Honor Newlin's wounds, to the achingly beautiful strains of the solitary piano.

"Chest: The chest shows evidence of significant trauma. There are five wounds in the chest area. Left to right, the first wound is postmortem . . . "

Brinkley made himself look. The woman's skin was as pure and unmarked as porcelain, now that it had been drained of blood. He looked away again, confused. He had seen a zillion bodies, all nastier than this one. What was bothering him? Maybe because Honor Newlin made him think of better things. Or maybe because he wasn't sure they had her killer yet.

"Abdomen: The abdomen is flat. There is no evidence of trauma . . . "

Brinkley glanced at her waist, which was small. Her stomach looked toned and supple, her belly button a tiny, refined knob. How had this happened? Could her husband really do this to her? Could her kid? *That* kid, with the big blue eyes and the long hair? Brinkley needed answers fast. He knew the news stories about no deals were trial balloons, and the public was responding. The man-on-the-street interviews were all hang 'em high.

"Now, the back." Hamburg motioned to an assistant and they turned the body over together, in one smooth, practiced motion. The woman's arms remained rigid at her sides, owing to rigor mortis. "The back is normal in contour," Hamburg continued. "There is no evidence of trauma to the back. Upper extremities: The upper extremities show evidence of defensive wounds. . . . "

Brinkley looked at the slashes to the woman's fingertips. The notion of somebody putting up their hands to protect against a knife always made him sad. The worst were defensive gunshot wounds. How many times had he seen Hamburg raise a body's hand to match where a bullet had passed through it? Brinkley knew it was reflex, but he couldn't help believing it was something else. Hope.

"Lower extremities: The lower extremities show evidence . . . hmmmm . . . "

Brinkley came out of his reverie. The body was lying on its back again, and Hamburg was bent over, his head down and his black yarmulke a punctuation mark. He squinted through his bifocals at the woman's feet and kneaded the large toe of her right foot. Without being asked, Brinkley turned and picked up the pink shoe with the torn strap, still bagged, and handed it to Hamburg, who reached up and turned off his microphone.

"I think our friend has a broken toe," Hamburg said, preoccupied. Brinkley couldn't tell if he was thinking about the toe or listening to the music, which was particularly dramatic, the notes gaining speed as they descended the octaves. Hamburg took the shoe and held it against the foot. "This is the right shoe, with the broken strap. Broken toe, broken shoe. Any theories, boys?"

Brinkley moved closer, intrigued. "You think she broke her toe the same time she broke the strap?" he asked, and Kovich listened quietly.

Hamburg nodded. "Seems reasonable."

Davis, joining them, shook his head. "Couldn't she have broken her toe another time? It's not like they treat broken toes. You just wait for it to heal."

Hamburg nodded again. "True, but there's a fair amount of swelling in the toe. I'd say it's a recent injury."

"How recent?" Davis asked, hugging his pad to a pinstriped suit.

"Yesterday or the day before."

"You don't put shoes like that on a hurt toe," Brinkley said, but Davis snorted.

"You don't know that. You can't assume that. She seems like a vain woman to me."

"How you get that from a body?" Brinkley asked, defensively. It seemed disrespectful.

"From the clothes. They're expensive. And she's thin, she stays in shape."

Brinkley paused. Davis was smart but he was still an asshole. "Look, it's a lot more likely that she kicked something hard enough to break her toe and her shoe. What do you say, Aaron?"

"Not my bailiwick, but it seems likely. You think she was kicking whoever was attacking her?"

"No." Brinkley was puzzled. "A defensive wound, to the foot? How often you see that?"

"From time to time," Hamburg answered thoughtfully. "In women, you see it. They do it out of desperation."

"Sure," Kovich agreed. "We've seen it in the rape cases. Remember Ottavio, Mick?"

Brinkley remembered. "But this isn't a rape case. In a rape case, the victim's on the ground and she kicks up. Tries to catch the guy in the groin or whatever. Here the lady is standing up, getting stabbed. If she kicks to defend herself, she destabilizes herself." He demonstrated and almost toppled over. "See?"

"She could have kicked up, being stabbed on the ground," Kovich offered, but Hamburg looked dubious.

"I can't say no, but I can't say yes. With this wound pattern, I can't make an exact determination about which is the fatal wound. But remember, she had been drinking heavily. Her blood alcohol was high, so any fighting she did wasn't that vigorous. If she was kicking from the ground, she didn't hit much. Not enough to break a toe."

Kovich said, "Unless she kicked Newlin before he started stabbing."

"If it's Newlin," Brinkley corrected, then caught Kovich's

annoyance. Davis, standing beside them both, said nothing and looked at the corpse. "Newlin didn't say anything to us about her kicking him."

"We didn't ask him, Mick."

"But it doesn't jive with his story. The way Newlin tells it, all she did was yell. She provoked him verbally and he got aggressive. Yelled back. Threw the glass at her."

"The toe's not that big a deal," Kovich shot back. "He overpowered her and she struggled. Anytime there's a struggle, things get broke."

"I'm with Stan on this," Davis said, speaking finally. His tone suggested a judge's ruling at the end of a case. "The broken toe is not significant. She was drunk, she flailed out at Newlin, it's some sort of defensive wound."

Brinkley eyed Davis. "You're acting like you got your mind made up."

"I do." Davis nodded, almost cheerfully. "I saw the tape, over and over, and I know how this went down."

"You know?" Brinkley frowned. "From a video?"

Hamburg waved them all into silence. "Separate, you two," he said, flicking on the overhead microphone.

After the autopsy, which ended routinely, Brinkley caught up with Davis outside the building. A squat edifice of tan brick with only a few slitted windows, the Joseph W. Spelman Medical Examiner's Building was situated on a busy corner, bordered by the Schuylkill Expressway and a complex of the University of Pennsylvania Hospital, Children's Hospital, and the Veteran's Hospitals. Wind swirled in unpredictable currents around the buildings and the traffic made a constant whooshing. "Davis," Brinkley shouted, knowing the D.A. was avoiding him. "Got a minute?"

"For you, sure." Davis turned, pad in hand, though he didn't break stride as he hurried across the parking lot to his car, a new white pool Ford. "What can I do for you, champ?"

"You said you saw the tape of the confession." Brinkley buttoned his jacket quickly in the cold air. Cars were parked willy-nilly in the lot, which was being repainted, and Davis was parked in a space with a sign that read PARKING FOR BEREAVED FAMILIES ONLY. "Did you see what I meant about—"

"Yeah, matter of fact I did. I think Newlin's lying, too. But I think he's the doer."

Brinkley didn't get it. "What do you think he's lying about?"

"The story he didn't plan it is bullshit. He's gonna plead out." Davis's determined chin cut the chill air. "Or so he thinks."

"Big mistake, Davis. I'm not sure he's the doer."

"You got anything to back that up?"

"Not yet. I'm just starting—"

"Lemme know you find anything, okay, my man? Keep me up to speed. I gotta roll." Davis opened the door of his car, but Brinkley held the door so it couldn't be closed.

"Listen, we talked to the daughter this morning, and I'm working on the theory that the father didn't do it. That he was protecting her, or somebody else."

"There's nothing to support that. Not a thing."

"I'll find it."

"You do that." Davis gave him a dismissive wave, closed the Ford's door, and disappeared inside. The car's engine started quickly, and Davis took off, leaving Brinkley standing there.

When he turned back, he spotted Kovich waiting at the front of the coroner's building, a distant silhouette.

21

Mary glanced around the cavernous warehouse, as large a space as she had ever been in, especially in the city. It was near the Delaware River, bordering New Jersey. In Philadelphia you had to go to Camden to get any room. Afternoon sunlight streamed through the floor-high windows, their security cages casting a diamond-mesh pattern on the rough concrete floor. In Camden even empty space needed protection. You couldn't win on the East Coast, in general.

Mary stood there with her briefcase and said "yo" to hear whether it echoed, but it didn't. The sound vanished into four tall stories of exposed brick. It was the shell of a furniture warehouse, completely empty except for the far corner, in which a little world had been created. She walked over, marveling as she approached. There were three distinct rooms of drywall, except that it looked as if the contractor had forgotten their ceilings and fourth walls. The first room on the left was an open dressing room, and young girls were changing clothes in front of everyone. Mary knew instantly that none of them was Catholic.

The room next to the dressing room was a makeup and hair salon, with two steel folding tables piled with an array of black makeup brushes and a layered box full of compacts and foundation. Models in lacy bras and slips sat on folding chairs, orange crates, and boxes while stylish men and women painted their eyes, contoured their cheeks, and styled their hair. One model was having a French twist combed out, and her head jerked back with each stroke. Mary winced. She was a lawyer, but she couldn't take that kind of pain.

Beside the makeup room was a final fitting room, with models going from one station to the next like a fashion assembly line, though Mary couldn't tell the order from all the milling around. In the corner stood a portable steam presser and movable racks of clothes, a quick glance revealing they were Young & Hip. From what Mary could tell, the Young & Hip biz was really thriving.

The operative word being Young. Mary got close enough to see the models and they looked like kids playing dress-up. They were preteens, starting at about age ten, up to fifteen or so. There wasn't a full breast in the crowd, though the kids appeared to be modeling slips that were supposed to be dresses. One model, a sprout of a blond with large blue eyes, looked barely twelve. She sat in a cloth-back director's chair while a man in black glued false lashes to her eyelids. Her feet, in strappy black sandals, didn't touch the ground and she clutched a Totally Hair Barbie, with coincidentally matching sandals. There was no mother in sight.

Suddenly shouting came from the largest room, which was merely a huge sheet of clean white paper hanging from a story-high steel brace. Background for the photographs, it curved onto the concrete floor like a paper carpet. The kids kept tripping on the paper's edge in their high heels, and a man kept yelling at them "not to rip the seamless." One of the mothers apologized for her daughter and grabbed her off the paper. Mary didn't get it. If anybody had spoken to her like that, her mother would have threatened to break his face. But Mary wasn't here to stop child labor. She had a client to defend.

She approached the closest man in black, a wavy brown ponytail snaking to his waist. He had his back to her and was bent over a large steel trunk of photographic equipment. Lenses, camera bodies, and flash units nestled in gray sponge cushioning, and Mary realized instantly that the cameras were treated better than the kids. "Excuse me," she said, but the ponytailed man didn't turn around. "I'm looking for the photographer, Caleb Scott."

"I'm his assistant, one of the million. He's over there but don't bother him. He's on the warpath for a change." The assistant glanced over his shoulder, through the smallest glasses Mary had ever seen. "I can tell you right now what he's going to say, honey. Save you the time."

"Go ahead," Mary said, surprised.

"You gotta lose thirty pounds, maybe more. You're too old for what he does. You need a nose job and you gotta do something with your hair. The color sucks and that cut is so last year." He turned back to the trunk, and Mary considered giving the finger to his ponytail.

"I'm a lawyer, not a model."

"Then you're perfect," he said, and didn't look back.

Caleb Scott simmered on the paper carpet, resting his Hasselblad on his slim hip like a gun. He was tall, reed-thin, and wore a black turtleneck, stone-washed jeans, and soft-soled Mephisto shoes. His spray of gray hair and a faux English accent served to distinguish him, in addition to his foul mood. Caleb Scott was angry about a yellow light on a tall steel stem, which kept firing at the wrong time. From the terrified attitude of the assistants struggling to fix the thing, Mary guessed that for Scott, anger was the status quo. But he didn't express his anger in a way familiar to Mary—shouts, tears, or the decade-long vendetta—he just got wound tighter and tighter.

"Mr. Scott, I have a few questions, but it won't take long," Mary said, hovering next to him.

"Take all day. I evidently have it."

"I represent Jack Newlin and am investigating the murder charge against him. You may have read about it in the paper. I need to know about Paige and her mother, Honor."

"I don't have time to read the newspaper. I have to get to work, where I stand and wait." Scott scowled at an assistant, hurrying by with a new lightbulb. The kids in slips held their position under the lights, and their mothers stood off to the side, watching them sweat.

"You didn't hear that Honor Newlin was killed?"

"I didn't say that. Of course I heard it, from one of my assistants. Everybody knows about it. If we waited for the newspaper to get news, we'd wither and die. Like me, right now." His thin lips pursed in martyrdom, and Mary figured he, at least, was Catholic.

"You photographed the Bonner shoot, didn't you?"

"I do all of Bonner's work, in town."

"I understand that Honor and Paige had a fight at the shoot, in the store dressing room. Did you know that?"

"Of course! Do you think that anything is a secret in this business?" Scott gestured toward his assistants, who swarmed around the offending light. It still wouldn't fire when they pressed a black button on top of what looked like a car battery. "We're the biggest group of gossips ever. You could dish all day if you had nothing better to do, but most people have better things to do. I, on the other hand, have to stand around and talk to lawyers. When I'm not baby-sitting."

"So you knew there was a fight in the dressing room?"

"Honey," Scott said, turning to Mary for the first time, "they fought wherever they went. That mother was the biggest bitch, and that kid was the biggest princess. When I heard the mother was killed, I thought, 'you go, girl.'"

Mary couldn't hide her shock. "What are you saying?"

"I'm saying that I thought the kid killed her."

"Because of the fight, is that why? What was the fight even about?"

"Not because of the fight, no way. The fight was about what they all fight about." This time Scott gestured at the mothers, sipping coffee near the paper carpet. Two were on cell phones, and Mary could hear them changing their kids' bookings now that the light had broken, delaying the shoot. "Look at them. Can you explain this? Mothers who would put their children through this? I can't."

She shook her head. She actually agreed. "They do it for money, don't they?"

"No, I'll explain in a minute. Look at the girls." Scott gestured at the kids, trying hard to stand in place, now going on five minutes. "They're beautiful, right? Each one of them."

Again, she had to agree, though their beauty was hidden by their makeup.

"None of this is about money, it's about a much stronger pull. It's about that their kid will become the next Claudia, Naomi, or Elle. That their kid will be the one to hit the jackpot. And after that, who knows? She can marry the prince. Or the rock star. Make movies. Be Julia Roberts. This is the lottery, with flesh and blood."

Mary scanned the young faces as he spoke. They were all so pretty, like a lineup of dolls. "But one of them will make it, won't they?"

"You mustn't interrupt." Scott paused, apparently to punish her. "The truth is, none of them will. They're kids from Philly and they look cute in catalogs and newspapers. Some of them will get go-sees to New York, but none of them is truly special. I have twenty-three of them here today and twenty-three tomorrow and twenty-three the day after that. They all have cute faces, but none of them have The Face. None of them will make it, and when they turn sixteen like Paige, it will be very clear. And the shit will hit the fan."

Mary was finally understanding. "Paige couldn't make it?"

"No way, but her mother didn't know that. 'If only you light her this way' and 'if only the makeup were better.' It was everybody else's fault. It always was, especially with Honor."

"You fought with Honor?"

"Each time I shot her daughter. Paige lost bookings because of her mother, I swear it. Nobody wanted to deal with Honor. It was about her, not Paige." Scott scoffed. "Soccer moms got nothing on model moms. This is the Little League for Anorexics."

Mary didn't smile. "Did you think Paige knew that she wouldn't make it?"

"Of course, at some point."

"Did you talk to her about it?"

"No, I don't talk to the kids, I shoot them. But I know. The kids are the honest ones. The kids know it before the parents do. They see the truth." Scott looked away, distracted by an assistant who was giving him a relieved thumbs-up. The light had been fixed. "Brilliant chatting with you. Back to the salt mines," he said, and walked off, raising his camera.

When Mary looked at the kids, she couldn't disagree. She lingered a minute to watch Scott work, clicking away as he shouted orders to them: turn your head three-quarters, no, less than that, somebody fix her bra strap, stop that giggling, stand completely still while I focus, not so much teeth, honey. When she turned away from the scene, she could almost understand why they'd grow up and want to kill their mothers. *She* wanted to kill their mothers.

She checked her watch and hurried for the exit. She had a lunch date to keep.

22

Thank God," Jack said, hoarse by the time a guard showed up in the lineup of holding cells. "I have to call my lawyer!"

"Shut up, Newlin." The guard was burly and young, with a brushy mustache and an angry expression. "You're nobody special in here."

"I have a right to call my lawyer, like anybody else." Jack was controlling his temper. He had to get to Trevor.

"Your rights. That's all I fuckin' hear all day." The guard took a ring of keys from his pocket as another guard appeared for backup. "Here's your rights, pal. You have the right to three frees a day, delivered to you like room service. You have the right to free heat and utilities and the right to be in the news like a friggin' celebrity." The guard shoved a key into the lock in the cell. "You got so many goddamn rights I can't count that high. Now turn around and put your hands behind your back."

"I need to make that phone call." Jack turned his back and presented his wrists, as the guard opened the door and slammed the cuffs on.

"Tell them at the house, counselor." The guard yanked him out by the elbow and shoved him down the hall, but Jack exploded in frustration.

"Goddamn! I've waited hours for one lousy call!"

"Shut up!" the guard shouted, and pushed Jack so hard he lost his balance, stumbled forward, and fell.

"No!" Jack cried out. He couldn't break his fall with his hands cuffed, and his chest hit the concrete squarely, knocking the wind out of him. His chin bounced on the floor and he felt dazed for a minute. When he looked up he was eye level with the laughing man.

Who abruptly stopped laughing.

23

The lab at the Roundhouse was busy, the criminalists bright-eyed except one. She was the one Brinkley had had working all night, liaising with the FBI and running the DNA tests he needed. He'd had to rush the report of the result, to stay ahead of Davis. Brinkley thought about saying thank you to the tech, but didn't. It was part of her job. If she didn't like it, she should find another. "What did you find out about the earring back?" he asked, standing with Kovich at the black-topped lab table. Before them was a row of microscopes and slides, which were carefully stored and numbered by case. "It's hers, isn't it?"

"The stiff's?"

"No, the daughter's. The earring back is Paige Newlin's, isn't it?"

"No, it's not. I took some flakes of skin off the hair you gave me and compared it with the earring back. There's no match."

"What?" Brinkley couldn't hide his disappointment. "You're sure about that?"

"Hair? What hair?" Kovich asked, but Brinkley ignored him.

"You *damn* sure about that?" he repeated. He would have bet his life it was the daughter's earring.

"Absolutely, Detective. I did a visual inspect and double-checked with a DNA analysis, just to make sure—"

"Hold on." Kovich smiled crookedly. "Let's get back to the hair."

"The hair's not your concern," Brinkley said, but Kovich pushed up his glasses.

"Excuse me, Mick, I'm very interested in this hair. You may not know this, but hair is a hobby of mine. In fact, if I get to see this hair for even one minute, I bet I can tell you where it came from. I am a fucking hair expert."

The criminalist looked from Kovich to Brinkley and held up her hands. "Don't get me in the middle, okay? I was told to look it over on the QT, so I looked it over."

"S'all right," Brinkley said, but Kovich held out his hand.

"Cough it up. Gimme the hair. I can carbon-date it. I amaze my friends, really. You oughta see me at parties."

"Here." The criminalist slid the bagged hair from an unmarked case folder and handed it over.

"Well, well." Kovich took the bag and held it up to the fluorescent lighting. "Yes, it's quite clear that this is a very special hair. Subject hair belongs to a gorgeous young model who is innocent of any major felony, but who is so good-looking she should be locked up."

Brinkley could hear the edge to Kovich's voice. He said to the criminalist, "Did you check what I asked you?"

"Yeh. Lookit." The criminalist turned around and peered into a large black microscope that rested on a white lab table. She took a second to bring the scope into focus, twisting the chrome knob. "Check it. It's a match."

Brinkley elbowed Kovich aside and looked in the microscope. A perfect circle of bright white stared back at him, and through the center of the circle was a thick stalk of red, with a line in the middle. "That's a hair? What's that line in the middle?"

"It's the cortex. The center of the hair, basically. Now look at this slide."

Brinkley watched as the circle went bright white and another red stalk appeared. "It looks the same."

"It is."

"Nice," Brinkley said, under his breath, and Kovich nudged him out of the way.

"Let me play." The heavy detective bent over the scope. "Ah, yes, even more hair, my specialty."

"A hair found on the decedent's body," the criminalist said. "One of several actually. It is the same hair as those in the bag."

"You dig, Kovich?" Brinkley asked. "We got the daughter's hair on the mother. What's that tell you?"

Kovich came up from the scope, his expression sour. "It tells me you and me are goin' for a ride, Mick."

"You know it's good, Stan."

"We'll talk about it. Let's not fight in front of the lady. Foul language may be involved." Kovich turned to the criminalist. "Thanks."

"You're not gonna make a stink, are you, Detective Kovich?"

"Nah. I'm just gonna bitch-slap my partner here. You wanna watch?" Kovich turned to go, with Brinkley following.

"Don't forget the reports," the criminalist called after them, and she thrust a set of papers at Brinkley. "By the way, the dirt in Baggie A, from the coffee table? It was gravel, soot, silica, and particulate of dog feces. Like you'd get off a sidewalk."

"I coulda told you that, Mick," Kovich said, as he led Brinkley out. "I am a particulate-of-dog-feces expert."

Brinkley didn't reply and tucked the reports unread under his arm.

It was impossible to keep a secret in a police station, so Brinkley and Kovich always fought in the Chrysler. It wasn't that they planned it that way, it was just that the fights always seemed to break out when they were driving. Or maybe that was the only time they talked to each other, Brinkley didn't know. "The hair on the mom is the daughter's," he was saying, increasingly exasperated. "You tellin' me that that doesn't mean anything?"

"No. It means something." Kovich was driving aimlessly in the north end of town. He squinted over the steering wheel into the bright sunshine. "It means the mom hugged her daughter."

"But the daughter told us she wasn't with the mom that day." The Chrysler, a shitwagon, hadn't warmed up enough to turn the heat on, so Brinkley kept his jacket buttoned up. The car was an '88 model, left over from another unit. Homicide got all the castoffs; their motor pool was a disgrace.

"So she hugged her mother another day. A day the mother was wearing the same blouse."

"What's the likelihood of that? They didn't live together."

"They worked together and they hugged."

"And the hair didn't fall off since then?"

"No. I'm the hair expert and I say hair sticks. Half the time, I got dog hair all over me and the dog's been dead a year."

"Shit. Come on, Stan. We wouldn't charge on that kind of evidence, but we'd sure as hell follow up. But we're not. We're lettin' the daughter go free."

"We already charged, Mick." Kovich slowed the car to a stop at the light. "We locked the guy up."

"So we unlock him."

Kovich laughed, his head jerking back like he had whiplash, though the car was at a standstill. "That's not happening and you know it."

"It should happen."

"Yeah, right."

"We go to the lieutenant and we say, look we got some doubts here." Brinkley gestured, palms up. "I tell him, gimme a day. Gimme two days. Let me talk to this kid and open her up. Lemme get down to it."

Kovich sighed audibly as the light changed and the car cruised forward. "Davis is sure of his case."

"He's wrong."

"He got the prints, everything."

"All staged."

Kovich steered right onto Broad Street, which thronged with Temple students in down jackets, carrying heavy knapsacks. McGonigle Hall and the university's other buildings lined the street, and its bright garnet flags, bearing a huge white T, hung from the streetlights, filling like sails in the wind. One was ripped. Kovich flipped on the heat in the car. Frigid air blew through the vents.

"You gonna back me up?" Brinkley asked, but Kovich was already shaking his head. Seemed to Brinkley he'd been shaking his head since the case began.

"No."

"Thanks." Brinkley looked out the window, watching the students. They walked in a throng from the Students' Pavilion, past the ivy-covered Mitten Hall, built with gray stones usually seen in medieval churches, and under the wrought-iron gate that led to Berk Mall. The college girls were young and pretty but Brinkley barely noticed. He fiddled with the air vent, trying to break it.

"Sorry, Cholly."

"Got it."

Kovich squinted hard. "I'm not a bad cop, Mick."

"I didn't say you were." Brinkley moved the vent slats this way and that.

"Just that there's somethin' you don't understand. This isn't about Newlin at all. Not anymore."

"What you mean?"

"Let's pretend that Newlin is innocent, like you say. I don't think it, but let's pretend. Like Gene London used to say."

"Gene London?"

"Kid's show. You don't remember *The Gene London Show*, when we were little? 'Let's pretend that it's story time'?"

"No."

"How about Pixanne? Chick in green tights? Flies around like a fairy?"

"No."

"Chief Halftown? Guy in an Indian headdress?"

"No."

Kovich frowned. "Where the fuck were you raised, Mick?"

"Not the same Philly as you. So what?"

"Forget it. Say Newlin is innocent. You think that matters."

"Of course. It's the truth."

"No." Kovich clucked as he swung the car onto a side street and powered it forward. "You wrong, home. Newlin used to matter, but he stopped mattering the minute he picked up the phone and told nine-one-one he did it. Then the case wasn't about him anymore, it was about dispatch, the uniforms, the techs, and us. You follow so far?"

"No."

"You do, too. Next it got to be about the crime lab and the bloody prints and then, shit, the D.A." Kovich hit the steering wheel with a palm. "The D Fucking A. Mr. Dwight Davis and his crew. Then the bail commissioner, and at the prelim it'll be the Municipal Court judge. Now it's about the American Justice Machine. Still with me?"

Brinkley stopped playing with the air vent. It was unbreakable. Nothing had been going his way, not since the lady left.

"Now Newlin's in the machine, and the machine is callin' the shots. And you know what? Newlin don't seem to mind very much. In fact, *he's* the clown who got the machine in motion. Cranked the sucker up. Engaged it, like a clutch. Poked that tiger with a stick. You understand?"

Brinkley's gaze fell on the reports in his lap. The daughter's hair was still in the folds of paper. Part of him wished he'd never taken it. Maybe he could forget about it then. Just let it go. He'd been wrong about the earring and the hummus. What was the matter with him?

"So, you get it, this is not about Mr. Newlin at all. He may have been a rich, powerful lawyer, but now he's the guy who switched on the machine, and it ate him up like it was the whale and he was Jonah. Ain't nobody can save Mr. Jonah now, not you and not me. Can't even see him no more. He's gone, Mick. All gone, and before you start cryin' for him, remember he brought the whole damn thing on himself."

Brinkley stared at the reports encasing the hair. CRIMINALISTICS LABORATORY REPORT. It was for nothing. If the truth didn't matter anymore, then Brinkley didn't know what did. It was like with Sheree. He could never convince her that she already had what all her new friends were looking for. Whether she called it God, Allah, or Jehovah, it was all about love. And Sheree already had love. With him.

"So my question to you, is if our Mr. Newlin wants himself convicted and the American Justice Machine wants him convicted, and even his own daughter wants him convicted, why you think you can try and stop it?"

The words on the reports swam before Brinkley's eyes. Was he losing it? Always thinking about Sheree, instead of business. Maybe that was his problem. The black letters on the crime lab reports came into sharp focus. It was the DNA comparison of the skin on the hair, Sample A, with the skin on the earring, Sample B. Lots of little letters that meant no match. Sample A indicated the DNA of a female. Sample B indicated the DNA of a male. Brinkley read the sentence again. The earring back was from a *man's* earring?

"Stan, pull over," Brinkley said, and the car came to an abrupt halt.

24

Mary sat on a frigid park bench behind Ray-Bans, on a busy Logan Square. Runners sprinted by in sweats and cotton gloves, heading to the river to do the eight-mile circuit. Catholic schoolgirls from Hallahan flocked together, their saddle shoes and blue uniforms out of a bad porn movie. Businesspeople hurried by, heading back to the office after lunch at one of the neighborhood restaurants like Au Bon Pain, Subway, and Mace's Crossing. Mary could count on one hand how many of them would have eaten at the Four Seasons.

"It's freezin' cold, Mare," Lou said, sitting next to her. Lou Jacobs was a retired cop who worked as an investigator at the Rosato firm. His thin hair had silvered like cedar shakes and his skin weathered from a lifetime of weekend fishing trips to Ventnor. He was compact, though trim and fit, with sharp blue eyes and a nose curved like a gull's beak. Lou and Mary had worked together on a previous murder case and had survived—each other. Mary, newly in charge, had called him and asked him to meet her here.

"I know it's cold, Lou. We bosses aren't bothered by cold. In fact, we welcome cold."

"Gimme a break." Lou shoved his hands into the pockets of a lined windbreaker, with a zippered neck. Underneath he wore a blue cotton shirt, knit tie, and corduroy pants. He liked to look good while he froze his nuts off. "Mare, let me give you a clue.

When I was on the job, I ran plenty of stakeouts. We always waited in the car, where there was heat."

"We can't do that. There's no parking around here."

"Plus if you can't bug the suspects or put in a tap, you have to get real close to hear them talk. Take it from me. I'm giving you the inside track here." Lou waved a wrinkled hand at the curved gray building that was the Four Seasons Hotel, perched on the corner across the street. The hotel restaurant faced Logan Square, and the Parkway encircling it was clogged with traffic. "This may be too much of a detail for a boss, but trust me. We're too effin' far away to see or hear anything."

"I know that. I'm working on that." Mary sulked behind the sunglasses. "I'll have a plan in a minute."

"Well, let's review. We came, we saw the girl, Paige, and the boyfriend hug hello, then we saw them go inside to the restaurant. Now we're sittin' here like ice cubes."

"Well, what do you think we should do? We bosses do use consultants from time to time."

"Thank you." Lou nodded graciously. "Now. This girl, Paige, she obviously knows what you look like. But she doesn't know what I look like."

"No."

"Well, it's late and I haven't eaten yet. So, I suggest I have lunch, right now, at the Four Seasons." Lou nodded, turning to the hotel. "Maybe a nice, thick steak. With a beer. Imported, naturally, to go with my steak."

Mary perked right up. "That's a great idea! What a good consultant you are! You go in and listen!"

"Heineken would be nice." Lou gazed at the hotel. "Or Amstel."

"You come back and tell me what you hear!"

"Maybe, for dessert, a little cappuccino. I like a little cappuccino with my imported beer." Lou turned to Mary with a sly smile. "I hear better when I have a little cappuccino, after my steak and my Amstel."

"Go, already!" Mary said, giving him an excited shove, and Lou rose from the bench stiffly.

"Should I bring you a doggie bag?"

"Bring me evidence! Evidence to go!"

Lou muttered something and walked off.

Five minutes after he had gone, Mary realized she could have waited somewhere toasty, but by then it was too late to leave the bench. She pressed her legs together for warmth and huddled deep into her coat. The skyscrapers blocked the sun. Wind from the Schuylkill River whisked down the wide boulevard. Passersby looked at her curiously. She caught sight of Lou in the warm restaurant, being seated at a table near Paige and Trevor. She edged forward on the bench. Her butt was frozen. Her pantyhose formed crystals.

Mary watched as Lou ordered, then was brought a meal. She shivered as runners, businesspeople, and even the homeless came and went. She was cold to her contact lenses, but she didn't want to leave. This was her shot. If her theory was right, Paige and Trevor were conspirators to murder. She prayed Lou was hearing something incriminating.

She got up and paced to keep warm and kill time. She walked around until her pumps got caught in the gray cobblestones and she had memorized the placards posted for tourists. She learned that Logan Square used to be a site of public executions, that the Swann Fountain was named after the president of the Philadelphia Fountain Society, and that the three verdigris statues at the center of the fountain—man, woman, and young girl—represented the three rivers of Philadelphia: the Schuylkill, the Delaware, and the Wissahickon. She hoped that Lou learned something more useful, or at least, more interesting.

An hour later Mary saw Paige and Trevor pay the bill and leave the restaurant. As soon as they were out of sight, Lou got up and went after them. She couldn't suppress her excitement. What had Lou overheard? What if they were both in on it? She shivered, this time with anticipation, and trained her eyes on the hotel entrance. In time Lou came out, crossed the valet parking area, and walked briskly across the street and toward the park bench.

Mary stood up. "Tell me, tell me, tell me!" she said, practically jumping up and down.

"Cheese and crackers! It's cold out here!"

"What'd you get?"

"A Caesar, to start, then I went with the Chilean sea bass, not the steak. For dessert, I had the chocolate chiffon cake with a decaf cappuccino. It hit the spot."

"No, I mean, what did you hear?"

"Nothing."

"What?" Mary was crestfallen. "You didn't hear anything?"

"I heard, but they didn't say anything that mattered. They talked the whole time about nothing. He talked about his French test and his track team. She talked about Wu-Tang."

"Wu-Tang?" Mary flopped down on the bench, dejected.

"That mean something to you?"

"It's music. A rap group."

"Rap!" Lou snorted. "Rap isn't music. Stan Getz is music. Or the Bird. Or Miles."

Mary was too disappointed to debate it. "So my lead doesn't pan out."

"Don't take it too bad." Lou sat down on the bench, tugging on his corduroy pants first so they didn't wrinkle. "You didn't ask me where they are now."

"Where they are now?" Mary looked over at him, then brightened. "Where are they?" She checked the hotel entrance. "They didn't come out. You came out but they didn't!"

"They're inside. They tried to get a room."

"A *room*?" Her mouth dropped open. She didn't know she was such a prude. Well, she kind of did. "They tried to get a room *together*?"

"No separate." Lou snorted. "Of course, together."

"That's disgusting. They're way too young for that."

"Not possible. Anyway, the hotel was booked and they didn't have a reservation. The room is beside the point, anyway."

"It is? Why?"

"Because they're having sex in the cloakroom."

"*What?*" Mary was astounded, but Lou checked his watch matter-of-factly.

"They should be done by now."

"Done?"

"He's young. What can I say? We all go through it."

Mary ignored him. "How do you know this?"

"I followed them after they got turned down at the reception desk. I thought they were going out to the atrium but they took a quick right into the cloakroom. It's right off the main lobby."

Mary sat back in the bench, appalled. "Her mother was just killed. When does grief-stricken start?"

"Hold off on that, Mare." Lou's eyes watered as he squinted against the cold wind. Sterling silver filaments of his hair flew around wildly. "Look, if she were my kid, I'd smack her one. The both of 'em are outta control, you ask me. Rich kids. They think they're entitled."

Mary nodded in agreement. Sometimes Lou sounded so much like her father it was scary. Mary decided that Italians and Jews weren't so different, except that Italians had even more guilt.

"It isn't good behavior, but it doesn't mean the kid killed her mother. I know, I've seen lots of victims' families. One father, when I told him his kid was dead, he just laughed and laughed. You can't judge by that. People show their grief in different ways."

"Sex in public is mourning?"

"Yeah, for some people."

Mary glanced at the hotel dubiously. "Wonder when they'll come out. She told us Trevor had a class at three." She checked her watch. It was almost three o'clock now. "She lied about that."

"Maybe she didn't lie. Maybe she talked him out of it."

"I don't understand."

"You're not a man. End of story."

"Hmmm." Mary watched the entrance, feeling torn. She wanted to see how long the two of them were there and what they did next, but she also felt guilty leaving Judy back at the office.

She explained the quandary to Lou as she reached into her bag for her flip phone, dialed the office number, and left a message. "She's not there," she said as she slid the antenna down with a flat palm. "So I should stay, at least."

"Stay? In this cold?"

"You go back to the office. I'll stay here." Suddenly Mary felt a surge of well-being. Dividing labor. Managing the case. Pushing old men around. Was this what they meant by empowerment?

"What are you gonna do here alone?"

"Watch when they come out, maybe follow them. *Surveille* them," she answered, but Lou was looking at her, his eyes blank pools of blue in a tan, lined face. Either he didn't understand real police lingo or resented her empowerment. "All right, Lou. You're the cop here. Help me out. Tell me what to do."

"I'll stick around. See what happens."

"Okay, good. I approve."

"Like it matters."

Mary smiled. "I think you enjoy our quality time."

"I think I got nothin' better to do. Plus I don't want you near that kid, the boy. I don't like him. He's a punk."

Mary felt her suspicions gain strength. Lou knew this stuff. "You think Trevor's in on it?"

"I don't know who's in on what. To me, the jury's out on the both of them. I don't know enough to make any conclusions, except that for kids with a lotta class, they got no class."

Mary didn't disagree.

Mary and Lou watched the entrance to the Four Seasons through two cups of hot coffee, three soft pretzels, and a hot dog with sauerkraut, which she had carted from a hot dog stand in front of the Academy of Natural Science. At three-thirty, she switched to chocolate water in a white Styrofoam cup. There was still no sign of either Paige or Trevor, although Mary saw the entire partnership of Morgan, Lewis and Bockius leave a firm luncheon, laughing and talking. They'd had a good year. Again.

"Why does everybody hate lawyers?" she asked Lou, sipping lukewarm chocolate water. She kept her eyes on the hotel entrance.

"Because they can," Lou answered. "It's like that dog joke. You know that joke."

"Yes, you told me that joke. The punch line is, 'Because they can,' right?"

"Right," Lou said, though he didn't remember telling Mary that joke. He would never tell a woman that joke, and even though Mary was a kid, she was still a woman. "Did I really tell you that joke?" he asked, to double-check.

"Yes," she said, watching and sipping.

If he did, Lou regretted it.

Mary was giving Lou a pop quiz. "Do you know what the three statues in the Swann Fountain are?"

Lou squinted behind him at the still fountain. "Naked."

"No. They're a man, woman, and young girl."

"Naked."

"No!" Mary's teeth chattered. "I mean, do you know what they represent? Beside the Newlins?"

"No clue."

"The three rivers of Philadelphia. Can you name them?"

"The *Niña*, the *Pinta*, and the *Santa Maria*?"

"No."

"Manny, Moe, and Jack?"

"No."

"Moe, Larry, and Curly?"

Mary waited.

"Okay, tell me," Lou said, after a time.

"It's them! They're out!" Mary leapt from the frosty bench when she saw Paige and Trevor materialize at the entrance to the Four Seasons, looking remarkably remote for a young couple that had just had sex in a coatroom. They weren't even holding hands, a fact that Mary couldn't help noting. "See?" she said.

"I see 'em," Lou said, rising stiffly and shoving his hands in the pockets of his corduroys.

"No, I meant, see, she shouldn't have had sex with him. He's not even holding her hand."

His eyes were trained on the hotel and he squinted against the cold. "What?"

"Forget it."

"Look." Lou frowned. "She's takin' the one cab, he's takin' the other."

"Oh, no." Mary watched as the doorman retrieved a cab for Paige and Trevor helped her into it, then waited until the next cab in line pulled up for him. "Where's he going? His school is three blocks away. What's he need a cab for?"

"Maybe he's late."

"It'll take longer in the cab." Mary snatched her bag from the bench. "I'll follow him."

"No, I will. I don't want you near him." Lou hustled to the curb and hailed a cab that was coming toward them down the Parkway. "You take her."

"No, she knows what I look like." Mary hustled in front of him at the curb and waved frantically at the cab. "I'm following him."

"Mare, wait." Lou grabbed her arm in protest. "Let me do it. You take her, I'll handle him."

"No!" Mary said, and as the cab slowed to a halt, she lunged forward to take it, flinging open the door even before the cab had stopped. "Follow her."

"Mary, stop!" Lou kept a wrinkled hand on the door handle. "This kid could be dangerous. Don't talk to him. Don't get close to him."

"I'll be careful. I'm not Judy or Bennie. You got your lawyers mixed up."

"Hah! You're all trouble," Lou called back, flagging the next cab, as Mary climbed into hers and took off.

25

Dwight Davis had gotten a job offer from the law firm of Tribe & Wright, so he remained uncowed by the grandeur of the place. Set at the pinnacle of a skyscraper, the firm occupied six floors, each one tastefully outfitted with light, custom furniture, giving the place a uniformly costly glow. As Tribe's managing partner, William Whittier had the largest office, and Davis was waiting for him in it. According to his secretary, Whittier had "stepped away," which was Tribespeak for went to the bathroom.

Davis sat with his flowery cup of coffee and suppressed his smile at the plush surroundings. Success at law firms was no longer measured in the number of windows—with modern architecture, even first-year associates couldn't be deprived of light and air—but in the number of desks. Second and third desks had become as important as second or third homes. Whittier had three desks; he not only ran the firm, he received the highest percentage of all fees it received. In other words, he was a major landowner, if not king.

Whittier's main desk was a huge, glistening affair of white oak whose raison d'être was to bear a single stack of correspondence, a shiny brass ship's clock, and a miniature walnut cabinet for a fountain pen collection. The second desk, to which Davis had been shown, was the Palm Beach house of desks, semitropical and relaxed. A large teak circle on a pedestal, it was as bare as the main desk except for a gray-green conferencing phone with foot-pads like a gecko. The third desk, tucked in the corner like a country home, was a computer workstation that held a slim laptop. For what it cost, Davis could hire an expert that would put some scumbag in jail for consecutive life terms, but nobody at Tribe thought that way, which was why he'd turned them down.

"You must be Dwight Davis," Whittier boomed, appearing at the door. Bill Whittier was a lanky six-footer, wearing a gray pin-striped suit and a broad, hale-fellow grin. He was middle-aged, but crossed the room with a sloppy step that reminded Davis of an overgrown frat boy, especially when Whittier clapped the prosecutor on the shoulder. "Brother Masterson's told me all about you," he said, and extended a loose handshake.

"You play tennis with a grip like that?" the D.A. said.

"Hah! Very good. Squash, actually. The bar's closer."

"There you go." Davis smiled. Of course. Squash. He eased back into his seat. "Thanks for your time today."

"No problem. This matter is top priority, with me." Whittier seated himself at the second desk opposite Davis and brushed back his pale blond hair with stubby fingernails, then twisted to the door just in time to see a second lawyer in an Italian suit coming in. "And here's Art, right on time as usual." The enter-ing lawyer was thinner and shorter than Whittier, with gaunt cheeks, slick black hair, and dark eyes sharp behind eyeglass frames the size of quarters. Whittier turned back to Davis. "You won't mind if one of my partners, Art Field, sits in."

"Of course not, he's welcome." Davis had expected as much and shook Field's hand before they both sat down. Field would function as Whittier's counsel, to make sure the frat boy didn't get himself or the firm in trouble. Field would also qualify as a human tape recorder, to back up whatever Whittier said he said, whether he'd said it or not. What else were partners for?

Whittier relaxed, crossing one strong leg over the other. "So tell me, how's your boss? Keeping the bad guys locked up, I hear. We're very proud of him, here at Tribe."

"I'm proud to work for the man," Davis said, wondering if Whittier was reminding him of the firm's campaign contribution. "But if I tell him we're proud of him, he'll tell us to go straight to hell."

Whittier laughed, a hearty ha-ha-ha signifying manners, not mirth. "He is a little cranky, isn't he?"

"I try, Lord knows I try."

Whittier ha-ha-haed again, then quieted. "Terrible news about Honor Newlin, just terrible. And Jack of course. He was one of us, you know."

"Yes, I do." Davis nodded, impatient. Of course he knew Newlin worked here; that's why he'd asked Masterson to set up the meeting. Every muscle in him strained to cut the shit, but if he did that, he'd get nothing.

"It's a terrible tragedy, just terrible. We're still in shock, my partners and I, and awfully conflicted. Jack's confessed, I understand. It was reported in several of the morning papers."

"I can't confirm or deny that."

"Of course." Whittier shook his head. "All over the news. Partner at Tribe & Wright, well, just terrible. Terrible for Jack, and for the firm." He kept shaking his head, though his wavy blond hair remained in order. "Impossible to understand, you see. Jack was such a wonderful partner. A responsible husband and father. Impossible, really." He sighed. "As they say, who know what goes on behind closed doors?"

"Yes," Davis said, for lack of something better, though Whittier didn't seem to be listening anyway. Davis couldn't shake the impression that Whittier was no Felix Frankfurter in the legal department and had become managing partner because of politics, not brainpower. And he undoubtedly had the right connections, which was all that really mattered in administrative jobs.

"And Honor Newlin was a lovely woman, a lovely woman. One of my wife's favorites."

"Oh? Did you see them socially?"

"Not much."

"How often?"

"Rarely." Whittier eyed Davis warily. "This concerns Jack, I assume. Not me or my partners."

"Correct," Davis answered, instantly wishing he had said something more casual. Once a D.A., always a D.A., and now Whittier had edged away, sitting farther back in his chair.

"Now, Davis, I'm no trial lawyer, I spent my long professional life in corporate law, as you may know. But I'm not so old I've forgotten what a subpoena is, and I understand that I am under subpoena to talk with you today. Is that the case, sir?"

"Of course."

"You have a subpoena with you, for the record?"

"Definitely."

"You'll leave it with Art before you go. I wouldn't want to be in the position of voluntarily doing anything that could harm Jack, if you understand."

"Understood. May I?" Davis picked up one of the blank legal pads from the table. He knew that yanking out his own pad would put Whittier on guard and the only way he could get what he needed was if nobody acknowledged what was happening. "Now, remind me, please. You are the managing partner here, and Jack Newlin headed the estates group, correct?"

"Yes, quite right."

"He reported to you as such?"

"Yes. All department heads report to me."

Davis made a note, to get Whittier used to it. He did it all the time in court so the jury couldn't tell what mattered and what didn't. "Now, Honor Newlin's family foundation is represented by the Tribe firm."

"Yes, the Buxton Foundation."

Davis nodded. "What is a foundation, anyway?"

"Damned if I know." Whittier laughed again. "Only kidding."

"I figured," Davis said, though he hadn't been so sure.

"Well, let's see, a foundation is simply a private charity, established in this case, by a family. The Buxton Foundation donates the Buxton family money to public charities. By law, the Foundation is required to give away five percent of the total fund each year. Our firm helps it do that, with the tax advice and filings and whatnot required by Uncle Sam. It's a real tangle of paperwork, you can imagine. You work for the government, in effect."

Davis ignored the slight, even if it was intended. "And Buxton Foundation matters were handled by Newlin?"

"Yes, Jack brought the Foundation to us when he married Honor, and he supervised its matters for the firm. Essentially, he ran the Foundation, sat with Honor on the board, and doled out its legal work to our partners in various fields, as well as associates and paralegals."

"How large is the Buxton Foundation?"

"Hah! Real large."

"How large?"

Whittier glanced at Field, who nodded imperceptibly. "The Buxton is one of the more substantial family foundations. Two hundred million dollars, approximately."

Davis blinked. *Large.* "How much does the Foundation pay Tribe per year, in fees?"

"Does this matter?" Whittier cocked a pale eyebrow, his good cheer gone flat as keg beer.

"Absolutely."

"Three and a half to four million dollars a year."

Davis made a note, as if he could forget that staggering a sum. "The firm cannot have many clients that bill as much, can it?"

"Frankly, the Foundation is our largest client, and that's all I'll say about the Foundation. Understood?"

"Understood." Davis switched gears. "As to Jack, did he receive a portion of the fees the Foundation paid the firm? I know that's typical in the larger firms."

Whittier nodded. "He did. Jack was the billing partner on most matters, so he received a percentage of his client's fees, as a billings bonus."

"What percentage?"

"It was substantial. Thirty-three percent, as I recall. We could supply you with the exact number under document subpoena."

"I'll look forward to it." Davis accepted the answer for now. So Newlin would get thirty-three percent, more than a highway robber but less than a personal injury lawyer. If the Buxton billings amounted to three million dollars a year, which they easily did, Jack would take home a mil of that. And it also meant that as between the Foundation or Newlin, the Tribe firm would choose the Foundation, never mind that they'd have to hang their own partner. "Let's get to the night of Honor's murder."

"Yes, let's," Whittier said, plainly relieved, and Davis thought it ironic that Whittier would rather talk about murder than money.

"You saw Jack the night of the murder, didn't you?"

"Yes. Let me think a minute." Whittier gazed out an immense window to the spectacular view of the city below. Davis was watching him so closely he saw his pupils telescope down in the light. "Around six o'clock, I think."

"How long did you two speak for?"

"About fifteen minutes, as I remember."

"Would you have billed that time?"

"Yes, we bill in six-minute increments," Whittier answered, without apparent shame. "My time records would reflect the exact time we spoke."

"I'd like to see your records for that day, if I can."

Whittier exchanged looks with Field, then said, "You're serving the firm with a document subpoena."

"Yes, it's already included."

"Fine, then." Whittier pressed a button on the conference phone and asked his secretary for the records. Davis was sure Whittier could have accessed them from his laptop, but that would have necessitated moving from the second home to the third. While they waited for the records, Whittier remained silent, taking in the view out his window as if neither Davis nor Field were there. In a minute, the secretary emerged with the records, handed them to Whittier, and vanished. Whittier slipped tortoise-shell reading glasses from his inside jacket pocket and popped them on the bridge of his nose. "I hate that I have to wear these now," he grumbled, almost to himself.

"What do the records show?" Davis asked, because he couldn't not. If something had gone wrong with Newlin's plan, it could have been the timing.

"Well, I was right," Whittier said, underlining one entry with his finger. "CI: JN re Florrman bill. That means I spoke with Jack Newlin from 6:15 to 6:30, regarding the bill in Florrman."

"May I see that, please?" Davis accepted the records, with-out remarking that Whittier would bill a client for discussing the client's bill. He knew it was common in the white-shoe firms. That was how they paid for the second and third homes. Davis skimmed the records. Shit. The timing was a dry hole. "Did you record this right after the conversation?"

"Yes, I always do." Whittier paused. "It does bring back my conversation with Jack, that night."

"I was just getting to that. Tell me about it."

"Well, I saw him walking past my door, his office is just down the hall, and it struck me as earlier than he usually left. I had been wanting to talk to him about the Florrman bill all day but I got tied up in meetings, so when I saw Jack I knew I had to grab him. I called to him and he didn't stop, so I went to fetch him in the hall. I told him I had some concerns about the bill in Florrman, that at six months it was an older receivable. It was time to dun the client in some effective manner. More effective than whatever Jack was doing."

"What did he say to you?"

"He loathed to dun clients, but he said he'd get it current and that he had to go. He said he had dinner planned with Honor."

"He said 'dinner planned with Honor'?"

"Yes, and he seemed agitated."

Davis wrote it down verbatim. "How agitated?"

"Very. He was preoccupied the entire time I was speaking with him. He seemed nervous, and in a hurry. It was evident, and I told him so. I asked him if anything was the matter."

Davis made a another note. It was so good for premeditation. "What did he say?"

"He said he was fine. Great. Never better."

"Would you testify to this conversation and your observations at trial?"

"If I were subpoenaed."

"Fine. Do you know how he and Honor got along?"

"Well, as far as we could tell. They were an intensely private couple, though, not the type to socialize or serve on boards other than the Foundation. Still Honor was a wonderful woman, a lovely woman. Devoted to her husband and daughter."

Davis paused. "She must have left a will."

"Yes, it will be probated as soon as possible."

"The will was prepared by this firm, right?"

"Yes. I supervised its preparation."

Davis wasn't surprised. A document that important would have to be blessed by the firm's managing partner, and Newlin was too smart to do it himself. It would look like a conflict of interest for him to prepare a will that named him the lucky winner of the Buxton lottery. "Who benefits under her will?"

"The beneficiary won't be released until we receive a death certificate, and that information is confidential."

"Again, I'll honor the confidence until probate, when it becomes public record. But I need to know now. Who benefits under the will?"

"Well, well." Whittier cleared his throat, setting his neck wattle jiggling above a stiff white collar. "The answer to your question is rather complicated, but in essence, Honor left a personal estate worth fifty million dollars. Now, as you know, that's separate from the Foundation's corpus, which would exist in perpetuity, even after her death. Only the fifty million descends under the will, and none of it was earmarked for charity."

Davis smiled to himself. *Only* the fifty million. "So Newlin gets the fifty mil."

"No." Whittier shook his head. "Not at all. The daughter does. Paige inherits the fifty million."

The prosecutor's mouth went dry. It couldn't be. His theory of motive flew out the window. "Newlin *doesn't* benefit under the will?"

"Jack? Not a penny." Whittier's lips set firmly. "He gets nothing."

"That can't be. Do you have the will? I'll keep it confidential and I did subpoena it."

"I have it right here." Whittier glanced at Field, pulled a thick packet with a blue backer from a folder in front of him, and passed it across the desk.

"Thank you," Davis said, snatching the will from the table. Its pages felt smooth under his fingers, which almost itched as he thumbed through the document. How could this be? He speed-read the provisions, all corporate boilerplate, until he got to the relevant provisions, which clearly explained the bequest. It provided that Paige would inherit one-third of her mother's estate at age twenty-one, one-third at age twenty-five, and the final third at age thirty. There was no mention of Jack Newlin at all. Davis looked up, speechless, but Whittier had taken a sudden interest in the cityscape outside the window.

"You may want to talk with one of our other partners, if you have further questions," he said casually.

"What do you mean?" Davis looked from Whittier to Field and back again. He didn't get what was going on. The will had thrown him off-balance. Were they trying to tell him something? And trying not to, at the same time? It was exactly what you'd expect from a law firm that wants to shaft one of its own partners and avoid massive liability therefore. "Who else should I speak with?"

"His name is Marc Videon. But you'll need a subpoena."

"I'll have it sent right over."

"We'll need it before you speak with him."

"Consider it done." Davis felt urgent. Where was this leading? "Who's Videon?"

"He's one of our more specialized lawyers at Tribe. *Sui generis.* A department unto himself."

"What's this Videon do?"

"Divorce," Whittier answered, and for a minute, Davis couldn't reply.

26

Follow that cab!" Mary told the cabbie and couldn't help but feel a little thrill.

The driver, a diminutive, dark-haired man with a curly mustache, turned around in the front seat. "No Eeenglish," he said, and Mary pointed at Trevor's cab, a trifle disappointed.

"Go! There!" she commanded. She kept her eyes on the cab ahead as it idled in the congested traffic on Market Street. The outline of Trevor's head was visible and he moved as if he were talking to the driver. In the next minute his hand emerged from the back window, halting a car that was trying to cut in front of them. He must have been in a hurry. Trevor's cab burst forward, going west, away from the city.

"Hurry, please!" Mary said. Trevor's school was behind them, so he wasn't going back to class. What was he up to? Something was going on; her lead hadn't been so dumb after all. Trevor's cab reached Seventeenth Street and took a left, a familiar jog that Mary took all the time, negotiating the one-way streets of her hometown. William Penn had laid out the grid two hundred years ago, and he hadn't taken cabbies and lawyers into account. She took a guess where Trevor was headed, and ten minutes later found out she was right.

Both cabs pulled up in the drop-off island at the Thirtieth Street train station, one after the other, as if unrelated. Both cab doors opened at the same time, and Mary left her cab only a split second after Trevor left his, and followed him into the station, keeping her excitement in check. Trevor hurried into the tan marble concourse past the left wing of the station, bypassing the suburban trains. Mary tracked him as he threaded his way through the crowd of travelers getting off the train from Washington. Trevor made a beeline for the ticket counter, and she picked up her pace.

The lines were long at the ticket windows, and Mary got behind Trevor in line, a zigzaggy affair cordoned with black tape. She looked at him up close, to see what she could see. Was he the kid who had bumped into her in the hall at Paige's condo? She couldn't tell. His hair was a light brown color, expensively feathered around the ears, and he wore a thin gold hoop in his ear. His eyes were large and clear blue, and in profile, he had a straight nose with a suspiciously perky tip. His shoulders were broad in a brown bomber jacket with a white T-shirt underneath, and he was easily six feet tall. Trevor struck her as a young prince, a type Mary disliked. Maybe because she couldn't pass for a princess. If Paige was the delicate cycle, Mary was distinctly regular.

NEXT AGENT AVAILABLE read the white blinking letters, and the line advanced. It moved unusually swiftly, with four agents working away and nobody asking for a complete oral timetable for a change. Trevor seemed impatient, even jumpy. His hand wiggled at his side and he kept shifting his feet from one brown suede Doc Martens to the other. What was his problem? Why was he in a hurry?

The line moved forward again, and though Trevor was three travelers from the front, he pulled a wallet from his back pocket and flipped it open as Mary peeked. It was a thin calfskin billfold and on the left were four credit cards, including a gold American Express card, VISA, and MasterCard. Mary didn't get it. Even she couldn't qualify for a gold Amex. Did this kid pay these bills himself? Where would a student get bucks like that?

Mary made a mental note, and the line shifted forward. She thought it was Trevor whom she'd passed in the hall but wanted to make sure. She cleared her throat and decided to shake his tree. "Excuse me, I hate to be rude, but do you live at Colonial Hill

Towers? I have a friend who lives there and I think I've seen you there."

"No." Trevor shook his head, jittery. "I live in the subs. Paoli."

"But have you been there? At Colonial Hill?"

The line shifted forward, putting Trevor at the front. NEXT AGENT AVAILABLE, blinked the sign. He turned to the ticket counter, and one of the agents waved him forward. "No," he answered, over his shoulder. "Never."

"Oh, sorry." Mary watched Trevor hustle to the agent. So he had lied; he had obviously been at Colonial Hill. Why would he lie about it? Or did people who lied lie all the time? And where was he going? She tried to overhear him at the ticket counter but it was too far away. Then the lighted sign started blinking again and an agent at the other end was waving her forward. Damn. She wanted to know where Trevor was headed. She stalled, trying to hear what he said to the agent.

"Lady, you goin' today?" a man behind her asked irritably, and Mary walked to the ticket counter.

"I don't really need a ticket, I have a problem," she said, when she reached the window. The Amtrak agent was an older woman in a red-and-blue uniform. Her eyes were overly made-up behind glasses with swirly gold-metal frames, and her smile was lipsticked a rosy red.

"Problem?" The ticket agent cocked an eyebrow penciled like a half-moon, and Mary inched closer to the glass.

"I'm in love."

"That's a problem."

"That guy over there. I just got in the ticket line because I thought he was so cute. Do you think he's cute?"

The agent's gaze slid sideways to Trevor and back again. "For a guy with a nose job."

"You think?"

"I know."

"I hate that. Why is it okay when women are vain but not men?"

The agent smiled, her lipstick glossy. "They don't teach us that at Amtrak."

Mary laughed. She kept an eye on Trevor, who was leaving the ticket window with two blue tickets in his hand. "Can you tell me where he's going? Look him up in the computer?"

"No. Forget about him anyway. It ain't happening." The agent pointed, and Mary turned around.

Trevor was rushing into the outstretched arms of a pretty blond girl with long, straight hair. She looked slightly older than he, but had a matching nose job, and Trevor embraced her, giving her a long, wet kiss. "Jesus, Mary, and Joseph," Mary said, under her breath.

"Looks like he's taken."

"You don't know the half of it." Mary shook her head and watched Trevor go down for another deep, lingering kiss.

"You gotta go," the agent said. "Remember, there's a lotta fish in the sea."

"Sure." She nodded and moved from the window as Trevor hugged the girl close. Then he checked his watch, put his arm around her, and they hurried laughing into the concourse.

Mary followed him to find out which train they took. She couldn't believe this guy. Scum, total scum. She lurked under the black information board in the middle of the busy concourse. "Metroliner to New York, all aboard Track Six," boomed a voice over the loudspeaker. The information board changed, its numbers flipping noisily around, and she watched Trevor and the blonde sprint into the line at Track Six, where the passengers were already showing their tickets to a blue-jacketed conductor.

So that was it. Trevor had another girlfriend and they were going to New York. Mary saw him and the blonde show their tickets to the conductor, then waited until they disappeared down the stairs to the train.

27

Lou, in an old black gypsy cab, trailed Paige's Yellow cab down Race Street. Behind them was the Parkway, ahead lay the red-lettered signs of Chinatown's restaurants. Paige's cab was heading east, away from downtown. Lou slid forward on his seat, his eyes on the Yellow. What kind of girl was this Paige? Eating at the Four Seasons? Takin' cabs everywhere?

Lou shook his head. When he was a kid on Leidy Street, he walked. Rode his bike. Took the trolley, with sparks flying from the wires that hung over the city like black lace. Or the subway-surface cars, with that burnt rubber smell. Forget cabs. He wasn't in a cab until he was twenty-five. It was a very special thing to take a cab. Lou still couldn't hail one without feeling rich.

"She's turnin' onto Race," the driver said. A young black kid, excited to be following someone. Lou didn't mind it. He liked enthusiasm in people.

"Stay with her," Lou said, his thoughts on this Paige. What kind of a name was Paige anyway? When did girls start getting named Paige? He understood names like Sally, Mary, Selma. But Paige? Lou's mouth set grimly. How you expect a girl to turn out when you name her Paige?

"She turned right on Twelfth, goin' up," the cabbie said, gesturing with his hand. A colorful braided string was tied to his wrist. "You want me to step on it?"

"Nah. Just don't lose 'em." The cabbie's shoulders drooped,

and Lou felt bad raining on his parade. "You like music?" he asked, just to make conversation as they sat stalled. Construction around the Convention Center clogged the street, the jack-hammers like machine-gun fire.

"I love music," the cabbie answered.

"What do you like?"

"Rap."

"Everybody likes rap, nowadays."

"It's good."

"It is? Who's a good rapper?"

"DMX. Dr. Dre. You know them?"

"I know Dr. Dre. Takes care of my prostate," Lou said, and the cabbie laughed.

Paige's Yellow cab took a right toward The Gallery, and Lou was surprised. She was going shopping? He had her figured more for Neiman Marcus than JCPenney, but the cab stopped on the right, short of The Gallery. He looked around. What else was there? The bus station. What, was she leaving town?

"She's gettin' out," said the cabbie, edging up in his seat, and Lou's cab slowed to a stop a half a block behind the girl's. The back door of the Yellow cab opened, and Lou quickly fished out a twenty and handed it to the cabbie, who looked at the money in astonishment. "But the fare's only three bucks."

"I know that. You gotta buy a record with the difference."

"A record? You mean a CD?"

"A CD, yes. Buy yourself *Stan Getz At the Shrine*." Lou could see Paige moving in the backseat of her cab. She must be paying, too. "Getz. You got that name?"

"Never heard of him. He new?"

"No, he's old. Very old. Old as me. Promise you'll get that CD."

"I promise," the cabbie said, and Lou climbed out of the cab after the girl.

But when Paige got out of the cab she didn't look the same as when she went in. She was wearing a black baseball cap that she must have put on in the cab and her red ponytail swung from an opening in the back of the cap. She slipped on a pair of dark sun-glasses as she walked. It was a disguise, strictly amateur, but why would she do it? To go shopping? To take a bus? What gives? True, the Newlin murder was all over the *Daily News* and the *Inquirer*, but nobody had published the girl's photo yet. The father was the story.

The girl kept walking down the cross street and even in the glasses and baseball cap caught plenty of stares from passersby and construction workers. Lou could see why. She wore a black miniskirt and legs. It was cold out, but you'd never know it from how she was dressed, in a navy pea coat that almost covered the skirt. She took strides so long he had to huff and puff to keep up with her, and the motion of her walk was something else. Even in clunky black shoes, she moved like the sidewalk was a catwalk. Lou didn't mind watching her, then felt guilty about it. She was way too young, and he liked young girls to be ladies, not to do the stuff this kid was doing. At the Four Seasons yet.

She crossed Market Street past The Gallery, and Lou followed her at a safe distance. Where was she going? Nowhere close. And why have the cab drop you so far from where you're going? Lou thought about it. Because you don't want anybody to know where you're going. And considering her disguise, he figured the girl was either paranoid or had something to hide.

They entered the old business district, abandoned now that most of the large companies had fled uptown to the new, glistening skyscrapers. Lou remembered when this part of town hopped, because of the Ben Franklin Hotel, the Old Federal Courthouse, and the busiest, the Post Office. Nowadays everything was e-mail and Chestnut Street was lined with car stereo outlets, credit unions, and Dollar stores. But Lou didn't have time to reminisce. He followed Paige to a sooty sliver of a low-rise and watched her disappear through its stainless steel door. Lou didn't know the building. Its sign was small and he squinted to read it.

PLANNED PARENTHOOD.

Lou halted in his tracks. He felt suddenly like he wasn't

allowed to enter, like it was a ladies' bathroom or a bra store. He thrust his hands in the pockets of his corduroys. Wind ruffled his hair as he stood in the cold sun. People hurried past, looking back curiously. Even if he was a man, he could still go inside, couldn't he? It was a free country. He smoothed his hair in place, straightened his tie, and went in.

Paige took an elevator to the fourth floor; Lou knew because he watched the old-fashioned numbers light up to track the single car, and he went up after her. Planned Parenthood's offices turned out to be brightly lit and painted a watercolor lavender, with matching cushioned chairs arranged in two rows in front of a TV mounted in the left corner of the room. The large reception desk was shielded by clear glass, which Lou figured was for security. Pastel pictures of women covered the walls, and women's magazines were fanned out on display on the side wall. On the rug under the display sat a large wicker basket in which Lou would have expected some artificial fruit. Instead were sample packets of Stayfree minipads.

Lou looked away, embarrassed, then spotted the Newlin girl. She had taken off her sunglasses but was still in her cap talking to a young, black receptionist behind the glass shield. By the time he found them, both women were looking at him funny. He guessed it was because of security, and not just because he was an old Jewish guy.

"Can I help you, sir?" the receptionist said, calling across the room, and Paige looked expectant under the brim of a cap that said GUESS. Lou didn't know what the hat meant, unless it was how he felt.

"Uh, no, but thanks," he answered. "I'm . . . meeting someone here."

"Who?" The receptionist was pretty, with big brown eyes and a sweet smile. Her hair had been marceled into finger waves, which Lou liked. He remembered when women wore finger waves the first time around. And pleated skirts. He liked them, too, but they were long gone.

"I'm, uh, waiting for my daughter. She asked me to meet her here, and I'm early."

"Does she have an appointment?"

"No, she was coming in without one." Lou took a few steps forward, and if he had a hat it would be in his hand. He noticed Paige watching the exchange, her mild impatience betrayed by a pursing of her lips. "Is that okay?"

"Well, some of our clients are walk-ins, but she'll need an appointment to use our services."

"Oh, sure. Right. I am in the right place, aren't I? I mean this is the place where you give out birth control, right?"

"We do perform that function, among other services." The receptionist permitted herself a smile as she gestured to a bank of pamphlets sitting on the counter in plastic holders. *YOUR REPRODUCTIVE SYSTEM, BREAST SELF-EXAMINA-TION, THE FIRST VISIT TO THE GYNECOLOGIST,* read some of the titles. "If you want to learn more about us, read the pink one."

"Thanks." Lou picked up the pink pamphlet, which read *SERVICES WE PROVIDE.* It would be useful and it was less embarrassing than *YOUR BREASTS.* "I'll study up."

"Feel free to take a seat. You can wait for your daughter, and when she gets here I can make an appointment for her."

"Sure, okay, I knew that. I'll just wait." Lou nodded and looked around the lavender sea for a seat. The last time he felt this funny was when he went to Rosato's law firm for the first time and all he saw everywhere was women. Now he was used to it; it had only taken him a year. He saw a chair near the reception desk and sat down, straining to overhear what Paige was saying to the receptionist. It sounded to Lou like, "lsisinwn sjduudun?" He'd had the same problem in the Four Seasons and was thinking it might be time to break down and get a hearing aid.

Paige finished her conversation with the receptionist and sat down in a chair a few away from his, against the same wall. If she recognized Lou from the Four Seasons, it didn't show. She opened her pea coat, crossed her legs in her black skirt, and picked up a *Seventeen* magazine. She began to read it, baseball cap bent over the glossy pages, as if she were memorizing it.

Lou's experience on the job told him to take it slow. The girl

was here for a very personal reason and part of him felt bad
prying into her life. Far as he knew, the girl was the daughter of
a murder victim and had been through hell in the past few
days. So what if she messed around with her boyfriend in the
coatroom? It wasn't his business, and if her emotions were all
confused, he could understand that. But why was she here?

He considered it. If she needed birth control pills or had
some plumbing problem, she probably had a real gynecologist.
One of those classy ones around Pennsylvania Hospital, closer
to where Mary said she lived. No reason for a rich girl to come
to Planned Parenthood in a half-assed disguise, unless it offered
something she couldn't get anywhere else.

Lou had a guess, but he wasn't certain. He opened the pamphlet and read: "*We offer reproductive health care for women
and teens. Every FDA-approved birth control method, gyneco-
logical exams, walk-in pregnancy testing, testing for sexually
transmitted disease, and first trimester abortion.*" The girl
could get all of the services at a regular doc, without a baseball
cap, except one.

Poor kid. She must be in trouble, big-time. Lou glanced over
at her to see if she looked pregnant, but he couldn't tell. She
looked skinny and gorgeous; maybe she wasn't showing yet.
He had two sons, both grown and moved away, and didn't
remember much about pregnancy except that anchovy pizza
was a definite no. It was a different time then. He wasn't there
when his kids were born; the nurse brought them out like UPS.

Lou had to confirm his theory. He got up, crossed the room,
and picked up another pamphlet from the counter. It was
white, entitled, *WHAT TO EXPECT IF YOU CHOOSE
ABORTION*. The receptionist was on the phone, and on the
way back he smiled at Paige, letting her see the pamphlet. He
eased into the chair with an audible groan and opened the
bifold. "This is amazing, what they do here," he said, to no
daughter in particular.

Paige didn't reply, but continued with her magazine.

"It looks like they really know their stuff." He turned to
Paige. "You think they do?"

"I don't know." She looked noncommittal under the GUESS.

"I mean, I'm kinda worried. My daughter, she's thinking she might have to have an abortion."

"Oh," Paige said, and her face flushed. Lou was struck by the fairness of her skin.

"I don't mean to get personal, it's just she's my only girl. She has lots of questions. She can't decide, and I don't want her to . . . to . . . well, it's not like this is a hospital, you know." He returned quickly to the pamphlet. "Well, sorry. I shouldn't have said anything to you."

Paige returned to her magazine with a quick swivel of her long neck.

Lou pretended to read the pamphlet and let the silence fall. If she had something to say, she'd come to him. He had seen it over and over when he questioned younger witnesses, on the job. Young girls, deep inside, just wanted to please. Sometimes silence proved the best weapon. So he didn't say anything.

Neither did Paige, who read her magazine.

Lou rustled his pamphlet.

Paige studied her magazine.

Lou worried that silence might not be the best weapon.

"She needs a counselor," Paige said, finally looking over, and Lou nodded.

"A counselor? Not a doctor?"

"No, not doctors. Counselors don't do exams or anything." Paige's expression had softened and she suddenly looked to Lou like an ordinary teenager, instead of a model. "They'll answer all your daughter's questions. They'll help her decide what to do. They'll just talk to her."

Lou waited, taking it slow. "They just talk to her?"

"Yeah." Paige nodded, the cap brim bopping up and down. "As many times as she wants, and they're really nice."

"They're nice?"

"*Really* nice." Paige broke into a smile. It seemed to Lou as if she wanted to talk to him, but part of her held back.

"So you think they'll help her decide? I mean, she's kinda confused."

"Oh, sure, that's their job. I mean, they don't push you one way or the other. They just listen and help you decide." Paige smiled again, with her eyes, too, this time, and Lou felt how young she was, how vulnerable. She knew too much about this process not to be in the same position herself.

There was a loud intercom beep at the receptionist's phone, and both Lou and Paige looked up at the sound. The receptionist put her phone call on hold, stood up, and picked up a manila folder from the desk. "Ms. Stone," she said to Paige. "You can go in now. I'll buzz you in."

Ms. Stone. Lou wasn't surprised at the use of the alias. This girl played it so close to the vest he wondered if anybody else knew she was in trouble. He watched as she squared her shoulders in her man's pea coat and followed the receptionist out of the waiting room. She was so in control for her age it reminded him of the young gangbangers he met on the street. Kids, with no mother and no father to speak of, who raised themselves. They got older but they never really grew up, and they stayed hollow at the core. And this girl, who musta had every advantage, didn't seem any better off.

Lou didn't get up from his chair, even though it was his chance to slip out of the place. He felt tired suddenly. He didn't know when kids had changed, but they had, in his lifetime. They got to be empty inside; they didn't care about anything. They listened to one-hit wonders, watched movies that weren't funny, and didn't read enough books. They didn't play ball in the street; they collected guns and shot each other. Lou didn't understand how it had happened, but it had, and it happened to Paige Newlin, too. There was something missing at her heart, and Lou worried that there was nothing in the world that could set it right.

It took Lou a few minutes before he could get up from the chair, but get up he did.

28

Kovich studied the criminalistics report, resting it against the steering wheel of the car, which idled at the curb. Temple students going to class flowed in front of the car but Kovich didn't notice. "The earring back is from a man?"

"That's what it says." Brinkley leaned over and pointed on the report with a cold finger. The heat still hadn't warmed up in the beat-up Chrysler and the tall buildings on Broad Street blocked the sun. "Contained sloughed-off skin cells from a male."

"Okay, so?" Kovich looked over, and Brinkley edged back into his seat.

"I don't know. Let me think. It's a surprise."

"Only because you figured it was the daughter's, which it ain't."

Brinkley collected his thoughts. "Take it step by step. We find an earring back next to the body, which suggests it came off after a struggle with the doer."

"The location suggests a *possibility* it came off during the struggle with the doer. It coulda come off anytime at all. Fallen off a rug cleaner who wears an earring. A gay decorator who wears an earring. Every guy in Philly wears an earring nowadays, maybe two. My brother wears one, for fuck's sake. Coulda been anybody, anytime."

"Okay, but it's possible that it came off in the death struggle."

"It's possible."

"Good. At least it's possible." Brinkley looked out the windshield of the car at the Temple students. Boys and girls flooded into the buildings in parkas, lugging backpacks like tanks. A couple of the boys had their arms around the girls, but the backpacks got in the way. Brinkley watched them idly. "I thought it could have been the daughter's because I'm working on the theory that she's the doer, and the father is taking the fall, right?"

"Also you are dumber than you look, in contrast to me. But yes. Right."

Brinkley was thinking too hard to ask Kovich what he was talking about. "If the location suggests the earring back came off during a struggle with the killer, then the killer was a male. So if you combine my theory with this physical evidence, it suggests that a man was at the scene with the daughter."

Kovich nodded. "Unless Newlin wears an earring, and he don't."

"Also, remember that there was dirt on the coffee table, put there by someone's shoe, and it had to be someone who put it there Monday after the maid cleaned. It's consistent with a male, since lots of women don't put their feet up on coffee tables."

"Mostly but okay. So what we got?"

"We got a man at the scene, brought there by the girl. Because I don't believe Newlin is the doer and there's no male in the picture he would protect, except a man he didn't know was there. A male his daughter brought in." Brinkley's heart quickened and he kept staring out the window. Two of the Temple students kissed. Young love, he could barely remember it. And then suddenly he could. "The daughter has a boyfriend."

"How do you know?"

"You saw her. She's a knockout. She's gotta have a boyfriend." Brinkley gestured out the window to the kids eating face. "Girl like that, she's gotta have a ton of boyfriends."

Kovich grew quiet, but Brinkley didn't notice.

"So let's say she goes over to dinner with the boyfriend and they kill the mother together. Or the daughter does it and the boyfriend helps, one way or the other. We got the wrong guy, Stan. We have to talk to the daughter again and find out if she has a boyfriend."

"No."

"What?"

"We're not bothering that kid again." Kovich shoved the report at him, and Brinkley knew he was in trouble.

"Why not?"

"Because she's a kid, Mick."

"So what? We question lots of kids. This kid's not from the projects, so we don't question her?"

"Don't go there, Mick. You know me too well for that." Kovich raised his voice a notch. "The girl lost her mother and now her father. You wanna find out if she has a boyfriend, find another way."

Brinkley thought about it. "Okay, let's go. Turn around."

Kovich leaned over and released the emergency brake. "Fine," he said, and Brinkley heard the winter wind in Kovich's voice.

It was never fine when Kovich said it was fine.

Brinkley scanned the lobby of Colonial Towers. Black marble, cushy tan chairs, and a classy security desk with a young white kid sitting behind it. His hat had slid back on his forehead and his neck sprouted like a stem out of his collar. Brinkley introduced himself and Kovich to the kid, who sat up straight when he saw the badges. "Homicide detectives? Sure, sure. How can I help you?"

"I wanna ask you a few questions about one of your tenants here. Paige Newlin." The guard's face changed immediately from fear to familiarity.

"You know who I mean."

"Sure, the model." The guard frowned. "I read her dad killed her mom. That's heinous."

Brinkley didn't comment. "We're investigating that murder,

and I need background information about her comings and goings."

"She comes and goes, nothing regular, for her job. But you notice her, you know." The guard smiled shyly. "She's totally hot."

"You ever see her with guys? You know, like boyfriends."

"Uhm, yes. She sees some guy, a prep, since she moved here." Bingo. "She's dating him?"

"Looks that way."

"He stay over?"

"I'm the night shift, not the morning. But I think so."

"What's he look like?"

"We call him Abercrombie Boy. He's like, right out of the catalog, you know."

Brinkley had no idea. "No, I don't."

"Tall, a jock. Good-looking. A rich boy."

"He got an earring?"

"I don't know. Mostly I look at her."

"You got a sign-in log?"

"Yeah, sure." The guard went behind the desk, pulled out a large black notebook, and opened it up.

"Turn back to the page for Monday," Brinkley asked, and the kid found the page and turned the book toward the detectives. It was a standard ledger, with signatures in a list and the time they signed in. Brinkley ran his finger down the page, stopped at the name of Paige Newlin, then jumped to the signature next to hers. Trent Reznor. "Trent Reznor, that's his name,"Brinkley said, satisfied.

"Huh? That can't be his name." The guard came around and peered at the logbook. "Trent Reznor's with Nine Inch Nails."

"What?" Brinkley read over the guard's shoulder, then thumbed back in time and checked every name written next to Paige Newlin's. "Ben Folds, Thurston Moore, Gavin Rosdale," he read aloud, and the guard took off his hat.

"Wait a minute. Ben Folds is with Ben Folds Five, Thurston Moore is with Sonic Youth. They're all bands. None of those are real names."

Brinkley went further backward in time, reading the log entries. "Dave Matthews, Eddie Vedder. Also rock stars, aren't they?"

"Yeah, older ones."

Brinkley tore through the book, checking each time he saw Paige Newlin's name on a line. The entries went back to December of last year and each name next to hers was different, as was each line of handwriting. Some slanted forward and some back, but he never wrote in the same hand twice. Shit! "Don't you read what these people write down?" Brinkley demanded.

"Uh, no." The kid colored. "I mean, not usually, I guess. We just ask them to write it."

"What's the point then? Why have them sign it if you're not going to check? What're you doin' the goddamn job for?" Brinkley raised his voice, and Kovich grabbed his arm.

"Excuse us," he said tensely. "Me and my partner are leaving now. Thanks for your help."

"Uh, sure," the guard answered, shaken, as Kovich steered Brinkley to the entrance door and out onto the sidewalk. The sun was bright but the wind gusted in currents in front of the tall building. Traffic whizzed by, moving smoothly at this hour, and two well-dressed older women approached. Kovich squeezed Brinkley's arm.

"You gotta calm down, Mick. You were screaming at the kid."

"He's a fuckup!" Brinkley heard himself shout, which he never did.

"He's ten years old, for Christ's sake!" Kovich yelled back as they squared off on the sidewalk. The two women picked up their pace past the detectives.

"Then he shouldn't be working the job! Security is supposed to mean something." Brinkley gestured at the women, who looked back, startled. "These people, they're payin' for security!"

"What do you care? You don't live here. You're losin' it on this case, don't you see!"

It only made Brinkley angrier. It was like nobody but him could see the truth. "The kid, the boyfriend, he's hiding something, don't *you* see?"

"No, no, you know what I see?" Kovich was shouting now, full bore. "The boyfriend is a wise-ass. A kid playin' games. Thumbin' his nose at authority. Who hasn't signed a fake name for a laugh?"

"Me!"

"Well I did, plenty of times, when I was young."

"What the fuck for?"

"For fun, Mick! For goddamn fun!"

"That's not fun!"

"You wouldn't know fun if it bit you in the ass, Mick. You don't know how to laugh anymore! You've been an asshole ever since Sheree walked out on you!"

Brinkley was about to yell back but he stopped short, his chest heaving, as soon as it registered.

Kovich blinked behind his big aviator glasses. "Aw, shit," he said quietly. His soft shoulders slumped.

Brinkley suddenly found it hard to swallow. Or even speak. He pivoted on his heel and walked away, ignoring the stares of passersby, so blind in anger and pain that he didn't notice the man in the car parked at the curb, photographing the scene on the sidewalk.

29

Davis knew who Marc Videon was the moment he entered the divorce lawyer's office at Tribe & Wright. Marc Videon was The Necessary Evil. Corporate law firms didn't want their CEO clients to go to elsewhere to off-load their wives, because there was a chance they wouldn't come back, so the firms were forced to employ a Necessary Evil. Davis had encountered one in every white-shoe Philly firm, and the suspect profile was so blatant it should have been unconstitutional: The Necessary Evil was always an outsider in a bad suit, nominally a partner and compensated on a salaried basis, and invite only to those firm social functions that the messengers went to, democratic events like the Christmas Party. Meeting Videon, Davis saw that he fit the bill, with his too-wide pinstripes that fit too tight on his squat form, a slightly greasy face with small features, and unnaturally dark hair that matched a pointy black goatee.

"Sit down, please," Videon said, seating himself. His office was as large as other Tribe partners, but in law firms, everything was location, location, location, and Videon's office was nowhere, stuck on the bottom floor of the firm near the duplicating department. Davis could practically feel the heat and hear the harsh *cathunka* of Xerox machines as big as oil tankers, belching paper like smoke. Nor was Davis surprised to see that Videon had only one desk, an undistinguished box of walnut veneer, with chairs and end tables that reflected only a mid-range furniture allowance.

"Thanks." Davis introduced himself, then sat down across from Videon's desk, which was cluttered with papers, cases, and scribbled notes. The Pennsylvania guidelines for alimony rested on the keyboard of a thick gray laptop, and Davis pulled out his legal pad. Next to him sat Art Field, the tape recorder with a law degree. Whittier had excused himself for this meeting, and Davis assumed he'd gone on to gouge the Fortune 500 in six-minute increments. "I appreciate your agreeing to meet with me on such short notice."

"What 'agreeing'? I'm under subpoena, *n'est-ce pas?*" Videon's neat head swiveled to Art Field, who was clearly annoyed at being acknowledged.

"Yes," Field answered. "There is a document subpoena as well."

Videon smiled. "Oh, goody. I like it rough." He ran a manicured hand through his thinning hair, which was nevertheless black as night. In fact, Davis figured that BLACK AS NIGHT was the name on the box. Videon had to be sixty, if he was a day. "I knew you'd come to talk to me sooner or later. Let's start with what a shame it is about Honor Newlin."

"It is a shame," Davis said, seriously. He wasn't so sure he liked The Necessary Evil, which would make sense. Evil shouldn't have a lot of running buddies.

"Yes, of course, a shame. A terrible shame. A terrible tragedy. Have I said 'terrible' enough yet to convince you of my sincerity? Put otherwise, are you buying this shit?" Videon paused as if expecting an answer, but Davis didn't give him one. "Yes, well, to the facts. Honor Newlin was in to see me on Monday. The day she was murdered. She wanted to divorce Jack."

"Begin at the beginning." Davis took out his pen and pad. "What time did you see her?"

"First thing in the morning, I think. Hold on." Videon moved the alimony guidelines aside, adjusted the laptop, and hit a few keys. Davis couldn't read the screen because of the angle. "Honor came in at 9:30. She was late and she'd already had a drink."

Davis made a note, hiding his surprise. He didn't dare look over at Field. "How do you know?"

"I knew her. Besides, I offered her one, and she turned me down. She said she'd already had one. Other than that, pure guesswork."

"What did you offer her?"

"She drank Scotch." Videon paused, then smiled. "You disapprove."

"Frankly, yes."

"Have you ever been divorced, Mr. Clean?"

"Yes."

"Good for you. Was it nasty at least?"

"Amicable."

"Lord, what a waste." Videon sighed. "Sorry you disapprove of my methods. I'm a divorce lawyer, son. I keep Kleenexes for the wives and Scotch for the husbands. Sometimes, there's a crossover, for women with more bucks than estrogen." He waved in the direction of a dark cabinet under a window that overlooked a rooftop parking lot. "You want a snoot?"

"I don't drink."

"I knew that," Videon said, and laughed. "What do you do for laughs?"

"I do justice." Davis smiled.

"Hah! I knew we had nothing in common." Videon shifted forward in his high-backed chair. "You try to change the world, right?"

"Perhaps," Davis answered, though he had never thought of it that way.

"Well, I try to keep it the same. The rich retain power and money. The poor try to get it and lose. You even up the odds, and I keep them out of whack, the way my clients want them." Videon eased back in his chair, his dark eyes scrutinizing Davis. "You aren't comfortable with my honesty."

"I'm comfortable with what pertains to the Newlin case," Davis answered, impatient.

"Oh, but it does. Honor Newlin walked in with all the money and she wanted to walk out with it." Videon turned to his laptop and hit a key to scroll down. "This year I saw Honor

Newlin twice, including the day she was killed. I'll give you a copy of what I'm looking at, it's my time records. Besides the day she was murdered, I met with her on January fourth, the first business day after the New Year. She said her New Year's resolution was shedding Jack."

Davis made a note. "Back up a minute. She called you, for the first appointment?"

"Yes, naturally."

"Tell me about it."

"The first time, she told me she wanted a divorce."

"Did she say why?"

"She felt her marriage was moribund. Things hadn't turned out the way she hoped. She had *l'ennui, la malaise*, and other French things. She was a victim of empty mansion syndrome and expected Jack to fill the void, to ascend the ranks to managing partnerdom. But he wasn't, even with the Buxton dough. Why?" Videon glanced at Field, seeking neither permission nor approval. "They used to say Jack was too much of a nice guy. That he didn't have the killer instinct. Hah! Perceptive, *non*?"

Field cleared his throat. "That's quite enough, Marc."

"I heard that Jack confessed to the police," Videon said to Davis. "Did he?"

"I can't comment."

"Of course. What a perfect answer. How do they make people like you? So upright. You're the good guy. I always wanted to meet a good guy, but I'm a divorce lawyer. Did I mention that?" Videon smiled at a joke only he knew. "As I was saying, Honor wanted the divorce, and she asked me, in our first meeting, to review her prenuptial agreement."

"She had a prenup?"

"Do I look stupid?"

"You drafted it?"

"I'm more than just a pretty face."

"What did it provide?"

"What else? That if they divorce, Jack gets *rien*. Nothing. Squat."

Davis made a note. "Isn't that a conflict? I mean, you worked with Jack, so why would she come to you for a prenup?"

"Jack asked me to draft the damn thing, and it was completely against him. Go figure. The Foundation has since become one of our most valued clients, heh heh."

"What's funny about that?" Davis asked, cranky, and Field looked miffed as well.

"Well, the Foundation is a private charity, as opposed to a public charity, like the Red Cross. That means there's virtually no oversight of the billings at all. It's even better than a corporate client because they watch the bills. The Buxton Foundation was a license to rape and plunder."

Field gasped. "Marc! Show some judgment!"

Videon scoffed. "As if it weren't common knowledge."

"It isn't," Field said. "Please excuse my partner—"

"—he knows not what he does," Videon supplied, but Field was visibly agitated.

"That's quite enough, Marc. Please. Mr. Davis, leave this subject or I end the interview."

"Fine." Davis nodded, though it confirmed his suspicions about the Foundation's value to Jack. "You were saying, about the prenup."

Videon sighed theatrically. "Anyway, the prenup was sound and I told Honor so. She asked me to prepare the divorce papers and came in to review them with me the day she was murdered."

"Did she get them that day?"

"Actually, no. There were two typos, both inconsequential, but she wouldn't wait for them to be corrected. I said we'd redo the papers and FedEx them to the house, but I got called into a meeting. I did have her sign the signature page for convenience." Videon searched his desk, rifling through yellow slips that littered his desk like autumn leaves. He produced a piece of white paper and handed it across the desk. "Here."

Davis skimmed the page. A standard verification, and at the bottom Honor's signature. *Honor Buxton Newlin.* Her handwriting was feminine, and Davis stared at it for a minute with sympathy. It was as if she had signed her own death warrant. He pondered its significance. "If Honor had lived to divorce Jack, would he have stayed at the firm?"

Videon fingered his stiff goatee. "Probably not."

"Even though he was head of the estates department?"

"Big fucking deal."

"Would he have been fired?"

"No, but he would have left on his own, public emasculation being an excellent incentive."

"How so?"

"Honor told me she didn't want to deal with Jack on a day-to-day basis, on matters for the Foundation. The management and billings of the array of Buxton matters would have shifted to somebody else in the firm, probably Big Bill Whittier, because we'd be damned if we'd lose it. Jack would have been shit out of luck."

Davis remembered his meeting with Whittier. He turned to Field. "If Honor divorced Newlin and he lost the Buxton billings, his draw would be lowered by about a million dollars a year? Ballpark?"

"Yes," Field answered.

Videon burst into laughter. "Rags to riches and back again," he said, but Davis was too intent to make light of it.

"Did Newlin have any other sources of income that you know of?"

"Not that I know of," Field answered, and Videon looked incredulous.

"Are you kidding?"

Davis considered it. "So the only way Newlin could keep his job and his income from the Buxton billings was if Honor stayed married to him. Or if she died before she could divorce him."

"I didn't say that," Field said quickly, and Videon waved his hand.

"I'm a witness. He didn't say that. If he said that, he'd get his ass sued."

Davis tuned Videon out, putting his case together. It no longer mattered that Newlin didn't benefit under the will. A million dollars a year and preservation of career were more than enough for motive. Of course Newlin had planned to kill her, to keep the goodies. But Davis's premeditation theory worked only if Newlin had known the divorce was coming. He turned to Videon, who had finally stopped laughing. "How often had they discussed divorce?"

"They hadn't discussed divorce at all."

"*What*? Of course they had," Davis said, and Videon smiled.

"How do you know?"

"I assumed it."

"Mr. Clean, you should know that 'when we assume, we make an ass out of you and me.' Camus said that. Or Sartre. Or my fourth-grade teacher."

Davis still wasn't laughing. "How could they not have discussed divorce?"

"They hadn't. I got the impression she had been thinking about it for a long time, then—*boom*—decided to do it. That would be Honor, impulsively destructive. She told me she was worried that Jack was thinking about it and she wanted to beat him to the punch. He had no idea she was planning to make the first move. She said she couldn't wait to see the look on his face when she told him."

"Do you think she could have mentioned it to him on the phone, maybe that day?"

"She could have, but she wouldn't have. That's not Honor."

Davis couldn't let it go. The state of Newlin's knowledge was the linchpin of his prosecution. Otherwise, the jury would buy Newlin's rage-at-the-divorce defense. "It doesn't stand to reason. People always talk about divorce for a long time before they file."

"Another assumption, *mon frère*." Videon shook his head. "Some do, but many don't. It's more husband behavior than wife, but it happens with some wives, too. They avoid the issue until they have to, then do it. The perfect clean break. In fact, where there's family money involved, I always advise a preemptive strike to maintain the advantage. Eliminate the fight over the prenup, like Pearl Harbor before the divorce war."

Davis thought about it. "Wait a minute. You work here, at Tribe, on the twentieth-fifth floor. Newlin works on the thirtieth. How is it that Honor comes to see you without him finding out?"

"He may have found out, for all I know. I asked her if she wanted to meet me somewhere else, both times. You can see, it ain't Versailles." Videon gestured to his office mock-grandly. "I was trying to respect her privacy and not tip off Jack. But Honor insisted we meet here."

Davis brightened. "So if Honor comes in to see you, the firm's divorce lawyer, everybody who sees her knows she's coming in to divorce Newlin. Secretaries, messengers, other lawyers, they'll all see her coming here. It would be a gossip item, wouldn't it?"

"*Very* dishy stuff. Not as cool as the sex-in-the-shower story I spread last week, but that's not pertinent here."

Davis ignored it. What a loon. "So it's possible, even likely, that Newlin could have found out that Honor had been in to see you that morning?"

"Correct, as you say."

Davis felt a relieved grin spread across his face. He could prove through Videon that Newlin knew he was about to be disposed of, and it would also support Whittier's testimony that Newlin appeared agitated when he was leaving to go home. Newlin must have guessed Honor would be breaking up with him at dinner and decided to kill her then. That was premeditation, for sure. The law was premeditation could happen in a matter of minutes; it didn't require weeks to plan. And Newlin couldn't hire somebody to do it because he didn't have time. Honor's murder was simply damage control. Davis almost jumped up in excitement as the puzzle fell into place. "I assume you would you testify for us in court?"

Videon looked at Field. "What's my line, boss man?"

"If you are subpoenaed, you must appear and give testimony."

Videon looked at Davis. "What he said."

But the prosecutor had one last question. "Why would the wife want to come here, to see you, for a divorce? Why risk it herself and why make it public? Why, even, embarrass her husband?"

"Again, you assume others see the world as you see it, but that is a critical mistake. You cannot imagine why Honor Newlin would humiliate her spouse because you wouldn't. And undoubtedly didn't. You had an amicable divorce, you said." The angles of Videon's face hardened. "You did not know Honor Newlin. She was a beautiful woman, a gorgeous woman, but not a kind woman. Not a nice woman, at all."

"Don't speak ill, Marc," Field interrupted, but Videon waved him off.

"You must understand, Honor Newlin was one of the meanest women on the planet. It was subtle, it was socially acceptable, but it was true just the same. She just didn't connect with people. Maybe men, but not even them for long. She had no enduring emotion except indifference. Honor Newlin was a sociopath in silk."

"Marc, Jesus!" Field cried, but Davis bristled.

"That's a little harsh, isn't it?" he asked. "She was a philanthropist. She did good works through the Foundation."

Videon scoffed. "Are you completely naïve, or just rehearsing for the jury? Honor Newlin didn't care about charity. The Foundation existed for generations before her and it will exist for generations after. She had no interest in where the money went. Jack made all those decisions. He actually cared about the causes. Honor couldn't care less."

Davis resisted it. "Did you know her that well?"

"Well enough. Women tell their divorce lawyers everything. We're the gynecologists of the profession." Videon leaned over his messy desk. "I tell you, Honor Newlin would have enjoyed humiliating Jack in front of his partners, the secretaries, the clients, the whole fucking firm. She had decided to cut his balls off with a dull knife, merely to alleviate her own boredom, and she would want everybody to see it. All the better, so they all knew that she wielded the knife. Except, surprise, Jack upped the ante. He's more of a man than I knew."

"Marc!" Field jumped to his feet. "I think that's enough, quite enough. Mr. Davis, you have the information you need, do you not?"

Davis nodded quickly. "From Mr. Videon, yes. But I do have one last stop before I leave."

30

"Trevor's gone," Mary said, bursting into the conference room, cluttered with papers from the Newlin case. It was after hours so the firm was closed and nobody was working overtime with the boss away. She slipped out of her coat, tossed it onto a swivel chair, and told Judy and Lou what had happened at the train station with the blonde and the Metroliner to New York.

Judy's eyes widened. "Sex in a coatroom with Paige? Then he hops a train with another girl? What a jerk!"

"I ain't surprised," Lou said sadly, smoothing out his pants and easing into a chair at the conference table. He had just gotten in himself and was wishing for a roast beef special, a bag of chips, and a Rolling Rock. "I knew the punk was bad news, only you two don't know how bad. I got a story to tell, too." He filled them in about Paige and Planned Parenthood. When he was finished, the three fell silent.

"It has to be an abortion," Mary said, after a minute. As much as she disliked Paige, she couldn't help sympathizing with her predicament. "Abortions are what they do, mainly. That's why they get picketed all the time."

Judy nodded. "I used to get diaphragm cream there, but I'm the only person cheap enough to do that. You're right, Mare. I think she's getting an abortion, too."

"Think she got one right then?" Mary walked to the credenza, where she poured a Styrofoam cup of hot coffee and powdered it with fake sugar and fake milk. She took a sip but it didn't thaw her nose. Italian noses took longer. "It could be, with the disguise and all."

"No way," Judy said. "She just had sex, remember? Who gets a pelvic after that, much less an abortion?"

Lou didn't want to hear this. Pelvics. Diaphragm cream. Breast exams. If it kept up, he could turn gay. Where was the beer?

Mary sipped her coffee. "So she's talking to a counselor. That makes sense. She's got no friends, her mother's dead, and her father's in jail. She needs someone to talk to. Since Trevor wasn't with her at the clinic, it sounds like she's not talking to him about it."

Lou stretched his legs, then crossed them. "I don't think he knows. I don't think a guy who knows his girl is pregnant does what they were doing in the coatroom, and they weren't talkin' babies at lunch." He sighed. "I feel bad for the girl, I do. Pretty girl like that, everything going for her. She's on her own and I think it's a crying shame."

Mary felt worse for Paige's father. "If Jack knows his daughter is pregnant, that gives him a stronger reason to protect her. He has to protect her and the baby. In fact, we're missing something here. At her age, doesn't she need parental consent for a abortion?"

Judy frowned. "Of course, you're right. Seventeen or younger, in this state. But if Newlin knew Paige was pregnant, he wouldn't let her abort at a clinic. If he's such a great father, he'd get her to the best doctor in the city."

"What if he knows about the pregnancy, but not the abortion?" Mary asked, thinking aloud. "That could be, especially if she's getting counseling about it. She wouldn't need the consent for that, not yet. If Jack knows only that she's pregnant, he'd take the rap for her."

Lou was shaking his head. "You never asked me, but I wouldn't take a murder rap for my kid. I'd want her to accept the consequences of her actions. How's she gonna learn anything otherwise? How's she gonna become an adult?"

Mary was again surprised. It was two to one. "What if you felt responsible for it? If you had let the mother abuse the kid over time. Not physically, but emotionally."

Lou puckered his lip. "Sorry, Mare. If she picks up the knife, she's responsible. She should do the time, even though she's my kid."

"My father would do it, and I think Jack would, too."

Judy's expression was tense. "Mary, isn't it possible that you've got Newlin on a pedestal? You don't know him that well and you're projecting all sorts of qualities onto him. He's not your father."

"I know that," Mary snapped, her face suddenly hot. This case was straining their friendship. "Jack is innocent, and I'm not going to see him convicted for a crime he didn't commit. We're close to something and we have to get to the bottom of it."

"But Bennie's been calling us." Judy gestured to a stack of yellow slips. "She may be out of the country, but they have phones. Do I have to tell you what she'd say about this? Working against our own client's instructions, to prove his innocence? Allegedly?"

"I don't care." Mary heard her voice waver and knew her emotion came only partly from the injustice of the situation. "We have momentum now. We're making progress."

Lou looked doubtful. "I wouldn't say that. All we're doin' is messin' around in people's private lives." He looked at Mary. "I think you should think about withdrawin' from this case, Mare. It's out of control, and Rosato pays the bills around here."

"We can't file withdrawal papers today anyway. Court closed a long time ago." Mary checked her watch. Seven o'clock. "Hey, it's about the time the murder was committed. It's the best time to visit a crime scene."

"The crime scene? You hate crime scenes!" Judy said, but Mary grabbed her coat and bag.

"That was the old me. The new me loves crime scenes." She

slipped back into her coat, which still felt cold, and looked at Judy with hope. Their eyes locked, and Judy surrendered first in their game of emotional chicken.

"Tell you what, Mare," she said. "I'll go with you on this, but just for tonight. If we find nothing, we're out. We withdraw tomorrow and refer the case."

Mary considered it, then nodded. "Deal. Let's go. If I have one night, I'm using it."

Lou didn't budge. "Hold on there, ladies. What about Bennie?"

Mary headed for the conference room door. "You don't have to come, Lou. We'll understand. Won't we, Jude?"

"Of course." Judy got her puffy white coat from a chair. "Stay here. Show common sense, unlike me. I could get fired twice by the same person." Judy looked at Mary. "One thing. We have to go home and walk Bear. Remember, I'm dog-sitting."

"Bennie's dog?" Mary headed for the conference room door. "Okay. She might not fire us if we show the dog a good time."

Judy snorted. "Oh she'll fire us, all right. She just won't kill us."

"Sure she will," Lou said, and reached for his windbreaker.

31

It had taken all day for Jack to be transferred and processed into county jail with a busload of other inmates; he'd been showered, shaved, sprayed prophylactically with lice treatment, and issued laundered and steam-pressed blues. By nightfall he found himself in a plastic bucket chair against the back wall of the TV room of Housing Unit C. A caged television blared from its wall mount in the corner and thirty-odd inmates ignored *Access Hollywood*, clogging a space that was smaller than most living rooms. The room was in constant motion, the noise deafening, and the air rank with body odor.

The inmates were large, muscular, pockmarked, and pierced. They had long hair, dreads, and Willie Nelson braids; one bald inmate had tattooed his skull with bright flames. Another huge inmate, a wiry blond ponytail snaking down his broad back, looked like a deranged Norse god. Jack didn't break eye contact when it was made by the inmates or the guards. He knew he was a novelty here; his photo was splashed across the tabloid on the bolted-down table, and the inmate who had piled mashed potatoes on his dinner plate that night had stopped serving to shake his hand.

"Why?" Jack had asked, astonished.

"I never met no millionaire before," the inmate had answered.

He had been thwarted in reaching Trevor. There was an "approved list" for calls from county jail, which contained only the inmate's attorney and one contact in the immediate family. He mulled over calling Mary and coming clean with his doubts about Trevor, but he couldn't sacrifice Paige. A commercial for Listerine came on TV, and in time Jack realized that his thoughts had stopped with Mary, which both worried and comforted him.

At the same time.

32

THE DEVIL'S INN, read the boxy white sign. It was illuminated from within and lightweight enough to be blown around by the wind, which set its old-fashioned drawing of the devil, wiry and red with a spiked tail and trident, whipping back and forth. The Devil's Inn was like every other run-down tavern that dotted Philadelphia's street corners, concentrated in the working-class residential neighborhoods, and Brinkley had been a cop long enough to disapprove not only of the bars but of the liquor billboards that popped up around them like mushrooms. That he disapproved didn't stop him from hanging in the Devil's Inn, sipping the whiskey they advertised on every block.

It was his favorite bar, in West Philly, on the corner and down the block from where he had grown up. He didn't go to Liberties, the bar in Fairmount where all the detectives went. He hated a bar like in *Cheers*, that TV bar where everybody knows your name. He went to the Devil's Inn because nobody knew his name there and he liked it that way. That was its only attraction for him, because it certainly wasn't a nice joint. It was small, dim, and smelled like dust and dirt. Stale cigarette smoke clung to the cocktail napkins and grit lay on the tile floor. The mirror behind the bar was too greasy to reflect anything, dust coated the few bottles of top-shelf, and a garland of dull tinsel festooned the cash

register. It was leftover from Christmas, five years ago. Brinkley
doubted it would ever come down.

He hunched over his shot and squinted down the knotty bar at
the other patrons. Aging black men, they all looked like him without a tie, and no one acknowledged him. He guessed they didn't
like *Cheers* either, and none of them were his old neighbors.
Those were long gone, surrendering what used to be a decent
black neighborhood to gangbangers, pipers, and crack whores,
emptying his old block. Sheets of plywood covered the windows
that used to have sheer curtains and Venetian blinds; the city
boarded up vacant rowhouses to keep trouble out, but the cops
knew it only hid the bad guys. Brinkley's childhood home didn't
even have plywood over the windows; the place lay exposed to
the elements as a nude woman. He didn't drive by the house when
he came to the Devil's Inn. He always took the other way around.

He sipped his booze and cupped his shot glass, which leeched
the warmth from his palm and then returned the favor. Brinkley's
hand never left his glass the times he came drinking at the Devil's
Inn and he wondered what that was about. He was in deep shit if
all he had in the world to hold on to was a shot glass. He downed
the last of his drink and when he looked up Kovich was sitting on
the barstool next to him. "Boo," Kovich said. "I'm Casper the
Friendly Ghost."

Brinkley didn't know what to say, it was so unexpected. He
had never brought Kovich here, never even mentioned it to him.
But there he was, with no coat on. Brinkley could smell the cold
night on him.

Kovich looked around the bar, layered with a visible haze of
cigarette smoke. "Is this a bad dream?"

Brinkley smiled crookedly. "How'd you know I was here?"

"I followed you."

"For real?"

"Only twice."

"Stalker." Brinkley smiled again. It was the whiskey that let
him.

"How else am I gonna find out stuff I need to know? You don't tell me squat." Kovich waved to the old bartender, who had his back turned, and called for a Miller Lite. Brinkley didn't tell him it would be a long wait. "I checked it out when you started getting cranky. I figured it was trouble between you and Sheree."

"How?"

"I'm a detective, remember? I *detected*." Kovich gestured again to the bartender, who was washing a glass in the grimy sink. "Hey, buddy, a Miller Lite for me and another shot for my lawyer." The bartender didn't turn around, and Kovich's heavy lips curled into an unhappy line. "What is this, Denny's? I'm too white to get a drink?"

"He's hard of hearing." Brinkley leaned over. "James!" he fairly shouted, and the bartender turned. "A Miller and another!"

"Lite!" Kovich added, loudly. When he looked over Brinkley was staring at him. "Portion size is key."

Brinkley laughed as the bartender came over with a sweating bottle and pilsner glass for Kovich and poured him another shot. Both detectives took a first sip.

Kovich cleared his throat. "So you're thinkin' the boyfriend is trying to hide something, the way he signs the logbooks. Right?"

Brinkley nodded. He was relieved Kovich didn't start talking about Sheree.

"That meant to follow up, we had to find out his real name. So while Goofus cries in his beer, Gallant gets busy." Kovich leaned down, picked up a paper grocery bag, and pulled out a stack of girls' clothes catalogs. He slapped them on the bar and spread them out like a winning deck of cards. There were easily ten, marked with yellow Post-its. "My kid saves these to bankrupt me." He flipped open the top catalog and inside was a photo of Paige Newlin. She wore a floppy hat with a fake daisy on it. "Recognize our girl?"

"Sure, yeah."

"So I call up the catalog company and ask about the girl but I can't get anybody who knows her. They give me the name of the photographer they use in Philly and I call him up. David

Something, his name is. He don't know much about her and he only dealt with the mother on the phone, but he says the boyfriend stopped by the shoot. He remembers the boyfriend's name in a flash, he says because it's an unusual name, but I say it's because he's queer as my dick is long."

Brinkley straightened on the barstool. "So what's his name?"

"Trevor Olanski. How's that for a handle?" Kovich took a gulp of beer. "So I check him out. Call Morrie in juvy on a flyer and ask around."

"What did you find out?" Brinkley said, his head clearing suddenly.

"Seems our Trevor got tagged for dealing coke, on Tuesday of last week. At Philadelphia Select, that ritzy private school in town. He goes there."

"No shit," Brinkley said, surprised. "Was there a complaint?"

"Don't show up in the file. The docket they keep shows it got withdrawn the next day. Smells like strings got pulled, but the officer in charge is on vacation. I'll find out when he gets back."

"So we gotta talk to this kid."

"I got an appointment with him tomorrow morning, at his parents' in the subs. You can come with, even though you're black."

"Damn!" Brinkley laughed. It was great news. Maybe they were on to something, with the boyfriend. "This mean you think I'm right?"

"No fuckin' way. I still say you're full of it."

"Good, then I know I'm on the right track," Brinkley said automatically, but it wasn't what he meant. What he meant was, I appreciate what you did for me.

Kovich put his catalogs away. "You're welcome," he said, after a minute, and Brinkley forced a smile.

33

Davis surveyed Jack Newlin's spacious, well-appointed office, on the top floor of Tribe & Wright. The wall of windows displayed the entire western half of the city, twinkling at night. A cherrywood Thos. B. Moser desk and end tables flanked a patterned sofa, and Newlin had two other desks: a polished library table in front of a matching file cabinet and, against the side wall, a modern workstation with a laptop. Three desks total; Davis would have expected as much. Atop them rested silver-framed photos of Honor and Paige Newlin. It was odd seeing a photo of Honor Newlin alive and it reminded Davis of his purpose.

He wanted to know all he could about Jack Newlin. He crossed to the file cabinet and opened the top drawer, which slid out easily on costly runners. He scanned the files, neatly kept, and all of them were Buxton Foundation matters. He reached into the first accordion, pulled out a manila folder of correspondence, and flipped through it. The letters concerned the tax structure of a charitable gift to libraries worth almost a million dollars. The D.A.'s eyes would have glazed over if it hadn't confirmed his belief that Newlin was a meticulous and patient planner. He marked the files for seizure by the uniformed cop waiting outside, with a warrant and a cooperative security guard from Tribe. He'd read the files at his office, to see the details they contained.

Davis opened the second drawer and zeroed in on the folder that said "CONFIDENTIAL—COMPENSATION." He pulled it out and skimmed the stack of papers inside. It was a listing of the partnership draw of the firm's lawyers from last year. They were ranked in order from the highest paid to the lowest, and he didn't have to look far to find Newlin's name. It was in second place, just under William Whittier's. Newlin's compensation was listed at $525,000 in partnership draw and a million dollars in billings bonus, from the Foundation business he'd brought to the firm.

Davis whistled softly. He had learned the information from Whittier, but it was something else seeing it in black-and-white. He flipped back through the years, fully expecting the most recent year to be the highest. But it wasn't. The previous year, Newlin was still number two, but his draw was $575 grand and his billings bonus was higher, $1.1 mil. The prosecutor double-checked, but he had read it right. He thumbed backward in time, to the previous year's compensation. Again, to Davis's surprise, it was higher than the more recent year, $625 in draw, $1.3 in billing bonus. And Newlin was number one in compensation that year, not Whittier. *What gives?*

Davis eyeballed Whittier's trend and that of some of the other highly ranked partners. All of them had partnership draws and billings bonuses that increased through the years. That would be the logical trend of the income of a successful lawyer; it was Davis's own salary history, though his pay was much lower. But Newlin's pay was going down.

Davis mulled it over. Given what Videon had told him, he suspected that Honor Newlin had been gradually decreasing the amount of work the Buxton estate was sending her husband and apparently beginning to funnel the billings to Whittier. She was costing Newlin hundreds of thousands of dollars and humiliating him in front of the entire partnership. In effect, Honor Newlin was firing her husband gradually, giving him every reason to want her dead before she cut him off completely.

Excellent, for motive. Davis slapped the folder closed, marked it for seizure, and searched the third drawer, which yielded nothing significant. He stood up, brushed off his suit, and was about to leave when he glanced at the third desk, the workstation. Newlin's laptop, he'd almost forgotten it. He went to the laptop and lifted its lid, which opened more easily than he expected. It hadn't been latched completely, merely closed to protect the keyboard from dust. Davis had the same careful habit.

The large screen was black, saving power, and he moved the mouse to wake it up. It came to life with Newlin's time records for the day of the murder, and Davis sat down and studied them carefully. Newlin's day in six-minute slices, spent on matters for the Buxton Foundation. The description of the billed time was detailed and complete: *prepare contracts, prepare documents for gifts to local college; revise press release with regard to computer-to-schools program; discuss joint gift to the Cancer Society.*

He checked the list for telephone calls and other items. All of the calls were related to the Buxton Foundation. The only non-billable time was for the Hiring Committee; Newlin had interviewed a law student for a summer job. The laptop wasn't much help, but he would seize it anyway, since it was arguably within the scope of the warrant. Davis was just about to shut it down when he noticed the task bar at the bottom of the screen.

He looked closer. The computer was running another program behind a minimized window. He moved the mouse and clicked on the box. A multicolored website popped onto the screen. It was an online travel agency, confirming travel to London, England. There was a ticket on British Airways, ordered that morning and leaving next week, with no return date. He checked the names of the reservations. JACK NEWLIN. A single ticket, no wife.

"Yes!" Davis said aloud and hit a key. That was it! Why wasn't Newlin taking his wife? Because she'd be dead, that's why. Newlin had been planning to leave the country alone after her funeral. Davis felt like he had won a marathon. With what he had learned from Videon, it was more than sufficient evidence to convince Masterson they shouldn't offer a deal, and after him the conviction would be a snap. The single ticket was just the sort of detail juries ate with a tablespoon. Newlin would pay for the crime he had committed.

Davis moved the mouse and clicked PRINT, just for a souvenir.

34

Mary, Judy, and Lou walked through the first floor of the Newlins' elegant town house, taking notes on its layout for trial exhibits and trying to orient themselves, but after a thorough search of the living room, dining room, and kitchen, they hadn't turned up anything that would support their defense. Mary was especially troubled, and it wasn't her usual revulsion at crime scenes. Even the blood that had soaked into the dining room rug hadn't fazed her, because she was so preoccupied. Nothing about the scene was supplying any clues about how the murder had been committed, other than what Jack had told them. "This is not going well," she said aloud, though Judy was drawing the layout and Lou was walking around in a professorial way, his hands linked behind his back.

"We shoulda brought the dog," Judy said, sketching. They'd left the dog tied up out front, on orders from the uniformed cop at the door. He'd been posted to keep out the reporters, but had made a spot ruling on golden retrievers.

But Mary was barely listening. It was odd, being in Jack's house and seeing no evidence of him. His presence was completely absent from the stone-cold living room, the overdecorated dining room, and the white kitchen that had no aroma whatsoever, a larger version of Paige's kitchen. Whenever Mary looked into this family, she kept seeing the troubled connection between mother and daughter, with Jack off to the side. She thought of the Swann Fountain in Logan Square, where she'd lurked all afternoon; the woman, daughter, and on the other side of the fountain, the man. So what? She had psychology, but what she needed was evidence. Maybe upstairs.

She ascended the carpeted stair with Judy behind her, sketch pad in hand, and Lou taking up the rear. At the top of the stair was a small library, which she quickly assessed as being for show, so she left Judy there. The next stop down the hall was a small home office, and she knew from its chilliness that it had to be Honor's, so she foisted it off on Lou and moved quickly down the hall to the master bedroom. The white double doors at the hall's end were closed, and she reached them with an undeniable tingle of anticipation. She had to find something here. Jack would be dead without it. She opened the doors.

The room was bare. There was a king-size master bed with the sheets stripped, a bank of dressers with the drawers open, an alcove with a window seat with the seat pad gone and all the novels taken from the shelves. The cops must have seized Jack's things as soon as he was charged. Mary's heart sank and she walked into the room like a sleepwalker. She should have come here earlier. Was there nothing left? She scanned the room and it was completely empty. Off the bedroom was an open door, obviously a closet, and she went to it.

A double walk-in with long racks on each side, also empty, even of hangers; the wood cubbyholes for shoes were bare, as if in move-in condition. Damn. She left the closet and eyeballed the room. In the corner were another two doors and she went to them though she knew what she would find. Two bathrooms, empty. She shook her head. She had blown it. There was only one chance. Paige's room.

She left the empty bedroom and hurried back down the hall the way she had come. She had to bet Paige's bedroom would be on the other side of the stair, the way rich people lived. Keep the kids separate. It seemed so foreign. In her parents' house, Mary and her twin had shared the bedroom across from her parents, so close they used to call to each other from bed. She hurried down the hall and to the end, where she opened the second set of white double doors and turned on the light.

The room had been left untouched. There were evidence tags on the dressers, but the cops hadn't seized them yet or hadn't given them the priority they'd given to Jack's belongings. She entered the room, which was the same size as the master bedroom, and it looked like every little girl's dream. A white four-poster bed dominated the space in the center of a large powder pink Oriental rug, and the bed linens were a custom white-and-pink-quilted pattern. White night tables flanked the bed and matching dressers lined the room on the left, near a closet.

On the right wall of the room stood white bookshelves and a white hutch, which caught Mary's attention. It was full of dolls, all of them six inches high with identically perfect faces, round eyes, and red cupid mouths. They were dressed in beautiful outfits, and she knew instantly what they were; she had seen them in the bedroom of one of her friends growing up. They were called Madame Alexander dolls, and the DiNunzios could never have afforded them. They cost fifty dollars apiece then; she couldn't imagine what they cost now.

She stood before them, momentarily enchanted. At least twenty dolls sat legs akimbo, in the top row, with their round Mary Janes in black velveteen, touching toe to toe. The German doll wore a dirndl, the French doll the French flag, and the Italian doll sported red and green ribbons flowing from her synthetic hair. In the center of the top row was a doll that was bigger than the rest, also a Madame Alexander but clearly the crème de la crème. Mary had to stop herself from picking it up. She was supposed to be working, not playing with dolls.

She walked over to check the rest of the bookshelves. The books looked like assigned reading and school textbooks; no novels otherwise. She always thought you could learn a lot about someone from their bookshelf, and this bookshelf confirmed what she thought about Paige. In the shelf above the desk was a large Sony CD player, which Mary found strange. Paige hadn't lived here in a year. Why would she leave a CD player behind? It would be expensive to replace, even for a girl with bucks. Mary walked to the desk area to check.

The CD player looked brand-new, and there was a stack of CDs next to it. Weezer, Offspring, Dave Matthews Band; music that Mary had heard about but didn't know. How old were these CDs? She picked a few up and squinted at the infinitesimal copyright dates. All last year. Paige had left these behind, too. Why? Then she noticed something in the middle of the desk, on a blotter covered with teenage doodles. Paige's driver's license, with a picture of the girl, posing prettily even for the state's camera. What kind of teenager leaves her driver's license behind? CDs you can replace, even a CD player, but a driver's license? That was a headache. Paige wouldn't have left that behind. Not if she had a choice.

Mary looked around the room, her thoughts racing. The bedroom was too neat to have been left in haste, but it was left abruptly in some way. She crossed the room and peeked inside the closet. It was completely full; a double rack of skirts and tops, matching sweater sets folded in shelves, and fancy shoes in cubbyholes. What gives?

She constructed a scenario. Imagine that Paige told her mother she was going to move out, even that she already had picked out a condo at Colonial Hill Towers. What would have happened? What could explain what Mary was seeing? Then she realized it. Paige hadn't left abruptly, or in haste, but she must not have been permitted back in. That was it. The bedroom was just as it was the day that Paige had told her parents—or her mother—that she intended to move out. Her mother hadn't let her pack anything; it was all here. And she hadn't let her back into the house. All of it, even the driver's license, had had to be replaced.

Mary felt her heart quicken. So much for the façade of the young model movin' on up. Maybe Paige had no hard feelings about moving out; her mother sure did. Mary was about to tell the others when she remembered she hadn't checked the bathroom. She should, just to be complete. She walked to it and flicked on the bathroom light, and looked carefully around.

Nothing unusual except for too much makeup and a complete line of Kiehl's shampoos, conditioners, and "silk groom," whatever that was.

She left the bathroom and walked by the shelves, pausing again at the dolls. They were so pretty; so perfect. Especially the big one at the top, with a blue gown and matching train spread around her, glistening and satiny. Her hair was a beehive of blond plastic; Mary guessed it was Madame Alexander's version of Cinderella. She itched to hold it just once.

Oh hell. What was the harm?

Mary tugged her shirtsleeve down over her hands to cover her fingerprints, so the cops wouldn't indict her for murder. It seemed professional, especially if you were doing something as dorky as playing with dolls at a crime scene. Once her hand was covered, she scooped up the doll by the hair. Then she gasped. Not at the doll. At what lay hidden under the doll's satin gown.

"Lou!" she called. "Judy! Come quick!"

A small, pink leather book sat on the shelf where the doll had been and its cover said "MY DIARY." The doll lay forgotten on the floor. Mary told them her theory of what had happened between Paige and her mother while the three of them gathered around the diary, deciding what to do.

"Let's take it and run," Mary said, excited. "Finders keepers, losers weepers. Isn't that a legal principle?"

"Shouldn't we tell the cop at the door?" Judy asked, but Mary shook her head.

"No, he'll seize it. He'll turn it in unopened, and we won't get to read it." She turned to Lou for verification.

"That's right. The uniform at the door won't open it. He doesn't have the authority, and once it's bagged, it's theirs." Lou's mouth set in the harsh bathroom light, emphasizing the deep lines of his jowls. Still he didn't look old to Mary, he looked experienced.

"If it helps Newlin's case, they have to turn it over to us, under the discovery rules." Mary was remembering from her cramming. "But I don't know when we'll get it. A lot of the cases suggest it could take months, if we ever get it back."

Judy looked grave. "It's true. I've read cases where they never turn it over."

"I'm opening it," Mary announced, reaching for the diary, but Lou stopped her arm.

"No. Let me, in case I gotta testify." He reached into the inside pocket of his windbreaker, withdrew a white cotton handkerchief, and deftly wrapped his hand with it. Mary was impressed.

"You carry that to pick up evidence?" she asked.

"No, I carry it to wipe my nose," he answered, and picked up the diary.

BOOK THREE

35

Mary sat opposite Jack in the tiny interview room, not six feet by six feet, with no partition between them. The walls were of cinderblock painted an institutional sea green and contained windows of bulletproof glass with a view of the guard station. A large button of bright red protruded from the wall, and Mary, who had never been in a prison before, knew it had to be the proverbial panic button. If it had been any other prisoner, it would have made her edgy, but with Jack she felt completely safe, if not completely professional. "We need to talk," she said.

"Sure, what is it? Is it about the preliminary hearing?" He smiled in a friendly way, despite the strain evident on his face. His color was pale and he seemed restless, his long legs crossed at the ankle, in dark blue pants with sneakers. A light blue shirt sat loosely on his shoulders, its V-neck deep enough to reveal a light tangle of chest hair and its sleeves short enough to show off sinewy biceps. To Mary's eye, he did more for a prison uniform and steel handcuffs than most felons.

"No, it's about the case. We need to start over. I don't think you killed your wife."

His smile vanished. "Are you serious?"

"Yes. I think Paige did it, with her boyfriend Trevor. You were supposed to be at dinner that night, but I think that when you came in, your wife was already dead. You made it look like you killed her, but you didn't. You're innocent."

"This is silly, Mary. I did do it."

"No, Paige did, and you're protecting her. If you tell me the truth, we can help her. They'll give her the deal they won't give you."

"I did it. You just don't want to believe it."

"I'd believe it if it were true, but it's a lie. All of it, from the outset."

"No it isn't. I did it. I confessed to it." Jack pursed his lips. "I even had blood on my hands, and you still don't believe it?"

"Not at all."

"Face it, Mary. You're not seeing me clearly."

"Of course I am. Why wouldn't I?"

"You know why. You tell me." Jack didn't bat an eye, and Mary's face flushed crimson. So he knew. She couldn't deny it, so she didn't try. She fumbled for words.

"You're right . . . about that. I have a crush, I plead guilty. And I may be embarrassed and humiliated, but I'm not wrong." Mary set her jaw, her neck still aflame. "You didn't kill your wife, and I know it. I can distinguish between the murder case and my personal feelings."

"No you can't. You can't separate those things. You're emotional and new at criminal law. You don't want to think I'm capable of murder, but you're kidding yourself. Is this why you don't want to negotiate my guilty plea?"

"Jack, give it up." Mary leaned forward urgently. She had to convince him. "I can tell you now, there won't be a deal in this case, not for you. It's all over the papers today. Masterson announced there will be no deals in this case. No plea bargains, understand? If they ask for the death penalty, you're headed straight to Death Row. Dwight Davis has put ten men there, and you'll be the eleventh. Tell me the truth and I can help you, before it's too late."

"I can't believe this." Jack's face colored with growing anger. "I shouldn't have hired someone with so little experience."

"I have enough experience to know that you're lying to protect Paige. Paige and your wife fought all the time, and your wife put enormous pressure on her, emotionally abusing her for years, as her manager, too. You ignored it, maybe denied it, for too long, and when you finally came to, it was almost too late."

"That's not true." Jack's brow darkened and his mouth grew tight.

"You supported Paige's emancipation but your wife didn't. You drafted the papers, but Honor wouldn't even let Paige back into her room. Honor kept everything that kid owned, stole it like a common thief. She even kept Paige's diary. I found it in her room."

"*What?*" Jack exploded. "You had no business doing that!"

"My guess is your marriage started coming apart a year ago, when you took Paige's side. You've been overcompensating since then, that's why you're protecting her now. I know guilt when I see it. It's my favorite emotion."

"Mary, what are you saying? Why are you doing this to Paige? Investigating her, reading her diary, accusing her of murder. You'll ruin her life!"

"Taking responsibility for a crime she committed isn't helping her. I understand that now. It's wrong for you and wrong for her. Let her take responsibility for herself. Otherwise, you raise a kid who expects her way paved her whole life, and the world doesn't work that way. She's like an orchid, Jack. She can live in a hothouse, but it's cold outside."

"Paige is not your business!"

"Then what about Trevor? You're protecting him, too. Paige lied about him, to you and to me."

"No she didn't!" Jack shouted.

"Bullshit!" Mary shouted back. She plunged a hand into her briefcase and thrust the newspaper at him. "A Roundhouse Divided," read the headline. "Did you see this morning's paper yet? Kovich and Brinkley having a fight in front of Colonial Hill Towers. Why do you think they were there?"

Jack grabbed the paper in handcuffed hands, his eyes scanning the article, his brow creasing as he read.

"They were investigating Paige and Trevor. I figured it out and so did the cops. You can't keep the wheels on this thing, Jack. They're gonna come after her, so why don't you give it up?"

"You're destroying my daughter, is that what you want?" Jack threw down the paper and jumped to his feet, and Mary stood up, too. They stood eye-to-eye in the cell, an instant and volatile intimacy.

"Listen to me, Jack. I know why you're doing this. I know Paige is pregnant."

"Stop it with Paige!" Jack erupted. "Stay away from my daughter! Stay away from me. You and your law firm are fired!"

"Trevor is already running around with another girl. Is that what you want to leave Paige with? How can you help her if you're in here? Or if you're dead? And don't you have your own life to think about? Aren't you entitled to that?"

"That's it!" Jack yelled. Suddenly he turned and slammed his handcuffed hands into the red panic button in the cinderblock wall. The alarm went off instantly, reverberating in the tiny interview room.

"What are you doing?" Mary shouted, bewildered, but the din drowned out her voice.

"That's it! I'll kill you!" Jack bellowed and reached for her throat, despite his handcuffs. His hands encircled her neck loosely and ersatz rage contorted his face. Mary realized instantly what he was doing. He was making it look like he was strangling her. Through the window she could see black-shirted guards sprinting from the security desk in alarm. "I'll fucking kill you!" Jack shouted again, his touch harmless. Up close his eyes were filled with pain.

"Jack, no!" Mary yelled, pulling his hands from her, but all hell had broken loose. The guards were at the cell window with their guns drawn. A huge guard burst through the door and brought his gun butt down onto the back of Jack's head. The sound was sickening. The blow stilled Jack's eyes. For a split second, he stared unseeing at Mary, unconscious on his feet. She caught him in her arms but he was too heavy and collapsed to the floor.

"Jack!" she screamed, but the sound was lost in the clamor of the alarm. Four armed guards swarmed over him and dragged him out the door, banging his cheekbone into the doorjamb on the way.

A young guard rushed to Mary and grabbed her arms, his eyes searching her face with concern. "Are you okay?" he asked, anxious.

"Yes, of course." Her eyes brimmed with tears of frustration. "I'm fine. He didn't really—"

"That asshole's goin' straight to ad seg."

"Ad seg, what's that?"

"Administrative segregation, isolation. Twenty-three hours in a cage. We'll call the cops for you. You can press charges for assault."

"No, I don't want to press charges. He was just pretending," she said, her voice thick, but the guard released her in disbelief.

"Lady, get real. He was trying to kill you."

"No, he wasn't. It was an act. He didn't mean it."

A look of disgust crossed the guard's features. "I don't get what you broads see in these cons," he said, but Mary didn't try to set him straight. She wiped her tears, straightened her clothes, and picked up her bag and briefcase.

She had to get going before it was too late.

36

Brinkley didn't touch the newspaper Captain Walsh threw across the desk at him and Kovich. He'd been shown it by the old man at his newsstand, the uniform at the desk downstairs, and the guys on the squad, who taped the photo to the wall in the coffee room. Somebody had drawn a mustache on him and had given Kovich a kielbasa dick.

"Explain this to me, you idiots!" Captain Walsh shouted, over the tabloid tenting his desk, where it had landed. The Cap was so pissed he could barely keep his seat. Dwight Davis, freshly shaved and suited, leaned against the credenza behind him. His expression was grave, and even though he was in the right, Brinkley still wished he could pop him one.

"I'm very sorry about this, Cap," Brinkley said, and met his boss's eye. Captain Derrick Walsh was a big man with curly black hair. A merlot-colored birthmark crept across his right cheek and bled into his right eye, but Brinkley always figured the Cap owed his toughness to growing up with that birthmark. "I take full responsibility for it, sir. It's my fault."

"It's my fault, too," Kovich added, but the Cap exploded.

"Goddamn right it's your fault! Who else's fault could it be? *Mine?*" The Cap's barrel chest heaved in his starchy white shirt, which bore the stripes of his rank and an ornate gold badge. It was the only decoration in the office, which was bare of the citations, awards, and honors the Cap had received on the job. Brink-

ley had always respected Walsh for not being a show-off, so his
criticism landed hard. It didn't help that Brinkley was completely
ashamed of his conduct.

"I lost control," he admitted. "It won't happen again."

"Goddamn right it won't! You think we got the wrong guy,
Reg? Article says so, somebody overheard you. But your girlfriend here thinks we got the right guy. Ain't that fuckin' terrific? First off, how can you be so stupid as to discuss an open
case *on the goddamn street*?"

"Sorry, Cap." Brinkley wanted to hang his head, but he'd be
damned if he'd do that in front of Davis. It was police business,
and the lawyer had no right being here anyway.

"And on this, of all cases? What are you, stupid?"

"It was my mistake. I started it. I'm sorry."

"Not good enough, Reg. You know an investigation is completely confidential. Not only are you broadcasting it, you're
fighting about it. In public!"

"It's my fault, Cap."

"So then this scumjob of a reporter goes and talks to the security guard at the desk, and he finds out that you roughed him up
over who signs the logbook at the daughter's apartment. Now
they're callin' you—" The Cap grabbed the newspaper and
flipped the pages madly.

"A hothead," Davis supplied.

Brinkley sighed inwardly. He had to hear it from the Lone
Ranger now. He could tell Walsh didn't like it either. He had
embarrassed the department in front of the D.A.'s office. Half
those lawyers thought cops were stupid anyway. Shit.

Kovich cleared his throat. "Just for the record, the security
guard wasn't roughed up, Cap."

"I don't give a fuck!" Walsh arched a furry eyebrow that lay
beside the birthmark like a wooded border. "This never should
have happened! None of it! We got elements of our investigation, whatever this logbook shit is, out in the open!"

Behind him, Davis crossed his arms. "The reporter called me
to verify. Of course I didn't give him anything, but I know this

guy. He covers the Criminal Justice Center. He told me off the record that he's got more than he reported, he just couldn't get the second source to confirm." Davis hesitated before telling more, but Brinkley knew it was just for show. "Said specifically that the two detectives were fighting about whether Trevor was involved, with the daughter."

"Jesus H. Christ, Reg!" Walsh yelled. "You're killin' me here! You're *killin'* me! What the fuck were you *thinkin'*?"

"It's me, too, Cap," Kovich interrupted, but Brinkley waved him into silence. He had to defend himself. It was now or never and it couldn't get any worse.

"Cap, I'll tell you, I'm worried that Newlin's setting himself up. I think he's covering for the daughter or the boyfriend, or both."

The Cap's eyebrows flew heavenward. "What the *fuck* is goin' on here, Reg? I read this file, I saw the lab work! The prints, the blood work, the whole shebang. We *charged* the father. What are you *talking about*?"

"The boyfriend had some trouble in juvy and we were about to follow up on that. We found an earring back near the body that may belong to him. We were about to check his whereabouts the night of the murder."

"You're tellin' me you're runnin' down another suspect, when you already got one in custody—*who confessed*?"

"He's the wrong man," Brinkley said, and the more he said it the stronger he felt.

The Cap turned to Kovich. "Stanislas. You don't think we got the wrong man, do you?"

"I'm willin' to check it out with Mick, Cap. I trust his judgment." Kovich nodded, and Brinkley kept his face front. If Brinkley weren't Brinkley he would have hugged his partner.

"That's very touching," the captain said. "Now what do you think?"

"It doesn't matter what I think. Brinkley is the assigned. It's his case."

"Christ, you people!" Walsh jumped to his feet. "Kovich, answer me! Did Newlin kill his wife or not?"

"Yes," Kovich said, after a minute.

"Good! Now *you're* the assigned, and that's an order!" Walsh shouted, and both detectives looked up. The assigned was chosen by wheel; it was whoever's number was up when the job came in. You couldn't start mickeying with that. Most of the detectives thought it was magic or fate whose number was up when the call came in.

"Cap, it was my call, and it's my case." Brinkley kept a civil tone, but Dwight Davis frowned and folded his arms.

"Reg, no disrespect, but you know what you're doin' here? Masterson's on record saying we make no deals, the case is so airtight. I'm on record saying it's a lock. It's in the same goddamn paper as this story." Davis gestured to the messy tabloid. "Then you come along and make us look like smacked asses. I gotta explain to Masterson, he's gotta explain to the mayor, the mayor's gotta explain to the public and the media. You know, Reg. The thighbone's connected to the hipbone."

"I know," Brinkley said, only because he was in the wrong.

"I got a prelim in *Newlin* today, in case you forgot. I gotta make out a prima facie case of murder, which in this case I could have done with my eyes closed, until today. If you're the assigned, how am I gonna put you up there? What are you gonna say? The defendant is innocent? Or is this gonna be the only case in history where the assigned does not testify at the prelim?"

Brinkley had considered it. "I'll have it sorted out by the prelim, one way or the other. You can count on me."

Davis raised a palm. "Not since this article. Now you're gonna get crossed like nobody's business. Now even DiNunzio will know what to ask you. You're fucked, Reg. You can't testify."

Brinkley felt it slipping suddenly away. His case. His life. His wife. Forget the D.A.; he faced Walsh. "Cap, listen to me. I'm not about to do anything that would hurt the department."

"You already did," the captain said sternly. "This is the problem. You shoulda come to me before."

Brinkley knew it wouldn't have helped. It was just something to say later, at times like this. He couldn't say anything that wouldn't get him in deeper, so he didn't say anything. He knew the way this was going, the way it had to go.

"I know you were only doin' what you think was right, Reg, but you're on suspension. You're off for a week, no pay, and you're off the Newlin case, too. I'll take whatever heat the union gives me, grieve it if you want to, but I can't have this, in the papers." Walsh pointed a thick finger at Kovich. "I'd suspend you, too, if I didn't need you at the prelim."

Neither Brinkley nor Kovich replied, but stood up in unison without a word. Brinkley flipped open his jacket for his badge, slid his gun from his shoulder holster, and set both down on the tabloid, covering his own photo. The department was taking guns ever since a suspended cop shot his wife two months ago, and he didn't want to make the Cap ask for it. It was bad enough.

"This should go without saying, but don't talk to the press, Reg," Walsh ordered. "You neither, Stan. Got it?"

"No comment," Kovich said, with a weak smile, but Brinkley wasn't about to make jokes.

He wasn't about to be stopped, either.

37

I need some answers about your father's case, Paige," Mary said, sitting on the chair across the coffee table from the young woman. A bouquet of white silk freesia in a glass vase sat atop the oak table, and the morning sun streamed though the windows, suffusing the living room with light. Mary didn't mention that she wasn't Jack's lawyer anymore. It was only a sin of omission, anyway.

"So early?" Paige blinked against the brightness, dressed in her blue chenille robe and slippers. Her hair fell loose to her shoulders, in a sleepy tangle, but gray circles ringed her blue eyes. "I'm not a morning person."

"Sorry about that." Mary felt a momentary twinge. If Paige were pregnant, she wouldn't be feeling so well in the mornings. She wondered if Paige had gotten an abortion, but she couldn't be distracted now. "It's important."

"All right, if you say." Paige sat before a cup of take-out coffee that Mary had brought her, for which she still hadn't been thanked, but she found herself less bothered by Paige's rudeness than before. Mary was seeing her differently, more fully. This was a girl who had been raised with both privilege and cruelty, and Mary felt she had less and less right to judge her. She just wanted to save her father's life.

"By the way, you're alone this morning, aren't you?"

"That's kind of personal, but yes."

"Sorry. I wanted to make sure that Trevor wasn't here. I thought you guys might have gone out last night," Mary lied. Okay, so it was a sin of commission. Drastic measures were called for.

"No, he couldn't meet me last night. He had to study."

So Trevor had lied to her, of course. Mary would save it for later. "Here are my questions. First, I was in your old bedroom, at your parents' house, and there's a lot I didn't understand." She pulled a pen, a legal pad, and a large manila envelope from her briefcase. The envelope held the diary, which puffed out its middle in a clear, square outline. She sat the envelope with the diary down between them like bait, but didn't refer to it. "Wonder if you can help me out."

"Sure," Paige said. If she noticed the puffy envelope, it didn't show. "I can help you, but why were you in my room?"

"As defense lawyer, I have to check out the crime scene. That's what we do, to help your father. You want to help your father, don't you?"

"Sure, yes."

"I figured as much." Mary glanced at her legal pad as if there were notes there. "Let's see, I saw your CD player and a whole bunch of CDs. How come you left that stuff?"

"I didn't need it. I got a new one."

"But this was a new one, and so were the CDs."

"I wanted an even newer one."

Mary checked the blank pad again. "Your driver's license was in your room, too."

"Oh? I thought I lost it."

"But it was right in the middle of your desk. I'm surprised you didn't see it there if you were looking for it."

"Well, I didn't." Paige shifted in her plush robe. "What's the difference?"

"Don't get attitudinal, I was just asking. It seemed like there were lots of things in that room that you would have taken with you if you could. I got the feeling that you didn't go back once you moved out, and you left things that mean something to you. Like your Madame Alexander dolls."

"My dolls?"

"Yes." Mary leaned back in the soft couch and watched Paige carefully. "I loved your collection. The doll from Africa, and from Italy. Take it from me, though. Italians don't wear red and green ribbons in their hair anymore. That is so last season."

Paige forced a smile, then her eyes fell on the manila envelope on the coffee table.

"You had the little *I Love Lucy* set, too. Lucy and Ethel, dressed for the chocolate factory. Do they give you the chocolates or not? Bonbons not supplied?"

"Uh, no." Paige eyed the envelope, guileless enough to betray herself. Mary could see her wanting to grab it and run.

"You have the doll in the black lace dress, with the French hat. I love that one. But my favorite was the big doll with the blue dress, from a fairy tale. Who was she? Cinderella?"

"Yes, it was Cinderella." Paige's eyes shifted from the envelope and met Mary's with resignation. "So. You found my diary."

"I did. I wasn't looking for it, but I found it. And I know your mother was horrible to you, growing up. I know that she was mean and abusive to you. I know that she put enormous pressure on you to succeed as a model and that you thought about leaving home for years until you finally moved out. She was furious at you for that, wasn't she? And your dad took your side, which caused even more problems than before."

Paige's lips parted in sad recognition.

"I know that she wouldn't let you back into your room and that's why everything was left behind. Everything you owned or had been given. All your stuff."

Wetness welled in Paige's eyes.

"I know that you two fought at the Bonner shoot. I know, too, that you're pregnant and thinking about an abortion. How'm I doin'?" Mary slid the envelope gently across the coffee table, and Paige reached out and picked it up.

"You read my diary." Her tone was hushed and she picked up the envelope only slowly, as if in shock.

"Open it," Mary said, and Paige fumbled with the brass clasp, opened the manila envelope, and reached inside. The diary came out with its latch hanging apart, and the teenager started at the sight.

"You broke it!" she cried.

"No, I didn't. Somebody else did."

Paige opened the diary and gasped. The first page was charred from a burn at the center, as if someone had burned it with a cigarette. The charring spread almost to the end of the page, obliterating the handwriting beneath. Paige turned the page carefully. The second page was burnt the same way, gone at the center and black around the edges. The only writing still visible was blackened. She flipped the pages frantically but they began to crumble in her hand. "Oh my God," she said, but it sounded like a moan.

"Your mother did this, didn't she?" Mary asked, and Paige nodded slowly, her eyes fixed on the cinders where the diary's pages used to be.

"Of course she did. She'd wanted to hurt me. She loved to hurt me. She knew I wrote in it when I was upset. She knew how much it meant to me. She must have done it when I told her I was leaving. She went crazy. Dad couldn't stop her." Paige looked at Mary with wet eyes. "You didn't read my diary. You couldn't have."

"No, I found it that way."

"Then how did you know everything?"

"I put it together. I tried to figure out what would make a smart little girl grow up into a very troubled young woman. You wanna tell me? I can help."

"Tell you about my mother, how it was with us? I mean, you've probably heard it all before, like on Jerry Springer or something." Page tried to smile but it quivered into a downturn. "But, you know, when bad things happen to you, it's like they never happen to anyone else in the world, ever. Even though they do, you know?"

"Yes." Mary thought instantly of her husband's death. "Well put."

"Um, you see, I think my mother, she hated me. No matter

what I did, she *hated* me. I was never good enough. And you know what? I hated her. I don't even miss her. I'm glad she's dead. Glad. That's the whole story, that's all I want to say." Paige tossed her head, her red hair falling back. "At her memorial service today, I should get up and dance around. She's history. It's all history. I don't want to talk about it anymore." Her eyes welled up again, but Mary ignored the waterworks.

"I understand, but we do have to talk about the truth. You have to tell me what happened the night your mother was murdered. Because I know your father didn't kill your mother, and I don't want to see him convicted for a crime he didn't commit. I have to believe that in your heart you don't want that, either. It's time for you to take responsibility for yourself."

Paige blinked back her tears.

"Nothing that your mother did to you justifies what you are doing to your father. You are letting your father take responsibility for your crime. And that's wrong, no excuses. So stop crying and talk to me, like an adult. Like a woman."

Paige swallowed hard. Mary could see her tiny dimple of an Adam's apple travel down her reddening throat.

"Did you kill your mother, Paige?"

She didn't say anything, and Mary resisted the urge to beat the truth out of her.

"Was Trevor involved in it?"

She still didn't answer, setting Mary's teeth on edge. If Paige had been on a witness stand, Mary would have torn into her, but that wouldn't work here.

"Look, Paige, I know you lied to me and that Trevor was with you that night. Why are you protecting him? Because he fathered your baby?"

"How do you know—"

"I know more than that, more than you. He's no good, believe me. You don't know everything about him."

"What do *you* know?" she asked, and Mary hesitated. The girl didn't need another shock, but Mary wouldn't get a second chance.

"After he left you yesterday, Trevor met someone else. Another woman. He went with her to New York last night. I saw them together at Thirtieth Street station."

"I don't believe you!" Paige shouted. Anger tinged her cheeks. "Trevor was home studying."

"No, he wasn't."

"He was, too!"

"How do you know? Did you call? Did he answer? I doubt it. Would you put your own father in prison to save a jerk like that?"

"He's not a jerk! You don't know him at all! I think it's time for you to go." Paige rose to her feet as quickly as Jack had, and Mary was getting used to being rejected by the members of the Newlin family. She reached down for her briefcase and legal pad.

"Think about what I'm saying, Paige. The longer you wait, the worse it is, for your father and for you. And Trevor, too. Read the newspaper today. The cops are on to you and Trevor."

"Get out! I won't hear this!" Paige hustled to the door and opened it wide, but Mary stopped at the threshold.

"Your father fired me this morning, for saying to him what I said to you. He is giving his life for you. And Trevor won't even return your calls. Is that the kind of man you choose? For you and your baby?"

Paige's only response was to look away, and Mary should have tried to convince her, if not throttle her. But instead she simply walked out on her, not wanting to be in her presence a moment longer.

38

Jack regained consciousness, lying alone in a small cell. Unlike his other cell, the door was solid except for a slit for food, and the sound of the other inmates was muffled. Ad seg; isolation. A stainless steel toilet, a bed, and twenty-three hours a day of alone; it didn't matter to Jack anyway. His cheekbone throbbed and he touched the warm wetness there with handcuffed hands. Blood covered his finger pads when he withdrew his hand.

His ribs ached and he fought to keep his breathing even. They must have whacked him around because he felt broken and his jumpsuit was ripped and dirtied. His head thundered but his thoughts were like lifting fog. Mary. The newspaper. The police were getting closer to finding out about Paige. And Trevor.

Jack felt his chest constrict. His plan was threatening to unravel. Mary was yanking hard on the string and it was coming undone. He had to keep it together. If Trevor was guilty, then he would find a way to deal with it, but not until he was sure. He wouldn't put Paige on the line, no matter what. It was the newspaper story that worried him now. If Trevor was in on Honor's murder, he would be starting to worry about his own vulnerability. And if Trevor started to worry, Paige was in jeopardy.

Jack struggled to a sitting position against the wall. His sides ached and he slumped forward, stretching out his feet slowly. He had to get out of prison, to protect Paige. He'd be freed after his preliminary hearing today, if he got bail. He'd need a new lawyer. A real criminal lawyer. One who would take direction. Mary was gone. He winced and shifted his weight to the other side. He wouldn't see her again.

Good, right? Right. Mary had been confusing him. Last night, in a moment before sleep, he'd caught himself hoping that the police would find out he was innocent, so he could go free. In one awful moment, he'd let himself realize that he had sacrificed his life when it had little value to him. Mary could have made it worth getting out of here. Now the prosecution was talking no deals. Jack would be going to trial, where he would lose. He had to; he'd rigged it that way. He froze at the thought, but he had no way out. The alternative would kill Paige. Even if Trevor were involved, Paige would be lost, too.

He was better off without Mary, he knew. She would have been his salvation. And his undoing.

39

"Miss DiNunzio, what happened at the prison?" "Miss DiNunzio, why did Newlin try to kill you?" "Mary, any comment?" "Mary, did you quit?" "Over here! Just one picture!"

It was overcast, gusty, and freezing, but for once the windchill wasn't the big news. The press thronged around the small brick chapel of colonial vintage, in the heart of Society Hill. Reporters spilled off the narrow brick sidewalk, and news vans clogged a cobblestone street meant to support only horse-drawn carriages. Mary and Judy fought their way though the media, which snapped their photos and shoved microphones in their faces. The news that Jack Newlin had attacked his lawyer at the prison was breaking, and Mary was the quarry.

She kept her head down and barreled through the crowd with the larger Judy running interference. They made it to the white wood entrance, grabbed a black-bordered program from a wooden stand, and ducked inside the chapel. Mary stalled at the sight; the pews were virtually empty. "Where is everybody?" she whispered, and Judy shook her head.

"I guess nobody but reporters liked Honor."

"At least Communion will be short." Mary entered the chapel, which looked more like a school than a church. The interior was small, bright white, and austere. The walls contained only a tasteful number of stained-glass windows, remarkably free of the crucifixion, cross-bearing, and bloody crowns of thorns that made

Mary feel so at home. She supposed you could have a religion without suffering, but she didn't know how.

She wouldn't have recognized the dais except that it was at the front. Instead of an elaborate altar that bore chalices, wafers, and wine, there was only a plain mahogany podium, an organ, and several polished wood chairs. The floor and pews had been milled from colonial walnut and were completely vacant except for Paige, her head bent in the front row, and a row of corporate lawyers that Mary was guessing were from Tribe & Wright. At the end of the row sat Dwight Davis.

"Trevor's not here," Mary observed. "But Davis came. Accept no substitutes."

"Maybe Paige confronted Trevor."

"Possible." Mary looked down the row and spotted the thick neck of Detective Kovich. Brinkley wasn't here, and she wondered if he'd been fired. The story in the newspaper couldn't have helped his career.

"The service is starting, Mare. Let's sit down."

"Go close to the front," Mary said, and they seated themselves in a pew several behind Paige and the lawyers. Mary wanted Paige to see her so she'd keep in mind what they'd said in the apartment. Maybe Mary's appeal would sink in. She could only hope, but she couldn't possibly pray. There was no ball of smoking incense, no cup of magic wine, and none of the other equipment essential to talk to God.

Paige sat in the front row of the service. The pastor was saying something but it didn't matter. She didn't know where Trevor was and she was worried that what Mary had told her was true. She'd left two messages for him but he still hadn't called. It was weird. This had been happening a lot lately.

She bit her lip and thought back to when it started. She had to admit it had been since she told him she was pregnant. She felt nauseous again but it wasn't the baby. She'd been going back and forth on the decision, but still couldn't make up her mind. She was running out of time. Trevor wanted to get married, and so did she. She hoped they would make good parents, not like the ones they had. She had even started to read about raising babies and she hadn't taken any drugs since the crystal.

The pastor was saying something else about her mother, even though he had never met her. Her mother didn't have any friends at all; supposedly a society lady, she had no society. Paige felt sorry for her until she realized that she was alone here, too. She didn't have any girlfriends either. Once Trevor had given her a button that said, I'M BECOMING MY MOTHER! She couldn't bring herself to wear it. She thought about that for a while, her head bent, her eyes dry. Out of the corner of her eye she spotted Mary, but looked away. She couldn't think about that now.

The service ended and Paige went with her mother's lawyers to the cemetery. When they slid her mother's polished casket out of the shiny hearse, Paige decided she wasn't going to pay attention anymore. The wind gusted, blowing her hair around, and she kept her head down and her lips tight. Men from the funeral home were the pallbearers, and for a while, it was easy to ignore everything, even at the graveside service. The short little pastor, the boring hymn, the rectangular hole, the important lawyer, Mr. Whittier, checking his watch; she didn't notice a thing.

The casket was lowered into the grave, and she became aware of the press photographers, kept at a distance. She turned to the cameras automatically and smoothed her hair, then caught herself. She didn't want to pose at her mother's funeral. She didn't want to pose at all anymore. She turned back just in time to see her mother disappearing into the earth forever, and the sight of it caught her by the throat. The harder Paige tried not to think about that, the harder she did think about it. The more she tried not to feel guilty, the guiltier she felt. The more she tried not to love her mother, the more she did.

And she started to cry and didn't stop until long after her mother was gone.

40

"The next matter is *Commonwealth v. Newlin*," the court crier called. "Defendant Jack Newlin is represented by Mr. Isaac Roberts, and Mr. Dwight Davis is here for the Commonwealth."

"Thank you and good afternoon, counsel," said Judge Angel Silveria from the dais. He flashed a brief smile, like a waning moon, and Mary, watching from her seat in the packed gallery, knew that it would be the last smile they'd see from him. A chubby, compact judge, Silveria was a former prosecutor who enjoyed his reputation as the most conservative on the Municipal Court bench. It didn't matter so much at this preliminary proceeding, but Jack couldn't have drawn a tougher judge for trial if he'd tried, and Mary wondered with dismay if he had.

"Good afternoon to you, Your Honor," Isaac Roberts said with a flourish.

Mary craned her neck to get a better look at her replacement, patron saint of sleazeballs. Roberts was one of the best-known criminal lawyers in town, although he had never tried a murder case. He plea-bargained for upper-echelon coke dealers, a specialty for lawyers wishing their fees in cash and their eternity in hell. Roberts wore the best clothes that cocaine could buy; a dark Armani suit, Gucci loafers, and a Jerry Garcia tie to complement his Jerry Garcia ponytail. Mary assumed that Roberts was confusing crackhead with Deadhead and began to simmer. He wouldn't care if Jack was innocent or guilty.

"Good day, Your Honor," Davis said, shooting up like an arrow at counsel table. "The Commonwealth is ready to begin."

Judge Silveria gestured to the sheriff. "Please bring in the defendant."

Mary suppressed a pang when Jack was brought in, in an orange prison jumpsuit, handcuffs, and leg manacles, and escorted to his seat by two sheriffs. A red swelling over his right cheek distorted his handsome features, and he walked with obvious pain.

"If I may proceed, Your Honor," Davis began, "the Commonwealth calls Detective Stan Kovich to the stand."

Mary watched as the beefy detective rose, punched up his glasses, and lumbered to the witness stand where he was sworn in. Kovich looked so earnest on the stand, four-square and forthright, that she knew he'd be a terrific witness for the Commonwealth. She wondered again about Brinkley and twisted around in her seat. He was nowhere in sight, and she wasn't surprised. She'd called the Roundhouse and left messages for him, but he hadn't returned her calls. No surprise there either.

"Good morning, Detective Kovich," Davis said. "I would like to direct your attention to January eleventh of this year. Did your duties as detective cause you to interview the defendant Jack Newlin at approximately nine o'clock in the evening?"

"Yes, they did," Kovich began, and Davis nodded.

"Please tell the judge, first, what you observed about defendant's appearance."

"I observed what appeared to be human blood on Mr. Newlin's hands and clothes."

The testimony continued with Davis taking Kovich through the high points of the videotaped confession, and Mary listened with increasing dismay. She counted only two objections by Roberts and a lame cross-examination, but nothing would have made a difference. At a preliminary hearing, the Commonwealth had only to make out a prima facie case of murder, the barest minimum, and they had that easy. The reporters scribbled and the courtroom sketch artists drew madly when Judge Silveria ruled:

"I find the Commonwealth has borne its burden of proving a prima facie case on all counts of the charge of general murder, and I order the defendant Jack Newlin bound over for trial." The judge banged his gavel. "Shall we set bail?"

Davis rose quickly. "Your Honor, the Commonwealth opposes bail in this matter. We believe Mr. Newlin poses a substantial risk of flight, especially in view of the fact that the Commonwealth has made a determination to prosecute Mr. Newlin to the fullest extent of the law in this matter. We have announced today that we are seeking the death penalty in this case."

In the gallery, Mary felt her heart tighten in her chest. So there truly would be no deals. The prospect horrified her. She looked for Jack at counsel table but all she could see was his profile, his bruised chin held high. His lawyer rose beside him in far too relaxed a manner.

"Your Honor," Roberts said, "regardless of the Commonwealth's scare tactics, Mr. Newlin poses no real flight risk. It is one thing to deny bail at the arraignment, but another to deny it after the preliminary hearing, Your Honor. I cannot recall the last case in which bail was denied at this juncture."

Judge Silveria banged the gavel again. "That much is correct, Mr. Roberts. Your client is hereby released on bail. Bail shall be set at $250,000. Next matter, please."

Mary felt relieved, despite the high number. She knew Jack could make the ten percent he needed to get free, and bail should have been granted, as a legal matter. She could use another crack at changing Jack's mind. Maybe a taste of freedom would influence him.

The gallery rose almost as one, with the reporters, sketch artists, and spectators filing out, but Mary remained behind. Roberts was packing his briefcase, but Jack had turned and was scanning the gallery. Mary didn't know why; Paige wasn't in the crowd, probably he'd told her not to come. She found herself rising to her feet as the gallery cleared completely and she realized Jack was staring at her.

Her heart lodged in her throat, a place it had no business being, and she didn't know what to do. He was looking right at her, his eyes betraying a tacit connection. Then they became guarded again, and he turned away. But Mary hadn't imagined it; it had happened. He had been looking for her.

She stood her ground in silence, which in itself made a statement. Jack was lying and he knew it, and if there was any justice in this city, all she had to do was keep standing up for the truth. She had to bear witness. She vowed never to give up and never to sit down and never to *let* down until she had brought the truth to light.

She remained standing in the empty gallery long after Jack had been led from the courtroom, and her eyes wandered over the judicial dais, the nylon flag, and the golden seal of the Commonwealth; the objects and symbols she took for granted in courtrooms and had never really looked at until now. She found herself believing in the objects in a way she had never believed in the chalices, wafers, and rosaries of her childhood, and she wondered if she believed in the gavel because she didn't believe in the crucifix. It might have been true; she wasn't sure. Mary knew she didn't have all the answers and wasn't better than anyone else. But for the first time in her life, she came to the conclusion that she wasn't any worse.

Fifteen minutes later, she was hurrying from the Criminal Justice Center and past City Hall, the cold wind pushing her along. The press thronged behind her in front of the courthouse; she had managed to duck most of them. She had to get back to the office to try to find Brinkley. He must know something that was making him investigate Paige and Trevor. Mary had to find out what it was.

The sidewalks were crowded and she threaded her way along, but when she got to the corner was surprised to see an attractive man approaching her with a plainly lustful look. She put her head down and hustled past him, but when she looked up again there was another man looking at her with naked interest. Mary didn't get it. Men never looked at her like that and they wouldn't be starting now. Her hair was messy, her coat was wrinkled, and her eyes were red from her contacts.

"Mary," said a voice behind her, and she turned. Standing right behind her, plainly out of breath, was Paige. "Do you have a minute?" the teenager asked.

41

There were worse things than being suspended, Brinkley was finding out. In truth it didn't feel so different, except for the money. He'd never felt a part of Two Squad anyway and had been on the outside looking in most of the time on the job. Now it was just official. Also it gave him more time to freelance. On the Newlin case. He stayed in the loop, thanks to the reporters who had gotten him suspended. The newspapers had the blow-by-blow of Newlin attacking his lawyer, and Brinkley knew instantly it was a scam. The man just did not have it in him. Brinkley had also heard that the prelim had gone down with new counsel, and that the judge had ruled for the Commonwealth and also set bail.

He was driving downtown in his black '68 Beetle, rotted at the doorjambs and chassis. The cold wind whistled through the rust holes, and he had to keep his leather jacket buttoned. Someday the Beetle's floor would fall out, but that was part of the fun. It ran great and the vinyl seats were still free of duct tape. Sheree had been too ashamed of the car to drive around in it and had dubbed it Shit Car. Brinkley used to call it that, too. Until today.

He cruised forward with the aftermarket CD player loud in the midday traffic, feeling like a kid playing hooky. Beside him on the seat was the FedEx package in a soft envelope. He stopped at the red light on Broad Street, where a brother pulled up in a cherry red 'Vette. Brinkley kept his eyes straight ahead. Just let him say something. A man can drive any damn car he wants to.

The traffic light turned green, and Brinkley hit the gas. The Corvette wouldn't approve of his music either. It wasn't rap or jazz; it was Elvis. Brinkley had a collection of over a hundred CDs and had been to Graceland three times. Each time he had been the only black detective from Philly in line, but he didn't care. Sheree hadn't gone with him on any of the trips. She didn't appreciate the King, which bugged him, and Brinkley clung to that thought. It was good to be having some bad memories of her. Maybe he could string them along, one after the other like keys on a ring, and not want her back.

He turned the corner, spotted the building up on his left, and slowed to a stop in front of it. Then he flicked on faint blinkers, grabbed the FedEx package, and climbed out of the Beetle.

42

Mary and Paige entered Captain Walsh's office, which was surprisingly bare for such top brass. She introduced herself and Paige, then took a seat in front of his regulation-issue desk and gestured to Paige to take the other. Mary had decided to go straight to the top with Paige's confession. The old Mary would have been intimidated, but the new Mary didn't think twice about the asking to see the manager. "Thank you for meeting with us, Captain," she said, and Paige nodded stiffly.

"Certainly." Captain Walsh nodded, his thick neck folding into the starchy collar on his white uniform. He wore a dark tie and gold badge and his hair looked permanently uncombed. Mary avoided staring at his birthmark, which matched the blotches on her neck. Captain Walsh gestured to the door, opening behind her. "Here's Detective Kovich. I think you know him."

"Yes, sure." Mary twisted around. Kovich entered the office in a short-sleeved shirt and spongy brown pants that revealed he hadn't cut down on portion size. Following him was a young man with spiky black hair moussed straight up and a black tweed jacket with baggy black slacks. Mary figured him for the Young & Hip version of detective.

"The good-lookin' one is Detective Donovan," Captain Walsh said, and Mary smiled politely.

"I also remember a Detective Brinkley, from our interview at Paige's apartment. Will he be coming?"

"No, Detective Donovan has replaced him on the case." Walsh addressed the young detective. "Say hello to the nice lawyer, Danny."

"Hello, Ms. DiNunzio," he said, with a mock half-bow, and Mary hated him instantly.

"Where's Detective Brinkley, Captain?" she asked.

"Detective Brinkley is no longer on this case. I'm holding a press conference later today about the matter. He was put on suspension for improper conduct."

Mary knew it was code for disagreeing with the boss and wondered how Walsh and Kovich would react when Brinkley turned out to be right. She paused until Kovich took a position at the right side of Captain Walsh, leaning against a credenza in the back. Donovan stood next to him, slipped his hands in his pockets, and looked skeptically at them. Mary ignored the boys-against-the-girls vibe and cleared her throat.

"Captain, as you know, I represented Jack Newlin in the early stage of his murder case, and after investigation I came to believe that he was innocent of the crime and that he confessed falsely, to protect his daughter. It turns out to be the truth, and Paige has decided to come forward."

Captain Walsh frowned so deeply his birthmark folded in two and he addressed Paige. "Is this true, young lady?"

"Yes, it is," she said. Her voice sounded soft and young, and Mary's heart went out to her. Mary could only guess at how frightened she must feel, turning herself in to face a murder charge. She had warned Paige that she might not be tried as a juvenile. "I'm very sorry for what I did, and I'm very sorry I let my father do what he's doing. I shouldn't have. He's innocent. I did it. I . . . killed my mother."

"Well, now. That's quite a mouthful." Captain Walsh's lips set like concrete. "I think at this point I should tell you your rights under Miranda. I think I still remember how." He went through the litany as Mary's stomach tightened. As bad as it felt for Jack to be in jail, it would feel equally lousy to have Paige there. It was a no-win situation, and Mary could almost understand why Jack had done what he did. Walsh finished, then asked, "Do you understand your rights, Ms. Newlin?"

"Yes," Paige said, her voice trembling, and Mary took her hand and squeezed it.

"Kovich, why don't you get us some waiver forms?" Walsh said, and the burly detective straightened and hustled out of the room. "Ms. DiNunzio, are you representing Ms. Newlin?"

"Yes, I am."

"Good, fine." Walsh clenched and unclenched his fist, as if he had a hand exerciser, until Kovich returned with a flurry of papers and handed them to Mary. "Ah, here are the forms," he said, as she read them and nodded for Paige to sign. She did, with a pen handed to her by the captain. "Now, Ms. Newlin, why don't you tell us what happened," he said.

"Sure. Right. Okay." Paige ran her tongue over dry lips. "I was going home to talk to my mother, to tell her I was pregnant. I told my dad on the phone that day, and he said he would be home to help me tell her. I brought my boyfriend over, but I told my dad I didn't." She paused. "My mother went nuts when I told her, like she went crazy. She was drunk and she hit me so hard I fell off the chair. Then she started kicking me in the stomach really hard, saying she was going to kick my baby out of me."

Walsh's dark eyes flared. "She said what?"

"She started yelling, 'You kill it or I'll kill it!' And then I just went crazy, too. I think it was the drugs." Paige halted and looked at Mary. They had been over this at Mary's office, and Mary had advised her to tell the whole truth, drugs and all. It had to come out, and Mary was hoping it could provide a diminished capacity defense or maybe reduce the charge.

"Drugs." Walsh sighed, his frown undisguised. "What were you high on?"

"Crystal meth."

Mary leaned toward the captain. "It was given to her by her boyfriend, Trevor Olanski. He was present at the crime and can substantiate everything she says. We've been trying to locate him but we can't. I have reason to believe he was in New York last night."

Walsh turned to Paige. "Please go on."

"Well, I never took meth before and I was so mad, like *raging*. It's hard to remember. I grabbed the knife off the table and I . . . I . . . stabbed her." Tears of guilt sprang to Paige's eyes but she didn't cry, and Mary felt proud of her. "I didn't even know I was so angry inside, but I got out of control and I stabbed her. I finally stopped and calmed down, and I dropped the knife. My mother was . . . on the floor, so my boyfriend picked me up and got me out of there. Well, then my dad came home and he must have found my mother and figured out what happened. He confessed, but he didn't do it. He didn't." Paige managed to hold back her tears, and Mary squeezed her hand. It was over. Paige had come through. Jack would be set free.

But Walsh still looked grim. "You know, Ms. Newlin, it's not unusual for a family member to come to us and try to cover for one of their own, especially in a homicide case."

Mary nodded. "We know that. That's why her father did it."

Walsh raised a palm like a traffic cop. "I'm talking to Ms. Newlin, Ms. DiNunzio."

"I understand that."

"So let me talk to her without interfering. If there's anything you don't want her to answer, you can tell her. But don't answer for her, understand? I muzzled my boy Donovan here, and if you think that was easy, you're nuts."

"It's not the same thing, Captain." Mary remained unintimidated, an act of will. "Detective Donovan isn't exposed to criminal liability. Paige is, and I'm her lawyer."

"And you were also Mr. Newlin's. Now, I don't know a lot about legal ethics, but I don't get how you can be his lawyer and her lawyer when their interests are in conflict."

"I'm no longer Mr. Newlin's lawyer and I know from my investigation on this case that what Paige is saying is true." Mary glanced at Kovich, against the credenza. "And before you question my ethics, look to the department's. It's all over the newspapers that you've broken ranks over this case. Yet your only response has been to punish Brinkley, not to release an innocent man."

"We haven't established that Newlin's innocent, Ms. DiNunzio. Maybe if you let me talk to his daughter, we can make some progress."

"Go right ahead," Mary said. She found herself respecting Captain Walsh, even as they fought.

"I'm so glad." Walsh hunched over his desk, closer to Paige. "Ms. Newlin, as you know, your father confessed to this crime and that's why we charged him. He confessed to nine-one-one, he confessed to the detectives, and we have it all on videotape. Nobody beat it out of him or made him say anything. He came in and told us what happened. You understand that?"

Paige nodded. "But he was lying, to protect me."

"You may not know that there was a substantial amount of physical evidence against your father. He had your mother's blood on his hands and clothes. We just received the coroner's report and he says it took a substantial amount of force to make those knife wounds. I wonder if a skinny girl like you could have done it."

"I did do it. I stabbed her," Paige protested, but Mary was getting a sinking feeling.

"There were a number of stab wounds, too. Do you know how many?"

"I think maybe two or three. I remember . . . two or three."

Captain Walsh shook his head. "There were five."

"Okay, whatever, there were five," Paige said, testy in a teenage way. "I don't know how many I did. I was high, I told you."

"I understand that." Walsh paused. "But five stab wounds into a chest takes time and effort. It's work. You wouldn't forget something like that."

"I was high, I told you." Paige was getting frustrated, and, standing behind Walsh, Donovan folded his arms.

"What about the cut on the hand, Cap?" he asked.

Walsh glanced back in annoyance, then returned to Paige. "You know, typically when a knife is used in a murder, the person doing the stabbing gets a cut or two on their hand, because the knife is so slippery. It almost always happens that way. Your father had a cut on his hand. Do you have any cuts on your hands?"

Paige looked down at her hands, spreading her fingers. They were pink and lovely, with not a scratch on them, and Mary felt stricken. She knew where this was heading. They weren't going to believe Paige. She wondered briefly if she should take Paige to confront Jack, but he would just deny it.

"But I did it, I'm telling you," Paige protested. The softness had vanished from her voice in her determination to be believed. "Do you honestly think I would make this up? Pretend I killed my own mother when I didn't?"

"Yes, of course." Captain Walsh nodded, his expression somber. "That's what you're telling us your father did."

Kovich shifted uneasily against the credenza. "I'm wondering about something, Captain. May I?"

"Can I stop you?" Walsh asked, with a stern smile, but Kovich wasn't taking no for an answer.

"Paige said her mother was kicking her stomach, hard. You saw the coroner's report, Cap. The mother's toe was broken, on the right foot. She could have done that kicking someone. We thought it was a defensive wound, but maybe it wasn't." Kovich's eyes sharpened behind his gold-rimmed glasses. "If Paige is telling the truth, she should have bruises on her stomach."

"Yes, she should," Mary said, eagerly. Kovich was helping them, obviously at some professional cost, and she nodded to him gratefully.

Walsh turned to face Paige. "Ms. Newlin, do you have any bruises on you?"

"I guess so, sure. My stomach hurt the next day. I was worried about the baby and I called Planned Parenthood. They said it should be fine, since it was so early."

"You understand, we can't take your word for it," Walsh said, his tone still heavy with doubt. "We'll have to see the bruises. Photograph them, too."

"Fine," Mary said. She wished she'd thought of it in her office, but she hadn't known about the broken toe. The prosecution hadn't had to disclose the coroner's report yet. "If you gentlemen will clear out of the room, maybe I can take a look at Paige's stomach."

The captain and the detectives rose and left. Kovich shot them a backward glance as he went out the door, which Mary read as encouragement. He must have realized that Brinkley had been right. With his information and Mary's, Jack would be exonerated. Mary jumped to her feet as soon as the police had closed the door behind them. "Paige, let me see your bruises."

"Sure." Paige began to unbutton her blouse, her long red hair tumbling forward. "I do have them. I mean, I didn't think to look, but I know I do. My stomach was killing me." Her fingers fumbled to open the middle button, then the next and finally the third and fourth. She parted her blouse. A lacy white bra peeked out and below it lay one of the flattest, prettiest stomachs Mary had ever seen. There wasn't a bruise or a blotch on her.

Mary's mouth went dry. "There's nothing," she said, stricken, and Paige looked down in confusion.

"I don't get it. Where are the bruises? She was kicking me and kicking me. I know it. I *remember* it."

"Then how could they not be there? How could you not know?" Mary tried not to sound accusatory, but it dashed her hopes for Jack's release. "Don't you look at your own body?"

"Not since that night, I guess. I've barely had time to shower. But she kicked me, I remember. I was worried she was going to kill the baby. She *said* she was going to kill the baby!"

Mary didn't know what to say or do. What was going on here? The captain would never believe Paige now, but she had been telling the truth. Her account was exactly the way she'd told it in Mary's office and all of it made sense. But Kovich, who had been trying to help them, had also been right. If Paige had been kicked with enough force to break a toe, she would have bruises to show for it. So the only logical conclusion was that she hadn't been kicked.

There was a soft rapping at the closed door. "Can we come in, Ms. DiNunzio?" asked Captain Walsh, and Mary felt panicky.

"In a minute," she answered, and Paige buttoned her shirt hastily.

Captain Walsh entered with Detective Donovan, and Kovich followed on their heels, holding a Polaroid camera. After him came a woman and he seemed excited as he introduced her to Mary and Paige. "This is Detective Andersson and she'll take photos of the bruises," he said, but Mary thought fast.

"We'll take the photos after we talk with her boyfriend. He can substantiate everything she says."

"What? What about the bruises?" Kovich asked, his shoulders slumping visibly, as Captain Walsh scowled.

"Are there bruises or not, Ms. DiNunzio?"

"No," Mary admitted, and she ignored the knowing look that spread over Donovan's face. "But maybe they haven't appeared yet, or something. The boyfriend was there, I know it. When we find him, he can corroborate what she says."

"I doubt it." Donovan folded his arms. "Paige is obviously trying to protect her father. She's lost one parent and she doesn't want to lose the other." He looked at Paige with sympathy. "I'm very sorry for your losses, Paige. But you are the victim of this crime, the same as your mother. Your father has to answer for her murder, not you."

"I'll handle this, Donovan," Walsh said. He returned to his chair and sat down heavily, looking up at all of them. "Tell you what, Ms. DiNunzio. You take Ms. Newlin out of here immediately and I won't press charges against her for filing a false police report and attempting to obstruct justice. Nor will I mention to the bar association that you're playing fast and loose with the truth. And mark my words, if either of you go to the press with this, I'll have *her* head." Walsh pointed at Paige. "*Capisce?*"

"Captain, as soon as we find the boyfriend, we'll come back." Mary couldn't give up. "Then he can tell you exactly what happened."

"I know where the boyfriend is, and he can't help you."

"What? Where?" Mary asked, in surprise.

"He's in federal custody," Captain Walsh answered, and Paige gasped.

43

Jack left prison in a cab, feeling strange in the gray sweat-shirt and jeans they'd issued him for departure. His face hurt from the beating he'd gotten and his eye was tender when he squinted against the sun, but his thoughts were filled with Paige. Now that he was free, he would protect her from Trevor and find out what the hell had happened.

The cab sped down the elevated strip of I-95, above abandoned rowhouses and graffitied warehouses, and he ignored the driver's cold eye in the rearview mirror. The driver had to know who Jack was, because he picked him up at the prison. Jack took his hostility in stride. He understood that people outside the prison wouldn't be quite so eager to shake his hand. Life as a confessed murderer wouldn't be easy, nor should it be.

The cab reached the city in an hour, and Jack directed the driver to his town house. He didn't know why but he was drawn to it. He didn't open the car door when the cab paused at the curb, as if he had just left a funeral service and was driving past the home of the deceased. It was apropos. Jack felt dead in a way; at least that part of his life was dead. Honor was dead, and he hadn't even gone to her memorial service. Ashamed of himself, he bent his head in a moment of silence.

The cab engine thrummed in the background as he thought about her. He mourned her, but he didn't mourn the life they had. He could only mourn the life they pretended they had, but there was no point to that. He looked out the cab window at the house, its front door crisscrossed with yellow crime-scene tape. He didn't have to be told he couldn't go inside, much less live there anymore. Everything he owned was there, but he owned none of it anymore. He had never wanted any of it in the first place. Sun bathed the colonial house in a million-dollar glow and though it shone like a sales brochure, Jack didn't want to see it ever again.

He asked the driver to take him to the hotel. He'd chosen a medium-priced one frequented by tourists because he knew no press would be there. The cabbie steered in its direction without responding and they arrived in fifteen minutes. He left the cab, entered the hotel, and pushed his American Express card across the wood counter, but again, the young woman at the reception desk didn't have to read Jack's credit card to know who he was. The newspapers stacked next to her bore a blowup of his photo, his face divided by the fold, his nose repeated twenty-five times. The young woman couldn't help but look horrified at the wounds on his face, not yet captured in news photos. He ignored it; he had to get going. Paige.

He quickly accepted his room key and card, hurried to the elevator, and punched the button, experiencing the same odd sensation his house had evoked. He felt disconnected from everything, as if he'd been unplugged from his own life. His home, his family. Mary. He tried to forget seeing her in court at his preliminary hearing. She had been there for him, to remind him to tell the truth, but there was no way he could ever do that, death penalty or no. He tried not to think about it.

Jack rode up in the elevator, spacious compared with ad seg. How could it be that in the same day he could be confined to solitary and later check into a tourist hotel? How could he so easily exchange prison blues for a sweatshirt? The disconnect Jack experienced extended even to himself, as if his body had become a hanger and he could change identities as easily as clothes. Father. Lawyer. Murderer. The elevator doors slid open and he stepped out.

He didn't know who he was any longer, but it was high time he found out.

Jack knocked at the door of the squat brick rowhouse, but there was no answer. It was cold outside but he felt warm enough in the football jacket he'd bought in the hotel gift shop. I LOVE PHILADELPHIA, it said across the chest. Still he didn't think his absurd jacket was the reason a little black boy stood on the sidewalk, staring at him. His silent gaze told Jack that few white people came to this section of the city.

Jack knocked again, then checked the address: 639 Beck Street. It was Brinkley's house; the address had been in the phone book. He had called and it had been Brinkley's voice on the machine, but he hadn't left a message. He didn't want to leave any evidence suggesting that he wasn't the killer.

He knocked again. He had to talk to Brinkley, face-to-face. It was a risk but he would take it if Paige were in danger. He'd been calling her but there had been no answer. He'd left a message with the name of his hotel and had told her to call there as soon as possible. He was worried about where she could be and who she was with. He hoped it wasn't Trevor.

Jack pounded hard on the door as the little boy wandered up to him. About seven years old, he wore a black knit cap pulled low over his eyes and his hands were shoved into a hand-me-down jacket. "He ain't home," the boy said. "I seen him go."

"Oh, thanks."

"He a cop."

"I know." Jack turned from the door, scanned the block, and walked back down the stoop. "I think I'll wait for him. Mind if I stay?"

"'S all right with me." The boy shrugged, staring frankly at Jack's battered face. "You get in a tussle, mister?"

"In a way." Jack smiled, then eased onto his haunches to strike up a conversation with the only person in Philadelphia who hadn't read today's newspaper.

44

I t's you!" Mary said, amazed. She took one look at the blonde with the nose job and recognized her instantly. "You're the woman who was at the train station with Trevor."

"Do I know you?" The blonde looked politely puzzled as she greeted them at the glass door of the bustling, modern offices of the FBI in the federal courthouse downtown. "I'm Special Agent Reppetto," she said, extending a hand, which Mary shook.

"*Special Agent?*" Mary couldn't help repeating. The woman looked more professional wearing a shiny FBI badge on the pocket of her blue blazer. Or maybe it was because her tongue wasn't buried in Trevor's mouth. "No, you don't know me. I saw you meet Trevor at the train station. I didn't know you were an FBI agent."

"You're not supposed to. I was undercover." Agent Reppetto grinned, apparently guiltless about her public make-out session, and Mary wondered if she were some new breed of Italian. "We've had our eye on Olanski a long time. He moves a significant amount of drugs out of New York and is distributing to a network of dealers here. Mostly he sells to dealers in private school. He sold to the wrong kid a few months ago, the son of a United States Attorney."

"Not a smart move. What will happen to him?"

"We'll charge him, but he'll make bail. We're gonna try our best to put him out of business, keep him away from other kids. It's mandatory sentencing and we'll prosecute him as an adult."

Paige groaned softly. "Does that mean he'll go to jail?"

Agent Reppetto nodded. "I can't discuss that with you. In any event, he should be out on bail tonight."

"I see," Mary said, but noticed that Paige's face fell. The teenager was going through so much and she was probably remembering Trevor's cheating on her. The least Mary could do was to clear up the confusion, however awkwardly. "Agent Reppetto, did you have some sort of affair with Trevor, to bust him?"

"No, I'm not a spy," Reppetto answered, with a laugh. "He wanted to make a buy in New York, then take me to Petrossian to celebrate. We never got to the caviar. I just wanted to go to the buy." She clapped her hands together. "Now, we've briefed the interrogating agent on your facts. Shall we go watch the interview?"

Ten minutes later, Mary and Paige gathered at one side of the two-way mirror into the interview room, and Detectives Kovich and Donovan stood on the other side. Mary had cautioned Paige not to say anything in their earshot as the FBI agents conducted the questioning. The agents had arrested Trevor on the "buy-and-bust," as they called it, but had been willing to cooperate with the Philadelphia police on investigating the Newlin murder. Trevor had agreed to talk with them, hoping for leniency. He slumped at the table in his brown leather jacket and white shirt, sullen as he fiddled with a can of Mountain Dew.

"I told you, I don't know anything about it," Trevor said, and the FBI agent sitting across from him nodded. The agent was a middle-aged man with dark hair, who looked fit in his dark suit. In front of him sat a can of diet Coke.

"You don't know anything about the Newlin murder?"

"No." Next to Trevor sat a white-haired man in a three-piece suit, whom Mary pegged instantly as his lawyer. She couldn't tell an undercover agent, but she could smell a lawyer through glass. The lawyer stayed quiet during the interrogation, taking occasional notes.

"Were you at the Newlin house that night?"

"No."

"Have you ever been in the Newlin house?"

"A coupla times."

"Why?"

"To meet the 'rents."

"Where were you the night Honor Newlin was killed?"

Trevor paused. "What night was that again?"

"Monday."

"I was home studying. I had a French final the next day, and you can check it."

"So you weren't there, with the daughter, Paige Newlin."

"No."

"Do you know if the daughter was at her parents' house that night?"

"She wasn't. She was at home. She gets migraines and shit."

"So you weren't there that night, but you were dating the daughter."

"Yes."

"The daughter is pregnant by you."

"So she says," Trevor said, and at the window Paige winced. Mary gave her a warning nudge.

The agent sipped his soda. "What do you know about the Newlin murder?"

"Nothing but what I read in the paper. That the father killed her."

"Did you give Paige any drugs that night?"

"No, I was home studying that night."

"Did you ever give Paige drugs?"

"Sometimes. It got her goin'," Trevor said, and it sounded so ugly that this time Mary winced.

"Did you help her calm down after the murder?"

"No."

"Didn't give her any drugs to calm down?"

"No."

"Did you tell her to tell the cops that you weren't together that night?"

"No."

"Did Paige kill her mother?"

"I don't know. Her father did, as far as I know."

"Did you?"

"Objection," said the lawyer, but Mary had heard all she had to. She took Paige's arm and led her away. When she left, Detective Donovan was smiling.

But Kovich wasn't.

It was a gloomy cab ride back to the office, with Mary kicking herself for not asking about Paige's bruises before they'd gone to Walsh. She'd been too eager to get Paige to the police and now Trevor was lying, doing his best not to implicate himself. She looked out the window at the chilly city, speeding by. She felt sick at heart. She had screwed up her only chance to help Jack. How could she have been so dumb?

Paige shifted in the seat next to her, looking out her window on the other side, and Mary could only guess how she must be feeling. Her father, in jail because of her, and her lover, betraying them both. Her perfect profile faced the city, but her eyes remained remarkably dry. And this on the day she had buried her mother. Mary couldn't fathom it. She reached over and patted Paige's hand, resting loosely on her coat. "I'm sorry I goofed up, with Captain Walsh."

Paige smiled sadly. "Don't worry about it. It was my fault, too, and I'm sorry."

"We're gonna figure this thing out, you and me. We have to."

"I know we are," Paige said, and Mary heard a new determination strengthen her tone.

"How are you feeling, Paige? I mean, I'm surprised you're not a mess after what Trevor just said."

"Not at all." Paige shook her head. "Trevor lied to save his own ass. I think I'm finally seeing him for what he really is."

"I was wrong about him cheating on you, and I'm sorry."

Paige waved her off. "You apologize too much, you know that?"

"Do I? Let's make a deal. I'll apologize less, and you say 'thank you' more. Fair enough?"

"Fair enough." Paige smiled. "And Trevor did cheat on me. He left me and went to New York with another woman. He didn't know she was with the FBI. That's cheating, isn't it?"

"Technically it's attempted cheating, but I won't bore you with the legalities."

Paige smiled. "So it's over with him. I want nothing to do with him."

"Good for you." Mary wondered what it meant for the baby, but decided this wasn't the time or place. Paige had enough to think about. The girl was growing up in only a few days, and Mary wasn't completely surprised.

Adulthood never had anything to do with age anyway.

45

Mary sat behind the conference room table like a judge while Paige stood up and told what had happened the night her mother was killed, and by the time she was finished Mary had almost succeeded in visualizing the scene. "Tell it again," she said anyway. "I want to see if there's anything inconsistent, telling to telling."

"Mary, I'm not making this up. It's the truth, I swear it."

"I believe you, but something's wrong. You have no bruises on you and you should, if what you're saying is true. Start over. You and Trevor go to your parents' house . . . "

Paige sighed without further complaint. "My mother started to fight with me, right off. Told me I looked fat and I shouldn't be eating. She started in on the Bonner shoot. How I looked like I was gaining. How I had to watch what I ate to get over."

"Get over?"

"You know, make it," Paige answered, and Mary flashed on the sweating kids under the hot lights, all hopeful but none with The Face. "I felt like who was she to tell me, I'm not a child, and now I was having a child. I'm going to be a mother, a way better mother than she ever was. So I said, 'I'm pregnant, that's why I'm so hungry,' and she hit me. I fell off the chair onto the floor."

"Then what happened?"

"I got up from the floor and I started to cry. Then she grabbed me and threw me down and started kicking me in my stomach. At least I thought she did." Paige paused, her forehead a knot of confusion. "I remember that happening. I swear, I remember she was trying to kick the baby out of me. She said so."

Mary shook her head, confounded. It rang completely true, especially the way Paige recounted it, but it couldn't have been. "What was Trevor doing?"

"He was trying to pull her off of me, I think. I don't really know."

"But he was in there, fighting?"

"Yes, I think. She was yelling, 'You kill it or I'll kill it!' I hurt, so much, and I rolled away, trying to protect the baby from her. But she kept coming at me, kicking." Paige looked like she wanted to cry but didn't. "I was so scared. Trevor said I was just crying and rolling on the ground."

Mary's ears pricked up. "Last time you didn't say, 'Trevor said.'"

"What?"

"Is it Trevor said, or you remember?"

"I remember. I remembered. Later. I mean, I remember crouching and rolling, trying to keep her away from the baby."

Mary frowned. "Do you remember really, or did he tell you? And when did he tell you?"

"I do remember, but we discussed it later, over and over. I couldn't get it out of my mind. I needed to talk about it. We talked after it happened, a lot. Until you came over. I was so upset, and he calmed me down."

"By talking about what happened?"

"Partly." Paige brushed a strand of hair from her troubled brow. "I think I remember. I needed to talk about it. Parts of what happened I couldn't remember. It happened so fast and I was so high. So crazy."

"What do you mean you couldn't remember parts of what happened?" Mary straightened, intrigued. "You didn't tell me that before."

"I didn't?" Paige's hand fluttered to her forehead. "Let me think. There were things I wasn't sure about, I think. Details. It was just so awful, the whole scene."

"You know it was awful or Trevor told you that?"

"I *know* that. I *remember*. It happened. Didn't it?" Paige's eyes flickered with bewilderment, and Mary dug in.

"You were high."

"Not so high that I don't know what happened to me."

"But think about it." Mary stood up, wondering aloud. "You go to dinner, you take a drug you never took before, and it makes you feel crazy. You and Trevor are together later and you go over what happened when you were high. How do you know what happened and what didn't?"

"I know because I remember."

"But how can you be sure you remember correctly? Memory isn't always reliable. It's like recovered memory. Those cases with the kids at nursery schools. They question the kids so much they forget what they remember and what they were told. The kids want to please the questioner. They remember what they're told to remember." Mary leaned forward. "Consider that there are drugs in this scenario. You were on drugs at the time of the murder and you told me that Trevor gave you a drug to calm you down after, right?"

"Yes. Special K. Ketamine, like a tranquilizer."

Mary thought about it. "How do you know it was Special K?"

"It looked like it. A pile of white powder."

Mary had never taken a drug in her life, except for Midol. "But aren't lots of drugs white powder?

"It made me feel relaxed, like K does."

"I would think lots of drugs do that, too. Maybe it wasn't Ketamine, Paige. Maybe it was some other kind of drug, to make you more suggestible."

"What?" Paige cocked her head, her hair falling to one skinny shoulder.

"Trevor gives you the crystal, or what he says is crystal, before you go over to your parents' house. By the way, why did you take it, if you had never taken it before? You knew you were going to an important dinner."

"I knew it would be hard. I didn't think I could go through with it straight." Paige flushed with regret. "I know it was stupid, but Trevor said the crystal would make me stronger."

"So he gives you the crystal, and you feel strong. Your memory is spotty. You feel out of control. You come home and he gives you another drug, then he tells you what happened. You said you two went over and over it." Mary's excitement grew. "What if you don't really remember what happened, you just remember what he tells you? In time it becomes the truth, but it's only in your mind."

Paige looked dumbfounded. "Is that possible?"

"Of course, given what you're telling me."

"So what really happened, with my mother?"

"Anything could have happened, but only one thing is the most likely. Trevor killed your mother and made you think you did it."

"What?" Paige's eyes widened. "*Trevor* killed my mother?"

"It makes sense, doesn't it? We have only your word that he didn't. No one else was there."

"I remember picking up the knife."

"But do you remember stabbing her, actually stabbing her?"

"I don't know." Paige raked her hair with her fingers, a gesture of Jack's. "I don't remember. I don't know what I remember."

"You heard what Walsh said. It takes force to kill somebody that way. Trevor is a big, strong guy. You'd have to remember stabbing your mother, actually bringing a knife down, five times. Do you? What were her reactions and yours? Did she fight you? Rip your clothes? How did you fight her back? Do you remember it?"

"I think—"

"Don't answer so fast." Mary held up a palm. "Concentrate. Think about it, every detail. Do you really remember? Can you tell it to me?"

Paige's eyes fluttered closed, then, after a moment, open. "I can't. I really don't remember what happened between when I grabbed the knife and when I found it in my hand, later, all bloody. I thought I had gone into like a trance or something." Paige shook her head. "But I would know if Trevor did it, wouldn't I? I mean, I would have seen him do it."

"But who knows what you perceived, under the influence of whatever drug he gave you? And who knows what you remember or what you saw?"

Paige blinked. "But why? Why would he do it?"

"You tell me." Mary's thoughts raced ahead. "He had to know your mother had money, didn't he?"

"Yes, and he knew I'd inherit it. Even as pissed as she got at me, she'd never disown me." Paige's blue eyes lost their focus as her thoughts slipped elsewhere. "He used to ask me about it, and I told him what I knew about my trust fund and all, and about the Foundation. His parents have money, but not that much."

"And you said he wanted to marry you."

"He talked about it all the time. He really wanted us to get engaged, but I wanted to go slower. I wasn't sure. I had just moved out and all. So I said we should wait."

"What did he say?"

Paige's face darkened. "Then we got pregnant." Her eyes glittered with a revelation, and Mary didn't have to ask what it was.

"You think he got you pregnant, on purpose."

"I always made him use the condom, for safe sex. I knew he got around before we started dating. The time we got pregnant, he said the condom broke."

"My God." Mary leaned back in her chair, recoiling from the knowledge. "Trevor's been playing you all along. He gave you drugs before you went over knowing they'd screw up your perceptions, maybe even put you out of it. I don't know enough about drugs, but I bet they have 'em. You may have heard your mother yelling, but it was him she was kicking. He killed your mother, then he told you that you did it."

"He planned on my father confessing?"

"I doubt it. Trevor couldn't have known your father would take the rap, but he took advantage of the opportunity. Either way, he gets your money. And if he's the killer, he's got the bruises to prove it. Did you notice any bruises on him later?"

"No, but I wasn't looking. How can we find out? Can we get the police to examine him, like with me?"

"No. You were volunteered, and I doubt very much he'll chirp right up. The cops can examine Trevor if he's under investigation for the crime, but he's not, so far." Mary kicked herself again. "I should have thought of it at the FBI, when they were questioning him. I'm sorry."

"Don't say that, remember?" Paige smiled. "You didn't suspect him then."

"I should have."

"He would have explained the bruises another way, Mary. He's a liar."

Suddenly the conference room door opened, and Judy walked in carrying a FedEx package. She was a welcome sight, even in a black corduroy jumper, white turtleneck, and red clogs. "News update, Mare," she said. "I ordered you both lo mein for dinner, I told our boss you're too sick to come to work, and most important, I brought you a present."

"What a woman."

"I'm more nurturing now that I have a dog." Judy handed over the FedEx package, and Mary opened it. Out slid a piece of white paper with a Polaroid paper clipped to it.

"Jesus, Mary, and Joseph," Mary said, amazed. CRIMINALISTICS LABORATORY REPORT, Philadelphia Police Department, read the top. She might have gotten it later, in discovery, but somebody wasn't making her wait. Brinkley. He was trying to help her, even if he wasn't returning her calls. She scanned the report, technical but understandable. "This says the DNA on something, Item B, was from a white male."

"Yowsa!" Judy squinted at the Polaroid. "Could this be Item B?"

Mary looked. It was a photo of an earring back against the field of an Oriental rug. What was this about? Where had she seen that rug? "Paige, isn't that the rug at your parents' house?"

Paige stood up and took the photo from Mary's outstretched hand. "That's our dining room rug."

"I thought so." It was where Honor Newlin had been killed. Mary scrutinized the photo. "If Brinkley sent this to us, it means it's a police photo. They take photos of the evidence at the crime scene. This must be an earring back they found there. And the lab report is saying it's from a male."

Paige pointed at the photo. "I know! I bet this is Trevor's. He didn't have his earring on later."

"What do you mean, later?" Mary asked.

"Later that night, after my mother was killed. I'd given him a new earring earlier that day, for a present. It was a gold cross with a post back. But when we got back to my place, it wasn't in his ear anymore. Somebody, I guess the police, must have found this back part."

Mary thought about it. "Brinkley found it in the dining room."

"That must be right," Paige said eagerly. "Trevor was freaked that he lost it. I thought he was upset because it was eighteen carat, but he must have been worried the police would find it at my parents' house."

Mary nodded grimly. "Maybe he lost it fighting with your mother, when he killed her."

"Does this prove anything?"

"The earring back? No. It's a given Trevor has been at your parents' house. He said so to the FBI, remember? That's probably why they asked. If he were confronted with it, he could say he dropped it some other time."

"No, he couldn't. He has been there before, but he never had that earring before. I gave it to him that day."

"But they didn't find the earring, they found the back of it. The earring we could identify, but the backs are all alike. It could be an earring back Trevor lost another time, even if it is his DNA on it. It doesn't prove anything except that there are good cops in the world."

Judy touched Mary's arm. "Cheer up. You'll think of something else."

"I will?" Mary said, but to her surprise, she already had.

46

Davis was at the office working on his laptop, outlining the Newlin case. He'd already gotten two calls from that scum-sucker Roberts, but hadn't returned them yet. Let him waste his own time. Roberts had yet to defend a murder case in an actual courtroom. He'd be even easier than DiNunzio. The phone rang and Davis picked up.

"Go away," Davis said, but it was the Chief. "What? They went to Walsh? Why didn't he call me, Chief? Doesn't he know we're on the same team? Left hand, meet the right hand." Davis laughed it off, but the news caught him by surprise. Newlin's daughter, trying to confess to Walsh. This was one wacky family. Newlin must have figured she'd do something like this. That's why he wanted to notify her himself. He wanted to play her, too.

"No bruises? I like that in a woman. Did they take Polaroids anyway?"

Davis reached for his Gatorade, almost buried in documents from Newlin's office. The wife's will was on top because he'd been studying it when the phone rang. Under the will, documents lay thick as the earth's strata; financials from Newlin's firm and partnership compensation, and the other documents they had seized. It was late but Davis would read through them before he went for a run.

"What? Then where? To the feds?" Davis's mood darkened. "Those idiots! They got a tag on the boyfriend. You think they could let me in on it? They're worse than the cops, Chief! Fuck no! I don't have time to call 'em and suck up!"

Davis didn't like his plans interrupted. On his computer screen was a list of witnesses they'd need to subpoena from the firm; Whittier, Field, Videon. He'd planned to have Whittier explain the compensation structure, then use Videon to take them through the prenup and his conversation with Honor Newlin. Davis hated to use the Necessary Evil, but he'd have to. If Davis spent the day preparing him, maybe he wouldn't mouth off on the stand.

"Of course the boyfriend said she didn't do it. She *didn't* do it! The *father* did, like I told you. Now let me work. Keep this up and I'll ask for a raise!" Davis said, and hung up.

Maybe it was time for that run.

Jack stood in Detective Brinkley's galley kitchen, his hand resting lightly on a chair of light wood at a round table. A fake Tiffany lamp over the table was the only light in the room and it cast long shadows on Brinkley's already long face. The kitchen was attached to the living room and, like it, was spare and uncluttered, with mismatched furniture. A black IKEA entertainment center dominated the area, with only a small TV above a stereo with tall, thin speakers and shelves of CDs. Jack was too intent to focus on decor for long. He had a plan for getting the information he needed about Trevor. "I have a beef with you, Detective," he said.

"Nice face." Brinkley was crossing to the refrigerator. "You run into a truck?"

Jack ignored it. "You've been saying things in the press, things that are hurting my family. The paper says you think my daughter and her boyfriend were involved in the murder. You have it all wrong. I did it."

"That why you came here? To tell me what a bad guy you

are?" Brinkley retrieved two bottles of Michelob from the refrigerator and two jelly glasses from a wood cabinet above the sink, then set everything on the table with a clatter. "Have a seat," he said, sitting down and eyeing Jack as critically as he had at their Roundhouse interview.

Jack remained standing. "The press is all over my daughter because of you. She can't go anywhere. I came here to tell you that you're ruining my kid's life. You keep this up, I'll file suit against you and the police. You don't have any evidence for what you're saying. It's not true, none of it."

"You know, you are a bad guy, Newlin. Even though you didn't kill your wife, you're a bad guy." Brinkley uncapped the beer with a church key that was already on the table. "You filed a false confession. You played my department for fools. You took public resources for your own personal use. Got everybody running in the wrong direction. And got me suspended, for doing my job."

"You didn't answer my question. You have any evidence for what you're saying?" Jack demanded. He knew what Brinkley was saying was true, but he couldn't admit it. The detective could report him to get his job back.

"You took the rap for your kid and her boyfriend, but that wasn't right. It was easy but it wasn't right. The right thing woulda been to let these kids answer for what they did." Brinkley took a sip of one of the Michelobs and slid the other one toward Newlin. "And you're a bad liar, pal. I'm thinkin' you're just about the worst liar I've ever seen, and I've seen some real morons. I picked up a guy, long time ago. He's standing on the street, talkin' to his buddies, holding a TV." Brinkley spread his arms wide, the brown bottle in one hand. "Like this big. I mean, holding the friggin' TV, right on the street. So me and my old partner, we're beat cops, we come walkin' around the corner just by chance, the worst luck of this guy's life." Brinkley started to laugh. "And we say, 'Hey, what are you doin' with that TV?' And the dude says, 'What TV?' I mean, '*What TV?*'" Brinkley burst into laughter.

Standing there, Jack didn't know what to do. He was trying to talk tough, but the detective was in hysterics. He felt like a complete idiot in his I LOVE PHILADELPHIA jacket, with a face that a truck hit, and he knew that Brinkley was right. Jack wasn't a good liar; he'd worried about that from the beginning. And he was so tired, and so worried, and so sick at heart, that he could do only one thing. *What TV?* He started to laugh. He laughed so hard that he had to sit down behind his untouched beer and glass. And when he finally stopped and wiped his eyes, Brinkley was wiping his, too, with a napkin from a stack on the table.

"Well, Newlin," the detective said, still smiling. "Let's get down to it. You got your tit in a wringer and you came to me for help. You're worried I'm gonna turn you in, but I won't. Anything we say is off the record."

"How do I know that?"

"You have my word."

Jack considered it. If he told the truth, Paige was on the hook for murder. If he didn't, she could be killed by Trevor. Momentarily stalled, he reached for his beer and took a swig.

"Let me make this easy, as my partner would say. We'll skip over how we got here and go straight to what happens next. I agree with you, your daughter is in deep shit. She's at least an accessory to murder, but I think the boyfriend is the doer."

Jack's gut tightened at hearing his suspicion confirmed. Trevor had killed Honor, not Paige. All this time. "If that's true, then Paige is in danger, from Trevor."

"Not yet. He's been in custody all day, on a drug charge."

"*Drug charge?*" Jack said, astounded. Paige's boyfriend? How had this happened? Had he been blind?

"The feds should be letting him go about now." Brinkley checked his watch. "Where's your daughter?"

"I don't know." Jack stood up in alarm. "I called but she's not home."

"She was at the FBI today with the lawyer, DiNunzio," Brinkley said, rising.

"Paige, at the FBI with Mary? That's not possible. How do you know that?"

"Friends in high places."

"Oh, no." Jack pieced it together in a flash. Paige must have decided to tell the truth, gone to Mary, and then to the police and the FBI. "We've got to get going," he said, but Brinkley was already reaching for his coat.

47

Cold air blasted Mary and Paige the moment they pushed through the revolving door of the office building and hit Locust Street. Mary felt her nose turn instantly red and her cheeks chap on impact. She finger combed her hair into place, knowing it was useless. She shouldn't have been worrying about how she looked anyway. Here she was, going to visit a client. Well, not a client anymore. Did that make it okay to have a crush on him? "Let's get a cab," she said anyway. "It's too cold to walk."

"The hotel is only ten blocks or so. Dad left the name of it on my machine." Paige flipped up the collar of her black jacket and squinted against the harsh wind. "We can walk."

"Of course we can, but we don't have to." Mary squinted up and down the street but there were no cabs. The street was dark, and traffic heading toward Broad Street was sparse. A man walked by in a wool topcoat and a knit cap, his muffler flying at his neck. At this time of night he'd be heading toward Suburban Station. Not a cab in sight. "Why are there more lawyers than cabs in the world? Cabs are more useful and often smell better."

"Come on, Mary," Paige said, buttoning a latch at the top of her coat. "Walking is good exercise."

"All right." Mary turned reluctantly toward Market and the hotel. "I'm not the type who cares if my hair looks like shit."

"Me neither." Paige fell into step beside Mary. "I've wasted too much time worrying about my hair. And my weight. And my eyes. And my hips."

Mary caught a faceful of city wind that would drive soot into her contacts and redden her eyes, for that Cujo look. "I never worry about what I look like."

"Kind of weird to think you've spent your whole life on all the wrong things. With the wrong people."

"You're only sixteen." Mary put her head down against the wind. If this kept up, she'd have bugs on her teeth. "Your whole life hasn't started yet."

"And I've screwed it up already," Paige said, her tone quiet, and Mary looked over, since it sounded strangely like something she would say. Paige's head was down, and her hair blew back in a silky sheet of red, as if she were standing in front of a photographer's fan. But she didn't look like a model anymore, with her hand carried protectively in front of her tummy. Behind her was a dark, closed-up store, and Paige seemed so alone that Mary took her arm impulsively.

"You know, I don't agree with you."

"No?" Paige didn't remove her arm.

"Not in the least." Mary kept walking with Paige's arm in hers, enjoying the chumminess of it. She missed working with Judy on this case, but this was almost as good, and for once, Mary was the smart one. "I think you have made a rather large mistake and are trying like hell to correct it. You walked into a police station today and begged them to arrest you for a murder that it turns out you didn't commit. That takes guts."

"Like father, like daughter," Paige said, and Mary laughed.

"You think it's genetic? You Newlins run around confessing to major felonies? Have excessive guilt complexes?" Mary's teeth chattered against the cold, and a crumpled newspaper blew down the sidewalk like urban tumbleweed. Another man hurried by on the street, his tartan scarf wrapped up to his nose. The cold and wind seemed suddenly hostile to Mary. She decided she didn't like the city in winter after all, and squeezed Paige's arm protectively. "You sure you're not Catholic?"

Paige smiled. "Can I ask you a question? It's kind of personal."

"That's the only kind I answer. The rest is all small talk, and who cares about that?"

"It's about abortion."

"Okay, I'm all ears." So much for feeling smart. Mary had her own views, but it was so personal. The wind blew harder on the other side of the street, making it rough going, or maybe it was the conversation. They reached the corner and crossed against the traffic light, since there were no cars. "Fire away."

"Well, you know I'm pregnant. What do you think I should do?" Paige looked over just as a gust of cold air hit them, and Mary couldn't take the cold anymore. She turned reflexively to put her back to the wind, which was when she saw him. A tall figure in a black ski mask and parka stood halfway down the block, aiming a gun at them.

"Get down!" Mary screamed. She didn't have time to think, only to react. She threw an arm around Paige, who was turning to her in confusion, and yanked her down to the sidewalk just as a gunshot rang out. Mary's chest slammed into the sidewalk and the heel of her palm skidded against the cold concrete. The explosive *crak* reverberated down the street, and she covered Paige's head with her arm.

"Mary!" Paige shouted in panic. "What's happening?"

"Stay down!" Mary raised her head to look back. Another shot sounded, echoing with a sickening report, and flame spit from the gun. Mary ducked reflexively. She had no idea where the bullets flew. Fear gripped her. She couldn't think. It was so sudden. The figure began to run toward them. There was no one else on the street. He would kill them. They couldn't stay here.

"Get up! Run!" Mary shouted and scrambled to her feet, yanking Paige up by her arm. "Help!" she kept screaming, and so did Paige, terrified, but there was no one around. They tore down the block, their coats flying.

Mary's chest heaved with effort. Her pumps slipped on the frigid sidewalk. Ahead lay the lights of the city center. She looked frantically around for escape routes. There were none. It was a straight line and they couldn't outrun a bullet. He'd hit them for sure.

She bolted down the street with Paige. Ahead lay an alley on the right. It had to go through to the street. Most of them did.

Mary glanced over her shoulder. The figure was running full tilt, holding his gun stiff at his side. He covered ground fast, his stride long. He was big and strong. His eyes were black holes. Who was it? Trevor, had to be. She should have known. Paige had blown his cover and now he was after her. Them both.

Mary streaked ahead with Paige running beside her. Trevor was gaining on them, a half a block away. The alley was steps ahead.

"Faster!" she screamed to Paige, who was lagging. They were at the alley. "Go!" she shouted. She grabbed Paige's sleeve and shoved her into it. Another *crak* sounded, closer this time, and she almost jumped out of her skin. She prayed the alley was the right move. It was too dark to see if it had an end. Had she steered them wrong?

It was dark inside and Dumpsters overflowed on either side. They ran through trash and frozen garbage. Mary didn't hear footsteps or gunshots behind her. Were they safe? She could see lights at the end of the alley. People!

"Help!" she screamed and so did Paige. The people at the end of the alley looked up, two young men in white uniforms. They were smoking outside the screen door of a restaurant kitchen. Golden light shone through the screen and the aroma of roasting lamb wafted into the night. Mary ran closer and heard voices inside. They were safe! Trevor couldn't shoot them in front of witnesses. She ran flat out, and even Paige put on the afterburners.

"Let us in!" Mary shouted to the uniformed men, but they turned and ran off down the other end of the alley. In the City of Brotherly Love, you're on your own. She ran straight for the door with Paige, threw open the screen, and darted inside, fumbling for the main door and slamming it closed behind them.

"*Quoi?*" said a startled sous-chef, from behind a glistening stainless steel counter, but Mary was bolting the door locked.

"Call nine-one-one!" she called out, but Paige had snatched her cell phone from her handbag and was flipping it open.

Mary sagged against the door, her chest heaving. Relief flooded over her so powerfully it brought tears to her eyes. She was never so happy to see such a scummy metal door. Trevor couldn't shoot through it even if he tried. The kitchen was warm and safe, filled with pungent smells and snotty cooks. She was alive. Paige was alive.

Mary didn't know how she had picked the right alley, but she whispered a silent thanks to anybody who was listening.

48

Jack and Brinkley rushed into the lobby of the office building, and Jack knew from the security guard's terrified
expression that she recognized him. A young woman, she
seemed to age on the spot.

"I know you two," she said. She backed away, her hand hovering at the gun holstered to her hip. "You're that lawyer who
killed his wife." Her frightened eyes shifted to Brinkley. "And
you're that cop who pushed that guard around. I read about
you in the newspaper. Either of you give me any trouble, I'll
shoot you down."

"Don't worry," Jack said, grabbing the edge of the desk.
"We won't hurt you. We won't hurt anyone. We need to see
Mary DiNunzio."

"She's not here." The guard looked nervously from Jack to
Brinkley and back again. "She's gone."

"When?"

"None of your business."

"She may be in danger. Tell me when she left."

The guard got more nervous. "About ten minutes ago. What
kind of danger?"

Brinkley was already backing up to go. "Was she alone? Or
was she with a young girl?"

"A girl. They left together."

"You know where they went?" Jack asked, heading out with Brinkley.

"No, and if I did, I wouldn't tell either of you. That's for damn sure."

49

It wasn't long before three squad cars arrived at the restaurant kitchen and Mary gave the cops a brief statement, then insisted on Paige and her being taken down to the Roundhouse. Mary wanted to see Captain Walsh and bring the whole case to light. En route she called Jack on Paige's cell phone, at the hotel number he'd left on Paige's answering machine. She couldn't reach him but left a message telling him to meet them at Captain Walsh's office. This time she didn't care how she looked. Okay, maybe she did.

She pressed the END button, stumped. She wasn't sure she should go to Walsh without Jack, but they were in the back of the squad car. She couldn't wait any longer anyway. Trevor was trying to kill her and Paige. She let the cruiser whisk them to the Roundhouse, where she was ushered in to see Captain Walsh for the second time that day. He greeted her with "long time, no see," and their meeting went downhill from there. She'd told him the whole story, from Paige's drugged memories to Trevor shooting at them, but he wasn't having any.

"Look," Captain Walsh said, from behind his bare desk. He looked more exasperated than he had earlier that day, if that were possible. "We'll do for you what we'd do for anybody, Ms. DiNunzio. Somebody chases you down the street with a gun, that's attempted murder, and we're on it."

"Not somebody. It was Trevor."

"You're not listening." Captain Walsh looked at Mary, his dark eyes frank and concerned. "We'll investigate, question witnesses, canvass the neighborhood, and see if anybody saw anything. We'll tell you as soon as we know anything about the shooter."

"But it was Trevor. It had to be."

"How the hell do you know? The shooter was wearing a ski mask, you said."

"Who else would it be? It's not like he tried to rob us. It was target practice, for God's sake. Right out in the open."

"Like I said, we're on it, but that's no proof it was Olanski. You know how many knuckleheads run around this city with guns? Did you see the last amnesty day? They turned in enough weapons to arm a small country."

"But he was shooting at us. It was directed, not random."

"We get that once a month. Guy takes a shot for no reason, drunk or high. In summer, it's the fish and gun club. Last week we had a guy, you must've read about it, takin' shots at people he thinks are Hispanic. We got him on ethnic intimidation."

"This wasn't a hate crime, take my word," Mary said angrily, and the captain's eyes hardened.

"I took your word once already, Ms. DiNunzio, when you told me Paige here killed her mother. But she didn't. Now you're tellin' me the boyfriend did it and she just *thought* she did it." Walsh hunched over the desk, his shoulders powerful beneath his shirt, which had lost its starch. "How the hell do you expect me to believe you? You can't tell a straight story one minute to the next. You think this is some kind of game?"

Mary took it on the chin. "Look, I was wrong, I'm sorry. I thought Paige knew the truth, but she didn't. Now she does. We both do."

Paige raised a hand like a schoolgirl. "Captain, it was Trevor. He had a body like Trevor. The way he ran was like Trevor, too. I've seen him play lacrosse."

"Thank you, Ms. Newlin, but we can't rely on that. This is what I have to go on." The captain held up the police incident reports, shaped like common traffic tickets. "All it says here is that the shooter was around six feet tall. We don't know if he was white or black. We don't even know if he is a he or a she. I can't pick up anybody because he plays lacrosse."

"Why not?" Mary broke in. "Not to arrest, just to question."

"Ms. DiNunzio, you of all people should know that. You're a criminal lawyer, right?"

"Of course." Mary figured she qualified by now. Not only had she studied, she'd been shot at.

"This kid has one of the highest-priced lawyers in the city, after you. The lawyer got him bail when they had him red-handed, pushing powder. You think he's gonna let me talk to the boy on this evidence? No way."

"You won't even try? He just tried to kill us. He did kill her mother."

Walsh's gaze shifted from Mary to Paige and back again. "With respect, we have the man who we believe committed that crime. He's Jack Newlin and he's going to trial for it."

"He didn't do it!" Mary cried, fighting the urge to pound the desk. She was in danger, Paige was in danger, and it was all her fault. "He'll explain it to you. I phoned him and he should be here any minute."

"Well, he isn't, and I have real work to do." Walsh squared the incident reports at the corners. "I think we've talked enough for one day, Ms. DiNunzio."

"You won't wait?"

"No." Walsh stood up behind his desk. "Thank you very much for your time. It's always a pleasure to talk with you. You have any more theories, feel free to call."

"Are we being thrown out?"

"Don't take it personal," the captain said, as he came around and showed them the door.

A sea of reporters surged toward Mary and Paige the moment they set foot outside the Roundhouse. They had undoubtedly picked up the news of the attempted shooting on police scanners and were waiting in force. "Ms. DiNunzio, any comment?" "Paige, Paige over here!" "Were there any injuries?" "What did he look like?" "Come on, gimme a break, Mary!"

There were TV cameras, microphones, steno pads, and handheld Dictaphones hoisted high above the crowd. Strobe lights seared through the darkness, temporarily blinding Mary. She felt paranoid, unsteady, and her eyes swept the crowd. Could Trevor be out there in the throng? Was he pointing a gun at them even now? He wouldn't be that bold, would he?

Mary grabbed Paige's arm and pushed their way through the parking lot to the curb on Seventh Street, where they ran into a wall of parked news vans. WPVI-TV. KYW. WCAU-TV. She couldn't see the street and shoved between two vans to reach it. She waved her arm frantically. They had no hope of getting a cab in this part of town and the buses ran few and far between this late.

"Mary, do they have a suspect?" "Mary, who do you think it was?" "Paige, does this mean the end of your career?"

Mary pumped her hand wildly in case a cab appeared in the traffic trickling onto the expressway. Suddenly a small dark car shot from the line and sped right toward them. Mary's breath stopped and she jumped back in fear. The car skidded to a stop right in front of her, and just when she was about to scream, she saw that it was a black man at the wheel. She wasn't afraid of black men, only white preppies. Then she recognized the driver, despite his cowboy hat and sunglasses, behind the wheel of an ancient black VW Beetle.

"Get in!" Brinkley called out. "Now!"

Mary grabbed Paige and they ran around to the passenger side and practically leapt inside, with Paige hopping into Mary's lap. Strobes flashed as they slammed the door and sped off, with a news van giving chase. Reporters rushed to their vans and cars, taking off after them into the night.

"All right!" Brinkley shouted. The Beetle accelerated toward the expressway. "Now where to, Newlin?"

"Let me think," Jack answered, popping out of the backseat.

"The press is probably at my hotel and they staked out your house and Mary's office."

"Dad! You're here! Hey, what happened to your face?" Paige turned around, grinding her back into Mary's nose, and Jack leaned forward in the speeding car to give his daughter a quick kiss. Mary hid her shock at his being there and tried to look attractive with a sideways nose. She couldn't see his face because of his daughter's back but she knew he was the handsomest beat-up guy ever.

"I'm okay. Had a small problem at the prison, but I'm fine now. I'm so glad you're safe, honey," Jack said, but Mary figured he was talking to Paige.

"Thanks to Mary, Dad. She saved my life."

Mary flushed, glad of the plug, then struggled for breath. Models were heavier than they looked. All that Evian weight.

"Hold the lovefest, people!" Brinkley said, as the VW tore up Callowhill. "Where we goin'? Any ideas?"

"How about Jersey?" Jack offered. "We can lose 'em in Cherry Hill."

"Too far. I know where they won't find us," Mary said, with difficulty, since her mouth was buried in Paige's leather coat.

"Where?" Brinkley asked, and Mary pointed around Paige.

"Turn left at the next light."

"Yeehah!" Brinkley shouted, and the Beetle bucked forward.

50

Davis, still in running clothes, stared open-mouthed at the TV in his office, over his messy desk of documents and notes. The Chief had called him from a union dinner and told him about it. On the screen was a reporter with a perky hairdo, holding a microphone. In the background was the curved shape of the Roundhouse and the reporter was saying, "A man in a ski mask reportedly chased the two women, Paige Newlin, daughter of the slain Honor Newlin, and her attorney, Mary DiNunzio, for several blocks, firing at them. Police are currently investigating to determine the reason for the shooting. Back to you, Larry."

Davis switched the channels with the remote, catching as many reports as he could. Then he flicked off the TV with the remote, eased back into his chair, and downed the last of his Gatorade. What the fuck? Who could be shooting at the daughter? Davis thought about it logically, his brain humming since his run. It had helped him to plan the Newlin case and he'd returned to the office to go through the documents from Tribe & Wright. He had almost finished reading them when he'd gotten the call about the shooting.

He tossed the empty Gatorade jug at the wastebasket, but it missed. Who was the guy in the ski mask? It led to the next question. Well, who would want the daughter dead? Answer: whoever benefits from her death. Well, who benefits? Then Davis remembered something he had read before his run. It hadn't seemed significant at the time but it certainly was now.

He flipped through the papers on his desk, looking for it. There it was, at the bottom. The document describing the trust fund that Honor Newlin had set up for her daughter. He yanked it out and flopped it on top of the stack. It wasn't long, maybe five pages, and its terms reiterated the fifty million Paige was set to receive, in scheduled increments. But there was one sentence that had caught his attention. Davis ran a finger down the smooth page until he found it: "In the event that Paige Newlin shall die before receipt of any portion of her inheritance under the terms of this trust, the remaining amount shall revert to her surviving parents. . . . "

Davis read it over and over. It was too good to be true. Follow the money, stupid! Under the mother's will, when the mother dies, the kid inherits. But under the terms of the trust, if the daughter died before she could inherit, the fifty million went to the surviving parent. In this scenario, that would be Jack Newlin. It didn't sound like the Honor Newlin that Videon had described, but she must never have thought it would happen.

Davis sat up in his chair, his foot wiggling with nervous energy. So the only way Newlin could get the wife's money was to kill the wife, then the kid. Then all of it, read *all of it,* comes to him. Davis clapped a palm to his forehead at the thought. Could Newlin have planned it this way? He'd have to! You'd have to be an estates expert to rig this result, will-to-trust. Fifty mil! God, this case was fun!

Davis grabbed the phone and his thoughts didn't break stride. Newlin was out on bail at the time the shooting occurred. Perfect! Motive plus opportunity! It had to be *Newlin* in the ski mask!

The phone rang on the other end and as soon as a voice picked up, Davis said, "Gimme the Chief."

51

"*Oh Deo! Oh Deo!*" Vita DiNunzio sobbed. She reached for her daughter the moment she got in the door, and Mary regretted instantly that she'd brought everybody here. The DiNunzio kitchen couldn't fit Mary, Paige, Jack, and Brinkley, in addition to her parents, shamelessly hysterical that their daughter had been shot at. Having a weeping mother wrapped around her waist wasn't a good look for Mary.

"Let's all calm down," Mary said, giving her mother a final hug and gentling her into a chair. Fresh coffee percolated on the stove and its aroma filled the kitchen. The table had been set with two mismatched cups and saucers. Her parents were just about to down their thirty-fifth cup of coffee before her mother went to bed. In the morning they would discuss why they couldn't sleep. "Everything's fine now. We're safe."

"Completely safe," Jack added, but her mother's lips trembled at the sight of Jack's swollen cheekbone.

"Oh *Deo*," her mother moaned. She took off her thick glasses, set them on the table, and dropped her small face into a knobby hand. Even her silver hair, teased into curls, swoops, and swishes, drooped sideways, listing like the top of a soufflé. Mary wondered if they had smelling salts. For hair.

"Mom, it's fine," she said, patting her mother's hand. "We're all fine. Me and Paige, we're fine. Fine, fine, fine. We even have a detective here to protect us." Mary handed her mother her thick glasses and made her slip them on, then gestured to Brinkley. "Look. See. Exhibit A. A real detective."

"A *detective*?" her mother said. She wiped her eyes with a napkin, leaving a reddish streak on her parchment-thin skin. Her eyes were as round as milky brown marbles behind the lenses, emphasizing their utter lack of guile, and Mary had to smile. If her mother was surprised at having a black man in her kitchen, it didn't show. They used to have her father's black crew home for lunch all the time, to the neighbors' disapproval. "You a detective, with the *police*?"

"Yes," Brinkley answered succinctly, from against the wall, and Mary's eyes flared at him with significance.

"Maybe you could elaborate, *Detective*," she prodded.

Jack laughed. "Reg, tell Mrs. DiNunzio how safe we all are because you're here."

"Yes, well." Brinkley's head bent to fit under the low ceiling and his arm cracked the Easter palm behind the switch plates. "You don't have anything to worry about, Mrs. DiNunzio. I have a gun."

"A gun? Oh *Deo!*" her mother wailed, and her father hovered. He kneaded her shoulders through her housedress until she got used to the notion of a Glock in a house with twenty-five crucifixes, two statues of the Virgin Mary, and a candle for emergency novenas. "A *gun!*"

"Coffee anyone?" Mary asked airily, and bustled over to the stove and grabbed the pot. She was just about to go for the cups when Jack opened the cabinet, grabbed a bunch, and began setting them on the table with a happy clatter. How could she have ever thought him a murderer? He reminded her so much of her father, who was still consoling her mother as she segued into Act III of *La Traviata*. Soon the wheezing would start. "Dad, I'm sorry about this, but would you mind going up and taking Mom with you?" Before her hair explodes. "We need to talk some business, and it might upset her." Call me crazy.

"Yes, good, no problem, Maria," her father said, his own tears subsiding.

"Thanks, really, Dad. Here, Mom." Mary set the coffee down and helped her father ease her mother up from the chair. Everyone said their good-byes as Mary and her father walked her mother out of the kitchen, through the dining room, and to the stairwell in the living room, with only slightly less effort than Christ bearing the Cross through the streets of Jerusalem. And after Vita DiNunzio was safely tucked in bed, with her husband at her side, Mary gave them both a kiss good night and fetched them their bedtime cup of coffee.

When Mary came back downstairs, Jack was enveloping Paige in a huge hug in the warm kitchen, his face buried in her glossy hair. "Thank God," he said, and Paige broke the embrace, standing away from him.

"Thank Mary, too, Dad. She really did save my life."

Jack looked over Paige's shoulder. He grinned with relief, his blue eyes frankly grateful. "Thank you, Mary," he said, advancing a step.

Mary stiffened, though there was a table between them. She didn't want him to hug her, did she? Yes. No. Of course not. In the kitchen, where her husband used to? She picked up the coffee and poured a cup for Brinkley, then went around the table until there were four steaming cups and nobody could ever sleep again. "No problem. I saved myself, too. So it wasn't so unselfish. Why don't you sit down?"

Paige looked between them. "That's not true, Dad."

"Everybody sit down," Mary said, waving her off, and pulled out a chair. Installed behind her aromatic cup of coffee, she felt safe and happy again and decided to attribute it to land memory and not Jack Newlin, who she was happy/sad to want to hug/not hug. It confused her. "We have a lot of catching up to do. Jack, let's begin at the beginning. You did not kill your wife."

"No, I didn't." Jack looked relieved to say it aloud, and Mary warmed to finally hear her suspicion confirmed. "I confessed because I thought Paige had killed her."

Paige looked grave behind her untouched cup. "I'm sorry, Dad. I shouldn't have lied to you about Trevor."

"Let's not talk about that now," Jack said quickly. "Let's hold the tears and I'm sorrys and get to the facts. Trevor killed your mother, didn't he?"

"Yes, we were high, at least I was. He told me I did it, so I thought I did it. I do remember picking up the knife, but I don't think I did anything with it. What I remember next was that it was in my hand, all bloody, and she was dead. But I don't think I killed her. I was angry at her, but I don't think I could ever do that." Paige told the story about her confession to Captain Walsh and the discovery that she had no bruising.

"And Trevor was arrested on drug charges," Mary said, but Brinkley was nodding as if he knew it. "Captain Walsh told us he was free on bail, so we think that it was him in the ski mask." Mary looked at Brinkley. "Thank you for the hint about the earring back and DNA test, by the way. It helped us figure out that Trevor was the one."

"Knew you'd put them to use."

"Trevor's trying to kill Paige because she knows what happened that night and he's still at large. Is that it?"

"I think so," Brinkley answered, but Jack, at his elbow, stirred and touched Paige's hand gently.

"Paige, why would Trevor kill your mother?" he asked, and Mary noticed he was sitting in Mike's chair to her right. She tried not to feel guilty, which was like not breathing.

"The money, Dad. He's wanted to get married a long time, like since we met. He's been pushing it. When I got pregnant, it got definite. I wasn't in love with it, but when I told Mom she freaked out."

"You should know why." Jack fingered his coffee cup. "Your mother got upset because that's what happened to her and me. She married me only because she got pregnant with you. I wanted to marry her. She was a prize to me, but she felt like she threw her life away when she married me. 'Married down,' as her family said."

Paige was silent, listening, her pretty features soft and sad.

"Now, here's the truth. You're not sixteen, you're seventeen.

Your birthday is March 18, a year before. We took a trip, like rich people did in those days, and we didn't introduce you around until you were about five. It was easy to pass you off as younger then. It was tricky, but doable since we didn't socialize much anyway. You know how your mom was. That's why you were born in Switzerland and why you were always more mature than your peers. They're not your peers."

Paige was stunned. "You're kidding."

"No, not at all."

"Dad, why didn't you just tell me that? It explains so much. About you, and her."

"Your mother didn't want to, and I went along with it. We're both to blame. Me, more so, because she was sick, at some level. I wasn't."

Paige shook her head. "I don't get it. Mom could have had an abortion, couldn't she? I mean, with her money, it would have been easy."

"She wanted the baby, and I did, too."

Paige laughed abruptly. "She didn't want the baby, Dad. I should know, I was the baby. What she wanted was to be miserable, and blame you for ruining her life. I heard her all the time, growing up. She always said she would have had a great career, if it wasn't for you. And me." Paige looked bitter. "Career as what? A professional victim?"

Jack winced. "Paige, that's not right—"

"But it is, Dad. She always blamed everybody else, for everything. She never took responsibility for anything. You should have seen her at shoots. It was the photographer's fault, or the clothes were wrong, or my lighting. Or at home. It was the maid, the accountant, my tutor. It was never her fault. Nothing was ever her fault." Paige fell quiet, and Mary let it lie, remembering what the photographer had said about dealing with Honor and about kids being the ones who see the truth. The two of them, father and daughter, would have to sort it out someday.

"The question is what do we do now," Mary said, after a minute. "Trevor is out there looking for Paige and maybe me.

He knows he doesn't have much time. He's not going to give up, and the police don't believe that he's the killer."

Brinkley cleared his throat, clearly uneasy. "I'll cover you and Paige. Tonight we can all get some rest. Here, if that's okay. We can sleep downstairs on the floor."

"Sure."

"Then first thing in the morning I take all of you to the Roundhouse."

Mary shook her head. "It won't do any good. I screwed that up so bad, the police won't believe anything I say now."

"Anything *we* say," Paige corrected. "I'm the one who doesn't know what's on my own tummy."

Brinkley shook his head. "They'll believe us this time because we'll be bringing in Jack. And Trevor."

"Trevor? How are you gonna do that?" Mary asked, and Brinkley hunched over the table.

"Listen up," he said, and they huddled around. "We got the earring back but not the earring. Now, we know from Paige that Trevor lost the earring and he doesn't know where. I didn't know that before. So we use that fact. We tell him we got the earring, that I found it at the crime scene. And does he want it, come and get it."

Jack looked doubtful. "Why would you do that? You need a credible reason."

"How about revenge?" Mary edged forward, certain that this was the first time a sting had been plotted at the DiNunzios' kitchen table. "And money. You offer to sell the earring back to him. You want to get back at the police department for suspending you. But how do we catch him?"

Brinkley shrugged easily. "I wear a wire. I get him to say what I need, then we take him in. No muss, no fuss."

"A wire," Mary repeated, because it sounded so cool, and Paige clapped in delight.

Only Jack looked worried. "It sounds simple, but things can go wrong. This kid's not that stable. He's a killer."

"I can't handle a preppie, I got no business in the business,"

Brinkley said with a smile, and Mary thought he should smile more often.

"Why don't we do it tonight?" she asked. "End this thing already?"

Brinkley shook his head. "Can't. Take me some time to get the wire. I have to figure a way to get court approval or any admission the kid makes won't come into evidence. I should have the wire by late morning, then we'll try to get hold of our boy."

"How do we do that?" Mary asked, and Brinkley smiled again.

"We start calling around. The boy's got to be pretty panicky right now. He reads the papers and he knows I'm on to him. If he hears my name, he'll come in." The detective reached for the coffeepot. "But first, we have some more of this fine coffee."

After they made the requisite telephone calls, Mary scrounged up four blankets and pillows for everybody and arranged them carefully on the living room rug, making sure Jack was farthest from her, then Brinkley and Paige. They all lay down, exhausted, and when Mary turned out the living room lamp she thought it looked like four sausages in a frying pan. In the morning they would hatch their scheme, catch the bad guy, and be home in time for breakfast.

Paige conked out first, then Brinkley, but Mary felt safe enough even with the detective asleep. Trevor wouldn't think to look for her at her parents' house and neither would the press. She was way too old to run home, and everybody but her knew it. What Mary knew was that she loved her parents more as she got older, not less, and appreciated them in a way she hadn't when she was young and time stretched ahead of her like a shiny sliding board. There was a limit now, an end point; Mike's death had taught Mary that. She didn't need her mother's thin skin or her father's ruptured spine to remind her. There would come a time when she couldn't go home again, not because the C bus had been rerouted, but because her parents would be gone. And when they were gone, home would be gone, too.

Mary shifted uncomfortably under her old blanket. It was a child's fear, she knew, the fear of her parents' death, and lying there she understood that every lesson her parents had taught her would be tested in surviving their passing. She didn't know how she would live after they were gone, but she knew she would, and only because they had taught her to. It would be their final, and their greatest, gift, and she thanked them for it in her dreams.

Jack heard Mary fall asleep, as he tossed and turned under the blanket. It wasn't the hardness of the floor that was keeping him awake. It was how everything had gone so wrong, not only from the night he took the blame for Honor's murder, but from the very beginning. From the moment he married Honor and started lying about their daughter, and to her.

Honor always thought it was a detail, what age the child was, but Jack was never convinced. He knew all along, even as he prevented himself from knowing, that it was profoundly wrong to lie to Paige about the circumstances of her own birth. He had taught her to lie from the cradle; she was swaddled in lies. How could he expect anything but a lie when she grew up?

Was Trevor with you, Paige?

Of course not, Daddy.

But all along, at some level, Jack had known that she was lying about Trevor. He had sensed that Trevor had been there and was responsible for Honor's murder, at least in part. In fact, if he were being completely honest with himself, it hadn't mattered to him whether Trevor was there or not. The truth was that he'd known it that night, when he asked Paige to lie to him and she did, and when he made the deal that he would protect her fiction, even serve it. As he had with her pregnancy.

Jack faced the darkness and found the truth. He hadn't been completely surprised when Paige told him she was pregnant, over the telephone at the office. He knew she was on a collision course with her mother, acting out against her from the day she'd declared she wanted to be emancipated. He knew that somehow, someday, Paige would figure out how to hurt her mother the most. Get pregnant, like her mother, replaying a past she didn't know existed, but perhaps suspected. So it wasn't Trevor's plan that got her pregnant at all. Paige was lying to herself about that, and to all of them.

Jack shifted on the hard floor. The more he thought about Trevor, the less likely it seemed that the boy could kill Honor as part of a long-range plan to get Paige's money. Trevor was a rash, spoiled, rich boy. A fuckup; the kind of kid who sold drugs and picked up blondes who turned out to be narcs. Something didn't fit; something just smelled.

In his mind Jack went over the day Honor was killed. He had gotten the call from Paige at work, then had been on pins and needles the remainder of the afternoon. He had packed his briefcase, by habit, and left in plenty of time to get home for his usual seven o'clock, but the rain and the traffic had stymied him.

Well, wait a minute.

He had been stopped in the hall. Whittier, wanting to talk about the Florrman bill. Jack had tried to get away, but it had made him late. And in that time period Trevor had killed Honor. Whittier's delay had given Trevor the time to murder Honor.

Jack sat bolt upright. Could it be? Had Whittier stalled him so Trevor could kill Honor? Not possible. There was no connection between Trevor and Whittier, was there? Jack thought about it, every sense alert and awake. It was at least plausible, and he had to find out. The responsibility for catching Trevor was his; it was his wife the boy murdered and his daughter he tried to kill. Jack's heartbeat quickened. He had a responsibility, not to a lie, as before. But to the truth. It might have been rash, but he had no choice.

He rose silently, slipped into his I LOVE PHILADELPHIA jacket and his shoes, and left the house, closing the door softly behind him.

52

J ack approached the glistening skyscraper that housed Tribe & Wright with anticipation. It felt so good to be taking action himself, free from prison. If Whittier was behind this, he would find out. He eyed the building. If there had been press around the building, there wasn't anymore; the eleven o'clock news was over and the reporters had crawled back under their rocks. It was dark, the street was empty. He hurried down the sidewalk and entered the marble lobby.

The security guard at the desk came to a nervous wakefulness when he recognized Jack. It had to be from the news; Jack didn't know the security guards on this late a shift. "Sign in, please, sir," asked the guard, righting his cap, his eyes glued to Jack's wounded cheek.

"Ran into a truck," Jack said, and walked to the elevator. His shoes echoed in the cavernous lobby and he stepped into an open elevator and hit the button for thirty. The elevator doors closed behind him with an expensive *swoosh*.

As soon as Jack was out of sight, the security guard reached for the telephone and punched in a number, as he had been instructed.

Jack had walked through the halls of Tribe & Wright a hundred times, even after hours, and the firm used to be as familiar to him as his home. But tonight it felt as foreign and unforgiving as the moon's surface and almost as lifeless. The lights were on but the reception area was empty, the front desk bare and unstaffed, and the offices vacant. Though his floor looked the way it always did, he couldn't shake the feeling that he didn't know where he was. Either the firm had changed or he had changed. Or both.

He walked by the foxhunting prints on the wall and scrutinized them as he never had before. He passed a side table made of tiger maple and wondered what it was doing in the hallway. It was just in the way. He passed the two large offices off the hall, one was Rossman's, but they weren't in, of course. He could do what he needed to do.

Jack's office was just down the hall and as he walked toward it, he sensed it would be his last time. He wouldn't be coming back to Tribe and he wouldn't miss the place. All he wanted from it now was answers. He was going to sit in his chair and use his correspondence, notes, and time records to reconstruct everything that happened the day of Honor's murder.

Jack's pace quickened. The police would have confiscated some files, but he hoped not all of them. Then he remembered. His laptop, with the single ticket to London. The prosecution would use it against him, but he had arranged the trip to give himself some time alone, to consider what was happening in his marriage since Paige's emancipation. It had all come apart before he had the chance. Jack arrived at his office, opened the door, and froze on the spot.

It was completely empty. Even the *furniture* wasn't there anymore. How could that be? The police would have seized files and computers, but not every file, cabinet, book, and law review. Where was his stuff? Photos of Paige and Honor? His personal papers? Diplomas, a citation from Girard? Then he thought about it. Only the firm could take these things and only with the approval of the managing partner. Whittier.

Jack felt his jaw clench in anger. What was going on? Was Whittier really involved in this? A man he had known and worked with all his life? And why would Whittier want Honor dead? It was unthinkable. She had chosen him to be her executor, she had trusted him so much.

Whittier's office was around the corner and down the hall. If Jack wanted answers, that's where he'd find them. He turned and strode down the corridor, more determined with every step. He'd tear the place apart. Ransack every drawer. Jack was halfway there when he heard voices. Strange. It was too late for the cleaning people. The voices grew louder as he got closer to Whittier's office. It sounded like shouting. The door was open. Jack broke into a run, and when he reached the office door, he got the surprise of his life.

Whittier and Trevor stood staring at him. Trevor looked disheveled, his eyes sunken and glassy. He was high, but Whittier surely wasn't. The managing partner, still in shirt and suit pants, stood open-mouthed. He looked merely startled, but completely in command.

"What the *fuck*?" Jack said, enraged, and suddenly everybody was in motion.

Trevor bolted in panic for the door, pushing Whittier out of the way. Jack lunged for Trevor but the teenager had enormous momentum and knocked him backward. He darted out the door, and Jack recovered and ran after him, his heart pounding. Jack wasn't about to let Trevor get away. He'd catch up with Whittier later.

Trevor thundered down the hall, a strapping kid in sneakers, but Jack ran quicker, fueled by a father's rage. He heard shouting from the reception area at the hall's end. He couldn't explain it and didn't try. Trevor bounded for the reception area with Jack right behind him, panting heavily.

"Stop, Trevor!" Jack shouted. He narrowed the gap between them, reaching for Trevor's sweatshirt, then veered around the corner. The sweatshirt was almost within Jack's fingertips when the elevator doors opened and a cadre of Philadelphia police flooded the reception area. Cops? Where had cops come from? What the hell was going on? Jack skidded to a bewildered stop but Trevor ran practically into the arms of the cops.

"He's got a gun!" Trevor screamed. "He's trying to kill me!"

"Freeze!" one of the cops ordered, drawing his gun on Jack.

"I'm unarmed!" Jack shouted, but in the next instant a crazed Trevor grabbed the gun from the cop's hand.

"No!" yelled the cop, jumping for his weapon. The cop flanking Trevor grappled for it, too, and they were wrestling for the gun when it went off, the sound reverberating hideously in the tony corporate setting. Jack held his breath and didn't know if anyone had been hit. Neither did the cops. And for a final split second, neither did Trevor.

"Shit!" said one of the cops, pained and angry, when the gun dropped to the plush Oriental.

Jack watched in horror as a strange smile appeared on Trevor's face, then went suddenly slack. Bright red blood spurted from a round hole in his neck, under his chin. His eyes rolled back in his head and he collapsed silently against the cops, who sprang instantly into action, trying to save his life. One palmed a radio while another ran to the reception desk for a phone. Two knelt over him, checking for a pulse and trying to staunch the flow of blood.

Jack, aghast, rushed to Trevor's side and knelt down beside the cops. Blood was everywhere, spurting regularly with each heartbeat, and they couldn't seem to stop it. They fell silent, their drawn faces acknowledging what they couldn't say. Even Jack could see how much blood Trevor was losing and hung his head over the boy's body.

"Shit, it's arterial," said the cop at Trevor's neck. Blood gushed through his fingers despite his grip. Trevor's face was ashen and his blue eyes still.

"The carotid," the other cop said, his voice heavy with regret. "Oh, jeez. Oh, jeez."

Jack couldn't believe it was happening. The kid was dying. He shook his head over his body, then spotted something. Trevor's shirt had been pushed up in the struggle and a purplish bruise peeked from the elastic bottom. Jack reached out and pressed his shirt to the side. *My God.* Bruises blanketed Trevor's stomach. It had to be the bruises Mary had told him about, that hadn't been on Paige. Jack was looking at the man who murdered Honor.

"No," he said, remembering Whittier, in a horrified daze. He had to make him account for this. And for Honor, and Paige. He rose to his feet but when he stood up his arms were grabbed from behind, wrenched together, and slapped into tight handcuffs. "What are you doing?" Jack demanded, twisting around in anger.

"Take it easy, Newlin," a cop ordered, shoving him to the elevator.

"I didn't do anything! I don't have a gun—"

"We've been looking for you. We're taking you down for questioning in the attempted murder of your daughter."

"What? Me, *kill Paige*? Are you insane?" Jack struggled against the handcuffs but more cops appeared. This was a nightmare. Him suspected of trying to kill Paige. Trevor bleeding on the floor. Whittier getting away with murder. "You can't stop me, you have no right! Get Whittier, would you? Arrest him! He's behind this and the murder of my wife!"

The cops shoved him toward the elevator. "Tell the detectives about it when you get there," one said.

"How *dare* you, Jack!" came Whittier's voice, from the entrance to the reception area. Jack twisted around in the cops' grasp, but Whittier remained composed, slipping into the pinstriped jacket he'd been carrying. "That's libel, and if you repeat it I'll sue you and the paper that prints it."

"Sue me, you asshole!" Fury constricted Jack's throat and he lunged for Whittier. The cops yanked him back and the handcuffs dug into his forearms. They shoved him toward the elevator but he stood his ground. "This boy's dying because of you! My wife died because of you! And my daughter—"

"Enough!" Whittier shouted. "As I told the officers, this *boy*, as you call him, has been blackmailing me over you. He told me you have been trafficking in cocaine, with his assistance—"

"That's a lie!" Jack shouted. He resisted the cops but they edged him to the elevator bank.

"—he was threatening to go to the press with it, destroying my law firm." Whittier tone quieted in the face of Jack's rage. "You must have known he'd be meeting me tonight, here, and that's why you—"

"*Bullshit!* You and Trevor killed my wife! You tried to kill my daughter!" Hearing himself raging, even Jack knew Whittier looked and sounded the more believable of the two. And he didn't have a murder charge hanging over his head. It infuriated Jack all the more. "I'm on to you, you asshole!"

"—came to my office, to kill him. You've lost control, Jack. You need help. Counseling. Are you an addict, too? You're not the man I knew."

"He's lying!" Jack erupted, lunging again for Whittier. He almost slipped free but the police tackled him to the rug, grunting and shouting. The wound on his cheek erupted and pain shot through his ribs. He thrashed and fought back to get to Whittier, but the cops subdued him.

"Get the fuck down!" they shouted. "On the floor! Get down!" They rained blows on his arms and legs. His ribs exploded in renewed agony.

Jack torqued his body right and left to get free, screaming Whittier's guilt until his ranting ended with a blow to the head and everything went black.

53

Mary peeked through the wired window of the interview room at the Roundhouse and felt her heart wrench in her chest. Jack sat cuffed to a steel chair that was bolted to the floor. A goose egg with broken skin swelled over his right eye and the wound on his cheek gaped. Blood dotted his tourist jacket and he slumped in the chair, in obvious fatigue and pain. Only his eyes had any life in them and they brightened the moment she opened the door.

"Jack!" she said, rushing into the grimy room. She didn't throw her arms around him, but knelt to be eye-level with him and touch his shoulder. She'd given up any pretense of sounding lawyerly, and his expression told her he had decided that he wasn't only a client anymore.

"Can I hire you back?" he asked, with a smile that reached her almost as deeply as a hug. A cut on his lip cracked when he grinned. "Now that I know you're from a nice family and all."

"You got it," she said, flushing with pleasure, then recovered her wits. They were alone in the interview room but it had a two-way mirror with a video camera. The cops and maybe even Davis were on the other side. Mary leaned closer to Jack so they couldn't be overheard. "They want to question you. The D.A. is convinced you were the one shooting at Paige. He had the cops looking for you. Let's just lay it out, okay? The whole truth and nothing but."

"It's about time," Jack whispered. "The inheritance has to be why they think I tried to kill Paige. I don't benefit under Honor's will but I do under the trust, if Honor is dead. Get to Whittier. He's the executor in both and the fees are worth millions to him and the firm. That's all I've got to go on."

"Don't worry." Mary stood up and faced the mirror, her hand on Jack's shoulder. It was warm and strong beneath her fingertips, or maybe it felt good to acknowledge her feelings for him. "Olley, olley, oxen free," she called out, and in the next minute, the door to the interview room opened and in came Detectives Kovich and Donovan.

Kovich took the chair across from Jack, and Donovan stood against the wall. Mary didn't wait for a Q & A and laid out the truth about Jack falsely confessing to the murder and about Trevor killing Honor and telling Paige she did it. Jack picked up the story about Trevor's being the one in the ski mask and his theory about Whittier being behind the murder. Mary noticed they both omitted Brinkley, to keep him out of trouble.

Kovich listened intently, but Donovan scowled throughout the account. "So, Mr. Newlin, you want us to believe that one of your partners, William Whittier, was in a conspiracy with Trevor Olanski to kill your wife and daughter?"

"Yes," Jack said, straightening in his chair with obvious discomfort. "That's what's going on."

"Sir, why would a partner in an important law firm conspire with a high school drug dealer?"

"I don't know that, I can't explain that myself. I was going to find out when I was brought here and I still can. Why don't you ask Whittier that question?"

Kovich looked concerned behind his overlarge aviators, but Donovan pursed thin lips. "We did question Mr. Whittier, and the story he told us is very different from yours."

"What did he say?" Jack's tone turned angry. "More crap about this supposed blackmail and cocaine scheme?"

"I'm not at liberty to discuss it with you, but we're investigating it. It conflicts directly with what you just told us."

"I'm not surprised, but what I've told you is true."

"That's what you said at your confession, as I recall. I saw the video." Donovan shoved his hands deep in the pocket of his fashionable black pants. "You said you were telling the truth then, but now you tell me it was all a lie. And your daughter, who went to Captain Walsh and said she was telling the truth, then later said she was lying, too. You put your own daughter up to protect you?"

"Of course not," Jack snapped. "We've explained it to you. You don't want to believe us, there's no way we can convince you. Trevor is dead now, so we can't ask him." He edged forward on the steel chair, his handcuffs pulled tight. "Let me go and I'll prove it to you."

"I don't think so. You're here to answer our questions," Donovan said, though Kovich appeared not to have any. "Where were you when Paige was shot at? We place the time of the incident at about six o'clock."

"I was trying to find her. I knew she was in danger from Trevor."

"Where exactly did you go to find her?" Donovan asked skeptically. "I assume we can verify who you talked to."

Mary knew the detective was getting into the time period when Jack was with Brinkley. She wondered if Jack would tell the detectives about him. It would help Jack's cause but put Brinkley on the hook. Taking evidence from a crime scene; interfering with a police investigation. They could charge Brinkley with obstruction of justice.

"Mostly I called around, from my hotel," Jack answered, and Donovan snorted in derision.

"You were so worried about your daughter that you picked up the phone and made a few calls?"

"It was my only option. I would have gone to look for her but I didn't know where to start, and I wasn't free to walk around the city, not with the press after me everywhere I went."

"Got it." Donovan nodded, and if a nod could be sarcastic, this one was. "So you sat in your hotel room and called people. Who did you call?"

"Her apartment. A few photographers."

Jack was making it up as he went along, and even Mary could see it. He wouldn't betray Brinkley, and though she admired him for it, she considered doing it herself. The choice between Jack and Brinkley wasn't an easy one, but there was no way Donovan would believe them now anyway. Exposing Brinkley wouldn't accomplish anything but hurting him.

"So you made some calls to photographers," Donovan was saying. "What did you find out?"

"Nothing. I didn't reach anybody. I left messages everywhere I could."

"Did you call nine-one-one, like you did after you killed your wife?" Donovan shot back, but Jack kept his cool.

"I told you, I didn't kill my wife. And no, I didn't call nine-one-one about Paige."

"Why not, if you thought she was in mortal danger?"

"There wasn't time and I thought I could handle it myself."

"Why would you think that, Mr. Newlin? You have police training? Firearms, self-defense, and whatnot?" Donovan cocked a thin eyebrow, and Mary guessed he was trying to learn if Brinkley was involved.

"No training, but she's my daughter. I was the one who put her in jeopardy. I was the one who was going to get her out of it."

"By making phone calls?" Donovan half smiled. "That means your phone records at the hotel would back you up."

"Yes they will," Jack answered quickly, though Mary knew they wouldn't. It was time to interrupt.

"Detective," she said, "you've asked enough questions to make it clear you have no evidence to support a charge of attempted murder against Mr. Newlin. It's the middle of the night, and Mr. Newlin is exhausted and in need of medical attention. This fishing expedition is over. Release my client." Mary rose to her feet, but Donovan stepped forward.

"Ms. DiNunzio, you don't tell us when we're done, we tell you. Your client is on bail for a murder charge. Now he's a suspect in an attempted murder of someone who may be a witness at his trial. So we got him on the attempt, obstruction charges, and witness tampering. We can hold him until we check his phone records and we will."

Mary and Jack exchanged looks. They both knew it was true, and in the morning the D.A. would probably have Jack's bail revoked. He'd be in prison until the trial, unless she could free him. Mary was on her own again, without him. She had come full circle. But it was different now, for lots of reasons. Not the least of which was that she was certain of his innocence and that her attraction to him had become undeniable, maybe even mutual.

"So I agree with you, the interview is over. But you're the one who's leaving, Ms. DiNunzio."

Mary rose to her feet. "You want to question Mr. Newlin further, you call me first. Nobody goes near him without me there. You get him the medical attention he needs. In the morning I'm filing a motion with the court complaining of police harassment."

"Somehow I knew you would say that," Donovan shot back, and Kovich got up and opened the door.

Mary noticed he avoided her eye when she walked out.

Dwight Davis stood with Captain Walsh on the other side of the two-way mirror. Davis felt fresh despite the late hour, but Walsh rested an arm wearily against the molding around the mirror, which looked onto the interview room like a window. "This case is gonna kill me," the captain said wearily, watching Kovich recuff Newlin through the window. "I don't work this shift anymore."

"Lighten up, Cap." Davis grinned, his legal pad hugged to his chest. He watched the two-way mirror as if it were great TV. "We caught Newlin in another lie, and as soon as I talk to the Chief, he'll pick up an attempted murder charge. I gotta find a way to get this before a jury. This man is going down big-time."

"Newlin's not the problem," Walsh said under his breath, but Davis picked it up.

"Who then?"

"What?"

"Who is the problem?"

Walsh sighed. "Brinkley."

"Brinkley?" Davis's neat head snapped from the window. "You think he's helping them?"

"I can handle it."

"Shit!" Davis was pissed. The fuckin' cops. From time to time he had to remind them who ran the show. Unlike lots of D.A.s, he didn't kiss up to the department. "Cap, I'll be straight with you—"

"Hold the lecture, counselor."

"No. If I find out that Brinkley had anything to do with Newlin or DiNunzio, I'll charge him with aiding and abetting, accessory after the fact, anything I can find. I will *not* have a rogue cop undermining my prosecution."

"Brinkley's not a rogue cop, for Christ's sake," Walsh shot back.

"Get him in line, or I will," Davis said, and walked out.

54

It was early morning when Mary hit the sidewalk outside the Roundhouse and waded into the throng of media. Despite the cold, their numbers had swelled from the night before. Trevor's death and Jack's arrest had whipped them into a frenzy. They mobbed her, clicking motor drive cameras, screaming questions, and thrusting videocams and bubble microphones into her face. They fogged the air with steam and filled it with noise and action.

Mary put her head down and barreled ahead, remembering TV footage she'd seen of her boss, Bennie, running the same gauntlet. Odd to think she was doing it now, too. Was this really her? And was it progress? Wasn't she really better off whining about her job? Reading the classifieds? Daydreaming about the life of a manicurist? At least on this case, she knew the answer.

She ran to the corner. She knew she couldn't get another cab and she hadn't convinced the one that had brought her here to wait. Brinkley couldn't risk coming out in daylight to pick her up, and so she'd had to plan ahead. She had, by checking the schedule. The white SEPTA bus rumbled by, this one spray-painted all over with DEGAS AT THE ART MUSEUM, and she ran for it, her briefcase bumping at her side.

The bus genuflected at the bus stop, a misnomer if there ever was one, but the pause did give her time to be seen in the driver's rearview mirror. The sight of a passenger running flat out usually cued SEPTA buses to zoom away, but this one stayed put. Either it took pity on her because of the media after her like a swarm of killer bees, or the driver didn't know the rules. She caught up with the bus, her chest heaving in the cold air. Its doors folded apart with a familiar rattle-and-slap, and she grabbed the steel handrail and leapt aboard. In Philly, real lawyers rode buses.

Mary watched two of the news vans take off after the bus, but the morning rush had started and in time one got lost in it. She slipped into a knit cap she had in her pocket, picked up a transfer slip, and got off the bus at the stop, then transferred to the C to get home. Nobody would suspect she was on the C. Nobody would bother with the C. It was the least suspicious bus route in Philadelphia. She watched the remaining news van get stuck in traffic, following the wrong bus, and she headed home. It would take her a little longer by bus, but it gave her time to think.

Jack had said that Paige's inheritance was the reason the cops thought he had tried to kill her. Mary had been pretty good at wills and estates in law school, and unlike criminal law, remembered it well. So the effect of Honor's will and Paige's trust must have been to have the Buxton money revert back to Jack. Mary knew that was almost boilerplate in wills. Whittier was the executor of both estates, a service generally performed for two percent of the total estate yearly, as Mary recalled. If it were a large estate, even two percent could amount to several million dollars, but it obviously wouldn't be collectable until after the deaths.

The bus chugged ahead, as did her thoughts. So Whittier would have wanted Honor and Paige dead for two reasons; either Honor was changing executors and he was in danger of losing the fees, or he simply wanted to hasten the day of collection, by killing them both. She shuddered. The bus hissed to a stop, taking on passengers as it approached the business district, and a young man in a tan baseball cap climbed on and wedged into the seat next to her. He let a heavy book bag slip from his shoulders and set it on his lap.

Mary returned to her thoughts. Only one thing didn't make any sense; Donovan's question. How were Whittier and Trevor connected? One was an important law partner, the other was a high school kid. Like the one next to her on the bus. Mary glanced over at him, for field research. Close-up, he reminded her of Trevor, either that or the outlandish possibility that all teenagers were dressing alike. His baseball cap had a bright red A on it, which she assumed stood for Abercrombie and not Adultery. He wore a hoop earring in one ear, and she speculated that they issued the earring at Abercrombie's. He was about sixteen or seventeen and he wore jeans, a T-shirt, and only a light jacket, to prove he wasn't cold.

She smiled. Boys hadn't changed much. He had clear blue eyes, looked clean-cut, and was obviously on his way to school in town. Maybe he even went to Trevor's school. "Excuse me," she said, "which school do you go to?"

"Pierce," he answered.

She nodded. Or not Trevor's school. But maybe he knew him. Philly was a small town. "You know anybody named Trevor Olanski? He goes to Philadelphia Select."

"No."

Of course not. So much for coincidences that broke the case. Mary had bad karma. She hadn't been to confession in eighty-five years. She gave up, looking out the window.

"What's your name?" the teenager asked, and she turned back to discover he was smiling at her.

"Uh, Mary," she told him, and he nodded as if she had said something incredibly interesting.

"That's a nice name."

"It is?"

"What's your last name?"

"DiNunzio."

"Mary DiNunzio. That sounds good together."

"I had nothing to do with it," she said, and he laughed warmly. She suppressed her smile. Was he trying to pick her up? The only time men looked at her like that was when a model was walking behind her. And he wasn't even a man, he was a man-child.

"Where do you go to school, Mary?" he said, and maybe it was her fatigue, but the first thought that popped into her mind was:

I'm old enough to be your mother. In fact, she wasn't, but she *felt* old enough to be his mother. And it gave her an idea about Trevor and Whittier, even though the kid didn't go to Trevor's school. She remembered something she'd heard in the last crazy days. Where had she heard it? Who had said it? *We've had our eye on Olanski. . . . He moves lots of drugs to kids in private school. . . . He sold to the wrong kid a few months ago. . . .*

Could that be it? Mary had found a connection between Whittier and Trevor, at least a possible connection, if it panned out. It shook her from her reverie. The bus was almost at her stop. She had to go. She couldn't wait to tell Brinkley. She could be right. She could break the case, all by herself. Anything was possible. It was America. She picked up her briefcase from the bus floor and jumped to her pumps.

"Mary?" asked the teenager, whom she'd forgotten. His face was flushed with embarrassment, and his eyes looked hurt. She couldn't do that to him. Scarred at such a tender age, he could turn into a lawyer. She bent down and gave him a quick kiss on the cheek.

"I'm taken, but thanks for asking," she told him, and made her way to the front of the aisle, where the driver steered the bus to a slow and safe stop. She didn't even have to hold on to the pole to avoid mortal injury. Definitely a rookie, she thought, and thanked him before she got off. It was the first time she meant it.

Mary hustled down Broad Street and when she turned the corner onto her block, broke into a run. She was so excited. She had figured it out. All they had to do was see if it was true. Brinkley could help.

She ran by brick stoops and marble stairs, past front windows with leftover plastic crèches and porcelain Christmas trees. Christmas lights were still strung across the street, rooftop to rooftop; they swayed in the stiff wind and glowed faintly against the morning sky, making a crayon canopy of red, blue, green, and yellow. Mary loved the lights. She loved life. She ran toward her house.

I'm old enough to be your mother. It was possible. She would find out if Whittier had a teenage son or a daughter. They would be roughly the right age. If Whittier had a kid, then maybe Trevor, drug dealer to preppies, had sold the kid drugs. And maybe that was the connection. It was possible, distinctly possible, especially in Philly. It was such a small town in many ways, and in her experience, the rich kids hung together and knew each other, even if they went to different schools. They went to the same exclusive camps, parties, even cotillions. This was Philadelphia, still.

Mary was going to free Jack, once and for all, and the certainty powered her to her front door. She reached the stoop panting, unlocked the door, and hurried inside. But she did a double take when she hit the kitchen.

She hadn't counted on the extra guest.

55

Mary dropped her briefcase in surprise at the sight. "Is the bus *that* slow?" she said, and laughed.

Detective Stan Kovich smiled sheepishly from behind the tiny kitchen table. His large frame barely fit the rickety chair. "I could have given you a ride, but then I would have been fired."

Mary slipped out of her coat. "Somebody want to fill me in?"

"That would be me." Brinkley gestured over a rather large plate of fried green peppers and soft scrambled eggs. She couldn't help noticing he'd been served first, so her mother and the Glock had made a truce. "Siddown, we got something to tell you."

"Yes, *sí*." Vita DiNunzio came over in her flowered housedress, with crisscrossed bobby pins holding the pin curls in front of each ear. She took Mary by the arm. "Maria, you sit and eat. Your friend Jack, he okay?"

"He's fine, thanks," Mary said, giving her mother a quick kiss before she sat down.

"You want coffee?" her father asked, but he was already scuffing over in his plaid bathrobe and slip-on slippers, bearing the steel pot. He poured her a cup, an arc of steaming brown.

"Thanks, Dad." Mary looked at Brinkley. "Okay, Reg, you go first, then I do."

Brinkley nodded. "We know that our boy Trevor deals coke to lots of rich kids at area schools. He was picked up for it last week, with a kid named Rubenstone. One of the kids he sold to was

Whittier's son, who goes to a private school in the subs. Kovich found out from a buddy of ours in juvy. That's the connection between Whittier and Trevor."

"Jesus, I knew it!" Mary launched into the story about the kid on the bus to show she had figured it out herself, but her mother kept glaring at her from the stove for taking the Lord's name in vain.

"Well, you were right. Here's proof." Brinkley passed a piece of paper over the table. It looked like an official form with redacted portions in the typed narrative. "Kovich had to wait 'til his buddy got back to find the papers, because the complaint was withdrawn. The next day, in fact. Christian Whittier was one of the kids Trevor sold to, and a William Whittier picked him up. We think Whittier paid to bury the complaint. It can't be an accident that the arresting officer's on vacation."

Mary frowned. "So let's think about this. Trevor and Whittier met last week? That doesn't give us anything."

"No, last week is the only time we know about, probably the most recent. But it isn't the first time Whittier's son makes a buy from Trevor, I guarantee it. Once a junkie makes a connection, they stay with it, especially these kids. They don't want to go a bad neighborhood to make a buy. They might get their hands dirty."

Mary glanced at Paige, silent behind an empty plate. The teenager had been beside herself when she heard Trevor had been killed and looked like she hadn't slept at all. Still, Mary had to press her. "Paige, do you know anything about this?"

"No," Paige said. She brushed a strand of red hair from weary eyes, trying to rally. "I didn't know Trevor was so into drugs and I didn't know anybody he sold it to. I just knew he had it all the time."

"It's okay," Mary said, patting her hand. The kid was going through hell, and judging from the empty plate, maybe having morning sickness. No matter what, Vita DiNunzio would force-feed her. Food equaled love in this household. Mary turned to Brinkley. "So, go on, Reg."

"We figure that Trevor and Whittier's kid were at least acquaintances, maybe even friends. Assume Trevor sells to Whittier's kid from time to time. Whittier finds out. He knows that Trevor is the boyfriend of Paige Newlin, Honor and Jack's daughter, and he blackmails Trevor into killing Honor."

"Where do you get the blackmail?" Mary asked, and Kovich raised his hand like a kid in school.

"That's from me. When me and Donovan interviewed Whittier, he told us that Trevor was blackmailing him over Newlin's drug use. It was the same thing he said at the scene, when Trevor got shot, the uniforms told me. Whittier had to have made that shit up on the spot, to explain what he was doin' at the office so late at night. And he ain't the sharpest tool in the shed, was my impression."

Brinkley nodded, picking up the story like a relay team. "People, when they lie, they make it up from something they knew. We see it every day. Like there's a grain of truth in it. Somebody was blackmailing somebody, it's just the other way around. If Whittier is behind this, like we think, that's how he gets Trevor to do the murder. He says, Kill her or I'll turn you in for the drugs you sell my kid. You can't pull strings forever, even in this town. Maybe Whittier pays Trevor, too, to sweeten the deal."

"That sounds like Trevor," Paige added sadly. "Sorry to say it, but he liked money."

Mary thought about it. "So now all we have to do is catch Whittier. That's up to me." Her mother glared at her again as she ladled scrambled eggs onto a flowered plate, and Mary recognized it not as the watch-your-language glare, but the if-you-get-yourself-killed-I'll-kill-you glare. Only a few Italian mothers had perfected it, all members of well-known crime families. Her mother said nothing as she carried a plate of peppers and eggs over and set it in front of Mary with more clatter than necessary.

"Eat," her mother commanded, but Mary knew she wanted to say, Choke.

"Mom, of course, I'll be very, very careful," she said, and her father smiled. "Now, as I was saying. I think it's up to me because I'm the lawyer in the group and I can go over to Tribe without suspicion."

"It's a start." Brinkley said. He finished the last of his eggs and turned to her mother at the stove. "Vita, this was terrific. Best breakfast I ever had."

"You deserve," her mother said warmly.

Mary smiled, mystified. Brinkley was getting along with her mother better than she was. "When did you two become such good friends, Mr. I Have A Gun?"

"Since I fixed the pilot light," Brinkley explained, and Mary laughed, as the doorbell rang and six heads looked at the front door in alarm.

Mary stood stricken at the silhouette of the police officers and Detective Donovan on her parents' marble stoop and felt instantly angry at herself for bringing this into her parents' home. "What are you doing here?" she demanded, though she suspected the answer.

"We're here for Detective Brinkley," Donovan answered, self-satisfied in his black wool topcoat. "May we come in?"

"Not unless you have a warrant," Mary told him, but his hard eyes widened when not only Brinkley but Kovich appeared behind Mary.

"Figured I'd find you here, Reg, but I didn't figure on you, too, partner." Donovan sounded sterner than his years. "I bought that dentist story."

Right behind Kovich and Brinkley hobbled Vita DiNunzio, flushed with anger and brandishing a wooden spoon clotted with scrambled eggs. "Whatta you doin' inna my *house*?" her mother demanded, but Mary held her back.

"Ma, relax, it's okay," she soothed, feeling the balance of power shift to the flying DiNunzios. It meant trouble when her mother had The Spoon. The cops had only guns. It was no contest.

Brinkley touched her mother's shoulder, dismay marking his

thin features. "It's okay, Vita's all right," he said. "Sorry this happened here, at your house. I'm going along with these gentlemen and I'll be fine."

"Excuse me, Mrs. DiNunzio, is it?" Donovan said, with smile that would get him nowhere. "We'll be gone in a sec. If Detective Brinkley doesn't resist us, we can avoid cuffing him."

"*Cuffing?*" Mary's mother repeated, making the g ring out like truth, waving the eggy spoon. "I cuffa *you* one! You no touch Reggie Brinkley. *No touch!*"

"Don't worry, Vita," Brinkley said again, as he grabbed his coat from the couch. On the way out, he gave Mary a hug close enough to slip something into her jacket pocket. She'd had a guess as to what it was, but would check later.

"I'll have a lawyer down there in an hour," she told him. In front of her parent's house idled five police cruisers, exhaust pouring from their tailpipes and turning to steam in the cold air. Uniformed cops hustled Brinkley and Kovich into the backseat of the closest car.

Donovan flashed a smile at the DiNunzios. "Thank you very much, and sorry about the intrusion."

Mary's mother snorted in a way you didn't have to be Abruzzese to understand. "*You!*" She waved the spoon. "You wanna good *smack?*"

Mary sat at her parents' ancient telephone table, holding the receiver of a black rotary phone that could qualify as a blunt instrument in most jurisdictions. She would be nagging her parents to replace it with a cordless if they weren't already so upset, huddling together on the sofa like a soft mountain of bathrobe, the wooden spoon back in its scabbard.

"Jude," Mary said into the receiver, when her best friend picked up. "Have I got a client for you."

56

The morning stayed clear and brisk, and Mary flowed with the foot traffic in the business district. Men hurried by with their heads cocked to cell phones, and women hustled along in conversation. She remembered when she had been one of them; an inexperienced associate dressed in her most conservative clothes, hands gripped around a briefcase that contained a legal pad, a Bic, and photocopied antitrust cases. Okay, so it wasn't all that different now. She was still inexperienced, her clothes remained conservative, and she had the same briefcase, legal pad, and Bic, though the antitrust cases had been replaced by something distinctly illegal:

The Glock that Brinkley had slipped her when he and Kovich had been taken away.

She tightened her grip on her briefcase handle, its shape and heft second nature. The gun had felt far less so when she tried to aim it in her parents' kitchen, where she pointed prudently away from any religious paraphernalia. Of course she hadn't fired the gun; the shot would have brought the neighborhood, the police—or worse, her mother—running. As much as Mary hated guns, she had to admit it felt better to have it along, even if it smelled faintly of oregano.

She stopped at the corner, keeping her head down in case anyone recognized her. The Newlin saga was all over the papers; the *Daily News* had run a small photo of her with Jack. It was a strange feeling, seeing yourself in the paper next to a man you had fallen for. The juxtaposition was more appropriate to engagement announcements than murder stories, but she was getting way ahead of herself. Must be the gun. It got a girl crazy.

The traffic light changed and she allowed herself to be carried off the curb and across the street, her thoughts focusing on Jack, in jail again, and what she had to do to get him out. It wouldn't be easy, but it was clear she had to question Whittier. She would be meeting with him as Jack's lawyer and start with the easy questions. Ask him about his talk with Jack the day of Honor's murder. Avoid mention of what happened with Trevor; don't put him on the defensive. If Whittier wouldn't cooperate, which was likely given that he hadn't returned any of her messages left with his secretary, she would confront him.

She sighted the glass spike that housed Tribe & Wright, a block away. Moussed heads bobbed on the sidewalk ahead of her, and the air was filled with the fog from cold breath and late-breakfast cigarettes. The crowd thickened as she approached the building, and her pace quickened, hurrying unaccountably to keep an appointment she didn't have. She hated the thought of Jack, battered, in prison. She worried what Davis would do next. Two men in front of her stalled. What was the holdup?

She craned her neck, apologizing as she jostled someone's cup of Starbucks. She was too short to see the base of the building. In the street, uniformed police were waving traffic away from the lane nearest the building, their squad cars parked haphazardly behind them. Lights flashed atop the hoods of the cruisers but the sirens weren't on. There seemed no immediacy; it was probably the aftermath of a traffic accident.

Mary threaded her way to the front, heedless about drawing attention to herself. Nobody was looking at her; they were worrying about being late for appointments. The crowd grew denser as she got closer to the building, brought to a standstill by whatever was going on. Over their heads she could hear their chatter and the shouting of the police. The block was suddenly buzzing with activity as two more squad cars pulled down the street, their roof lights flashing, followed by a news van. If it was an accident, it must have been a serious one.

She wedged herself between wool-clad shoulders but couldn't go forward, the crowd was too packed. She didn't know how much time she had. Whittier had been in when she called, but he might have gone out. He'd certainly want to avoid her, knowing the questions she'd have. She had to get going. She stood up on tiptoe and looked around. One way out. The street.

Mary broke free and headed for the street, then ran along the gutter beside an ambulance that was moving slowly, despite the lane evidently cleared for it. Its driver waved her off in alarm but she sprinted ahead, trying to forget she was bounding along with a concealed deadly weapon. She was out of breath by the time she reached the cop directing traffic.

"How can I get into the building?" she asked him. Behind him was a sea of uniformed cops in caps and black leather jackets. They clustered on the sidewalk on the near side of the building. The ambulance stood parked a few feet away, its back doors flung open and its powerful engine idling.

"Lady, get out of the street!" the cop directing traffic shouted. "Can't you see we got a situation here?"

"But I have to get into the building."

"You can't. Now get outta here!" The cop turned his back at the sudden blare of a horn, and Mary sprinted behind him and pushed her way toward the building, just in time to see the cluster of cops breaking up. From the center of the group emerged two paramedics in blue uniforms, carrying a stretcher between them. On the stretcher lay a black body bag, zipped to the top.

Mary stood appalled at the sight. The paramedics loaded the body into the van and the doors slammed closed with a final *ca-thunk*. Someone had died here, right on the street. A heart attack maybe. "What happened?" she heard herself say, and one of the older cops turned around.

"A suicide," the cop said. His expression was somber and his eyes strayed skyward. "A man jumped out a window."

"My God." Mary looked up, too, squinting against the searing blue of the sky, or maybe to soften the impact of the sight.

An empty pane of jagged glass marred the shiny, mirrored surface of the building, and the sky reflected in its mirrors looked like someone had torn a hole in heaven itself. A few business papers floated from the shattered window, caught crazily on the crosscurrents of city air, and fluttered to the crowd. She watched them fall, drawing her gaze down to the sidewalk, visible now that the cops were moving away. A large white tarp had been thrown over the pavement but blood still soaked through the material. "How terrible," she said, horrified, and the cop nodded.

"Not a pretty sight. He was a big deal, too."

She looked over, suddenly stricken. Something was very wrong here. She thought of her phone calls to Whittier. "Who died? Who was he?"

"Don't think we've notified next of kin yet, miss," the cop answered, with a quick glance over his shoulder. Behind him the cops had begun redirecting the pedestrians around the tarp, now that the body had been removed. But Mary wasn't thinking about getting inside the building any longer. She had a terrible hunch.

"From what company, what firm?" she asked, urgent. She couldn't explain how she knew, but she did. "Was the man from Tribe & Wright?"

"Can't say, Miss. Now please, move along." One of the officers behind him was listening, and in the next minute she understood why. Captain Walsh, standing out from the uniforms in his bright white cap, navy dress jacket, and dark tie, was eyeing her warily from the center of the group.

"But I'm supposed to see somebody at Tribe. His name is Whittier, William Whittier," Mary said.

The cop didn't answer but his eye registered a reluctant, but unmistakable, recognition just as Captain Walsh strode toward her.

57

Mary felt Captain Walsh grip her arm and steer her toward an empty white-and-blue police cruiser. "Step into my office, DiNunzio," he said under his breath.

"It was Whittier who committed suicide, is that right, Captain?" she asked, as he placed her bodily into the passenger seat, slammed the door closed after her, and went around to the driver's seat. The legal term "custodial interrogation" popped into her mind, but she shooed it away. Everything was happening too fast for her to process, but the suicide only confirmed Whittier's culpability. And it might have been the final key to Jack's freedom.

"DiNunzio, you are one royal pain, you know that?" Walsh climbed into the cold car and tore his hat off. "First you get two of my best detectives in hot water, then you show up here. What were you doing with Reg? Did he help you?"

"Reg who? Now tell me about Whittier."

"'Reg who?' The Reg we tagged in your parents' house. That Reg."

"Tall, black guy? Likes peppers and eggs?"

"That's the one."

"Don't know him." Mary would be damned if she'd incriminate Brinkley. "Talk to me about Whittier. I need to know what happened."

"No you don't. We got Brinkley and Kovich in custody because of you. You think that's good for the people of this city? You think it's easy to run a homicide squad with two detectives out? We're understaffed as it is."

"I'm not talking to you about Brinkley or Kovich. I'm talking to you about Whittier. You don't want to talk about him, I'm on my way." Mary put a hand on the door handle and hoped she was convincing.

"You wanna talk about Whittier? Okay, explain to me what you're doing here and why you been calling him all morning."

"How did you know that?"

"We interviewed the secretary." Walsh glared at her from the driver's seat, which barely accommodated his burly frame. "In fact, a big cheese like Whittier was, I came down and questioned her in person. What did you want him for? She said you told her it was important. You had to see him about Honor Newlin."

"I was coming to confront him. Whittier was responsible for Honor Newlin's death. He blackmailed Trevor to do it. That's what the fight was about last night, in Whittier's office. The one Jack broke in on."

"*What*? This a new theory? And it's *Jack* now?"

"Look, I swear it. Trevor sold drugs to Whittier's kid and Whittier must have known that I knew that." Mary checked her urgency to convince him, but his eyes narrowed with trained skepticism. "I was onto him, and he knew it was only a matter of time before it all came apart. It must be why he—"

Walsh cut her off with a chop. "DiNunzio, don't give yourself so much credit. Whittier killed himself because *you* were on to him? Get real."

Mary felt an undeniable pang of guilt. "Not that I'm proud of it. But it proves that what I was telling you is true. Whittier knew it was over and he couldn't face it. This proves Jack Newlin is innocent."

"Newlin confessed!"

"He recanted!"

"They all recant when they realize they can get out of it! As soon as they find a lawyer young and gullible enough to buy their rap. I saw you two in the interview room, makin' eyes."

Mary ignored the slight. You get a crush on your client, you have to take the heat. "It's the truth, Captain. Honor Newlin's murder just got solved."

"Oh please! You don't know what you're doing. You're pingin' around like a Ping-Pong ball, and in the end good people get hurt. Don't you get it? You're an amateur!" Walsh looked away, obviously trying to keep his temper, but Mary couldn't let his words hit home.

"Captain, I know this seems crazy to you. I know I haven't had it figured out from the beginning. I'm not a professional detective, I know that, too. But I'm right. I'm really right this time, and this suicide confirms it."

"Please." Walsh harrumphed audibly and his eyes scanned the scene around the squad car. Police officers milled around, controlling traffic and ushering in a snub-nose yellow truck with hoses to wash down the sidewalk. Walsh appraised their progress, then turned to Mary. "You honestly think we're gonna let Newlin go, because this lawyer committed suicide?"

"It's proof! Didn't Whittier know I was coming?"

"Yeah, he got the messages, but so what?"

"How soon after my last message did he kill himself?"

"Fifteen minutes, okay?"

"So there. Not much time, is it? What happened?"

"He sent his secretary down to the cafeteria for doughnuts. When she came back, he had jumped. A lawyer down the hall heard the crash. He broke the window with a chair first."

"What did the note say?"

"No note."

"So we don't know the reason for sure."

"Wrong again." Walsh laughed, without humor. "You think he's gonna write, 'I'm a bad guy, I'm scared of DiNunzio, this is me jumping'?" Walsh shook his head, eyes focused again on the scene through the windshield. "And we *do* know the reason for sure. The secretary told us Whittier came in late this morning and she smelled booze on his breath. He looked so low she asked him what was the matter and he told her he was ashamed of being all over the newspapers. He thought he embarrassed himself and the firm. She said that Whittier had already lost four of his biggest clients. I'd jump outta the building, too!"

"But that's not the reason. He knew it was going to get worse, when I proved he killed his own client."

"Come off it! You got proof of nothing! You can't have! Whittier didn't kill the wife, Newlin did."

"Captain, hear me out," Mary said, and told him the whole story, omitting the aid of Brinkley and Kovich. As she spoke, she experienced a sinking sense of déjà vu. She had no credibility with Walsh and she knew, even as she tried to convince him to the contrary, that she had no hard evidence against Whittier. It sounded like supposition, especially without Trevor's record in juvenile. She knew it was true, she just couldn't prove it. "Captain, you're holding an innocent man."

"According to you. I'll pass it along to Davis. I hear he liked the one about the daughter and the bruises, too."

"You want evidence, I'll get it." Mary opened the passenger side door. "I'll make you let him go."

"Not with your track record, kiddo," Walsh said, but Mary was leaving.

She hurried from the squad car and broke into a light jog, running upstream against the swarm of businesspeople, some of whom stared at her curiously as she ran by. She didn't know where she was running. She let her feet carry her away from the bloody tarp on the sidewalk and Walsh's words. *Not with your track record, kiddo.*

Her pumps clattered on the cold concrete. The sun was cold on her back. The chill stung her nose and made her eyes water, but still she kept running, her bag and briefcase flying at her side. Her emotions churned within her. Her chest felt bound with cold and fear, making it hard to breathe.

She had felt so close to the solution, right at Whittier's door, and now he was dead. She had succeeded in nothing except forc-

ing the man's hand. Driving him to end his own life. Fresh tears
sprang to her eyes and she didn't pretend they were from the cold.
As dreadful a man as Whittier was, he didn't deserve to die. She
had wanted to bring him to justice, not suicide. And not that way.
Not with your track record, kiddo.

She kept running, blinking wetness from her eyes. A woman
hurrying toward the business district looked at her with a flash of
recognition. Mary didn't care. Jack was back in jail, and with
Whittier's suicide, his fate could be sealed. She didn't have the
proof to free him, and with Whittier dead she was no closer to
getting him out, but farther away. Now both conspirators, Whittier and Trevor, were gone. How could she prove dead men guilty
of murder?

It made her run faster. Brinkley and Kovich were in custody,
too. Could Judy keep them out of jail? Mary kept running, the
gun in her briefcase. Would the police find out about that, too?
Would that make it worse for Brinkley? Was Walsh right? Was
Mary just an amateur, doing damage?

The crowd thinned as she fled the business district. The pavement grew emptier the farther south she went. She didn't know
where she was going at first. She had nowhere to go. She couldn't
go home and upset her parents. It wouldn't serve any purpose to
go to the office or even to see Jack.

Her heels rang out swift and certain on the concrete. Her ears
were filled with the sound of her own breathing. She was on her
own. She couldn't call on Judy or Lou; she didn't want to. Mary
was meant to get to the bottom of this, it would have to be her.
She had to think, she had to plan. She had to keep moving and
not give up. Most of all, she had to succeed.

And when she finally stopped running, she was only partly
surprised at where she found herself.

58

A theists never feel completely comfortable in church, and Mary was no exception. She had returned to the city church of her childhood and thirteen years of schooling, coming back even to the same pew. She wasn't sure exactly why she had come to Our Lady of Perpetual Help. She was praying, if anything, to figure out what the hell she was doing there, much less on her knees.

She couldn't puzzle it out. She didn't believe in the perpetual help part and she knew it didn't do any good to put her hands together in prayer, thumbs crossed like a staged Communion picture. But she did these things in this place, her feet having followed routes only they remembered and her hands obeying messages of their own. Mary was a Catholic on autopilot.

The church was completely quiet, as it would be during a weekday afternoon, if there wasn't a funeral. She knew the schedule and rhythms of the church as well as her own. Only a few older people sat in the front pews, and Mary knew they would be stand-ins for the same older people who prayed every day when she was little, who most often now were her parents and their friends, like Tony-from-down-the-block. She squinted at the outline of the silvery heads, but none of them was related to her, which was good considering the gun in her briefcase, by the padded knee rest.

Mary breathed easier. The church was as gloomy as it always was, Our Lady of Perpetual Darkness, because the overhead lights were so dim, the light from their ancient fixtures squandered in the vaulted arches of the ceiling. The darkness emphasized the votive candles that flickered blood red on either side of the altar and the vivid blues, greens, and golds in the stained-glass windows, depicting the Stations of the Cross. Bright lights over the white marble altar set it glowing, and no stage was ever lit to more dramatic effect. The brightest spot in the church, illuminated by a white spotlight, focused on a singular, martyred image.

He hung from an immense gold crucifix at the front and center of the church; a life-size, lifelike statue of Jesus Christ. His blue eyes were lifted heavenward in fruitless appeal. Painted blood dripped from the crown of thorns on his head. Even now, an adult and a lawyer, she had a hard time looking at it. As a child, she used to obsess about what it must feel like to have a crowd of thorns forced down onto your forehead and nails driven clear through your ankles and wrists. But as she gazed at the statue, her hands folded against the smooth back of the pew in front of her, Mary realized why she had come.

Because the church was the same as it had always been, since as long as she could remember. The cool, slippery wood of the pew. The hollow echoes of someone's cough. The splotches of dense color. The white-hot image at center stage. Everything outside the church's stone walls had changed—Mary had lost a husband, seen her parents age, changed jobs, ducked bullets, and met an interesting man—but this city church had remained the same.

And that everything stayed the same implied that it would always stay the same. Why? Because it always had been. As a lawyer, Mary recognized that the logic was circular as a Möbius strip and the exemption from change applied only under this roof, but she found herself comforted nonetheless.

As it was, is, and ever shall be, world without end, were the words of the prayer, and she found herself murmuring them quietly, and then, after them, other prayers. The words summoned themselves from a place in her brain she didn't know existed, the useless information lobe, where she kept the lyrics to "Good King

Wenceslas" and the commercial paper provisions of the Uniform Commercial Code. And though it was sunny and busy and bustling outside the church, inside it was dark and still and familiar. The words were the same as they always had been, as were their rhythms, falling softly on her ears.

In time Mary could feel her heartbeat slow and her muscles relax. She eased back onto the pew, linked her hands in her lap, and let her thoughts run free. She said the words that came to her lips and breathed in the smells and sounds of the world without end, and that world was good and generous enough, even after all this time, to give her peace and room to think. And when she opened her eyes it was growing dark outside the church as well as in and afternoon had faded to dusk. And though it was still strange and new beyond the walls, Mary was no longer afraid.

Tears she couldn't quite explain came to her eyes and as she brushed them away she realized what they were. Exhibits A, B, and C. Mary had been looking for evidence all this time, but it was streaming down her face. A lawyer naturally wanted proof, was trained that way, and now she had finally found it. Evidence that she had been lying to herself for quite some time. And it wasn't a time for lies anymore; it was a time for truth.

So Mary spent one last moment whispering a thank-you to someone she always had believed in, and when she got up to go, with her briefcase and her gun, she knew exactly what to do.

Streetlights and lighted offices illuminated the street corner where Tribe & Wright rose from the concrete, and Mary was relieved to see that the crowd had gone, so her waiting had paid off. No police, no press, not even a sawhorse to mark the spot where Whittier had died. She looked up to the broken window and found the bright square of plywood. She gripped her briefcase and strode to the building in the chill night air. She felt refreshed and determined, with Walsh's words a faint memory. She might have been an amateur detective, but she was a professional lawyer. And this was lawyer's work.

She conceptualized her task as a legal case, about to be tried. The case she had to prove was that Whittier had made Trevor kill Honor Newlin and that he had done so to get the money from the Buxton estate. She needed exhibits to make her case and there had to be a paper trail in Whittier's office, some document, accounting records, or something in the wills. Anticipation quickened her pace. The paper trail had to begin, or end, with Whittier.

She checked her watch as she hurried along. Eight o'clock. Late enough. She hoped everybody would be gone and she couldn't wait any longer. She would search all night if that's what it took. She wouldn't stop until she made her case, piece by piece. Paper by paper. As she approached the building, she reached into her handbag and popped on her sunglasses in case anybody recognized her. She had already pulled her hair back into a low ponytail to complete a sketchy disguise, which was all she needed. The rest she would accomplish with sheer attitude.

Mary drew herself up to her full five feet two inches, reminded herself she had attended an Ivy League law institution, and pushed open the glistening door to the lobby like a self-important lawyer, which was redundant. The lobby was opulent and the young security guard decorated with gold epaulets, but Mary hurried past him to the elevator with her newfound professionalism.

"Miss? Miss," he called after her. "You have to show building ID after hours."

"Oh, no. Sorry." Mary hustled halfway toward the desk, then stopped in fraudulent agitation. "I don't work here, my sister does."

"I knew you weren't a lawyer."

Mary forced a hasty smile. So much for professionalism. "Listen, you gotta help me! Call nine-one-one!" She hurried back toward the last elevator bank, which serviced the twenty-third to the thirtieth floors. Tribe & Wright was on twenty-five to thirty. "Hurry!"

"What?" The guard looked alarmed. "Why?"

"My sister's on the twenty-third floor, in labor! She's having her baby! She just called me on the cell phone!" Mary slammed the button for the elevator and the doors slid open. "Call nine-one-one! See you on twenty-three! Don't forget! Twenty-three!" She leapt into the elevator and hit the button to close its doors. "Hurry!"

"Okay! Tell her don't push!" called the guard, and she heard him pick up the phone as the doors slid closed.

Mary hit the button for thirty, the top floor of Tribe's six floors. If Tribe were like the other big firms, Whittier's office would be on the top floor. Nearer my God, to thee. The elevator whisked her skyward, and she leaned against the cab wall with relief. The security guard would go to twenty-three; she would go to thirty. Sufficiently far apart to give her time to search Whittier's office and run. As relieved as she was that her plan was working, she felt a prick of conscience that she had lied, and so effectively, right after church. What turned a good Catholic into a good liar?

Law school.

TRIBE & WRIGHT, read the gilt Roman letters on the paneled wall. Mary knew she had the right floor as soon as the elevator doors opened. The smell of fresh paint and the newness of the rug tipped her off; the aftermath of Trevor's shooting. The firm would have wanted to put that incident behind it quickly and overnight repairs would be in order.

She hurried off the elevator. The reception area was elegant, and the overhead lights in the common areas had been left on. Under glass on the reception desk was a map of the floor layout, and she crossed to it quickly. She didn't have much time before the security guard and paramedics came looking for her and her allegedly pregnant sister. In the meantime, she'd grab any documents that looked relevant and get the hell out of there.

Mary checked the floor map, running a finger down the row of partners' offices, past Jack's name to Whittier's. It was right down the hall. She paused, listening. It was silent and looked empty; no sound on the Power Floor. Of course, nobody at this level would be working this late; those lawyers worked on the Loser Floor. She hustled down the hall straight ahead and passed one huge office and the next until she reached the one in the corner. Whittier's.

She flicked on the lights. The office was well-appointed, with a huge mahogany desk and end tables, brass lamps rubbed to a soft finish, family photographs in heavy sterling silver frames. Though she didn't have time to assess décor, there was something visually incongruous about the tasteful mahogany desk in front of the rough-hewn plywood expanse over the broken window.

It stopped Mary in her tracks, wordlessly posing an excellent question. Was Whittier the kind of a man who jumped out a window when the shit hit the fan? It didn't fit the picture. If he had known Mary, or the law, was closing in, why didn't he take off to Brazil? Get lost in Europe or the Caymans? He had the money. Mary blinked, pondering it. She recalled what the D.A. had said about Jack at his arraignment. *A wealthy partner in a major law firm, the defendant possesses financial resources far beyond the average person and poses a significant risk of flight. He can use his resources to flee not only the jurisdiction but the country.* The argument had the force of common sense. It was the reason she had lost the bail petition. So why didn't it apply here, as well?

Mary stared at the clash of mahogany and plywood in the still office. Had Whittier really jumped from the window? She recalled what Walsh had told her: Whittier had sent his secretary down to the cafeteria, and when she came back, he had jumped. A lawyer down the hall had heard the crash of the chair against the window. A suicide would be a logical conclusion. But now Mary had seen the layout of the hall. Somebody could have come into Whittier's office from one side of the hall, knocked him out and pushed him out the window, then kept walking down the other side and never have been detected. Was that possible? Was Whittier pushed out the window? But who would have killed him, and why?

"Turn around, very slowly," came a commanding voice from the door.

59

Hello," said the short man standing on the threshold of Whittier's office. He aimed a black gun at Mary's chest. "My name is Marc Videon and I'll be your lawyer tonight."

Mary stiffened with terror. She couldn't speak. She didn't know who he was. She didn't know what to do. She couldn't believe it was happening. She didn't want to die.

"You must be Mary DiNunzio behind those Foster-Grants." Videon smiled, his thin lips curling unpleasantly. "You're practically famous. Got a talk show yet?"

The sunglasses. She had forgotten she was wearing them. For some reason she snatched them off her face and saw him better. His eyes were small and slitted, his hair dark, and his goatee came to a waxed point. He reminded Mary of the Devil himself, but she had just come from church. Or maybe it was his gun. Her stomach felt cold and tight.

"Congratulations. You have found your way to my partner's office, having identified him as the malefactor. You were half-right. Or is it half-wrong? Is the glass half-full or half-empty?" Videon cocked his head as if he were actually considering the question. "I say half-empty, but you look like one of those relentlessly perky, half-full types to me."

Panic told Mary to bolt, but she knew she wouldn't make it. He'd fire as soon as she moved. She had to think of something. Brinkley's gun was still in her briefcase. The security guards and paramedics would be here soon. Stall him. "I thought Whittier was the bad guy," she said.

"Of course you did. I planned it that way. Big Bill Whittier had the stature and the pedigree but he didn't have the brains or the balls. I'm the one who drafted the prenup, wills, and trust documents." Videon licked his thin lips with amusement. "I made Whittier rich. As Honor kept sending him more matters, he collected from the Foundation as billing partner, as managing partner, and soon as executor of Honor's personal estate. He kicked back half to me, and I fed him what he needed to know about Honor. Surprised? You're in good company. The firm thinks I'm the skanky divorce troll with the office under the bridge. I'm not one of the Tribe, you know."

Mary could see Videon wanted to brag, and she needed time. "Did you kill Whittier?"

"Of course not. The fall did. All I did was push." Videon smiled. "Aw, don't look at me like that. Big Bill had to go. He got all worked up when he found out that I had the boy kill Honor. He said he'd steal, but not kill. A lawyer with scruples, no?" Videon's smile vanished. "Dumb fuck. He actually thought Jack did it. That's what the boy—Trevor—was doing in the office last night. Tattling on me."

"But Whittier told the police Jack did it—"

"He lied. Thought the truth would make the firm look even worse in the newspapers. Nobody could malign Tribe when Big Bill Whittier was around. Not to mention that his livelihood— and pension—would vanish if the firm went under." Videon laughed, an audience of one. "And your meddling got to him, my dear. He was actually worried about *you*. I couldn't rely on his discretion. I had to make sure he never went to the police."

Mary felt a stab of guilt. "How did you get Trevor to kill Honor?"

"I bought him out of his first drug charge, for a criminally high sum, for dealing to Big Bill's kid. Told him to get there before Jack got home. But *why* did I have Honor done away with? That's a better question than how, isn't it? Aren't you curious?"

Mary nodded. Where were the paramedics? Where was security? She could have had a baby by now.

"I knew that when Honor divorced Jack, she'd take the Foundation business elsewhere eventually, and I couldn't lose that cash cow. She was pushing for those divorce papers, and I had to stall her by having typos in the draft. Sure, we'd shifted a lot of the Buxton business to Whittier, but why would she stay with her ex-husband's firm? Where's your Tribe spirit?"

Mary gathered it was rhetorical. The gun was pointed right at her chest. He stood only four feet away. Even a lawyer couldn't miss. Especially a lawyer couldn't miss. How could she get to Brinkley's gun?

"I can see I'm boring you, even at gunpoint. You've been reviewing your options, but you have none. I gotcha. I was coming up to gather a single loose end and I ran into you. Had to go back for my gun." Videon took a step closer, raising his gun point-blank over Mary's heart and she could swear she felt it stop beating.

"You can't kill me here. You can't explain another body."

"That's why you're coming with me."

"No!" she shouted suddenly, and threw her briefcase at Videon's gun with all her might. The gun exploded with an ear-splitting sound but Mary sprinted out of the office, running for her life.

"Help!" She started screaming as soon as she hit the hall. Where to run? She flashed on running from Trevor that night, but it was close quarters this time and Videon was smarter. He hadn't missed a trick and he wouldn't start now. His footsteps pounded the soft carpet behind her as she turned the corner. He was waiting for his shot.

"Help!" she shouted. She raced past the reception area, breathing hard from fear. The security guard and the paramedics had to be searching for her by now, didn't they?

Where was the fire stair? She tried to remember the layout she'd seen at the reception desk. Where had the stair been? Left? Right? She took a chance. Right. Yes!

Ahead lay the red exit sign for the fire stair, past a lineup of secretaries' desks with lawyers' offices behind them. The hall was a long, straight line. It would give Videon a clear shot. She glanced back. A squat figure, he stood at the end of the hall, aiming at her with a two-handed grip.

"No!" she screamed. She hurtled forward, zigzagging to throw him off, tears of fright in her eyes. She was at the fourth desk when she heard the gun go off, an explosive *crak*.

The pain arrived before the sound. Jesus God, she heard herself say. Heat shot through her right calf, stalling her in mid-stride, but she pitched forward and didn't stop running. She banged through the fire door and hit the concrete stairs. She couldn't die now. She had the bad guy. She had Jack. Her parents needed her. She had to take her father to the doctor and her mother to church. She grabbed the banister and slid her hand down it as she half stumbled and half ran down the stairs.

30TH FLOOR, read the stenciled paint on the fire wall. A caged bulb threw dim light on her stair, and she spotted bright red spurting from her leg. She grabbed it reflexively and felt its slick wetness. Her own blood. She felt faint. She broke out in a sweat. Her stomach turned over as she ran around the landing and kept going.

She hit the next stair and saw a red fire alarm with a lever. She yanked the lever on the fly. The siren sound was instantaneous, screaming in her ears, but she kept running downstairs. It would tell security where she was. But it would tell Videon, too.

29TH FLOOR. He would be after her. Down the stairs in a minute to finish her off. There was a red door on each floor but she decided not to take it. She had to get closer to twenty-three to help. Where was Videon? She couldn't hear the closing of the exit door over the siren.

28TH FLOOR. Would he take the elevator? Meet her from the bottom up? She suppressed her scream. Her leg gushed blood. Each movement brought agony. She didn't know if she could go on. She had to. Where was security? Where were the paramedics? Didn't the fire alarm matter?

27TH FLOOR. Suddenly a shot rang out. Mary flinched and

stumbled down the stair and past the red door. She didn't know at first if she'd been hit. She didn't know where the shot had come from or where it had gone.

26TH FLOOR. She glanced at her arms, whole in an intact suit. She was fine. He had missed. She felt herself laugh, hysterical with relief and terror as she flew down the stairs. Out of breath, in pain. Weeping with fright.

25TH FLOOR. She was almost there! She pitched down the stair and stumbled as her bloodied leg buckled under her.

"Help!" she shouted as she went down, but the siren swallowed her cry. She hung on the steel banister and almost swooned when she saw fresh blood staining her suit on her right side, near her hip. Videon had shot her in the side. He hadn't missed; she'd been too adrenalized to feel it. Jesus, God.

She looked up in the dim stairwell. Videon was scurrying down the stair, only a floor up. Terror paralyzed her but she hoisted herself to her feet. Dots popped before her eyes. She couldn't see but she started to run. She must be losing blood pressure. She kept her bloodied hand on the banister as she ran past the fire door and down, down, down.

24TH FLOOR. It was getting darker. Was it getting darker? Was she going the right way? She was in such pain. Was it worth it? She ran down the stairs, at least she thought she was running.

"Help!" she screamed, but even she couldn't hear it over the din. She fell again, in the dark, and her hand slipped free of the banister. She didn't have the strength to get up. The red door was right there but she couldn't make it. Everything hurt so much. She was drowning in the sound of a siren that hadn't brought help.

Her eyes fluttered closed as a dark figure stood above her. The last sound Mary heard was the sickening *crak* of a gunshot.

60

Brinkley stood on the concrete landing of the fire stair, behind a smoking gun. He'd taken a single shot at the man about to shoot Mary, and Brinkley's bullet had found its target.

"Oh!" the man screamed, as his hand exploded. He doubled over, howling, and his gun clattered to the concrete stair.

"Freeze!" Brinkley shouted. He ran the few steps between them, collared the man by the scruff of his neck, and kicked his gun over the stairwell. "Get your face on the floor!" he ordered, and the man obeyed, moaning like a little girl.

Brinkley didn't know who the asshole was but he kept his aim on him as he rushed to Mary's side and felt her neck for a pulse. Blood soaked her suit and blanketed her leg. Her eyes were closed. Her skin was too pale.

"Mary, wake up!" he called to her, desperate to keep her conscious. He couldn't let her die. He couldn't do that to her parents. He couldn't explain why, but the DiNunzio family mattered to him. He counted his blessings that he'd guessed she'd go to Tribe, following the connection from Trevor to Whittier, and that her friend Judy had bailed him out in time.

"Mary! Wake up, Mary!" he called again, his fingertips on her neck, trembling too much to feel a pulse. He was about to lift her when a security guard burst through the fire door, followed by a group of uniformed paramedics. He couldn't explain that either and he didn't try. "She needs help!" Brinkley shouted.

But the paramedics took one look at Mary and didn't need to be told.

61

It was the wee hours and the hospital cafeteria was practically empty. Brinkley slid his too-small turquoise tray along the stainless steel runners and went through the line, numb with fatigue and tension. He picked up four triangles of prepackaged tuna sandwiches for himself and the DiNunzio family, who were upstairs in the intensive care waiting room. He grabbed four Styrofoam cups and filled them with hot coffee from a black-handled spout. By the fourth cup he was yanking hard on the handle to drain the last of the coffee, which trickled through dotted with grinds.

"You got more coffee?" he shouted, even though there was nobody behind the counter except posters of dancing apples, happy peas ringing a carrot maypole, and a fluffy head of lettuce with a manic grin. None of the healthy food bore any resemblance to the processed crap for sale, and if Brinkley had been in any kind of mood, he would have laughed at the irony. But he couldn't, not with Mary still in surgery and the DiNunzios so upset. Brinkley couldn't figure out if they had adopted him or it was the other way around, but as unlikely as it was being a tall black detective in a short Italian family, Brinkley found himself liking it. Even tonight, with Mary.

He grabbed a handful of Half-and-Half cups from a bowl of melted ice and sugar packets from a basket, then played mix-and-match with the coffee lids, wondering how smart you had to be to distinguish a large lid from a medium. Shit. He eventually lucked out and pressed the plastic lids onto the coffee cups, then got to the end of the line and handed a twenty to the girl who finally showed up to take his money, then left with only her attitude. Brinkley packed the stuff into bags himself and wedged the cups carefully into a cardboard carrier, and when he was leaving, stopped, because he recognized a man in a suit, hunched over his own cup of coffee.

Dwight Davis. Boy Wonder. The D.A.'s rep tie was undone and his oxford shirt wrinkled under his suit jacket. There was no fresh legal pad in sight, and Davis's head was bent, his eyes bloodshot and his gaunt runner's cheeks even more sunken than usual. The man struck Brinkley instantly as a burnout case, though the detective couldn't scrape together any sympathy for the prosecutor.

"What are you doin' here?" Brinkley demanded, standing over the turquoise table, and Davis finally looked up.

"Reg. She the same?"

Brinkley was so surprised, he couldn't answer. Was Davis asking about Mary? Was that why he was here?

"That's two hours she's been in surgery," Davis said, and Brinkley felt a knot of anger tighten in his chest.

"Who told you that?"

"How do I know? I keep calling the desk, different nurses answer, and they tell me."

"They not supposed to do that." Brinkley's tone stayed calm but he was shouting inside.

"Huh?"

"They're not supposed to tell you." Brinkley wanted to deck the man, but he tried to remember himself. He was a professional. They needed him upstairs. He had the tuna sandwiches, cream cups, and the cardboard carrier.

"You're right, Reg. They're not supposed to tell. I stipulate to that. Okay?"

"No. Why do they?"

"Jesus, Reg!" Davis voice sounded hoarse. "I tell 'em Masterson wants to know and they tell me. What's the friggin' difference?"

"It makes a difference. You're not immediate family."

"I'm the *D.A.*"

"So what? That don't matter. They shouldn't tell you." Brinkley could barely control himself. Why did it bother him so much? Then he knew. "Because you don't have a right to know."

Davis leaned back in his plastic bucket chair. "You're wrong, Reg. I have more of a right to know than anybody."

"How the fuck is that?"

"I put her there."

Since Brinkley could neither deny Davis's guilt nor take pleasure in it, he left the man with it and walked away.

62

A somber-faced Brinkley shifted uncomfortably on the wooden dais, his arms linked behind his back, standing next to Kovich. He blinked against the harsh flashes from the Hasselblads and avoided the black lenses of the video cameras pointed at him. He hadn't slept the rest of last night and had barely had enough time to change clothes for this morning press conference, which was a total waste of time. He'd much rather be with the DiNunzios, who needed him, but he was on orders.

Microphones sprouted from the podium at the center of the dais, their thick black stems craned toward Captain Walsh. The Cap was wearing his dress uniform, since this was official, and to his left stood Dwight Davis. Davis wouldn't even look at Brinkley, which was fine with him.

Captain Walsh raised his hands to settle the reporters packing the large press room. "Okay, people," he said, when they had quieted, "we'd like to make a short statement about recent events in the Newlin case. Bottom line, we've dropped all charges against Jack Newlin. We have charged Mr. Marc Videon for the murder of Honor Newlin and the murder of Mr. William Whittier." Walsh nodded once, as if to punctuate his speech. "We'll take a few quick questions at this time." The reporters shouted and waved at once, but the Cap pointed at a woman reporter in the front row. "You," he said.

"Captain Walsh, did the police department really charge the wrong man? And if so, how did that happen?"

"No two ways about it, we made a horrendous mistake. We accepted Newlin's confession and we shouldn't have. The credit for correcting this mistake goes to our own Detective Reginald Brinkley, of Homicide." Walsh gestured to Brinkley, who looked immediately down at his loafers. He had changed them at home. His sneakers had been stained with Mary's blood. *Mary*. He bit his lip.

Walsh continued, "I would also like to give credit to someone who is not here with us tonight, Mary DiNunzio, Mr. Newlin's attorney. Next question?" He pointed again. "You, John."

"This is for Dwight Davis," the older reporter said. "Mr. Davis, you thought the Commonwealth's case was so strong that you announced earlier this week you would not offer Mr. Newlin a plea bargain. How do you square that with his ultimate innocence?"

Davis edged forward to take the podium. "John, I have to agree with Captain Walsh," he began, and Brinkley looked up, listening. He'd never heard a D.A. admit he was wrong and couldn't believe he was about to hear it from Davis, in front of everyone. It was one thing to fess up in a hospital cafeteria and another to do it in public. "My prosecution of Mr. Newlin was a complete miscarriage of justice, and the fault is entirely mine. I am announcing effective today my resignation from the Office of the District Attorney."

Brinkley looked over, stunned. Davis had changed his view of lawyers in one shot. Almost.

"I was overzealous in this case and I think it's time for me to take a breather. Beyond that, I have no further comment." Davis stepped away from the podium, as strobe lights flashed like gunfire.

The reporters immediately began shouting again, and Captain Walsh picked one in the back of the room. "You have the last question, Bill."

"Thank you, sir," the reporter said. "What's the latest on DiNunzio's condition?"

EPILOGUE

Sunlight filtered through oak trees in full leaf, and Jack felt the late-summer sun on his shoulders through the worn cotton of his oxford shirt. He crossed his legs on the park bench, gazing across Logan Square at the Four Seasons Hotel. In one hand he held the red tape leash of a fuzzy golden retriever puppy, who was chewing happily on the looped shoelace of Jack's sneaker. The traffic around the hotel flowed steadily on this Saturday afternoon, affording him and his partner on the bench, Lou Jacobs, a decent view of the restaurant.

"I remember the day I was here, with Mary," Lou was saying. His eyes looked flinty in the sun, and his tanned hands rested on the pressed crease of his khaki pants. His white polo shirt was a neat concession to Philadelphia's humidity. "It was right after she met you, on the case. She was tellin' me about the fountain."

"Swann Fountain?" Jack looked behind him. The fountain spurted and bubbled at the center of the cobblestone plaza, sending graceful arcs of frothy water into the circular pool and misting the air with cooling droplets. "What about the fountain?"

"She liked it."

"I can see why." Jack smiled at the sight. Two little boys played in the fountain in front of an indulgent mother, squealing with each cold splash. At the sound, the puppy's neck swiveled and his wavy-haired ears lifted to attention. Jack breathed in the fresh smells of the greenery and the faintly chlorinated scent of the fountain water. He had so much to be grateful for and so much to regret. "Tell me what she liked about it. Do you remember?"

"Sure. The statues around the fountain are a man, a woman, and a young girl. See?" Lou's eyes remained fixed on the hotel. Filaments of his silvery hair caught a passing breeze. "Mary said it reminded her of you, your wife, and your daughter."

"She said that?" Jack felt touched that Mary had been thinking of him even then. He had been thinking of her that early, too, but he had been lonelier than she, he just hadn't known it. "What's going on now?" he asked, turning to the hotel.

"Hold on." Lou raised the binoculars to his eyes and aimed them at the hotel restaurant. The baby shower, taking place two months after the baby had arrived, was going on inside, and through the window he could see the hen party was breaking up. "Finally they stopped yapping."

"It's sports, they're crazy about sports," Jack said, standing up and eyeing the hotel entrance. He could barely see inside the restaurant. Paige was hostessing the shower, for the baby's adoptive mother. "Seems stupid they don't let men into these things, still."

"Nah, who wants to go? Not me." Lou stood up, too, and let the binoculars hang at his neck. "I'd rather sit out here and tell dirty jokes."

"Agreed," Jack said, with a smile. He watched the hotel entrance, and Judy came out first, her height helping him identify her even across the street. She would be wanting her puppy back, and he would happily off-load it. Raising a daughter, especially belatedly, was enough for him. He'd spent the last few months trying to undo his past mistakes with Paige. "You see my kid yet?"

"There." Lou pointed as Paige appeared. Her new haircut, a shiny red wedge, was a bright spot in the sunlight. Her arms were full of baby gifts, which she was loading into the couple's minivan. The baby was at home with his adoptive father, a teacher. Jack's heart warmed at the thought. Paige had grown up so much in the past few months and with counseling had taken the hardest step of her life. She'd decided the most responsible thing she could do as a mother was to offer her baby to a couple who could love and raise him. Jack hadn't disagreed with a word.

"There's Mary!" Lou said, with a smile, and Jack looked over.

Mary had managed to abscond with not one, not two, but with five centerpieces of roses, daisies, freesia, and even an orchid or two. She moved with the bouquets like the most petite float in the Mummers Parade. Jack smiled. "Why do women take centerpieces?"

"Because they can," Lou said, and they both laughed.

AUTHOR'S NOTE

They call publishing companies "houses," and I have only recently come to understand why. I have written seven novels, including this one, for the same publishing house, HarperCollins, and it has come to feel like home to me. Not because I can finally find it in New York (though that helps) but because of the caring people who reside within, and I owe them all a huge debt of gratitude.

Thank you so much to Jane Friedman, President and CEO, who has imbued the house with her warmth, grace, and wisdom, and has mothered me from the day we first met. Thank you so much to Cathy Hemming, who took the time not only to improve this manuscript, but has even come—slinging a backpack of manuscripts—to one of my signings. Heartfelt thanks, as always, to Carolyn Marino, my editor, who is completely invaluable for her expertise, taste, and friendship. If you like my books, it's because of her. If you hate them, it's when I didn't listen.

It takes a village to raise an author. Deep thanks to my wonderful agent, Molly Friedrich, who is the truest sort of intellectual. She loves books without pretense and cares about them with passion. I am forever grateful to be one of her charges, and she is the most fun mom an author could ask for. Thanks, too, to Paul Cirone, for his advice, help, and good looks.

I need help with the facts, too, though when I get them wrong the blame is on me. For this book I turned first to Commissioner John Timoney of the Philadelphia Police Department, who let me follow him around for a day. Commissioner Timoney is rightfully a hero in my city, and I consider the good cops in this book a thank-you to him and to all of those who serve and protect. Thanks to Lieutenant Martin O'Donnell and the officers of the Civilian Police Academy; my baseball cap is off to you.

Thanks, too, to Art Mee of the District Attorney's office, for his good-humored advice and sartorial splendor, and to Glenn Gilman, public defender extraordinaire. For estates advice I turn to the expert, Robert Freedman of Dechert, Price & Rhoads. There is none better, nor more generous with his time and expertise.

Personal thanks and all my love to my family: my husband, daughter, and stepdaughters Sarah and Elizabeth. And to return briefly to the importance of mothers, my deepest thanks go to the best one of all. Mine.

Thanks, Ma.